CONTENTS

Also by D.E. Greenfield   v
Acknowledgments   vii
In Memory Of   ix
Historical Timeline: 2030 and 2086   xi

Prologue   1
Chapter 1   11
Chapter 2   39
Chapter 3   55
Chapter 4   59
Chapter 5   79
Chapter 6   89
Chapter 7   97
Chapter 8   105
Chapter 9   123
Chapter 10   139
Chapter 11   147
Chapter 12   157
Chapter 13   165
Chapter 14   173
Chapter 15   183
Chapter 16   191
Chapter 17   199
Chapter 18   207
Chapter 19   217
Chapter 20   225
Chapter 21   235
Chapter 22   245
Chapter 23   253
Chapter 24   261
Chapter 25   271

Chapter 26   283
Chapter 27   291
Chapter 28   297
Chapter 29   313
Chapter 30   321
Chapter 31   331
Chapter 32   345
Chapter 33   363
Chapter 34   379
Acronyms & Terms   389
Acronyms & Terms-2   391
Acronyms-Terms-3   393

Characters   395
About the Author   397

Please purchase only authorized electronic editions, and do not participate in or encourage electronic piracy of copyrighted materials. Your support of the author's rights is appreciated.

Please visit my website: www.degreenfield.com

Sign up for my newsletter and get the latest news before the public.

❀ Formatted with Vellum

ALSO BY D.E. GREENFIELD

Every word I have written and published is from my noggin (brain, in case you don't know what noggin means). My fiction is all make-believe, from the deep dive into my wild imagination. All my nonfiction books have been researched until my brain has scrambled.

Nonfiction	
The Puppy Baby Book	Mastering Your Money (2022)
Puppy Adoption and Beyond	Writers Preparation Handbook
Mastering Your Money (2008)	What's Breaking Your Budget
Online Classes	
Writers Preparation Handbook	How to Format Word Docs Like A Pro
Cozy Mysteries	**Sci-Fi-Fantasy**
The Alcott Family Adventures	**The Thol Series**
Hot Chocolate	Prophecy of Thol
Bitter Chocolate	Gifts From Thol
Spicy Chocolate	Love of Thol
Nutty Chocolate	King of Thol
Katz' Cat Series	Earth Calling Thol
Katz' Cat	**Sci-Fi Romance Adventure**
Bill Hill's Pills	Forced Dreams
The Detectives	**Dystopian**
The Pact	The Last Dog
Discreet Conversations	Texmexzona
Books by my Alter Ego ~ DG Ireland	
Bonded Shapeshifter Billionaire Series	
Bonded	
Tothars	
Tilted	
Unforeseen	
Connected	
Need A Notebook?	
See my 54 themed notebooks on my website www.degreenfield.com/notebooks	
Screenplays formatted as books	
Plan B (Dark Comedy)	Where's Ralphie? (Family Comedy)
The God Child (Action Adventure)	Standing Dead (Drama/Tragedy)
The Far Corner (Sci-Fi/Psychological/Creatures)	Block Captain (Action Comedy)
Screenplays as TV Episodes	
Hot Chocolate ~ Episode 1	Prophecy of Thol ~ Episode 1
Bonded ~ Episode 1	
See my screenplays and awards on my website: degreenfield.com Filmfreeway, ISA Network	

ACKNOWLEDGMENTS

This book was born in 2010. I had never written a dystopian book before and I had to make sure my concept was solid. I hired Erin Niumata to edit the book and she gave me great feedback. Then she up and moved to London.

After I waded through all the changes, I wanted to make sure I had my head on straight and that the book was still solid. In marched Barbara Price. Her insight was so helpful. Then my brain shut down on The Last Dog. I was so stuck from working on it that even Peggy Stautberg couldn't get me out of the crater.

The book sat on the shelf until late 2016, at which time I climbed out of that deep pit and read everyone's notes and began a cohesive rewrite that I finished in 2017.

I shipped TLD off to Michelle DeLaBarre and April Hoffman, my proofreaders/fact checkers out in California (mother and daughter I've known for decades). I had to make a few changes from their findings. Now, FINALLY, after years of trying to get this book out of my computer, it has marched out the door (2018)!

Cicely Wynne from my critique group has been knocking me on the head to get TLD out the door all this time. Many thanks to the original test readers from 2011 for all the feedback.

And last, but not least, Brandon White, my visionary son

who designed the covers (original 2010 and new 2024).
Thanks, son!

WINNER OF THE BOOK EXCELLENCE AWARD •
READERS' FAVORITE 5-STAR WINNER

IN MEMORY OF

My parents, George and Dorothy Daigle Greenfield, my big sister, Robin, and my middle sister, Sheryl.

Shasta Annie Ireland, my furry sidekick for 16-1/2 years, and from whom I drew the character of Abby.

My best friend, Joseph C. Feduccia, and my best bud who was also one of my bosses, Colin Talbot

You are all missed so much!

The Last Dog
Historical Timeline: 2030 - 2086

Year	Event
2030	New World Order (NWO)
2030	Declaration of Life
2032	Deportation Act of 2032
2032	Welfare system overhaul
2034	World Obesity Prevention Act (WOPA)
2035	Social Security Administration overhaul
2042	Collapse of megachurches
2044	Republic of Texmexzona (TMZ)
2045	All Beliefs Celebration Day (March 27)
2045	Unified World Pact
2045	World Guild, the new global government
2047	Mag Car created by Brandon Lyons George III
2076	9.2 earthquake along the West Coast of the US, aka "the Incident", creating the New Islands, also referred to as the Ragged Edge
2077	The Dot, invented by William (Bill) Maxwell
2080	The Dot, mandatory in humans
2084	The Dot, mandatory in dogs and cats
2085	The HoloRemote Canine Upgrade
2086	Current year

Then and Now
AD 2030—2086 NWO*

The year 2086 marks the beginning of the New World Order (NWO*), which significantly impacted humanity. To understand the before and after of this single year, it would be advantageous to take a step back in time and peruse the vast changes of the past fifty-six years.

Many people have an inner struggle with change. They don't want to move an inch out of their comfort zone. The familiar, whether it's good or bad, is easier than learning new rules, especially when it concerns everything about their daily life. Some welcome change with open arms. They are optimistic about crossing the bridge and enjoying what's waiting on the other side.

After more than a decade of people wondering whether they would have Social Security (SSA) when they retired. SSA was finally overhauled in 2035. A new numbering system incorporated a genealogical data gathering/compilation that left nothing private.

The old nine-digit number grew. Depending on an individual's ethnicity, religion, sexual grouping, and medical criteria, the number ranged from fourteen to twenty-five digits. Memorization was a chore.

Also on the horizon, a global government was emerging and the lineup of powers shifted for another decade. The USA dipped and regained top power, but the United Kingdom teeter-tottered among China, India, Japan and Germany.

Several important things changed between 2030 and 2035. These changes paved the way for vast shifts in the United

States of America's practices, beliefs, expectations, and quality of life. As the rest of the world watched these US events unfold, changes spread globally with unstoppable, viral swiftness.

Everyday people woke up one morning in 2030 and decided that they would not sit still while their government ran amok, the FDA and pharmaceutical companies poisoned them, and the media churned out paid news for the deep pockets of corruption. United States citizens took back their country and government in a public, non-violent war that shook the world.

What started in the mid-2000s with protests and petitions, quietly but quickly became an organized party that literally stormed government offices across the country just before noon on September 9, 2030, and escorted public officials out of their offices.

It helped that the top military brass led the new party. Time seemed to stand still as there were more than a few shaky moments where the usurpers faced soldiers and weapons, but the military was forced to stand down via orders from the top. Everything happened so quickly that the public didn't have time to blink or think.

A new Declaration of Life was created that included the following provisions:

1. Everyone deserved basic living standards: food, water, shelter, education, and health benefits.
2. All recreational drugs would be cheap, legal and readily available, thus saving grandmothers growing and selling pot to try to survive the economy.
3. No money, goods, or services would leave the US until infrastructure was one hundred percent in

place from coast-to-coast and top-to-bottom of the
entire land.

4. The US would not support any country or cause
that went against its policies for human rights.

5. English was the language of the US. Period.
Citizens learned it or they could leave the country;
there was no choice.

6. Revolving prison doors screeched to a halt, with
massive rehabilitation and education programs.
Prisons were torn down and replaced with condos.

Provisions (4) and (5) spurred the Deportation Act of 2032.
The old Homeland Security had secretly scanned people with
a radiant blue light, too faint for the human eye to detect, in
grocery stores, gas stations, and Walmarts.

The Blue Light report captured precise details, including
fingerprints, and no one ever suspected.

Unfriendly illegal immigrants were shipped back to their
home countries, which had been a mixed blessing. Once
scanned, any person whose picture was not found in a database
containing photos of US, naturalized or legally accepted citizens, was rounded up at the exit where they were scanned
again and taken for a ride.

Foreigners who had caused massive grumblings were
shipped out of the US by the plane-full.

The labor force to replace those workers was almost non-existent. Real Americans didn't want to mow lawns, become
maids and janitors, or work in convenience stores.

That's when the welfare system was yanked.

Generational welfare families received letters instructing
them to report to work stations where they would be assigned a
job. There was no accepting or denying; only complying.

Provision (6) required that prisoners be sorted. Non-violent inmates, petty thieves, drug addicts and the like became the new groundskeepers, working off their time. By contributing to the workforce, they earned their way back into society.

To cut down on supervision, prisoners were fitted with newly developed programmed collars that enforced the coordinates of the assignment, tasks to be performed, breaks allowed, and the return to the prison pickup point.

If a prisoner tried to escape or sit down on the job, a jolt of electricity sped through their veins, making them model citizens.

Violent criminals who underwent successful rehabilitation were collared and joined the workforce. Those who failed rehab underwent a brain swipe and started over, and were monitored closely.

During this tumultuous time in the 2030s, the government took a serious look at its citizens. Obesity was running rampant. The World Obesity Prevention Act (WOPA) became one of the most feared programs.

It had taken eight years for nations to agree on the universal weight, height, and body type charts for men, women, and children. And during that time, healthy eating and exercising regimes—discounted as useless to fat people—were examined by doctors from around the globe, and the solution to the obesity problem was planned. Once the details were hashed out and the WOPA act took effect, the United States, once the fattest nation on the planet, became the poster child for physical fitness.

Back when all the scanning by Homeland Security was taking place, if anyone bought anything, they, and everything in their possession at the time of their transaction, were scanned by the nefarious radiant blue light.

The scanners captured images. There was no opportunity

to lie about weight, hair color, whether teeth were real, or if eye color had been enhanced with contacts.

Families began hiding their overweight family members from prying eyes. If someone turned them in, or they were discovered, they were picked up by authorities for treatment.

WOPA-approved treatment consisted of heated fiber optic wires that were wrapped around the person, mummy-style, from head to toe. Steam rose off the fiber optic wires as the fat melted and drained from shunts into a vat.

The Blue Light diagnosed spending habits and eventually found a few secret stuffers hiding behind friends and family. Once the signal was sent through the network, they were rounded up one by one. The old term fat farm took on new meaning. It was a messy affair.

Another shift that transpired between 2032 and 2042 was the flip of the Mexican government. There were so many Americans living in Mexico that the standard of living changed remarkably. Gone were drug lords and all the murderous feuds from the 1990s up through 20-teens. Gone were the corrupt politicians who had raped, pillaged, and plundered their country of its resources and revenues.

The American-Mexicans demanded and brought about change throughout that land and in 2044 Texas, New Mexico, Arizona and the country of Mexico merged to form its own independent district. It was not a state or a country. The United States government declared that Texmexzona (TMZ) was an outlaw district and if citizens of the US moved there, their US residency was yanked.

During this troubling time, religion changed almost overnight when mega-churches collapsed. Members reevaluated their core beliefs and decided (1) they did not need to pay to pray anymore; 2) they sure didn't need to support a multimillionaire preacher while they themselves tithed ten percent of their highly taxed income while; (3) the sexual abuse scandals continued decade after decade involving priests and ministers.

By the time 2045 rolled around, mainstream religion was almost non-existent. The Vatican was torn down and sold off in pieces, similar to the old Berlin Wall. March 27 was set aside for an All-Beliefs Celebration. People could worship however they pleased on that day.

After the Unified World Pact of 2045 was signed, people lived in a state of peace and prosperity previously unknown in human history. The World Guild, the new global government, managed all the needs of humanity and the animals it loved.

Technological innovations flourished. Many industries that were solid footholds for decades, and even centuries, vanished because of major changes in technology. As the computer chip became smaller and more powerful, computing technology changed. Gone were desktops, towers, laptops, iPads, and everything in between.

The world went virtual and holographic. People loved it because this new world was finally, truly interactive and it took little brainpower to figure out how to use new devices.

With technology shrinking and morphing, things that 20th Century and early 21st Century people swore would never be affected simply went away. Forever. Gasoline, natural and other gases, oil, and coal became obsolete as natural resources became cheaper and easier to use. Fossil fuels would stay in the ground forever.

Solar, wind, and new power from the universe outside of Earth's atmosphere (space) became cheap, clean, and easy. As microchips shrunk, so did the cells required for solar collectors. Wind farms sprang up across the globe along with the new collecting dishes that satellites used to beam the gathered energy from space.

At first, all forms of vehicles changed over from gas and oil to solar and hydrogen (water). Then, when Brandon Lyons George III successfully demonstrated a sleek, sexy, silver vehicle that operated using the Earth's natural magnetic system at the 2047 Chicago Auto Show, the face of transportation changed forever.

The Mag-Car appeared to hover, tireless, about a foot off the dais on the show floor. Over time, the Mag-Car evolved into the gliders that whizzed through the air in 2086.

Airspace was divided into zones appropriate for specific types of gliders: 1) individual and family; 2) commercial; and 3) industrial. There were gliders for every function or industry.

And then the incident of 2076 occurred.

An earthquake that officially registered as 9.2 on the Richter scale tore the US West Coast apart. The tectonic plates along the San Andreas Fault didn't just shift; they jumped and screamed, shook and cracked the earth as if a bomb had been wedged beneath the surface.

Miraculously, San Diego remained unscathed, as did Vancouver, BC. Everything else between those two destinations—approximately twelve hundred and fifty-five miles of pristine real estate along the Pacific Ocean coastline—split away from the mainland as if the Earth spit them out and dropped huge globs of land into the ocean, before slowly bobbing to the surface.

The land had been cleansed of all civilization caught off-guard in the seventeen minutes of the foremost terror that the United States had ever experienced.

The resulting tsunami fanned out across the Pacific Ocean, wiping out the Hawaiian Islands. The wall of water continued westward and roared over Japan and Korea, leaving debris in its wake.

Hong Kong was obliterated, as were Taiwan, the Philippines, Malaysia, and Indonesia. Miraculously, Vietnam, Cambodia, Laos, and Thailand were spared.

The New Islands, as the surviving land masses off the western coast of the United States were now called, were made up of sixteen California islands, four Oregon islands, and two Washington State islands. Survivors of the disaster divided into two groups: those who saw the advantage of being apart from the mainland, and solid-land lovers who evacuated the islands in herds.

The US and the rest of the world slowly recovered. Some areas rebuilt; others remained wastelands—constant reminders of the mysterious workings of Mother Nature.

After the chaos settled, a young man named William Maxwell wowed the world with his inventions in 2082.

Bill and his wife Teresa were childless, as were many people in the 2070s and 2080s because of decades of toxic forms of birth control—hormone therapies and sperm inhibitors promoted heavily by the disbanded FDA and pharmaceutical companies.

The long-ago problem of dog and cat overpopulation underwent a reversal. People fought to adopt dogs and cats, and waiting lists spurred bribery and black-market adoptions.

Bill was a genius. His forward-thinking, practical mind churned out many patents, but two would stand out as his most brilliant ideas: The Dot and the PawBoard, precursors of the HoloRemote.

The Dot solved many societal problems: It contained those long ID numbers no one could memorize, and it aided the Sky Angels in finding lost animals and human children or a wandering super-centenarian. Eventually the Dot made money obsolete since anything anyone required or desired could be purchased via a Dot scan, which became commonplace at every shopping facility and distribution center.

Bill worked diligently for six years (2076-2082) expanding the Dot's functions to make it possible for dog and cat children to communicate with their human family members. It had been a challenge to solve the myriad of interspecies language translation problems.

After that, it was a simple matter of tweaking the voice coding in the tiny transmitter that worked with a nano-receiver that was injected into the larynx to translate animal thought into a synthesized voice. Dog-thought sent electrical signals to the transmitter, which triggered the larynx to respond with the pre-selected voice. Bill's Dot technology was a stepping stone in the intelligence evolution of the canine species.

Cats, while intelligent, proved to be less than desirable Dot subjects, as some parents discovered. Most felines had no interest in learning to communicate on a higher level. They rather enjoyed keeping their human companions in a constant state of guessing.

To encourage a more well-rounded education for animal children, Bill created a paw-friendly keyboard called the PawBoard that connected to the Universal Connection Platform, or UCP, which the Twenty-First Century Internet had evolved into.

The PawBoard, while considered a rather large, awkward device, was another leap for dogs and cats in understanding the modern, technological world of humans. Bill's device enabled a dog or cat to step on a button and connect to the UCP. From there, they could choose from approximately 5,000 programming options, most of which were educational.

A week after the PawBoard debuted, Bill and Teresa's adoption application was approved and they happily became the parents of Lilith, a Bull Terrier newly weaned from her mother, Arabella.

The work on the HoloRemote took a back burner while the new family settled down, then Bill tackled the canine Dot to implement his latest wonder.

CHAPTER ONE

Aberdeen Tallulah Maxwell, nicknamed Abby, and fondly called Puppy-dup by Teresa and Bill Maxwell, her human mother and father, tottered on six-week-old puppy legs across an expanse of slippery terra cotta tile in the vast kitchen that never seemed to end.

She lifted her black nose to the air and sniffed, then whimpered woefully as she looked about. No whelping box here. Everything was big and way over her head, and she didn't recognize any of the skinny furniture legs or the wooden walls of the curved counter.

Her back shone like rich brown velvet in the sunlight that warmed the floor from the rays pouring through the high kitchen windows. Abby's two white toenails looked opaque in the sunlight, one on her front right paw and the other on her left rear foot.

Her little angular face showed a resemblance to Lilith, her bull terrier mother.

Jimbo Smythe, Abby's canine father, was a purebred black Labrador who had an uncanny ability of climbing any wall or fence in pursuit of romance. He breached fences throughout the neighborhood and was as far away as three miles. Some thought Jimbo must be part cat since he always landed on his feet no matter how high the fence was.

Unfortunately, Jimbo jumped one fence too many and mindlessly careened into a low-flying glider, thus abandoning his family in an untimely death.

Abby plopped down in the middle of the kitchen floor, stuck her nose in the air, stretching the elongated white star on her chest, and wailed.

"Abby!" Lilith called from the whelping box.

Ejonia Matthews, the beloved house manager for the Maxwells, stood in front of the food console, her stout body draped in a brightly colored flowing dress that cascaded almost to her sandaled feet. Thick brown braided hair was wrapped around the back of her head, and a beaded, braided loop hung at the center back of her head. Fingers and toes were adorned with colorful rings and bands.

She watched as Abby stood with her ears perked and turned in a half circle and barked in her biggest puppy voice.

"Go find your canine mother," Ejonia said.

Abby looked up at Ejonia's eyes and whined.

"That way." Ejonia pointed toward the hallway.

Lilith barked once and warbled in normal dog-talk.

Abby galloped toward her canine mother's voice, her feet slipping and sliding on the tile around the table and chair legs, down the hallway on the slippery wooden floor and over the threshold into her human father's combination office and lab.

Ejonia crept after Abby and peeked into the lab. All the puppies, except for Abby, were sound asleep.

"Come to bed," Lilith scolded.

Abby scampered over the ledge of the whelping box that had kept the puppies inside the box until two days ago when they learned how to climb. She barked playfully, two feet on the fleece bed and two feet planted firmly on the office floor.

Lilith gently lifted Abby by the scruff of her neck and placed her in the bed. Abby pawed at Lilith's face and bit her ears until she wore herself out.

"Settle down, little girl," Lilith said. She licked Abby's face.

Abby cuddled down in the bed with her sisters and brothers and yawned. Within minutes, she was asleep.

Lilith looked at Ejonia. "Finally!" she said.

"We're going to have to put up a gate so they can't get out of the room," Ejonia said.

"They'll figure a way," Lilith said, knowingly.

BILL MAXWELL, the thirty-three-year-old founder and CEO of Maxwell Industries, walked across a crushed rock surface outside the new main building where a fountain sprayed a fine mist. A couple of dog-children romped through the water until their parents whistled for them. They jumped down from the fountain and then shook their coats, soaking their human parents.

The sprawling four-story multi-building complex spanned a park-like setting equaling ten football fields, with the Santa Cruz Mountains as a backdrop. Bill had jumped at the opportunity to purchase the land after the incident of 2076.

He approached the door, spotted a bunch of tourists, and snuck around to the side door to gain access to the building. He ran undetected up the stairs to his office and labs, which contained many guarded prototypes unknown to the government or the general population. Bill had developed robotic bees that flew around the complex and his home, in and out of power connections, air ducts, and any crevice or opening to explore, detect, and report any spyware or probes.

If the bees discovered any abnormalities, robotic wasp-ants were dispatched to defuse, destroy, or capture the infiltrators and tow them back to a holding case where Bill could study them. Most were silly, unsophisticated units that were no challenge to decode. Sometimes Bill rewired their circuits and used them as double agents to gather information for him.

Toby, one of Bill's trusted employees, had a lot of fun with the physical characteristics of the bees and wasp-ants. He was well-known for his sense of humor.

THE CROWD of tourists swarmed around the lobby, fascinated with the information while taking in the virtual storyboards. The company history was displayed on the wall monitors and contained several of Bill's most prominent inventions, including the Dot.

A middle-aged woman with the latest chrome beauty mark near her lime green lips stood beside one storyboard. Her bright green, red and purple caftan with embedded glitter flowed and sparkled with her movements as she conducted a virtual tour for the group of people.

"William Maxwell is a technological genius who owned several successfully developed patents at the age of twenty-three. When Maxwell Industries announces a new product, the world listens." She pressed buttons on a hand-held device that started a virtual player on the first storyboard.

"The Dot is a microscopic disc less than 0.0396875 centimeters in diameter. It contains your entire history—medical, genetic, home location, workplace, and, when required, will aid the Sky Angels in finding you if you are lost or injured. The Dot is a safe harbor for animal and human children or wandering super-centenarians."

The second storyboard showed a Dot insertion procedure and explained that Dots became mandatory in 2080. A man in a white lab coat smiled as he held a compressor syringe over the palm-side of a woman's wrist. He pressed the plunger on the syringe and painlessly inserted the Dot. The woman smiled at the man at the end of the procedure.

The next storyboard showed how the Dot had made paper money obsolete. Employers bought into the government's idea that "income credits" could be incorporated into the Dot. Anything anyone required or desired could be purchased via a Dot scan if a person had the credits. Dot scans became commonplace at every shopping facility and distribution center.

Viewers watched a holographic clip of Bill and a team of programmers and technologists working diligently in a lab setting in an old building. They were intent on expanding the Dot's functions to make it possible for dog and cat children to communicate with human family members. Each segment of the holograph was date-stamped showing the year of research and development, sometime between 2076 and 2080.

The brightly dressed guide touched the thin screen and showed the group a file which contained the code that had been a challenge for Bill and his team. A holographic narration continued with a discussion about how language experts and software programmers had to solve the myriad of interspecies language translation problems.

The visitors murmured among themselves as thousands of lines of code flew by on the screen.

Visitors giggled as various dog and cat children spoke in different voices on the screen as their speech was tweaked. The first attempts produced nothing that could be translated into any recognizable language.

Their tour guide pointed to the various buttons on the wall and encouraged the group to press them and listen to the selection of voice examples. While the visitors pressed buttons and laughed at some of the voice responses, the tour guide explained how it worked.

"The programming sends electrical signals to the transmitter, which triggers the larynx to respond with the pre-selected voice that is transmitted to a special collar with speakers, thus allowing a conversation to take place," she said.

A lady raised her hand. "I don't understand how that could work."

"There's a tiny transmitter that works with a nano-receiver in the larynx," the guide explained.

"Oh," the lady said.

The guide had to further explain what and where the larynx was and that the Dot technology was a stepping stone in the intelligence evolution of the canine species.

After the group finished playing with the buttons, they meandered down the storyboard wall to other inventions.

TERESA MAXWELL WALKED into Bill's home office and approached the whelping box. While she and Bill were only months apart with birthdays in January and July, she looked barely twenty-five. The puppies were sleeping in the curve of their canine mother's belly. Lilith raised her head. Teresa cupped one of Lilith's cheeks.

"Mommy's going to the office to meet Auntie Gayle. I'll be back this afternoon, okay?" she whispered.

"Okay," Lilith whispered. "I'm going to take a nap."

Teresa bent over and kissed Lilith on the head.

MYRA-JUNE MEYER, Teresa's front-office assistant, greeted Teresa and Gayle as they entered the newly constructed fourth-floor office suite. The tiny red-head wore a fitted fine-knit charcoal colored sheathe as she arranged office tools in her work space.

"Hi, Mrs. Maxwell. Hi Mrs. Goanflower," Myra-June said.

Gayle's hair and eyes, as dark as polished opals, and flawless skin, a creamy tan, made her unforgettable. She came to a dead stop as she took in the white walls with tan, gold, and gray accents. She ran her hand across the back of a gold-tone chair and admired the gray fleece dog beds precisely stationed on the Berber carpeting to balance the room.

A chrome dog-and-cat faucet and a water bowl were against one wall a few feet from the co-species animal bathroom closet.

"Is that bathroom closet new?" Gayle asked. "I don't remember seeing this one in your old office."

"I wanted to upgrade for my new office," Teresa said.

Gayle stuck her head in the bathroom closet open doorway. The floor was covered with spongy artificial grass that smelled like real grass. The fine sand area was freshly raked, and the shallow wading pool contained about an inch of circulating water.

Gayle turned and took in the reception area. "I like your command center, Myra-June." The curved tan, white, and gray desk console was a focal point of the outer office.

The perky assistant bounced up from her chair and flung her arms out. "Isn't this a great room?"

"It's spectacular!" Gayle said.

"Any messages?" Teresa asked.

"The Trident Group would like to discuss a research project. I sent you all the details, but also put a hard copy on your desk," Myra-June said.

"Hmm," Teresa said. "I'll look it over."

Teresa linked her arm through Gayle's and walked her past Myra-June's desk and opened the door to a hallway.

They passed two closed doors on the left side of the well-lit hall and one on the right. At the end of the hallway, a closed door beckoned. Teresa opened the door to her spacious office and ushered Gayle inside.

"Oh, my Great Earth! This is beautiful, T!" Gayle said. "I wish I were a dog!"

The room did not contain a desk. Virtual pictures hung on the wall, one row at floor level for animal children and another row several feet higher at a human adult eye level. Leg-less overstuffed sofas and dog and cat beds formed a half-circle and did not obstruct the pictures.

Dog and cat toys were stowed in boxes, and another chrome dog-and-cat faucet and a water bowl were positioned to the right of the doorway. There was ample room for animal children to romp around without crashing into anything that could hurt them.

The lower virtual pictures contained stimulating action views of butterflies flitting through the air, rabbits hopping, lizards creeping, squirrels going about their busy business, and other animals doing things that a dog or cat child would find interesting.

Teresa flopped onto one of the floor sofas and patted the cushion for Gayle to join her.

"You're not going to psychoanalyze me, are you?" Gayle asked.

"Only if you bark, meow, or pee on the floor," Teresa said.

They giggled.

"I can't believe this day has arrived!" Teresa said. "It seemed as if the construction would never end."

Gayle looked around the room. "It was so worth the wait, T. Your other office was okay, but this is so vibrant, open and inviting. Like I said, I wish I were an animal-child so I could come here for therapy."

Teresa's smile faded as a bad thought crossed her face. Not a day went by that she didn't curse the old drug-pushing FDA and those doctors of the past who only prescribed drugs instead of trying to heal people. Only one in a hundred women could conceive now, and she was not one of them. Everyone knew that if someone didn't come up with a solution, humans might become extinct in the next couple of hundred years.

Teresa shook off her melancholy moment. "My calendar is full for the next two months," Teresa explained.

"That's wonderful!" Gayle said. Her demeanor changed from glowing and happy to troubled.

"What's wrong?" Teresa said.

Gayle grasped one of Teresa's hands. When she met Teresa's gaze, her eyes were suddenly apologetic.

"Harold has accepted a position with Hycore Security in New York," Gayle said.

Teresa stared at her friend in disbelief, and then she became teary. She gripped Gayle's hands.

"Why didn't you tell me Harold was looking for another post?" Teresa asked.

"We've discussed it for a long time, but we didn't want to say anything because you know how difficult it is to move to another state and sector," Gayle said.

Gayle appeared fraught with indecision. "I've known you my entire life. You're not only my very best friend, but you're like my sister, and now I'll miss seeing the puppies grow up."

"When...?" Teresa asked. She tried hard to be brave.

"Two months. July fifteenth. There's a lot of preliminary preparation on both ends," Gayle said.

Teresa took a deep breath. She had a feeling that July 15, 2086, would be one of the worst days of her life.

~

TERESA LOUNGED on the end of the large gray and gold-flecked sectional sofa in the living room. A smile played on her face as she watched Lilith sleeping on a round fleece dog bed, her legs kicking periodically as she chased a dream. Teresa thought Lilith was probably relieved to be away from her puppies for a moment of peace.

Bill joined Teresa on the sofa and pulled her legs onto his lap. He leaned in and kissed her, then really looked at her. "What's wrong?"

Teresa dropped the smile and unleashed her full emotions. She looked very sad. "Have you talked to Harold lately?" she asked.

"No. He's been pretty busy," Bill said. "What's going on?"

"Gayle told me he's accepted a position with Hycore Security and that they're moving in July," Teresa said.

Bill pulled back several inches and stared at Teresa in disbelief. "What?" he said. "Hycore—in New York?"

"One and the same," Teresa said.

"I wonder how he got approval to move?" Bill asked.

Teresa frowned. "Gayle tells me everything, good and bad. For her to keep this secret doesn't add up."

"She's never mentioned anything before? Never hinted that Harold was recruited or seeking this post?" Bill asked.

She shook her head. "Makes no sense, does it? My best

friend since we were seven years old, and she kept this secret from me."

"Why don't we have them over for dinner? Maybe they'll open up," Bill suggested.

"That's a good idea. I'll ask them over for next week," Teresa said.

TERESA SAT AT THE SMALL, square, blond, natural wood breakfast table in the kitchen with a mug of organic hot chocolate. Lilith romped on the terra cotta kitchen floor chasing a small rubber scatter ball that rolled haphazardly and bounced off surfaces to keep her entertained and exercised.

The ball whizzed past the table. "Go get that ball," Teresa encouraged with a laugh. Lilith took off after the ball and careened around the table and chair legs, skidding.

The Advanced Multi-Media Device (AMD) was concealed under a moving picture of a flowing mountain stream on the kitchen wall, which added a warm touch to the room. Within the two-by-three-foot frame, water flowed over rocks. A deer drank from the stream, and birds flew in the bright blue sky. The nature sounds of the water and the birds were soothing.

"Call Gayle Goanflower," Teresa said.

The AMD engaged, and the mountain scene swirled and dissolved as a communication portal opened. Within moments, Gayle's face filled the screen. She appeared to be in her glider.

"Hi, Gayle," Teresa said. "Where are you off to?"

"Hi, T," Gayle said. "Going to the distribution center to pick up something Harold ordered."

"Can you two come over for dinner Tuesday?" Teresa asked.

"Oh, that sounds so good. We could use a break from all of this chaos surrounding the move," Gayle said. "What time?"

"Let's do an early dinner. Say, six o'clock?" Teresa said. "It'll force Bill home early, too."

"Our men," Gayle said.

~

TUESDAY AT FIVE FIFTY-EIGHT, the front door sensor announced to the visitors, "Hello, we will be with you shortly. Please wait patiently." The message repeated.

Bill went to the front door and deactivated the security system at an imprint panel to the left of the door. He placed his hand into the mold. A green light activated around his hand as it read his fingerprints and the lines in his palm. The system responded authorization authenticated, and the many front door locks unlatched in sequence.

He opened the door wide to Harold and Gayle. "It's about time, Injun Jim," Bill said.

Harold fake-punched Bill. He looked at his timepiece. "It took you two minutes to deactivate security, for Earth's sake. We were here right on time, Golden Eagle," he said. Harold Goanflower, an American native with thick black hair, dark eyes, and a six-foot eight frame, made an imposing figure. His face was smooth with a strong jaw. He could trace his family back before Columbus ever set a toe on the east coast.

"An unexpected teleconference of the highest importance almost made us late," Harold said.

A foot shorter, Gayle walked beside her husband, a wide smile on her lovely face.

Bill looked at Harold quizzically, but left his unspoken question silent. He snickered as he stepped back to allow them into the house. He and Harold shook hands warmly, and then he and Gayle hugged.

"As funny as ever," Gayle said. "Where's Teresa?"

"In the kitchen," Bill said.

Gayle left Bill and Harold in the living room and went to the kitchen.

"Hi, Ejonia," Gayle said.

Ejonia wiped down the counter. "Oh, hi, Mrs. Goanflower; you look nice." She noted the pale green, loose-fitting ensemble that Gayle wore. "That color is striking with your eyes."

"Oh, you're always so colorful. Where's Teresa?" Gayle asked.

"She's watering the new tree," Ejonia said.

"How's the new food console?" Gayle asked.

"Mrs. Goanflower, this is not just any food console. It's the Capresso Jura Premium Epicurean Gourmet Center! I can finally put my professional training to good use," Ejonia said. She stroked the stainless-steel pillar before her. "Did you know I can specify a 'pinch' of an ingredient and it understands what I mean? This is a dream come true! I never thought I'd ever get to use something like this."

"I can't wait to see what you delight us with tonight." Gayle crossed the terra cotta floor, stepped outside, and saw Teresa.

Teresa, in a light gray silk pants outfit with a pink and gray fine-knit scarf around her neck, rushed over to Gayle. They hugged in a tight, best-friend way. She stuck her hand through Gayle's arm and ushered her back into the house. They joined the men in the living room.

"T, I can't get over your new office space! Your decorator is brilliant," Gayle said.

"All my clients like the new atmosphere," Teresa said.

Ejonia entered the room carrying an elaborate painted tray

with crystal goblets of sparkling water and a plate of mushroom appetizers.

"Make sure you save your appetites for the main event," Ejonia said.

"Ejonia's debuting new food console creations," Teresa said.

"Dinner's almost ready," Ejonia said.

"What are you cooking up for us tonight?" Bill asked.

"Tilapia almandine, wild rice with cranberries and mandarin oranges, and steamed squash," Ejonia said. "But first, the appetizers."

They each took a glass from the tray. Ejonia set the appetizer plate on the coffee table and returned to the kitchen.

Bill raised his glass. "Sounds like a couple of toasts are called for. To the new food console!" He lightly tapped his glass with Harold's, then Gayle's, and Teresa's. "Harold, here's to your new post with Hycore." They all clinked their glasses again.

As he sipped water, Bill glimpsed Harold giving Gayle a warning look. Bill studied Gayle's unhappy expression, and for a split second he thought she was on the verge of tears.

"So, don't hold us in suspense. Details," Bill said, turning to face Harold and Gayle.

BILL, and Teresa approached the master bedroom. The overhead lights came on as they entered.

"Dim lighting," Bill said.

The lights adjusted to his command, and the room was bathed in low light.

"Something's not right about this Hycore thing." Bill closed the door behind them.

"I know," Teresa said.

"Gayle seemed to put on an act, trying to be all happy, but I caught a glimpse of a look between them," Bill said. "Harold won't let her tell us something. I don't like it."

Teresa pulled off her shirt and slacks and hung them in the smart closet. She stood in bra and panties and faced Bill, hands on her slender hips.

"What in the world could it be? Will he be spying for the World Guild or something?" she said. Her periwinkle blue eyes sparked with anger. "I can't imagine a secret so deep that they can't tell us."

She held her hand out toward Bill. He slipped off his shirt and handed it to her, then his slacks. She hung them in the smart closet and pressed the control button.

The glass door sealed with a low hiss, and a green mist swirled inside the closet. A bright white light shone for approximately thirty seconds and faded, leaving the clothes clean and free of odor-causing bacteria.

"I don't know what to think," Bill said. "But I'm going to ask some of my contacts if they can find out something."

Teresa unhooked her bra as she walked into the bathroom. She deposited the bra and her panties into a stainless-steel lingerie cleaning drawer and then stepped into the misting chamber.

Bill followed Teresa into the bathroom, naked. He watched for a moment as the mist soaked Teresa's exquisite body, and then he joined her.

THE SUN SHONE through the window in Bill's home office. Lilith was having a hard time keeping up with her puppies.

"Mandy, put down that pencil; it contains lead, and it's

dangerous!" Lilith said. She turned to see Bob stalking his brother. He chomped down on Larry's tail. Larry howled. "Bob! Leave your brother alone!"

Lilith went over to Larry and sniffed his tail. "You'll be okay, Larry. Go play with Jasmine."

Lilith let out a short huff. "Nap time!" The six puppies romped all over the place, ignoring her. She rounded them up one by one and put them in the whelping box. She crawled in after them and flopped down. The puppies settled, and they all conked out for a nice nap.

BILL STEPPED OFF THE ELEVATOR, then he entered Teresa's office suite.

"Hey, Myra-June, is Teresa finished up?" he asked.

"She's all yours," Myra-June said.

Bill went around the desk to Teresa's office, tapped on the door and opened it.

Teresa was holding a portable electronic reader against her bent knees on one of the low sofas. She pressed a button, and the reader made a "swish" sound of a page turning

"You ready to go see the landscapers?" Bill asked.

"Ready, but we'll have to take separate gliders," Teresa said. "I have another session scheduled today." She set the reader on the floor, stood and stretched.

Bill came in and closed the door. He crossed the room and embraced Teresa, burying his face in her hair and breathing in her lavender scent deeply. She ran her fingers through the hair on the back of his head. They swayed slightly.

"I love you," he said.

"I love you more," she said.

Bill took her hand and tugged her to the sofa. They sat facing each other in the middle of the sofa.

"I received a ping from the east coast," he said.

Teresa tensed; her face a mask as she waited.

"There doesn't seem to be anything mysterious about Harold's new post or any of the arrangements," Bill said.

Teresa let out a breath of relief and sat in thought for a moment. "Maybe we were reading too much into Gayle's stress. She's most likely just having a difficult time leaving."

Bill shrugged. "I thought for sure something bad was happening, so I'm glad I was wrong."

TWIN AZURE-BLUE GLIDERS with clear bubble roofs arrived within moments of each other at the Maxwell's large Southwestern-adobe-style home. The gliders slid silently into the holding area, formerly known as a garage.

Three men in drab gray jumpsuits, each with a thin copper-colored band around his neck denoting their non-violent prisoner status, were having a heated discussion in the front yard as Bill and Teresa exited the holding area and approached them.

"What's wrong, Dion?" Teresa asked the tallest of the three as she and Bill approached the trio.

"Hi, Mr. and Mrs. Maxwell."

"So, what are you guys fussing about?" Teresa asked.

"Acid bugs, Mrs. Maxwell," Dion said, shaking his head. He pointed to the grass at their feet.

"Again?" Bill bellowed.

"Johnson's has inferior inventory compared to Origins," Gregor said.

"We see so many infested plants and grasses that have come from Johnson's landscaping," Dion said.

"I wonder how they stay in business," Teresa said.

Bill squatted and poked through the silky grass that rarely needed maintenance. As he parted the lush grass, dozens of brown, hard-shelled bugs with long feelers and a hundred legs scooted out of the way.

"Careful, Mr. Maxwell, the lawn is infested," Brody said. "I've already been burned twice."

Brody showed two blistered fingers.

"We need to report to the Tranquility Force so they'll reassign us," Gregor said. He pawed his neckband nervously.

"That's it," Bill said. He stood, rubbed his hands together to remove loose dirt, and put his fists on his hips. "Take it out of here tomorrow. I'll have Johnson's pick it up and credit us."

"Why don't we try an oasis setting, Bill?" Teresa asked. "We were going to do that before Johnson's talked us into this premium hybrid grass. We would have been better off with that ugly perma-grass."

Teresa scanned the immediate neighborhood. Residences were all shapes and sizes, and without the old streets, houses seemed plunked down at all angles. Gliders didn't need roads, and after thirty years of zooming through the air, roadways, bridges, and the old stacked interstates were demolished.

There were a few standard World Guild-approved box dwellings similar to a shipping container, only larger. The color palette was eclectic, at best, with an orange house next to a purple or green one. Teresa shuddered slightly as she turned her gaze to her beautiful light taupe-colored stucco home.

The men gazed across the expanse of houses to the hideous fake lawns that were one notch up from the old Astroturf.

"Yoo hoo!" Becky Smythe hollered. She stood in front of a small purple and green house and waved to Teresa.

Teresa squinted against the sun and waved back exuberantly.

"Who's that?" Bill asked while shielding his eyes from the sun.

"Becky," Teresa said. "Wave."

Bill turned and looked across the many yards. He waved at Becky.

"An oasis would look nice," Dion said. He activated the command center on his wrist and a holographic landscaping application appeared in the air in front of the group. Dion tapped keys on the hologram, and a picture of Bill and Teresa's house floated before them. "We could do a small koi pond with those nice flat, polished rocks, some colorful grasses and bright, flowering plants."

The hologram changed as Dion tapped the keys. The koi pond, rocks, and plants looked as solid as the ground on the hologram.

Teresa and Bill looked at each other, conferred silently, and came to an agreement.

"Do other grasses have a problem with these acid bugs?" Teresa asked.

"You could get the Bolero dwarf fescue for the backyard so Lilith and the pups can play safely," Dion said. "The new modified variety is bug–resistant, and acid bugs hate the stuff."

"Good suggestion, Dion," Teresa said. "Bill, send the Tranquility Force the new assignment, and place an order for the new grass. We should make Johnson's remove this infested grass. We don't want the guys to get any more acid burns."

Gregor's copper neckband glowed lightly, followed by Brody's and Dion's. "We've been idle for too long," Gregor said fearfully.

His neckband turned an angry orange. Gregor cried out in anguish as he grabbed the neckband to no avail. He collapsed to his knees, making agonizing sounds, followed quickly by Dion and Brody grasping their neck bands.

"Bill! Call the Tranquility Force!" Teresa said, agitated.

Bill quickly tapped a shiny patch on his shirt. He touched a button on a holographic communication device as it hovered in the air in front of him. He tapped Judicial Assignments, and a virtual officer appeared.

"Please stop stunning my workers! We were having a meeting," Bill said through gritted teeth as he tried to moderate the edge to his voice.

The virtual officer made no verbal commitment or acknowledgement, but the shocks to the inmates ceased.

"I would also like to modify the assignment," Bill said.

"Commence," the Virtual Officer said.

"Tomorrow, June 2, 2086, send my workers to Maxwell Industries for their normal duty roster. On June 3, 2086, the Maxwell residential landscaping project will continue," Bill said.

Everyone listened as the virtual officer repeated and logged the assignments.

"Brody, come inside so I can treat your fingers," Teresa said.

After the inmates mustered at the pickup point, a Tranquility Force transporter arrived and took them away.

TERESA HURRIED BACK to her office in time for her appointment. After the hour session concluded, she hugged a short, red-headed woman, then held her at arm's length.

"I'm glad you're going to apply for adoption, Estelle. It will take several months before you hear anything from the agency, which will give you time to grieve Frieda's passing," Teresa said.

Estelle sighed deeply, her eyes red-rimmed. "Thanks, Teresa. I'm so glad I kept the appointment today."

"Me, too. You need time to reflect, but you also need to be around people so you don't dive into depression," Teresa said. "Eat a handful of cashew nuts every day. They stave off depression."

"I'll try," Estelle said, tears flowing. "I'd better go. Blessings to you."

Teresa walked Estelle out the door and down the hallway to the outer office. She patted Estelle on the back, then returned to her inner office and sank into a sofa.

Myra-June sat at her desk in the outer office, creating a virtual picture on the monitor-easel for animal children clients when Estelle entered the outer office. Myra-June saved the purple rabbit she had created and turned her attention to Estelle.

Estelle passed her wrist over the Dot reader on Myra-June's command center without saying a word.

Myra-June smiled brightly at Estelle. "Take care, Mrs. Ford."

Estelle nodded and quietly exited the office.

Teresa engaged her communication device. "Call Gayle Goanflower."

The AMD engaged, and the mountain scenery dissolved into a connection scene with a giant Sprintcast logo. An avatar appeared on the screen.

"There is no record of Gayle Goanflower," the avatar said.

"Connect with Harold Goanflower," Teresa said. She spelled Goanflower for the avatar.

"There is no record of Harold Goanflower," the avatar said.

"Of course there is," Teresa argued. "Specifically look in New York city."

"There is no record of the name Goanflower in the state of New York," the avatar said.

"Disconnect," Teresa said. She shoved her chair back and

marched into the schoolroom. She poked around in a drawer in the wall shelving and pulled out a slip of paper. Gayle's elegant handwriting provided the new location details. She slipped it into the pocket of her slacks.

She called Bill.

"There's something screwy going on. I know you had this Hycore thing checked out, but I haven't been able to get in touch with Gayle," she said. "Should you try calling Harold?"

"Do you get a personal message at least?" Bill asked.

"No, there's no record of her or Harold in New York," Teresa said.

"What? Even though the Hycore transfer seemed to pan out, I think something happened," Bill said. "You may have to just wait to hear from her."

Teresa fretted.

LILITH SLIPPED OUT of the lab unnoticed after a two-hour nap as the puppies played. Bill had cordoned off the area beyond his desk so the puppies couldn't get into trouble amid his lab equipment.

The puppies tried to break through to the forbidden area. Bob, Abby and Jazz gnawed at the sturdy gate, keeping them on the safe side of the lab while Mandy and Frankie played tag. Abby turned in time to see Lilith's brown tail disappear into the hallway. She took off running after her canine mother and skidded, bonking into a kitchen chair while the flap of the dog door slapped back and forth and finally locked into place.

Abby romped over to the dog door and pushed the flap with her head, like she had seen her canine mother do. Without a Dot to activate the mechanism, the flap would not budge. Abby huffed, exasperated, and pawed the flap. After a few minutes, she gave up and trotted away toward her next adventure: an opaque door. She pushed her head against the door, and it opened. Abby slipped inside and the door shut with a click.

TERESA MAXWELL WALKED out of Happy Tails, her animal psychology business in the downtown business hub, and stepped into her glider.

"Glider ready. Destination: Maxwell Industries," she said.

The glider lifted off the ground and zoomed through the air at a normal speed. Ten minutes later it came to a stop in front of the corporate campus of Maxwell Industries, her husband's company. The glider settled on the ground, and Teresa stepped out and approached the front door.

Bill was descending the stairs as Teresa entered the building. They smooched and smiled at each other.

She reached over and smoothed the stand-up collar on the back of Bill's black silk dress jacket. The stand-up white shirt collar was perfectly displayed a half-inch higher than the jacket collar. His matching slacks fell atop his dress sandals that were reminiscent of the old Birkenstock shoe line created 309 years earlier in 1774 by Johann Adam Birkenstock in Germany.

Her communication device dinged. She removed it from her shirt and looked at the opaque two-inch square screen. Myra June, her assistant, was contacting her. The light tap on the communicator patch triggered a holographic menu port that opened and hung in the air a foot in front of Teresa's face. She dragged it through the air with a finger and repositioned it a little lower, then studied the menu. She found the communications portal button and tapped it.

"Did you forget an appointment?" Bill asked when he saw the message was from Myra June.

"No, my calendar was clear for lunch. Maybe there's an emergency. I'll only be a minute," she said. She tapped the screen, and Myra June's face appeared.

"I'm sorry to bother you, Mrs. Maxwell, but Mr. and Mrs. Abunce requested an emergency session for Jitterbug. She's being aggressive towards them again," Myra June said.

Teresa grimaced. "What's the calendar look like for this afternoon?"

"You can fit them in at two-thirty," Myra June said.

"Two-thirty it is. They'd better not have one of their conflicts," Teresa said.

Myra June giggled. "I'll contact them and set it up. Have a nice lunch with Mr. Maxwell."

"Do you want Teresa to bring you back some baklava, Myra June?" Bill asked.

Myra June gave a gleeful smile and a thumbs-up, then she disconnected the call.

Teresa replaced the communication device on her shirt. "Okay. Let's head out."

"I'm glad we don't need lunch reservations," Bill said.

LILITH FINISHED her business in the bathroom closet and stood, nose to air, sniffing the warm July summer breeze. Extremely loud emergency alert alarms startled her.

Lilith hunched close to the ground, and then stood warily. She turned in different directions, trying to track the racket while curiosity crinkled her brow.

The kitchen door opened and Ejonia stepped outside.

"What's that noise?" Ejonia asked.

"I don't know," Lilith said. "It's scary."

The gate slammed opened and Bruno, the head security detail for the Maxwell's, ran into the back yard. He was dressed in the Proteus low-risk commander's form-fitted silver and blue suit with minimum weapons and a molded helmet with exposed facial features.

Ejonia scratched her arm. Skin blistered and peeled off in long, bloody strips. "What in blazes..."

"Poison!" Bruno gasped out.

Ejonia pinched her nose with her fingers, too late. She gagged. Her face turned red. Her whole body erupted in blisters and boils. Chunks of flesh dropped to the ground. She collapsed.

Lilith sniffed, and then coughed deeply, once.

Bruno sprinted toward Lilith and scooped her up in his arms.

"What's poison, Bruno?" Lilith said, frightened. She coughed again.

He lunged five long paces, his lungs giving out, and then he stumbled. As he fell, he flung Lilith closer to the house. His expression clearly showed agony while blood seeped out of his eyes and nose. His body jerked in spasms as his face blistered. Then he was still.

Lilith struggled to her feet and sucked in her breath, and felt her throat constrict. Her skin erupted all over her body. She stared at Bruno's lifeless form in horror. Blood filled her mouth and seeped out of her nostrils. She made a choking noise as if she were drowning.

She looked on in fear as Ejonia's body seemed to boil right in front of her. Blood stained Ejonia's dress, and her hair fell out of its neatly coiled bun. Blood splattered the grass as what was left of Ejonia crumbled to the ground.

The sensors of the security system detected the threat and

triggered the titanium window shields that covered the few small windows on the house, two feet under the eaves. The shields ratcheted closed in rapid succession, snapping like a deck of cards.

~

ABBY PLAYED with Lilith's toys in Mommy Teresa's home office. She started as the loud clacking of the window shields sounded throughout the house. The fur on her back stood up as she looked this way and that. She growled at the unseen threat.

~

LILITH TOOK A WOBBLY STEP. "Puppies... Momma... Da...," she struggled to breathe as blood poured from her nostrils and her skin heaved and boiled.

She stumbled back to the house blindly, blood oozing from every orifice. Lilith frantically bumped her head against the house repeatedly while blindly searching for her dog door that was hidden by the titanium shield. She finally found the door, collapsed in front of it, and struggled to her feet.

Lilith's Dot triggered the release of the locking device, and she pulled herself through the door. She staggered through the kitchen and down the hallway to the whelping box in Bill's lab. Lilith collapsed in the bed, blood oozing from everywhere as her skin boiled and chunks dropped off.

Mandy and Bob romped and played while Frankie and Jazz worked the gate with their sharp little baby teeth.

Bob saw Lilith and puppy-galloped over to the whelping box. He scooted over the edge and plowed into her. He bit one of her ears and noticed the blood dripping and the huge blisters on her body. He licked at the blood. Bob's little body trembled and shook. He fell to the floor of the whelping box, dead.

Mandy, Frankie and Jazz ran over to the whelping box and climbed inside. They snuggled to Lilith's belly and suckled at their dead mother's bloody teats. One by one they shuddered as they lapsed into comas and died, as Abby tugged happily at a rug in Teresa's home office, oblivious to what she had lost.

CHAPTER TWO

B ill released his hand from the front door as the emergency alert sounded. The Maxwell Industries security system kicked in and security shutters covered all windows and doors. The contained air system switched on.

A smattering of employees converged on the ground floor of the main building. Other employees gathered at each floor, looking down at the lobby. The emergency generators kicked the lights on.

"What the hell happened?" Bill asked the Communicator at the front desk.

The top-of-the-line robotic Communicator was perched on a swivel stool behind an expansive curved counter in the middle of the lobby. Her face was dazzling white with large dark blue eyes, long poly-lashes, a delicate nose and chrome lips.

The Communicator's brilliantly painted trunk of a body with white-silver poly-skin was built into the chair. Her tentacle arms swayed like Medusa's hair, and a gleaming metal alloy and glass halo, three feet in diameter, crowned her head and was supported by a steel framework that rested on her shoulders.

Colors rippled across the Communicator's halo. A virtual storyboard on the wall came to life. Two newscasts played: GNN, and GCAUGHT, which was classified a rogue channel.

GNNie, the Global News Network literalist, hovered in airspace as she floated around the GNN headquarters in New York City amid floating event recording globes (FERGs) that zoomed through the air capturing action. GNNie's holographic avatar beamed from the closest GNN media satellite and broadcast the captured live event to every corner of the planet. She was a new model equipped with a curved, radiant face-shield which left only her stationary, brushed chrome lips exposed. She appeared as a glowing white and silver, androgynous mannequin. The GNN news team had classified her as female at her public debut in 2082.

People stared at GNNie's luminous white robe infused with the latest nanotechnology truth-bits as it fluttered in the air as if fanned by a breeze. Literalists were designed to be impartial bearers of the news. Their face shields transcribed speech quickly, displaying words nanoseconds after they were spoken.

All their reports, including speeches, were scrutinized through an intricate web of technology using fact-finding Nbits. These nanobits worked with the truth-bits and verified information so quickly that spoken words were determined to be true (green) or false (red) as the speaker verbalized them.

People looking out of office windows watched as anyone outside collapsed into bloody clumps of pulp. Gliders that flew on programmed journeys carried dead passengers to their destinations. Others that flew on manual, crashed to the ground. Literalist avatars from several newsgroups hovered several feet above the crowd in their designated positions. They silently recorded and reported the facts to their audiences as the news unfolded.

The GCAUGHT human literalist was heavily geared up in a Level Ten biohazard suit. She cumbersomely walked with difficult strides as if on the Moon.

"Whatever biological agent was released is an instant killer."

She showed an unfortunate man blistering, boiling and erupting chunks falling to the ground as he stumbled around, eventually falling into a bloody pulp on the sidewalk. A glider chose that moment and location to crash-land, clipping the GCAUGHT Literalist. The tear in her suit was instant acknowledgment of her imminent demise.

Bill, Teresa, and Maxwell's employees watched the screen in horror. Bill suddenly snapped alert and commanded action.

"Show Maxwell Industries locations," he roared at the screen.

The other buildings in the complex were in lockdown mode as well. The grounds were littered with the bodies of people who had been moving between buildings or working at outdoor workstations.

"List Maxwell Industries casualties," Bill barked out.

Thirty-seven of the five hundred employees' names appeared on screen. Bill, Teresa, and the onlookers moaned in sorrow.

"Define quarantine," Bill said.

"Security breach at Xavier Labs in Colorado released the deadly experimental agent XSKL435. High shifting winds from two storm systems have carried the poison from coast-to-coast.

"XSKL435 is deadly upon contact. It becomes inert after

twelve hours. Because of weather conditions, XSKL435 drift may continue for another twenty-four hours.

"Zheng Industries, one of Xavier Labs' top competitors in China, was also breached. Stay tuned for death tolls."

As the news was digested by all, Bill took action. "Open comm ports between buildings," he directed the Communicator.

"Comm ports opened," the Communicator stated.

"This is Bill Maxwell. We will be in lockdown for forty-eight hours. Everyone try to communicate with your families. We do not know who is left alive outside these walls."

Teresa frantically tried to contact Ejonia to no avail.

Soft music played.

"Your party cannot be reached," the mechanical voice responded.

Bill called Proteus Security after not reaching the security detail at their house.

"Proteus," a man answered. He sounded harried.

"This is Bill Maxwell. I've been trying to reach Bruno and the team at my house," he said, keeping a calm tone to his voice.

"Mr. Maxwell, we can't reach them either. There's a possibility that only a dozen of us at headquarters are all that's left in our company," the man said.

"Oh, no!" Bill said. He was shell-shocked. "We're in lockdown, so I don't know if my dog-daughter and her pups survived."

"Let us know when you're released and can get back home," the Proteus security man said.

"I will," Bill said and ended the call.

The large screen came to life. "This is an emergency broadcast from the World Guild. Fleets of eliminator drones have been dispatched across the globe. Do not leave secured locations until instructed to do so. Eliminator drones must disintegrate all casualties. Burying casualties will poison the Earth. Under penalty of death, no casualty shall be interred in any form. Disintegration is mandatory."

The World Guild, in Washington D.C., consisted of 204 nations. It was led by a President, six Sub-presidents (one each for North America, South America, Africa, Australia, Europe, Asia and Russia), the secretary of nations, and a war consular. The guild's bureaucracy involved more governmental positions and titles than the average person could keep track of.

The giant screen showed a swarm of drones zapping the fallen outside of GNN's headquarters.

"Oh, my Earth," Teresa said. "How will anyone know they've lost someone?"

Bill stared at the action on the screen. "That's the good thing about the Dot. If a life force isn't detected, they'll know that Dot was a casualty. They'll cross-reference the numbers to the names and build a list."

ABBY FOUND her way back to the whelping box. She stopped a couple of feet back from it as she detected something wrong. Her tail curled down between her legs. She noticed that her canine mother was a big, bloody mess with only patches of fur remaining. Her siblings didn't look right either.

Abby sniffed. She smelled death—an instinct that seemed to be wired into her DNA. She backed away slowly, then turned and ran from the room.

She stopped in the kitchen, panting in fear. Abby noticed the canine feeding and water stations on the floor against the wall. She approached it with caution. As she stepped up to the two devices, water ran in a gentle trickle into a stainless-steel bowl. She stretched her neck and lapped at the water running freely. Abby let out a little huff of satisfaction. She studied the second device. Several nuggets dropped into that bowl.

Abby snatched one nugget and dropped it on the floor, and sniffed it. It smelled good. The nugget was a little big for her mouth, but she managed to gnaw off a small chunk.

She now had a dilemma. She had to go potty, and the potty pads were in the bad place. Abby looked down the hall toward the whelping box and whined. She looked around the kitchen. There was a dish towel hanging off a big metal thing. Abby stood on her hind tippy-toes and stretched her neck. She could not reach the towel. Her forehead creased in thought.

She hopped on her hind legs.

Hop. Hop. Hop.

Finally, she snagged the towel by a corner and pulled it down to the floor. She squatted and peed, turned and looked at her new potty-pad then pooped.

~

THE FORTY-EIGHT-HOUR DEADLINE HAD PASSED. Everyone at Maxwell Industries waited, tense for the security shutters to lift. Bill communicated to all his employees in all buildings.

"Do not leave the premises without protective covering once the emergency has passed and we're allowed to leave," Bill warned. "Our personal gliders are not toxin-resistant, so stay suited until you reach your destination and are once again inside."

They waited another four and a half hours before the security shutters lifted and people could exit the buildings.

Bill and Teresa, suited in white head-to-toe bio-gear suits rated for deadly toxic contaminants, labored under the strain of the weight and bulkiness of the suits as they exited the main

Maxwell Industries building. Running was out of the question. Teresa headed for her glider. Bill tapped her and shook his head.

"We won't be able to sit in these suits," he said.

Bill guided her to a building off to the side where several maintenance gliders were parked. They moved as fast as the suits allowed to one of the maintenance gliders.

"Glider ready. Destination: William and Teresa Maxwell's home, maximum safe speed," Bill commanded in a tense tone as he and Teresa stepped onto the boarding platform of the vehicle cab area.

The cab sealed shut, and the glider rose off the ground, banked toward the west and scoped the course, and took off at a high-moderate speed.

Teresa reached up and pressed the decompress button to remove her helmet.

"No!" Bill shouted as he grabbed her gloved hand. "It's impossible to know how toxic this poison was. Everything will have to go through a cleansing, including the interiors of the gliders."

"Oh, My Earth! I didn't think about that." Teresa reversed the decompress function and locked her helmet back into place. She punched a button on the dash. "Call home."

"Unknown command," the mechanical voice responded.

"Uh, wrong vehicle." Teresa cleared her throat. "Call William Maxwell's residence."

Soft music played.

"Your party cannot be reached," the mechanical voice responded.

Teresa felt her heart hammering as she turned from the console and glanced out the windshield, then the side windows.

"What is that?" Teresa said. She peered through the windshield and pointed to the ground. "Are those bodies?" She heard her voice quivering.

Bill looked at the landscape in a one- hundred - and -eighty-degree area. The ground was scattered with dead bodies—both human and animal. He placed a gloved hand on Teresa's arm. "Yes."

As the glider flew across the sky, a swarm of eliminating drones scattered across the landscape. Bill and Teresa watched as the dead were disintegrated.

"I wonder if they've reached our neighborhood yet?" Bill asked.

Teresa cried. "Oh, please... Call Ejonia Matthews," Teresa commanded voice control.

Seconds ticked as music played. "Your party cannot be reached," the mechanical voice responded.

They approached their neighborhood. People were outside in their off-the-rack bio-suits. Bill and Teresa's horror grew as they gazed down at a smattering of bodies.

"Our friends and neighbors," Teresa whispered.

Bill rested his gloved hand on Teresa's hand as the glider banked a curve and their house came into view.

As soon as he saw them lying on the ground just feet from their glider, Bill knew that all the Proteus guards were dead.

"They must have tried to reach their glider," Bill said, his voice cracking behind the bio-mask. "I'm not sure if they would have been safe, even if they'd made it. Proteus should have had them in full headgear."

Teresa sobbed. "Oh, Bill."

"Land here," Bill commanded. The glider eased to the ground outside the holding area. "We need to go to the back-yard first. There are only five guards here and no one answered my call."

They awkwardly exited the glider and approached the gate

to the backyard and kitchen door. "Emergency override," he commanded. He rattled off a twenty-four-character sequence and answered security questions. Then the gate opened.

"Do you want to wait here?" he asked.

Teresa didn't answer. She lumbered past Bill and entered the backyard, her eyes darting wildly from one area of the yard to the next.

"Ejonia!" she moaned. She stood at Ejonia's side and reached out toward the dead woman.

Bill grabbed Teresa and pulled her away. "Don't touch her! Don't touch anything."

"Oh no. Bruno!" Bill said in anguish. He stared at the fallen guard that he considered his friend.

"Bill. Come on," Teresa was tugging on his arm. He followed her into the bathroom closet and stuck his head in the door, terrified at what he might find.

"Clear." He and Teresa stared at each other for a moment before they both exited the gate and returned to the front of the house.

ABBY WANDERED into the living room and found Lilith's old red scooter ball. She sniffed it, and then snorted, and the ball rolled toward the front door. Abby romped after the ball until she heard loud voices and crying noises on the other side of the door. Her ears stood up straight. She gave a little bark as she stared at the door.

The electronic unlocking sequence beeped, and the locks clacked open. Abby backed up a couple of steps and stared at the door.

The front door flew open and banged against the wall. Teresa and Bill tore into the house in a panic.

Abby barked nonstop, afraid of the strange vision before her. Her little heart pounded double time at the scary situation.

Teresa lumbered into the house and tripped; she stepped over Abby, barely missing her tiny feet. She and Bill pressed the decompression buttons on their helmets, then the jumpsuits.

"Throw everything outside. I'll get them to the smart closet later," Bill said.

The helmets released their docks to the suits with a swish. Teresa lifted the helmet off. Bill tossed his outside. Teresa followed suit.

"It's okay, honey," Teresa said.

Abby wagged her tail as she recognized Bill and Teresa. She barked happily but kept her distance from the strange suits.

Teresa flung the gloves after the helmet and eased out of the suit, pulling the arms inside-out and stepping out of the jumpsuit. She flung the suit out in the yard, bent and scooped up Abby, letting out a wail of pure joy.

"Bless the Earth!" she cried. "Oh, Abby, thank the Earth you're okay."

Bill shucked his suit, closed and secured the door, and ran past Teresa and Abby. He raced down the hall to the lab. "Lilith!" he roared with grief.

Teresa's smile crumbled. Her face twisted in anguish as she tried to stifle emotions. She held Abby protectively and ran into the office.

"Lilith!" She choked as she saw the horrifying scene in the whelping box.

Abby barked ferociously in her puppy voice.

"She knows," Teresa said.

Bill grabbed Teresa's shoulders and turned her away from the lifeless form of their beloved dog-daughter. The rest of the pups, so full of energy just hours ago, were now dead at their mother's belly.

"I can't believe this is happening," Teresa moaned, tears streaming down her face. "Why is this happening?"

"I'll have to call for eliminator drones, then we'll most likely have to leave the house while this area is decontaminated," Bill said, crying.

Teresa sobbed as the pain of a mother's loss ripped at her heart.

"Oh, Bill," she finally said between sobs. "It's not just about us. We have to call Ejonia's family. And then call Bruno's and Frank's and the others."

Bill and Teresa cried uncontrollably for several minutes. "He must have tried to save her," Bill said, thinking about Ejonia's proximity to Bruno's on the ground outside. "His arms were outstretched."

"Becky and Percy... they're going to be devastated. Abby is all they have left of Jimbo," Teresa said. "If they're even still alive!"

Bill put one arm across the back of Teresa's waist and maneuvered her out of the lab and shut the door. He leaned against the door for a moment as if to gather strength, and then he and Teresa headed down the hall to the kitchen. A half-chewed nugget was on the floor, water was in the bowl, and they saw the soiled dish towel.

"Abby has survivor instincts," Teresa said.

They went to the living room, where they collapsed on the sofa and cried, taking turns stroking a traumatized, whimpering Abby.

"GNN on," Bill commanded in a shaky voice.

The liquid moving picture of a flowing mountain stream on the wall swirled and the AMD panel appeared. A newsroom came into view on the wall screen, and a literalist appeared.

The same broadcast played that they had watched forty-eight hours ago.

Four-star General Emil Gootenberg appeared on the White House lawn, in full bio-gear, amid a frenzy of literalists and media from around the world, all encased in bio-suits.

"These biological acts of terror have not been traced back to their source," General Gootenberg said. "The Chairman of the Coalition of Middle Eastern Desert People is beaming into our broadcast."

A holographic image of the MED-P Coalition Chairman, in standard white robes and his head sporting a keffiyeh, appeared on the White House lawn. He was standing in a bomb-proof protective chamber at his home with his entourage of protectors in bio-gear fanned out on both sides.

"We are not responsible for this atrocity," the Chairman said. Eliminating drones disintegrated corpses in the background. Thousands were dead.

"Damn you to hell!" Bill exploded. "They had a population problem. Now it's solved."

"Bill, we don't know if they were responsible," Teresa said in a neutral voice.

Abby whined and trembled at Bill's outburst.

The literalist continued with the news while visuals appeared across the screen.

"Because most of the world's food-producing crops and animals are housed in structures with simulated day and night, there will not be a shortage of the world's food supplies."

Background pictures showed gliders helter-skelter on the ground where they had either crash landed, or arrived at their destination with dead passengers.

"It is estimated that approximately forty million people have been killed in the US alone."

"GNN off!" Bill said.

~

A LOUD POUNDING on the front door caused Teresa to jump. The front door sensor announced to the visitors, "Hello, we will be with you shortly. Please wait patiently. Violence is unnecessary." The alert repeated.

"Security, show exterior front door," Bill said, coming off the sofa.

Becky and Percy, who wore over-the-counter biohazard suits and headgear, stood at the front door, clutching each other's hands.

Bill walked to the front door and disengaged the locks.

"You're alive!" Teresa cried. Tears streamed down her face, and her body shook slightly as she tried to process this bit of positive news. Abby licked her teary face.

Becky and Percy's faces were filled with trepidation as they gestured toward Bill's lab.

Bill shook his head.

Becky sobbed as she and Percy stood on the doorstep and removed their headgear, then their suits, and tossed them a few feet from the door. They entered the house.

"Can we see them?" Percy asked, overcome with emotion.

"It's better if you don't," Bill said. "Abby is the only one who survived."

"I'm going to make arrangements for the eliminator drones," Bill said with a big heave to his chest.

They went to the living room and sat, Becky and Percy looking longingly at Abby.

The AMD switched from the mountain stream to communication mode. A local World Guild attendee appeared on the screen.

"WestUS World Guild," the man announced. "How can I help you, Mr. Maxwell?"

Bill explained the problem.

"I'll dispatch a unit to your address," the attendee said. "I'm sorry for your loss."

The AMD closed and the mountain stream appeared.

"I'm going to take the latest backup of Lilith's Dot and transfer the data to Abby's Dot. We'll want Abby to share her memories when she's a little older," Bill said.

"That would be so nice," Becky said. "She's so young she may not remember her canine mother and siblings in a few more months."

Teresa stood. She gained control over her heartache and handed Abby to the Smythes. Becky and Percy cried with a mixture of grief and joy as they fawned over her. Abby rewarded them with baby licks.

"I've got to call Ejonia's family," Teresa said.

Becky reached out and grabbed Teresa's hand. They clutched each other's fingers for several moments; then Teresa left the room.

TERESA'S SKIN prickled as the front door sensor announced visitors. Bill looked up and saw that her face was very pale.

"I'll get it," he said as he hurried to the door.

He opened the door to a World Guild Eliminator worker in full bio gear with one drone hovering close by.

The worker announced his orders.

"Come on in," Bill said.

The worker came inside, the drone following. Bill led them down the hallway to the lab and opened the door. The worker scanned the area. A holographic image hovered in front of them showing the complete whelping box.

"Will we have to leave for decontamination?" Bill asked.

"That won't be necessary," the worker said. "After forty-eight hours, the hazard is completely inert. All that will be necessary is washing the floor.

Bill watched as the drone received the holographic mapping and zapped the area. The whelping box, his dog-daughter and her dead pups vanished as his eyes blinked. He walked the worker and the hovering drone to the front door.

The drone got busy eliminating the guards from the front of the house. Bill stepped outside. "There are two bodies in the backyard. I've unsecured the gate for you."

The worker dipped his head somberly. "We were so sorry to hear about Lilith and the puppies."

Bill bowed his head and retreated to the house.

Becky returned Abby to Teresa, and they all went to the lab.

Abby lifted her little head and howled.

Bill, Teresa, Becky and Percy clutched each other's hands as tears streamed down their faces.

Bill steered Teresa, Becky and Percy to the sofas where they cried, unable to control their grief. Abby whimpered and howled, too young to understand what had happened, but she picked up on the atmosphere of grief.

CHAPTER THREE

Bill wrapped his arms around Teresa on the sofa. Abby slept against Teresa's chest. The somber mood was interrupted by a GNN broadcast.

"Worldwide statistics are now calculated from the recent tragic displays of aggression," the literalist said. "Of the five-hundred twenty-eight million canine companions, only four life forces have been detected. The World Guild requests parents of all canines who do not currently have their Dot installed at the requisite four months of age to report and register their canine child, or recent litter."

Bill and Teresa squawked their disbelief. Abby whimpered.

Teresa cooed her back to sleep as she and Bill listened intently to the rest of the broadcast.

"Bill, how could that be possible?" Teresa appeared shell-shocked.

"Think about it, honey," he said. "Lilith probably died going to the bathroom closet. Most are outdoors. Plus, they come and go through their private doors. If they were outside, they're dead. And don't forget, most people take their children everywhere so they died along with their humans in unprotected gliders, or on the ZoomBus."

"You know how curious Lilith was," Becky said. "She would have gone outside to see what the racket was with the emergency alert. I can't see how those numbers are accurate though."

"I bet countries like China, India, and the African continent were probably hit hard. Many people in those countries don't even have gliders. They either walk or ride glide bikes everywhere," Percy said.

The screen showed a world map. Mountain and forest areas across the planet were highlighted.

"GNN science officers are sending teams across the planet to remote areas to gather census information. Mountain, forest and other indigenous people may not possess reporting technology," the literalist said.

The broadcast was interrupted by an incoming call. A GNN statistician avatar appeared on the screen.

"This is a World Guild request for undocumented canine survivors per household," the statistician stated in an authoritative tone. "Please state your identification number, followed by species as the reporting citizen."

"97922AJ734668210," Bill said.

The avatar looked coolly at Bill. "You did not state your species."

Teresa laid her hand firmly on Bill's thigh.

"Human," Bill said. His jaw clenched.

The statistician avatar repeated the data. Bill confirmed.

The avatar turned her impersonal gaze on Abby. "State the birthdate, sex, and name of your undocumented canine."

Bill's icy glare bore into the statistician as he began with the information. "Aberdeen Tallulah Maxwell, female, born June 4, 2086."

The statistician avatar repeated the data, and Bill confirmed. The transmission terminated.

"Request, my ass!" Bill snarled. "They'll break your door down if you don't comply. And what's this about species? The numbers clearly discern human or canine."

"It's over," Teresa said. "Please calm down."

Percy and Becky stood. "We'd better go home and let you have some space,"

Bill and Teresa walked Percy and Becky to the door.

"Just leave the suits. I'll dispose of them," Bill said.

"Shouldn't we take them with us?" Becky asked.

"These over-the-counter suits are for onetime use only," Bill explained. "Their seals aren't industrial strength and would let in contagions that could kill you."

"Looks like we'd better buy another set," Percy said.

Percy and Becky waved and went home.

Bill and Teresa returned to the living room.

"They'll find more dogs, but in the meantime, I think we'd better prepare for the worst," Bill told her. His shoulders slumped in an attitude of defeat.

Teresa felt her heart race. "What do you mean? Abby's not in any danger."

Anguish washed over Bill's face. "If there are only four documented dogs on the entire planet, the World Guild will confiscate the remaining dogs for a reintroduction program."

Bill put his arm around Teresa's shoulders.

She didn't even know that the woman screaming was her.

CHAPTER FOUR

Teresa struggled with her emotions and dropped to the sofa. She sat like a rock as sheer terror knocked the wind out of her and left her speechless. Her reasoning and rationale shutting down, a vacant expression froze her face. Without warning, she shot to her feet.

"They can't have her!" she roared.

Abby jerked awake and looked up at Teresa, then across to Bill. She knew something was going on. She chewed on Teresa's fingers.

"I'm going to implant Abby's Dot," Bill said.

"She's just a baby, Bill! She's too young!"

"I'll encode it to become effective when she's four months old. At least we can prepare her with critical data and memories of her family. If I don't implant her Dot now, she may never have access to those memories, hon."

Teresa thought for a moment, and then agreed. "You're right." She pressed two fingers at the bridge of her nose and squeezed her eyes shut. "Bill, I don't think I can live in a childless world. I don't know what I'd do without Abby. Lilith's gone. She's the only child we'll ever have! And what about all the childless people across the planet that lived for the moments they watched Lilith on her show?"

Lilith had been the wonder dog: the first canine to use the PawBoard, the first dog to talk through the Dot. The UPC had developed a weekly thirty-minute program where Lilith entertained the world with her charming personality. It was extremely popular, especially with people who were on waiting lists for adoption.

Bill pulled Teresa into his arms. They clung together in silence, with Abby wedged between their hearts. Bill rested his forehead on Teresa's head. The pain of her words sliced through him as the reality slammed home.

A NEIGHBORHOOD CHANNEL opened on the big screen in the living room. Bill and Teresa recognized one of their neighbors.

"Hi everyone. A few of us have organized a memorial for our fallen neighbors. If you feel up to it, please join us in our park area tomorrow afternoon at 2:00. May the Earth comfort you!"

The channel closed and the mountain stream appeared.

"That sounds nice," Teresa said. "I'll see if Myra-June can come over to watch Abby."

"You don't want to bring Abby with us?" Bill asked.

Teresa shook her head. "I think it would be too traumatic for people who have lost so much."

Bill thought about what she said. "Yeah, I think you're right."

"I'm going to see if Becky and Percy want to go with us," Teresa said.

MYRA-JUNE WAS RETRIEVING a snack for Abby from the food console when the kitchen door opened. Teresa entered first, followed by Becky, Percy, and Bill. Their downcast expressions brightened as Abby rushed out from under the table and barked a greeting.

"Was Abby any problem?" Teresa asked. She swooped down and captured Abby in her arms.

"Are you kidding?" Myra-June asked. "She's a bundle of fun."

"Hi, Abby," Teresa said as she crushed Abby to her heart and rocked her. Abby licked Teresa's chin.

Becky scratched Abby's butt, which triggered a rear leg scratching reflex.

"How would you like some tea or coffee?" Myra-June asked.

"That would be lovely," Teresa said. "Who wants what?"

"I'll have some hot chocolate," Bill said.

"That sounds good," Becky said. "What do you want, Percy?"

"Yeah, hot chocolate sounds good."

"Four hot chocolates," Teresa said.

They all sat at the kitchen table in a numb silence. Myra-June worked the food console.

"I'm thinking of closing my practice," Teresa said calmly.

Everyone stared at her in stunned silence, including Myra-June, who stopped preparing the beverages. "But Mrs. Maxwell, people are going to need you more than ever to overcome their grief."

"My patients were animals and their parents," Teresa said. "They're all dead. Any human parents who survived need to talk to human therapists who are better equipped to help them."

"But those parents need you, not a human therapist who has no experience with dog children!" Myra-June exclaimed, near tears.

"As a therapist, you know you should not make any rash decisions following a crisis," Becky said.

Myra-June turned back to the food console and blinked back tears. She retrieved two cups of hot chocolate and brought them to the table, and returned for the next two.

Bill laid his arm across Teresa's shoulders and pulled her to him. He rested his head against her flowing blonde hair. "Becky's right. No quick decisions. Take some time off. Myra-June, you can come over to Maxwell Industries. I'll find a place for you until Teresa thinks this through."

Teresa shook her head. "No. They're going to take Abby away from us, and I have to prepare her and us for that loss."

THE NEXT DAY, Teresa was more settled. She sat in her home office and began creating lesson plans for Abby. Bill wandered in.

"I'm going to take Abby to Maxwell Industries," he said.

Teresa looked up, startled. "You're going to take her out of the house? Why?"

Bill sat on the edge of her desk and placed his hands on her shoulders. "I want her to see and experience what we have, and since Maxwell Industries provides for all our comforts, she needs to go there."

Teresa sat and thought for a moment. She bobbed her head.

"I guess you're right. I know you'll keep her safe. Just promise me you won't stop anywhere along the way. She's vulnerable in not knowing her status."

Bill kissed Teresa on the forehead. "I promise."

~

BILL CARRIED Abby up the stairs to his office on the second floor. "This is the big office where Daddy works when he doesn't work at home, Abby."

Abby's tail wagged and her butt wiggled as she sniffed the floor, walls, shelves at her height, stuck her head in the trash can, and checked out everything possible.

"Let's go over to the other building where Angelica works," Bill said. "Come with Daddy."

They walked to the elevator and entered the car. Abby raced out of the elevator on the ground floor. She skidded to a stop several feet from the Communicator and watched as the tentacled arms waved through the air with the halo rapidly changing colors.

"Stay close to Daddy, or I'll have to carry you," Bill warned. They walked past the Communicator to the front door. Abby looked over her shoulder at the Communicator again before they exited the building onto a crushed gravel path.

"This way, honey," Bill said. "Stay on the path. There are security sensors."

Abby scampered down the path near Bill, her tail in the air. Every few yards she stopped to sniff an interesting scent on the gravel.

A tiny alligator lizard scooted across the path inches in front of her. She jumped back, recovered, and then took chase after the scampering lizard off the path through the land-scaping.

"Abby! Get back here!" Bill shouted from the edge of the path.

Security globes whizzed through the air from concealed locations throughout the complex when Abby stepped off the path. The silver and sky-blue orbs hovered over Abby and glowed brightly. They beamed spotlights on and around Abby.

"Return to the path at once. Authorized personnel and registered visitors must stay on the path. Trespassers will be arrested in accordance with the Trespassing Act," the globes announced.

Abby stopped her frantic search for the lizard. She looked up and saw the security globes hovering in the air over her. She stood up on her hind legs, dog-paddling the air for balance, and touched her nose to one of the globes.

"Abby, NO!" Bill roared.

An electrical discharge erupted from the globe.

Abby yelped, dropped to all fours and rubbed her nose across the grass, whining.

A few employees rushed over to Bill. "Is she okay?" someone asked.

Bill slapped the shiny communication patch on his shirt and canceled the alarm through the holographic screen in front of him.

"Yeah. It should only be a minor shock, but I know it must sting," Bill said.

Abby ran to Bill and pawed his legs, yelping. He picked her up and inspected her swollen nose.

"Your mother's going to be pretty upset about this," he said. "I'll fix you up as soon as we're in the lab."

Abby pawed at her nose and whined pitifully.

"When Daddy or Mommy tells you to do something, there's always a good reason. You need to pay attention," he said.

One of the guys looked at Abby's nose. "That doesn't look good."

Abby buried her face in the crook of Bill's arm and whined.

Someone scratched Abby's butt. "I hope you feel better soon."

"Lesson learned, I hope," Bill said.

Bill carried Abby to the development building. He placed his hand in the security system's imprint panel hand mold beside the door. The door clicked open. Bill entered the building.

"Just a few more minutes, honey. Daddy just has to answer the security question," Bill said.

The foyer was a five-foot by five-foot brightly lit area. A single door stood to the right, barely visible. No imprint panel was present. Bill turned and faced the door. He blew a steady breath into the air in front of him. A holographic screen appeared in front of the door.

A woman's face became visible on the screen. She scrutinized Bill and Abby. "Yes, may I help you?"

"I would appreciate your help," Bill replied in a steady, clear voice.

The door popped open. Ten feet in front of him was an escalator. Bill hurried to the escalator and rode to the next floor.

Angelica, the woman on the holographic screen, met Bill at the top of the escalator. She looked at Abby's swollen nose. "Oh, no! What happened?"

"She didn't listen and got zapped," Bill said.

"Should I call Teresa?" Angelica asked in a mild panic.

A fleeting look of guilt crossed Bill's face. "No! She's stressed to the max already!"

"Let's go to the Virtual Healing office," Angelica said.

"We don't have anything here to fix her?" Bill asked.

Angelica shook her head. "She really needs to see the virtual veterinarian."

Abby let loose a pitiful wailing sound. Bill and Angelica cringed.

~

BILL AND ANGELICA hurried through the main lobby of Maxwell Industries, past the Communicator and elevators. Abby's nose was buried between Bill's arm and his shirt, and she whined pitifully.

The Virtual Healing Office (VHO) was tucked into a nook at the back of the building with a large, brilliantly lit caduceus symbol above the doorway.

A large blue mold in the shape of a human stood in the center of the small space. Smaller blue molds in the shapes of a dog and a cat, both facing the human mold, were on either side of the human mold.

"Okay, Abby. Don't be scared. This is the Virtual Healing office. You need to stand right here in this dog mold," Bill said. "It will close in on you a little, but it will be okay—it doesn't hurt one bit."

Bill set Abby on the floor in the recessed shape of the dog mold. A white light lit up around the shape of the dog mold, and the shape shrank to within two inches of her body.

"Welcome, Abby Maxwell," the virtual veterinarian said. "Please state the reason for this visit."

"An electrical shock to the tip of the nose," Bill said.

Abby turned to face Bill, her brow furrowed.

"Please place your face into the canine form," the virtual veterinarian said.

"Honey, you have to keep your face here so the veterinarian

can make your nose feel better," Bill said. He gently moved her face into the correct position.

Abby mewled pathetically and looked out at Bill and Angelica with a sad expression on her little face.

Bill moved her face again and held his hand against her cheek. Angelica squatted and patted Abby gently on the rump.

"It's going to be all right, Abby," Angelica said.

The snout area of the dog mold lit up with a bright red light. Then it changed to white, then peach, and finally black. After twenty seconds, the black light shut off. Abby wagged her tail.

"The healing is complete. Avoid all unsupervised activity while in the proximity of electrical currents, as this may constitute a similar condition," the virtual veterinarian said. "Please scan your Dot at the credit panel."

"Uh-oh. Forgot about that," Bill said as he picked up Abby. He turned to the credit panel on the inside wall of the VHO and presented his wrist. "Guess I'll have to confess to Teresa after all. She'll see the VHO charge on our credit statement."

The credit panel read the Dot on Bill's wrist. A green LED appeared on the screen. "Credit accepted. You owe zero balance. Thank you for your business," an automated voice said.

"Let's get going so we can get some work done," Bill said.

"Can I hold Abby?" Angelica asked.

"Sure," Bill said. He passed Abby to Angelica.

Abby wagged her tail and licked Angelica's chin.

"See, that didn't hurt at all, did it? You're getting so big!" Angelica said.

They walked back over to the development building. Angelica put Abby down when they stepped off the escalator on the second floor.

"Here you go, Abby. Feeling better?" Angelica asked.

Abby barked up at Angelica.

"Don't forget, when Mommy or Daddy tells you to either do something or not to do something, you have to pay attention," Bill said.

A FAINT DING SOUNDED, and Teresa glanced down at the communication device on her wrist. She touched the small screen and tapped a button. She frowned as she saw an entry for veterinary services. Twenty seconds later, she placed a call.

"Hi, Angelica. What happened?" Teresa asked.

"No point in asking. You know I'm not going to tell," Angelica chided.

"One of these days you may cave in," Teresa said with a chuckle.

"What, and get fired?" Angelica said.

"Bill would rather cut off his nose than fire you," Teresa said. "But you know that."

Angelica tittered. "Okay, I'll cave. You can beat him when he gets home. Abby chased a lizard off the path and got her nose zapped."

"Oh, no! Is she okay?" Teresa asked.

"She did really well at the VHO. You can be proud of her," Angelica said. "Bill's showing Abby around. They should be home in a couple of hours.

BILL AND TERESA stood at the black glass transfer surface in Bill's office lab in their home. The twenty-five by forty-inch intuitive machine was the envy of many scientists. Bill's inventions had added to the comfort and convenience of humanity, and he and Teresa would never want for anything. The only thing he had never been able to perfect or invent was how to have a human child.

The transfer surface was one of the best pieces of technological advances to be perfected over a forty-year period. It lit up, turned an opaque white, and displayed a control unit with a number pad, alpha key controls, along with various LEDs and buttons.

The innovative machine was used to transfer any type of data from one device to another. It determined what each device was and how it would transmit the data. If translation was required, it happened automatically during the transfer.

An electronic storage device was in the sending circle on the transfer surface and was busy downloading massive content. A tiny red Dot flashed in the receiving circle as hundreds of files uploaded.

It was time to pick Abby's voices. Bill and Teresa listened to various synthesized voices, from infant to teen to adult voices. They played voice stages several times trying to make clear decisions.

"That's a sweet little-girl voice," Teresa said. "It seems the right type of voice which would be equal to a little girl three and a half human years old."

"Yeah, I like that one." Bill made a note of the file name, then pressed another selection. The voice was tinny and abrasive.

"Heaven help our blue planet!" Teresa said. "Who in their right mind would choose that, Bill? You should delete that from the selection process."

"I have no idea who programmed that voice," he said. He pressed another button, and the voice of a little older girl sounded.

"That's nice for when Abby is around one-year-old, which

would be between nine and ten years old in human years," Teresa said.

Bill noted the file. They continued until all their selections had been made. Bill set the voice preferences for Abby's Dot that would change through her growing process. He completed the procedure and the transfer surface indicated it was ready for another task.

"I'm going to upload the voices, language, history, geography, art, health, science, social skills, and mathematics—you name it, including pictures and holographic clips of you and Lilith playing educational games, learning manners, proper protocol and verbal expressions along with Lilith's entire three-year history," Bill said.

"Good. She needs all of that," Teresa said.

"It should take two to four days for the integration to take place, so we're sure to be surprised when she talks," Bill said. "It's going to be very interesting to see how much of this information she can assimilate and how she'll use it growing up."

"She's already bright," Teresa said.

They both looked down at the floor. Abby was gazing up at them with a big smile filling her face.

"Daddy's going to insert your Dot today. You'll be talking like a big girl soon," Teresa said.

Abby wagged her tail.

"I'll come get you when all the files have been uploaded and cataloged," Bill said.

BILL WATCHED the transfer surface in his home lab. A tiny red Dot winked in the receiving area of the transfer surface. Another Dot flickered in the sending area. He stared at a monitor while pictures and information flashed past as Lilith's memories were transferred to Abby's new Dot.

Bill slowed the progress to watch snippets of Lilith. He clenched a fist and checked a sob from escaping.

All the love that was showered on their beautiful dog-daughter had been captured in full detail. Then the goofy, yet resourceful, Jimbo Smythe had sneaked into Lilith's life, along with her human in-laws Becky and Percy. Abby and her siblings followed, and the entire birthing process was recorded. They were so young and happy, romping and playing, nursing and sleeping. It was all there—including Bill's notes on the cleanup with the eliminator drones.

Bill thought about deleting the cleanup and the GNN announcements about the tragedy and deaths, but felt that Abby needed to be aware of the circumstances of this critical time in her life. His gut told him that her time with them was short.

The computer screen announced that the upload was complete and awaited acknowledgement and instructions. Bill pressed *procedure complete*.

Bill used long-handled scientific tweezers to pick up Lilith's Dot and placed it in a tiny, clear, circular container, which he then placed in a plastic case. He pressed a button on a multi-tiered, temperature-controlled cabinet, and a thin drawer slid open. Bill placed the memories of Lilith in the drawer and closed it.

He sighed deeply and returned to the work at hand. Abby's Dot flashed up at him. He typed data on the virtual keyboard with grim determination.

Bill used the tweezers to pick up Abby's Dot and placed it on a slide on the countertop. Then he picked up a small blue vial capped with an eyedropper. He carefully squeezed one drop of the formula from the vial onto the Dot.

The red Dot turned opaque. Bill blew on the Dot for a minute, then picked up a scanner and powered it on. Bill passed the scanner over the Dot repeatedly, but the scanner did not detect the Dot. He tried a different type of scanner with the same result. He set the scanner aside.

"Perfect," he said.

Bill gathered up the insertion tool that contained a supportive liquid for the Dot properties to adhere on the organ and sucked up the Dot. He went in search of Teresa and Abby.

BILL FOUND Teresa and Abby in the schoolroom. Teresa was sitting on the floor, showing Abby some of Lilith's old toys. Abby snatched up Lilith's stuffed lamb.

"That was Lilith's favorite toy," Teresa told Abby. Her voice shook with emotion.

Abby growled and shook the lamb, then dropped to her belly and licked her new treasure.

Bill joined Teresa on the floor. "She probably detects Lilith's scent," he said.

Abby grabbed the lamb and raced up to Bill to show him her prize.

"Is that your new baby?" Bill asked as he scratched the top of her head.

Abby deposited the lamb in Bill's lap and yipped. She crouched down with her butt in the air, waiting for Bill to play.

Bill grabbed the lamb and tossed it across the room. Abby took off running and retrieved her new toy.

"I finished the Dot," he said.

Teresa sighed. "Come here, Abby."

Abby pranced across the room, the lamb gripped in her

teeth. Teresa picked her up and cuddled her, kissing the top of her head. "Let's put your little lamb on the floor for now, okay?"

Teresa took hold of the toy. Abby would not give it up.

"Let go," Teresa said.

Abby reluctantly gave up her lamb. Teresa placed it on the floor. "It's right here, and no one is going to take it."

"Daddy is going to insert your Dot, Abby. It won't hurt. You'll feel a little sting, like a pinch, at the back of your neck, but it will be okay. Daddy would never hurt you intentionally."

"I'm not inserting her Dot in the typical place," Bill stated.

Teresa looked quizzically at Bill. Then it dawned on her.

"I'm not taking any chances," he explained. "Only you and I will know where Abby's Dot is implanted. I want to keep it that way."

"Where are you going to put it then?" Teresa asked.

"At the bottom of her white patch."

Abby's white patch started on her chest and finished between her two front legs.

"If she's ever scanned, they'll miss it," Bill said. "I coated the Dot with the new formula I've been experimenting with. It is virtually invisible to the naked eye and undetectable to the scanning devices that the Tranquility Force uses."

"Are you sure it's going to work?"

"I created the technology and Maxwell Industries updates all the GNN, UCP and World Guild hardware and code. Thank the Earth that we own all the patents; otherwise, I wouldn't be able to protect Abby. This is the trial run."

Teresa cradled Abby in her arms so her belly was exposed. "Daddy isn't going to place your Dot in your scruff, Abby. This may sting a little bit more because you don't have a lot of baby fat on your chest, honey."

Bill placed the tip of the Dot insertion device on the hair at the bottom of Abby's white patch. Then he pressed the plunger.

Abby yelped.

"All done," Bill said as he ruffled her head. "I'm sorry that hurt, baby, but Daddy wants to make sure that you have all of this important history and information. Lilith was loved just as much as we love you, and one day you will understand the things that are happening now a little better."

Abby squirmed to get down. Teresa placed her on the floor. She shook herself and looked at Bill rather indignantly. She snatched up her little lamb, walked four or five steps away and flopped down on the floor, resting her chin on the fluffy toy.

"How about a treat?" Bill asked.

Abby batted her angelic eyelashes at Bill and Teresa in a forgiving moment and raced out of the lab and headed to the kitchen, pain and suffering forgotten.

TERESA WALKED into the schoolroom the next day. Abby walked at her heels, hauling her lamb. "We are going to have so much fun," Teresa said. "Lilith loved the schoolroom, Abby. Everything your canine mother learned, you will learn."

The schoolroom walls were covered with digitally live pictures created by Myra-June that stimulated a dog's immediate reaction.

Teresa sat on the floor in front of the old-fashioned PawBoard. She pulled Abby onto her lap. "This is the old PawBoard, Abby." She held her hand out over the PawBoard, then the monitor. "This is the screen. I'm going to teach you how to choose your meals and select portion sizes. Then I'll teach you manners and communication skills."

"Once you understand the PawBoard, I will teach you how

to use the HoloRemote. For that to work, you need to be four months old and your Dot activated. So, we'll start with old technology first," Teresa explained.

Abby's attention span was a direct reflection of her age. She squirmed to get at the rabbit on the screen. Teresa held firm to her young charge while Abby reached out toward the screen, trying to make contact with the hopping animal.

"Abby," Teresa said firmly. "Concentrate on what I'm saying. I know you're not used to learning and you don't understand all of my words, but if you pay attention, you'll understand more each day."

Abby let out a loud sigh and settled down. Teresa scratched the top of Abby's head and began the lesson. She pointed to a big key with a bowl of steaming food. "This key is for hot food."

When she pressed the big key, the screen filled with pictures of hot food plates. A bowl of beef stew was currently highlighted. Abby looked from the PawBoard to the screen. She lifted her nose to the air and sniffed. She wagged her tail; she was following the explanation.

"This is an arrow key. If you step on the arrow key, you can move to the next picture, and you'll smell what that food is like if you don't recognize the picture."

Teresa demonstrated by pressing the right arrow. A plate of scrambled eggs, ham, and potatoes was highlighted. Abby sniffed the air and wagged her tail. She looked up at Teresa with a glowing face. She liked this part of the lesson.

"Come down here and try to select something," Teresa said. She cleared the screen of the food pictures, returning to the main menu.

Abby climbed out of Teresa's lap, her tail held high in anticipation. She studied the big board in amazement. She sniffed the key with the bowl of steaming food—no smell there. Abby pounced on the key.

"Don't jump on the keys," Teresa said. "Just use one paw and step on the key."

Abby stretched her neck toward the screen where several delectable dishes appeared—no smells there either. She turned her head toward Teresa for encouragement.

"Remember the next step?" Teresa quizzed.

Abby looked at the PawBoard and walked over to the arrow keys. She stepped on the right arrow. The beef stew aroma wafted through the air. Abby wagged her tail. Her little face lit up with excitement.

"Don't stop there. You have a lot to explore," Teresa said.

Abby pressed the down arrow and more good things showed up: a pasta stew with lots of cheese and ground meat. Abby sniffed and wagged her tail. She drooled on the plastic-coated keyboard.

After about ten minutes of food exploration, Teresa let Abby place an order for her dinner meal.

"Chicken and pasta with vegetables, a good choice," Teresa said. "The next step is to choose the portion size."

Teresa pointed to the screen. "See this, Abby? There are four sizes of dogs: puppy, small, medium, and large. What size are you?"

Abby pressed the arrow and chose medium.

"You goof; you aren't a medium dog. You're a puppy! You don't want to gorge yourself or you'll end up making yourself sick."

Teresa reached over and hit the left arrow key, and the previous screen appeared. She had Abby select puppy from the menu, and her meal selection was completed.

Abby's face lit up; she was proud of her accomplishment. Teresa scooped up Abby and hugged and kissed her. She settled her on the floor in front of the PawBoard.

"See this key? This is GNN. It's for important information

on what is happening right here in WestUS and the rest of the world," Teresa explained. "The World Guild tells us when something important happens, and they announce it on GNN. Do you remember how we sat and watched for news about the bad thing that happened?"

Abby remembered. Dread washed over her face. She missed her mother and her playmates. She looked at the GNN key on the PawBoard. Sniffed it, memorized its location.

Abby yawned. Teresa picked her up and held her close.

"I think that's enough for one day, don't you?"

Abby licked Teresa's chin.

CHAPTER FIVE

Teresa stood in front of the food console at the kitchen counter; her flowing two-piece silk pantsuit appeared loose. The new machine was much more complicated than the old and she was grateful for Ejonia's notes, which appeared holographically when Teresa touched the machine. She scanned the controls. Press D2 for dinner. Press B3 for breakfast. Press A for Lilith's choices. Teresa stared at that note, a little sad. She'd have to figure out how to change the label to Abby's name.

She touched the screen and chose the A category. Teresa perused the choices and selected a compressed vegetable and egg treat in a puppy-sized portion shaped like a bone. The food console bell tinkled, announcing that the food was ready to be served. The treat appeared on the receiving shelf of the food console.

Abby lifted her nose to the air and sniffed; she pranced about the kitchen, excited.

"Your manners are unbecoming, little girl," Teresa scolded.

Abby stopped in her tracks and looked toward Teresa, her brow furrowed with wonder.

"There are times to run wild and there are times to sit politely and wait," Teresa said.

Abby immediately got the message. She scrambled over to Teresa and sat by her feet, keeping her focus on Teresa's hands. Good things came from the food console, and she wanted to be the recipient. She beamed a smile at Teresa, who tried to suppress a smile, but Abby batted her lashes at the right time.

Teresa squatted down beside Abby and grabbed her in a bear hug. "You are so precious, Aberdeen Tallulah Maxwell-Smythe!" She held out the dog treat. Abby used polite restraint and gently reached for the dog treat, but then gobbled it down.

The front door opened and closed. Bill, wearing a short-sleeved, loosely tailored deep blue shirt, black slacks and sandals, joined Teresa and Abby in the kitchen. He wrapped his arms around Teresa and nuzzled her neck. They pecked each other on the lips and shared a quiet smile. Bill then stooped and hugged Abby.

"How are my girls?"

Abby squirmed and rubbed Bill's arm and chest with her snout. She lifted her face and howled a little greeting.

Bill rubbed Abby's head with his knuckles and smiled as she beamed in delight. She treated him to a dog-smile.

"You're such a little cutie."

He picked her up and kissed the top of her head, then cradled her in one arm while petting her with his other hand.

"Want to go to Daddy's lab for a while?"

Abby squirmed to get down. Bill settled her on the floor, and she pranced around.

"Don't jump on Daddy," Teresa said.

Abby remembered and pranced around in circles.

"You can see her little mind working. I can't wait for her Dot to kick in," Bill said.

Teresa chuckled. "She's going to have a lot to say."

Bill and Teresa headed to Bill's home lab with Abby at their heels. At four months old, she stood seven inches high, about half of her potential height. The female was the smaller of the dominant breed—in this case, Lilith's lineage. Abby had the triangular face and the clownish personality of her bull terrier mother, and loved water in all forms like her black Labrador father.

Bill opened the lab door, and Abby darted ahead of him. She raced around the tables, workbenches, and chairs, skidding on the slippery tile floor.

"I think she does that on purpose," Teresa said. "She loves to run and slide."

Bill flipped a switch, and pictures of Lilith, the puppies, and Jimbo appeared along the floorboards. Abby trotted up to the picture of her canine mother and stared at it, her nose twitching, sniffing but not picking up any scent. She touched the picture with her nose and then stepped back.

"Lilith," Abby said.

Teresa gave a chuckle. "Oh, my sweet Earth, Bill, Abby can talk!"

"Four months, right on the dot," Bill said. "Yes, that is your canine mother, Lilith, your siblings, and your father, Jimbo. Do you remember them, Abby?"

Abby sniffed each of the pictures and returned to stand in front of Lilith's photo. "She was my real mother."

"What a big girl you are... you can talk now!" Teresa exclaimed. She was momentarily overcome with longing and sadness.

Bill enfolded Teresa in a hug, and they shared a moment of

silence, each lost in their thoughts, drifting back to the day of death and turmoil.

Teresa dropped to the floor and swooped Abby up in a hug. "Now that you can talk, we can have some real fun, Abby."

Abby squirmed out of Teresa's arms and pranced about. "Fun, fun, fun."

"Don't wear it out," Bill said. He bent and scratched the top of Abby's head as she skidded to a stop at his feet. Her angelic face glowed with happiness.

Bill's security device pronounced a short warning alert of three beeps that indicated an incoming transmission from the World Guild. The atmosphere in the lab changed abruptly. Teresa sucked in her breath, and Bill stood ramrod straight.

"Don't say anything, Abby," Teresa said. "Just be very quiet."

"Okay," Abby said.

The AMD swirled the liquid moving picture of a snowy mountainous landscape on the lab wall, and a World Guild statistician appeared.

"Please state the sex, breed, and general health of 5344212RK3002805," the statistician requested.

Teresa flinched as if she had been slapped. "5344212RK3002805 is a female canine of mixed heritage: bull terrier and black Labrador retriever. The subject is in good health."

"Report acknowledged," the statistician said, and the screen dissolved back to the peaceful landscape.

The room was anything but peaceful as Bill exhaled loudly. "They'll be coming for her soon."

An agonized sob escaped Teresa. "It's not right! Let's leave!" Teresa looked wildly around the room and started grabbing small pieces of equipment and putting them in a pile.

Bill grabbed Teresa and made her stand still. He took a

small microscope out of her hands and placed it back on the counter.

"Where would we go? You know as well as I that our every move is traceable," Bill stated.

"You made Abby's Dot undetectable. Why can't you do the same for us?"

"Ours is a little more complicated. I'm not saying that it can't be done, but the time it would take to work out the correct sequencing so we don't lose our wealth is time that we don't have," he explained.

Bill walked over to the transfer surface and opened files and looked at schematics. His fingers glided over the smooth white surface as he opened and then dismissed drawings, documents, and scientific calculations. He absorbed and then calculated scientific data on the number pad on the white surface.

"I would have to trick the World Guild into believing that we were in our domicile as usual, and then we would have to get a transport glider to load up the most important equipment, which means I would have to make the glider undetectable," Bill explained. "We would have to move in the dead of night and be cloaked with shielding so that detection beams would pass through us as empty air space."

"You can do this, Bill. Ask Percy to help."

"Time is against us, Teresa. Percy doesn't have the mathematical skills to help with this. I would need a top scientific mind to work alongside me."

Teresa appeared downcast. "There has to be a way. I wish we had thought of this scenario two months ago," she moaned. "We could have gone to Texmexzona. That's completely out of their reach."

"Texmexzona? That is a completely lawless place. It's not even considered a state anymore. Once you move there, the

World Guild considers that you've renounced your citizenship and you can't return home," Bill said.

They were lost in thought, silently analyzing the impending problem and searching for a more realistic solution when the silence was interrupted by a news announcement.

The security system sounded the GNN news tone, alerting them that important world-event news was taking place and being reported.

A GNN literalist appeared, an unreadable news-face pasted on, completely neutral. "This is a special broadcast by Global News Network," The literalist reported. Her gaze seemed to bore into Teresa and Bill's. "Global Health has announced that three of the surviving four canines have succumbed to the after-effects of the toxic agent that was released. Every effort was taken to preserve the lives of the three canines, but their neural systems were compromised beyond the point of repair. There is one remaining canine in known existence."

The screen showed pictures of mountains, forests, and deserts. "Data-gathering from remote locations is incomplete at this time. There is no indication that other canines exist."

Bill and Teresa stared in horror as the news transmission completed and the literalist dissolved.

"Abby!" Teresa called.

Abby looked up from where she had flopped down on the floor with a synthetic chew bone. She immediately jumped to her feet and ran to Teresa, her face full of questions.

Teresa sat on the floor and pulled Abby in front of her. Bill joined them. Abby looked from one to the other. Her ears drooped as she determined she was in some sort of trouble.

"I didn't do it," Abby said.

"Honey, you didn't do anything wrong," Teresa said. "It's

important that you pay very close attention right now. Daddy and Mommy love you very much, do you know that?"

Abby licked Teresa's hand and beamed at her. She then licked Bill on the nose as he bent to kiss her.

"I love you too."

"Strangers called Tranquility Force are going to come and take you away from Mommy and Daddy. You did nothing wrong, and I know this will be difficult to understand," Teresa explained.

"I'm not supposed to go with strangers," Abby said, confused.

Bill picked Abby up and held her close. Abby licked his ear. "You'll have to go with these strangers. When they come to get you, you must not talk. This must be a very big secret. You cannot talk until a man in a white coat installs a new Dot in your scruff," Bill said. He rolled her scruff on her neck to demonstrate.

"I love you. I want to stay with you," Abby said.

"Puppy-dup, we love you so very much. It will break our hearts when they take you away from us, but the Tranquility Force is going to come and take you away. We can't stop that from happening," Teresa said.

Abby squirmed out of Bill's arms. "No, no, no!" Abby bawled. "I'm not going! I'll run away!"

Abby ran out of the lab. Bill and Teresa jumped to their feet and pursued her.

"Abby, stop! We need to talk!" Teresa called.

They ran into the kitchen and found Abby cowering by the permanently closed dog door. Bill and Teresa dropped to the floor.

"Listen Abby, you may not understand this right now, but in time you will recall our words and as you grow up, you will be able to retrieve the conversation in the special Dot that Daddy implanted in your white patch," Bill said.

He rubbed the white patch on her chest. "Never tell anyone about the Dot in your white patch. That is where all the information and memories from Lilith, Mommy-Teresa and Daddy-Bill, and Grandma Becky and Grandpa Percy are. We don't have much time left together. The World Guild will most likely have the Tranquility Force take you to a governmental scientific building. You must be brave. In time, you will find someone to bond with. You must grow up quickly and learn how to detect good humans from those who don't have your best interests in mind."

Abby whined and looked forlorn.

"When I created your Dot, I gave you the ability to communicate with us secretly through the HoloRemote," Bill explained. "No matter what governmental facility they take you to, there will be an uplink to satellites and communication outlets. We will be able to communicate back and forth without anyone knowing."

"How do I do that?"

"You will have to get quiet. Pretend you're napping. Then you will have to internally look at the file structure in your Dot and find the communication portal that is called Wise Owl. It contains high encryption that only Daddy has access to. You will be able to use your brain to tap letters and words and send us messages."

Abby cocked her head in thought. "I'd better try that out."

"Good idea," Bill said. "There's something else. I have your Dot programmed on my locator system; it's a GPS tracking system. When we see where they take you, I'm going to work on a way to get you out of there."

Teresa picked up Abby and held her close. Her lower lip quivered, but she held her tears back. "Let's get to work, Bill.

I'll be able to do some of the work, but the burden will be on your knowledge and skills. I have a lot of information to impart to Abby right now."

"I'm going to the complex," Bill said. He kissed Teresa and Abby and hurried out of his home lab.

The front door sensor announced visitors. "Hello, we will be with you shortly. Please wait patiently. Violence is unnecessary." The announcement repeated in a loop.

Bill and Teresa looked at the monitor and saw two Tranquility Force enforcers at the front door.

"Are they here for Abby?" Teresa almost screeched.

"No way. They'd come with an entire platoon." Bill looked at Abby. "You stay here and be quiet. Do not come to the front door, do you understand?"

Abby crawled under a low table. "Okay. I'm hiding."

Bill and Teresa went to the front door as the system repeated the arrival of visitors. Bill went through the security checks, then opened the door.

The enforcer didn't waste time on greetings. "We are looking for Harold and Gayle Goanflower."

Both Bill and Teresa balked. "What do you mean? They moved to New York."

Becky and Percy hurried across the yard. "What's going on?" Becky asked, out of breath.

Teresa reached out to Becky. "Harold and Gayle are missing!"

"Oh, no!" Becky said.

"They moved to New York, didn't they?" Percy asked.

"They never reached their destination," the enforcer said.

"That can't be right," Teresa said. "Gayle told me Harold had this great position at Hycore."

"You have not heard from them?" the enforcer asked. "They have not communicated in any way?"

Teresa appeared stricken with fear. "I've tried and tried to contact her, but the AMD system doesn't even have a listing for either of them."

Bill seemed thoughtful. "The last time I spoke with Harold, he told me they were taking everything in a transport glider."

"Maybe air pirates got them!" Percy said.

"Oh, no!" Teresa moaned.

"We will keep searching," the enforcer said. He and his companions returned to their glider and took off.

"Let me make you some tea. This is quite a shock," Becky said.

They all went inside.

CHAPTER SIX

B ill entered the private lab on the fourth floor at Maxwell Industries. The windows between the lab and the work floor were in secret mode—he could see out, but no one could see in.

The immense room was stark white with bare walls. White counters with suspended monitors were positioned throughout the room along with high-backed captain's chairs with side wings that completely enveloped their occupants. The front of each chair contained what looked like vision testing equipment suspended on a pole, and white gloves.

Bill slipped into one of the captain's chairs and pulled the Vision Core to his face. He adjusted it until he could see clearly out of the two large eye viewers that wrapped around the contour of his head. He grabbed the gloves and slipped them on. Bill moved his fingers and hands as if he were typing, then pulling at something.

He diagrammed a transport glider in the virtual reality mode. Bill hesitated for a moment as a thought passed through his mind.

"Hmmm," he said. Bill quickly pulled up a map of the planet with an overlaid grid system in bright red. He zeroed in on WestUS and set the grid in motion.

Blue lines appeared.

He honed in closer to the grid to populated areas. Green lines appeared, and then white, yellow, and orange ones. He studied the map in front of him through the eye viewers.

"Risky, but it will work." He entered data on the virtual keyboard. He jotted numbers, equations and notes on an electronic notepad and sent them to himself through the interconnected system, encrypted in red-level code.

A few minutes later, he removed the gloves and pushed the Vision Core unit away, then slipped out of the chair. Satisfied, he unsecured the door and walked out of the lab and headed across the large workroom to another closed, secured door with windows in secret mode.

Three employees were completely engrossed with special research projects in the spacious workroom and didn't even look up as he passed by.

Bill approached the lab door and blew into the breath collector, which determined that it was him. The door clicked open, and Bill stepped inside.

"Lights up," Bill said. The quiet, bare white room illuminated. In the center of the large room stood a work surface with a thick glass top. A thin, two-inch square piece of metal, etched with gleaming copper, was embedded into a mold of a patented material under ten-inches of unbreakable glass.

Bill passed his right hand above the glass surface. A low humming sound filled the room. Unnoticed seams in the walls opened, and several flat-paneled screens extended and illuminated. File drawers that required top-security access lined one portion of the wall. A small refrigeration unit was nestled under the space where one of the flat screens had extended.

"Find camouflage reflective spray files," Bill commanded. A monitor filled with data: text, scientific formulas, diagrams and drawings, tables of numbers, and color codes.

"Transfer data to Bill's private account using red-level encryption," he said.

He watched as the data transferred.

"Back-secure and shut down," Bill commanded.

All traces of his request and transmission evaporated.

Bill thought for a moment. He woke the transfer surface. "Ping TMZ."

He watched as the system sent beams toward Texmexzona. He saw deflector beams stopping his pinging. "Ping TMZ. Capture the code of the deflector beams."

The transfer surface monitor became loaded with code.

"Stop!" Bill commanded. He watched as the code swallowed his inquiry and continued to flood his system. Bill manually shut down the transfer surface. "Have to study this."

He rebooted his system. "Show visuals of TMZ." Blue skies and an arid desert appeared with no sign of civilization. "I know this is a farce, but I'm going to get through this if takes my entire team to tear down this smokescreen."

Bill sent a message to his top team of code breakers. "Any luck on breaking into TMZ?"

Multiple messages responded. The gist of them stated the obvious. TMZ was shielded so thoroughly that it was practically invisible. "Keep working on it," Bill typed.

He crossed the room and blew into a security decoder at the refrigeration unit. The door popped open. He perused the vials and containers until he found a vial with blue liquid in it. Bill withdrew a small padded pouch from a drawer and secured the vial into the pouch.

Stepping back to the transfer surface, Bill passed his hand over the surface once again. The monitors retreated into their hidden cabinets, and the walls appeared smooth and solid once again. He unsecured the door and left the quiet room.

~

TERESA HAD an oversized calendar on the floor in front of Abby in the schoolroom.

"When you wake up in the morning, the sun is shining, or the sky may be gray because of rain. Then you eat breakfast, play, learn in the schoolroom, play some more, take some naps, eat supper, and then you go to bed," she explained.

Abby sniffed the calendar and looked at Teresa.

"That is one day, Abby," Teresa explained, and held up one finger.

Teresa pointed to one of the calendar squares. "Every square is one day."

"One day," Abby said.

Teresa pointed out one week. "One row across is one week."

Then she encompassed the whole page. "All the days on this page equal one month. This is how we measure a year. There are twelve months in a year and twenty-four hours in a day. We will talk about time a little later."

"A month?" Abby stared at the calendar and wagged her tail. She raised her face to Teresa's, all aglow in wonderment.

Teresa smiled at Abby. She ran her finger along the border of the square for that day. "This is Sunday," she explained. She went through the days of the week a couple of times, skipping around, trying to make learning a game.

"Where's Friday?" Teresa asked.

Abby pounced on Sunday.

"No, that's Sunday, silly girl. Let's say the days of the week together, okay?"

"Sundy, Mundy, Toosdy," Abby said in her child-like voice as she bounced on the days of the week.

"Very good so far," Teresa encouraged.

"Wensdy, Thirsty, Fridy, Saderdy," Abby exclaimed.

Teresa clapped and scooped Abby up and whirled her around.

Bill clapped from the doorway. "What a smart little girl."

Bill stepped into the room and kissed Abby on the head. He enclosed Teresa in an embrace and kissed her head as well.

"Come into the lab. I want to show you something," he said seriously.

They left the schoolroom and walked down the hall and over to Bill's lab. Teresa still had Abby in her arms, and when they stopped at the transfer surface, Abby was intrigued by the colorful lines that seemed to jump off the surface, like magic. She turned her head this way and that, looking at the grid.

"What is this?" Teresa asked.

Bill took a deep breath. "Controls."

He let that sink in.

Teresa knitted her brow and stared at the grid. "What do you mean?"

"Tracers. All movement everywhere is tracked. The different colors are for different controls," he explained.

"My Earth, Bill! How could you have been a party to this?" Teresa said, whirling around to face him.

Abby looked from Teresa to Bill, studying their faces.

"It started off innocently enough: to find lost animal and human children or a wandering super-centenarian. Then the World Guild and Global Health got together and expanded the use of the system," Bill said.

Teresa nervously glanced toward the door. "Are you supposed to have this grid?"

"Teresa, I've created things I'm not proud of, but I promise... when we get through this crisis, I'll make some major changes," he exclaimed.

Teresa sank into his chest. "Oh, Bill."

Abby squirmed and pushed on Bill's chest.

"I'm sorry, Abby. Mommy didn't mean to squash you against Daddy like that."

Bill gently took hold of Teresa's arms and eased her back a few inches. He turned to the transfer surface and brought up the numbers and data. Then he manipulated some settings.

The picture on the transfer surface changed to take on a holographic, 3-D layering hanging in the air over the counter.

"You can see the positioning of the lines better in this view and should have a better understanding of the tracking and processing," Bill explained.

He pointed at a group of lines. "This is ground level with incremental stages for all sizes of humans, animals, and all low-flying family, single gliders, glide bikes, and the ZoomBus."

Bill moved his fingers up. "This space is housing and buildings."

He made some adjustments to get a different perspective, raising the holographic map and looking at the grid at an upward angle. Teresa stood beside him. Bill pointed to a higher layer in the grid.

"This is the flight squad's air space," he explained, wiggling his fingers in the area of the lines. "It's reserved for the Military, Tranquility Force, Sky Angels and Privateers." He then pointed out a space between the topmost grid for buildings and the airspace of the flight squad.

"Here it is. A slight flaw in their strategy that will work to our advantage," he said. "For several months, I've been working on a special formula that hasn't been through the patent process yet. I was going to present it at the Global Scientific

Gathering next year, but now I can see that this formula is what we need in order to leave here."

"What formula?" Teresa asked.

"Just like the Dot formula. I'll give you a demo when I've tested it," Bill said.

"Wait a minute," Teresa said. "If you're going to make the transport glider invisible, why do we have to fly so high?"

"Because we will have to make sure we avoid collision with transport gliders going fast while avoiding satellites and other things," Bill said.

"Oh," Teresa said.

Abby reached out to touch the colorful lines of the grid. She sniffed.

Teresa stared at the grid and then turned to Bill, exasperated. "A transport glider can't operate at that height, can it?"

"I'm going to devise a mechanism that will use the energy of the grid and the planet's magnetic forces to provide buoyancy to keep the glider balanced until we're out of the city grid."

Bill paused in thought. "As we travel east, toward TMZ, we'll be able to drop down to normal transport glider levels for a while. As we approach urban areas, we'll have to rise again."

"This is way too dangerous... we could get killed," Teresa said.

"It will be okay. We have to take this risk to get out of here undetected," Bill said.

Abby's ears perked up. She squirmed to get down. Teresa set Abby on the floor.

"There's too much to do. You have to make our Dots invisible, you'd have to make the transport glider invisible and now create some type of device to keep the glider balanced?" Teresa asked. "Bill, you're just one person. I don't have the technical or scientific skills to be of any help at all."

"We need a solid plan for Abby," Bill said. "Yes, it is a lot to do, but it isn't impossible."

Teresa shook her head. "I don't know."

"Mommy, Daddy, don't worry. I'll find you," Abby said.

Bill and Teresa were stunned into silence by Abby's simple statement.

"You will find us, won't you?" Teresa looked at Bill. "Okay; get started. I was just panicking."

Bill pulled Teresa into his arms. "You have every right to panic. Our life will never be the same, and we will have to leave those we love behind."

Teresa silently stared at the grid for a moment. She looked at Bill and let out a tense breath.

"Abby, let's go talk about time," she finally said. Teresa left the lab with Abby prancing after her.

CHAPTER SEVEN

Teresa sat on the floor of the schoolroom with Abby teaching her how to tell time. There were two big pictures of clocks in front of them, an old-fashioned round analog clock with a standard clock face, and a digital clock.

Teresa moved the hands on the round clock and then pressed buttons on the digital clock.

"Okay Abby, this may be a little confusing but you'll get it," Teresa said. "Remember, on this clock, you have an hour hand and a minute hand. The other clock only has numbers."

Abby looked from one clock to the other, and then looked at Teresa.

"What time is it?" Teresa asked.

Abby studied the clocks. "Twelve-two!"

"Almost," Teresa said. She suppressed a giggle as she leaned forward and pointed to the number twelve on the round clock. "When the big hand is on the twelve, we call that 'o'clock'; when the big hand makes its way around the clock and lands on the six, then it's 'thirty'."

Abby sat on her haunches and stared at the clock. She let out a 'hhrump.'

"It's not that hard, honey. The little hand is on the two, so you were right. It's two o'clock, not twelve-two. The twelve means o'clock," Teresa explained. "See the digital clock? It says two o'clock. Let's try another time."

Teresa maneuvered the hands on the manual clock and then set the digital clock.

"Four thirty!" Abby shouted.

Teresa clapped. "Hooray for Abby! Yes, that's the right answer!"

Abby pranced around the room and skidded back to Teresa's side.

"Momma, can you show me where Tex-Mex-O is?" Abby asked.

Teresa stared at Abby in amazement. "Nothing escapes you, does it?" She stood and walked to where the PawBoard was.

"Do you remember which key to push for GNN?"

Abby studied the large keyboard. "This one." She walked down the gutter between rows and stepped on a key with the GNN insignia.

"Very good; now you have to watch the screen and push arrows or keys," Teresa coached.

Abby looked at the big screen at floor level. There were menus with pictures. She walked over to the arrows and stepped on the up arrow until it moved the highlight to the picture of the earth. She stepped on the Enter key, and a picture of the planet appeared on the screen.

"Very good," Teresa said.

More choices as menus appeared. Abby returned to the arrow keys and stepped on the down arrow until WestUS was highlighted. She walked to the enter key and stepped on it. She faced the screen.

"Good work, Abby. WestUS is where our family lives. Texmexzona is to the east of us," Teresa said.

Abby pressed the arrow, and the screen adjusted. An extensive area made up of the former states of Texas, New Mexico, Arizona, and the country of Mexico was highlighted in blue and labeled Texmexzona.

Abby looked at Teresa for confirmation.

"That's it, Abby. Texmexzona." Teresa and Abby stared at the screen.

"I'll find you and Daddy," Abby said. "I promise."

Teresa gathered Abby into her arms and held her close. She squeezed her eyes shut tight, trying to stop the tears from flowing, but failed.

Abby licked Teresa's fallen tears.

"I know you will find us, Puppy-dup. You're one smart little girl. Lilith would have been so proud of you," Teresa said. She kissed the top of Abby's head and then set her on the floor. "You can never ever tell anyone you know about Texmexzona. It is another very big secret."

"I like secrets."

Teresa ruffled the tuft of hair on Abby's head. "Let's go see what Daddy is doing, okay?"

Abby raced out of the schoolroom ahead of Teresa. She careened around corners and galloped into the lab. Beakers and bottles stood in holders on the counter as Bill worked with formulas. He stirred a glass carafe that contained a pale blue liquid.

"Hey, slow down there, Abby!" he said. "Daddy doesn't want you to crash into something important."

Abby pranced up to Bill and sat by his feet, her tail wagging. "What're you doin?"

"Daddy is working on an important solution," he said.

"What's it for?" Abby asked.

"Gliders," Bill explained.

Teresa came into the lab. She pecked Bill on the lips. "How is it going?"

"Not good," he said.

"You'll get it—it's just going to take a little time," she said.

A red light flashed on a monitor, and the screen filled with the jack-booted squadron of Tranquility Force enforcers, their heads encased in black and silver combative protection helmets with built-in heat-seeking sonar weapon detection sights. Their muscular bodies donned gray, black, and silver uniforms with a blue and gold WG patch on their shoulders. They were outfitted with an array of deadly weapons.

A team of six was approaching Bill and Teresa's home. Three other monitors showed the team spreading out. Two approached the front door, two ran to the back of the house, and two were positioned on each side of the house.

"They're here!" Bill said.

"No! It's too soon!" Teresa bellowed, frantic.

Bill grabbed Teresa by the arms. "You don't have time for an emotional meltdown."

Teresa swooped Abby up into her arms and crushed her in a hug. She kissed Abby's face. "Abby, the scary time we talked about has come. The Tranquility Force is here to take you away."

Abby balked in fear. "What time is 'scary time'?"

The front door sensor announced visitors. "Hello, we will be with you shortly. Please wait patiently. Violence is unnecessary." The announcement repeated in a loop.

Bill lifted Abby's chin. "Abby, remember two things. Do not talk until someone inserts a Dot in your scruff. You'll have to act like a puppy with no voice. Can you remember that? It is a very big secret that you can talk. You can't talk until you get a new Dot."

Abby squirmed in Teresa's arms. "I will not go!"

Teresa patted Abby's behind with a quick tap. "You don't have a choice. You will have to go with the Tranquility Force. We can't protect you. Now listen to Daddy. This is the most important moment in your life."

Bill kissed Abby on the head. "If you escape from where the Tranquility Force takes you, never return to this house. Mommy and Daddy are going to Texmexzona. If you get there first, you'll have to wait for us. If we get there first, we will wait for you. Mommy and Daddy love you very much."

Abby licked Teresa and Bill. "I promise not to talk, or come home again."

"Have you tried out the Wise Owl program?" Bill asked.

"No. Mommy was teaching me about time," Abby said.

"Try to send a message as soon as possible," Bill said. "We have to be able to find you."

Teresa inhaled sharply, and the dam burst. She wailed as she held her dog daughter.

"Mommy and Daddy, I'll find you. I love you," Abby said. "Try not to worry."

Bill slipped Abby out of Teresa's arms and held her close. "Daddy loves you very much. You are a smart little girl. Remember, you have the secret Dot in your white patch and will be able to communicate with us in secret. Protect your secret. Don't let anyone know. They may try to trick you. Never tell."

Teresa reclaimed Abby. "You will be a big girl when Mommy sees you again, Abby. Make me proud, honey."

Teresa and Bill walked to the front door.

"My baby!" Abby cried, twisting and turning in Teresa's arms.

Bill looked around and spotted Abby's little stuffed lamb toy on the floor. He scooped it up and handed it to Abby. She snatched it out of his hand.

Bill opened the door.

Percy and Becky ran across the yard to Bill and Teresa's house.

"Wait! Wait! We want to see our granddaughter!" Becky screeched.

"Please, just let us have a moment with our granddaughter," Percy begged.

The Tranquility Force did not respond to or acknowledge Percy's request. Two of them roughly grabbed Percy and Becky, preventing them from approaching the door. Percy and one of the Tranquility Force enforcers scuffled for a moment, but Percy was overpowered as another enforcer stunned him with his wand. Percy fell to the ground and convulsed.

"Percy!" Becky shrieked. "How dare you stun my husband!" She struggled to release her arms from the steely grip of the Tranquility Force enforcer.

"Bill! Make them stop," Teresa said.

The captain presented Bill and Teresa with an electronic order.

The other four Tranquility Force enforcers joined the captain at the front door, two on each side, their faces hidden behind the molded protective masks with slits for eyes, nose, and mouth.

"Captain Simon Day, Tranquility Force Unit 4105. We have orders to confiscate Aberdeen Tallulah Maxwell, 5344212RK3002805," Captain Day announced. He shoved the electronic order at Bill. "Acknowledge transfer."

Bill clenched his jaw. "Let her grandparents through."

Captain Day considered Bill's prominence and connections. He raised a hand and twirled his fingers. His people stood down.

Becky helped Percy to his feet, and they pushed their way through the squad of Tranquility Force. They took turns petting and kissing Abby.

Abby raised a front paw and touched Becky's face.

"Try to remember Grandma and Grandpa," Becky said. "Be brave." Her voice cracked, and she inhaled deeply, but it didn't stop the torrent of tears that followed. Percy struggled to stay calm with his emotions. He failed.

Bill took the electronic order and looked it over. He placed his hand on the screen, and the pattern of the lines on his hand was digitally captured and compared to the print on file.

"Exact match," the machine announced.

Teresa kissed Abby on the head. "Remember what Mommy and Daddy told you," she whispered. "You have to be a big girl now. We all love you very much."

Bill held Abby for a moment. His pain was evident as he kissed her face and stroked her back and sides. He returned her to Teresa.

One enforcer approached with a small acrylic cage with air holes. Captain Day turned to Teresa. He carefully extracted Abby from Teresa's arms and slipped Abby, who clutched her lamb by her teeth, into the cage.

Abby dropped her lamb on the clear acrylic floor. She lifted her little chin and howled at the top of her voice; a wail that started low and rose to a high pitch. Abby faced her family as she howled and yipped, her face an abyss of sadness.

Bill pulled Teresa toward him. They clung to each other as the Tranquility Force squad turned and retreated down the walkway to the silver and black glider with the large black Tranquility Force symbol on all sides. Every step of their march, Abby howled in anguish.

Teresa sobbed as she watched her beloved baby being taken away. The enforcers slid into their seats in the glider. Then they were gone.

CHAPTER EIGHT

On the journey in the Tranquility Force glider, Abby clawed the clear enclosure to try to stand up on her hind legs to see where they were taking her. She experienced new countryside scents along the way, but since she had never been outdoors beyond her own backyard and the one time she went to the Maxwell complex, she could not identify the smells.

Lost in despair, she howled and whimpered.

A helmeted enforcer rapped her cage with a big, shiny stick. "Shut up, will you?"

A different helmeted face peered inches away from her on the other side of the acrylic cage. "If you don't shut up, I'll stun you."

Abby shrank back from the stench of his foul breath. She crouched in a corner of the cage, resting her chin on her lamb.

After about two hours, the Tranquility Force glider approached a red-brick complex with a high chain-link fence and an electronic gate. Abby could not see anything from where her cage sat. The big squadron surrounded her.

She heard the facility gate's electronics scanning the vehicle. After just a second or two, tweets and beeps emitted from the scanning device, and the gate slid open. The glider entered the compound and docked at a parking area.

Abby watched as the Tranquility Force team slid out of the glider. Captain Day reached inside the glider and took possession of her cage. He transported her to the main building while the others hung around the glider.

Captain Day stopped at a doorway and pressed his hand onto a scanner surface. Abby watched everything he did. The door popped open, and Captain Day entered the building.

The Communicator was having a busy day. Abby barked at the robotic receptionist—she thought it was creepy.

Captain Day approached the desk and placed the cage on the counter. "Please contact Dr. Roberts and let him know that Aberdeen Tallulah Maxwell is present."

The Communicator signaled her acknowledgement; colors rippled across the halo, which then turned green, showing that the message had been delivered. The halo continuously changed colors as it exchanged information silently.

After a short wait, a door to the right of the Communicator popped open and Dr. Julian Roberts entered. He was a middle-aged man in a long white lab coat. His brown, slicked-back hair showed just a fleck of graying at the temples.

Spotting Abby in the acrylic cage, he rubbed his hands greedily together as if expecting a feast. He approached Captain Day and Abby.

"Any problems?" Dr. Roberts asked.

"No, sir," Captain Day said. He slid the cage across the counter to Dr. Roberts, who bent down and peered in.

Abby growled low in her throat and slid her tail between her legs. She lunged at the doctor, teeth gnashing, with all the pent-up emotions of the past few hours. She growled fero-ciously, like her bull terrier mother would have.

Dr. Roberts straightened up. "Good job, Captain Day," he said.

Captain Day presented the electronic transfer order, and Dr. Roberts placed his hand on the surface.

"Delivery acknowledged and accepted," the machine-voice announced.

Captain Day saluted, turned on his heel, and exited the facility.

Dr. Roberts took hold of the cage and walked back to the door he had come through. He pressed his palm to the security surface, which turned green—an acknowledgement of autho-rized personnel. The door popped open, and he entered the secured facility.

Abby watched, fearful, as Dr. Roberts approached a thick glass door and repeated the process. There were people, tables, machines, and equipment in the cavernous room. The door opened, and they entered.

Dr. Roberts placed the cage on a work surface. Abby looked around and could not see the end of the place; it was so large.

Two technicians approached with smiles on their animated faces. Gene had a trimmed beard and mustache and a kind face. Carole wore her hair in a long, thick braid that reached her waist. Both were younger than Dr. Roberts. Abby sniffed the air and sensed that they were more loving in nature than the doctor.

Dr. Roberts opened the cage. Abby snatched up her lamb and backed into the corner of the small, confining space, to no avail. The doctor grabbed her by the scruff of her neck and dragged her out of the cage and plopped her on the counter like a specimen. Abby squealed in terror.

"Abby. I'm Dr. Roberts. I knew your canine mother, Lilith,"

he said. "Lilith was the very first dog to communicate through the Dot and the PawBoard that your human father invented."

Dr. Roberts picked up a scanning wand and scanned Abby's back from head to tail. "Looks like we got you just in time," he said. "Your dad didn't insert your Dot yet. Just as well. We would have had to override anything he programmed."

The doctor picked up a Dot insertion device and held Abby's scruff roughly. He inserted the Dot into her scruff.

Abby yelped from the sting and from Dr. Roberts holding her scruff so tightly. She panted with fear from the ordeal.

Dr. Roberts removed Abby's rhinestone collar and threw it in the trash. "You won't need that anymore," he said. He placed a special collar around her neck.

"Say hello to Gene and Carole. They'll be your new friends," Dr. Roberts explained.

Carole petted Abby's head and scratched her chin.

"When can I go home?" Abby asked.

"Looks like you're going to be a chatty little dog," Dr. Roberts said. "This is your new home, and you have a lot of work to do. Gene and Carole will make sure you have everything you need."

"I want to see Mommy and Daddy," Abby said as she looked at the doctor.

"Carole and Gene are your new parents," Dr. Roberts said. He spoke directly to Carole with strict authority. "Take Abby to her new home."

Carole presented her hand to Abby.

Abby sniffed the extended hand and gave Carole a little kiss. "Would you put my pretty collar on my lamb?"

Carole retrieved the shiny collar from the trash can and slipped it over the lamb toy's head. "It's a little big, but I'll fix it." Carole adjusted the collar and slipped it back onto the lamb's neck. "There."

Abby licked her lamb.

Carole gently picked Abby up in one hand and scooped up her lamb in the other. "Come on, Abby. Let's get you settled in. I'll bet you have to relieve yourself after that long trip."

Gene walked ahead across the facility to an eight-foot by eight-foot glassed-in room. He stood at the door and pressed his hand onto the scanner. "Authorized personnel. Exact match," the computerized voice announced. The door swung out, away from the magnetic locking mechanism.

Carole entered the house and placed Abby on the floor. "Here you go, Abby. You have a nice fluffy dog bed, a dog faucet, and your own bathroom closet."

Abby walked to the bed and deposited her baby. She went to the faucet and drank some water, then wandered into the bathroom closet. She walked over to the fine sand area, squatted, and peed. Then she waded through the shallow wading pool, got out, and shook herself off.

"Abby, do you know how to use the PawBoard?" Gene asked.

"Mommy taught me," she said.

Abby walked up to a device near the dog bed. It looked like a bookstand with an attached metronome. "What's that?"

"That's a reading device," Gene said. "When you learn to read, you will be able to read books and journals—anything with words. This device turns pages."

Abby ignored the toys on the floor. She climbed onto the dog bed and cuddled with her baby. Carole and Gene exited the glass house.

About an hour later, Carole returned to Abby's house with a plate of food. She scanned her hand, and the door popped open.

Abby sniffed the air and climbed out of bed, her little tail wagging slightly. Carole placed the plate on a low table for

Abby. "After you eat, you can activate the PawBoard and place your food order," Carole said.

"I love beef stew," Abby said as she gobbled the food. It had been hours since her breakfast meal at home, and she was used to having a snack in the middle of the day.

"Would you like to go for a walk?" Carole asked.

"I can go outdoors?"

"No, we have a walking path around the interior of the facility," Carole explained. "It is very important that we keep you safe. You are the very last dog on the entire planet, Abby."

Carole walked to the door and held it open. Abby trotted after her. They approached a walkway of black tread about four feet wide and about a foot or more from the wall. It wound around the entire facility.

"This is the walking path. You must stay on the path so you won't get lost or stepped on. It will lead you right back to your house," Carole explained.

Abby sniffed the path. She looked to the right and to the left. She went to the left and started her walk at a trot. She passed technicians working on machines that she did not recognize from her home environment. Abby saw test tubes and equipment that her human father had in his lab.

As Abby passed people, they stopped what they were doing and watched her. Every once in a while, someone called out, "Hi, Abby" but she did not deviate from the path.

When she approached the far end of the path, about a quarter of the way through the facility, Abby saw something running towards her at a fast pace, from the other side of the facility.

Abby ran down the path, away from whatever it was. She looked over her shoulder, and it was still coming her way. Abby ran at her full capacity. Something passed her. She slowed down and then stopped.

The mystery thing turned around and came back, slower. It stopped in front of Abby. She recognized a dog's form, but there was no dog smell. She stuck her nose out and smelled metal and plastic.

This dog had red lights for eyes and a spiked collar. Abby's hair bristled along her spine, and she raised her tail to its highest position. She laid back her ears and growled low in her throat.

They circled each other, the metal dog's circuitry and mechanical structure making little creaking noises as it followed Abby's lead. A hinged piece of metal on the dog's chest popped open and hung down, exposing a dark cavity. The metal swung back and forth, emitting a little squeak.

Abby stopped and sniffed the hinged door and the dark hole. She snorted.

A technician ran up and stopped several feet away from the dogs. "Rex, stand down," he said; he was joined by Gene a moment later.

"Let's observe," Gene said.

"Abby. Lilith's pup," Rex said in a mechanical voice. "Lilith's pup."

"What are you?" Abby asked.

"I'm a dog-bot. All dog-bots are to study Abby so they can be just like real dogs," Rex said.

"You are not like me." She nudged him with her nose. "You are hard and you don't have dog hair. You are not a real dog. You're a machine."

"Rex is going to be a dog-child," he boasted. "We are learning to be just like real dogs—companion dogs, children dogs."

"Rex will never be a real dog," Abby stated. "Real dogs have fur and blood. Dogs are warm and soft. Real dogs have a Mommy and a Daddy."

Abby's hair relaxed and her tail lowered to a friendly posture as she and Rex talked, facing each other.

"Rex will get a new soft dog-skin upgrade soon," Rex said.

"People want real dogs, not a machine-thing that looks like a dog," Abby stated. "My Mommy and Daddy cuddle-kiss me. They wouldn't cuddle-kiss a hard thing like you."

Rex absorbed the information with a series of whirs and electronic noises.

"What do you think Rex is thinking about?" the technician asked Gene.

"He's processing information that is unknown to him. We did not program a human-dog love concept," Gene said. He appeared lost in thought as he pondered this complex subject.

"I'm going to have to bring this up in the next process meeting," Gene said. "We may have to make some adjustments. How did Rex know about the dog-skin?"

"He must have overheard someone discussing design and implementation plans," the technician said.

Gene shook his head. He looked at Abby and Rex. "Abby, it's time to return to your house."

"Rex, back to home base," the technician said.

Rex dashed back to where he had come from.

Abby looked at Gene for a long moment. "I want to go for my walk!" She turned and ran down the path in the opposite direction from where Gene stood.

"Abby! Return to your house immediately!" Gene said. His voice echoed in the giant room and sounded loudly through a transmitter in her collar. He took off, running after her, unable to close the distance between them.

Abby ran at full throttle. She passed workbenches with electronics, test tubes, tool chests, and computers. Desks and trash cans and workers became a blur as Abby made the curve around the room and ran down the path, making a complete circle.

She ran past her glass house where Carole stood, circled it and stopped in front of it when Gene finally caught up with her. He was not happy. Abby panted from the exercise. Gene, out of breath, rammed his hand on the scanner, and the door to Abby's house opened. She went inside and quenched her thirst at the dog fountain and then entered the bathroom closet to do her business.

"We should begin behavior modification," Gene stressed.

"There was no harm done," Carole said. "Rex interrupted Abby's walk, and now she's back."

Dr. Roberts stormed over to Abby's glass house. He was clearly steamed from observing her behavior. "Gene, why didn't you take control of the situation? Why did you allow Abby to run away when you gave her a directive to return home?"

Gene stammered from the rebuke. He realized that running after Abby was not in his best interest, nor hers. "Carole and I were just discussing behavior modification."

"I don't want to see this again," Dr. Roberts said. "This could have an adverse effect on the dog-bots' imprinting."

Dr. Roberts turned to Abby and stared hard. "Abby, you are never to run away from Gene or Carole again. Do you understand?"

Abby's tail lowered between her legs. Her lips twitched. She met Dr. Roberts' stern expression. "I know. Sorry."

Dr. Roberts accepted her apology with a clipped nod. He glowered at Gene, turned and went back to his work.

Gene and Carole stood in uncomfortable silence, arms tightly crossed across their chests. Abby walked up to Gene and nudged him with her nose. "Follow the rules," Gene said.

Abby looked up at Gene and Carole. "I don't like Dr. Roberts."

Carole quickly swung around to see where Dr. Roberts was. She saw him clear across the room, talking to a scientist. She turned back to Abby and whispered. "Abby, be very careful about what you say. You don't want the wrong person to overhear."

"I want Mommy and Daddy. I don't like it here," Abby said.

Gene squatted and rubbed Abby's ears. "I know it's tough being taken away from your home, but there isn't anything anyone can do about that. Dr. Roberts is in charge. This is your new home now."

Abby made a huff sound. "Is Rex, the machine-dog, a good dog?"

"Yes. Rex is the pack lead. All the dog-bots follow Rex's lead," Carole explained. "Dogs have been an integral part of people's lives for thousands of years. It's important to provide humans with replicas of dogs. Losing human-children and now dog-children means that dog-bots must be the best they can be. There's nothing else to replace dog-children. Rex has an important place in this new dog-bot society."

THE FACILITY WAS BLANKETED in darkness, and all was still. Abby lay on her dog bed, her chin resting on her lamb. Her brow furrowed as she internally mind-clicked on Bill's communication program to send a message. Each time she tried, a 462-error message appeared that stated: You are currently disconnected from Wise Owl. Reconnect?

"Yes!" Abby said out loud, angrily. She lifted her head and looked around to see if anyone was in the lab to hear her. Abby grumbled in frustration as she settled down again and went inside her head to try the program again.

Error 462.

Error 462.

Error 462.

Abby stood, shook herself and finally stopped trying. She went to the bathroom closet, then drank from the water faucet and returned to bed. She settled down with her lamb, sighed loudly and finally drifted to sleep.

Dreamland kept her busy. She twitched, and little sleep-barks escaped, but did not wake her. At six-fifteen in the morning, the secure door between the lab and the reception area emitted sounds. Abby jumped to her feet, blinking back sleep and clearing her head. She faced the secured outer door and barked a long warning in big-girl dog-talk.

Tinny-sounding barks arose from the other side of the lab. They were computer-generated and hollow-sounding, not real dog barks. Abby craned her neck toward the barks but could not see Rex.

The door opened and the lights came up. Dr. Roberts entered the lab. He walked over to Abby's house, not saying a word; just looking at her. They stared at each other for a moment, and then Dr. Roberts walked away. Abby's lips twitched into a silent snarl as Dr. Roberts turned his back to her.

She sat, then eased down and rested her chin on her front paws. She watched Dr. Roberts' every move as he went from one table to another, switching on one machine here, another machine there.

The secure door emitted sounds again. Two lab technicians came through the door. Abby watched as a steady stream of men and women in white lab coats entered the room over the next hour. Carole arrived at seven-thirty and brought Abby her pre-selected breakfast of oatmeal, eggs, bacon, and blue-berries.

Abby was fond of blueberries, but now they made her a little sad. Mommy-Teresa had played a little game with Abby, rolling a blueberry across the kitchen floor. Abby would chase the blueberry and gobble it up and wait for the next one so she could chase it down.

After breakfast, Gene strode to Abby's house with Rex by his side. "Want to go for a walk with Rex?"

"Can we go outside?" Abby asked, hopeful.

"Nah, too dangerous," Gene said. "You'll have to walk the track." Gene opened the door to her house.

Abby huffed a snort of displeasure and went for her morning walk around the lab, accompanied by Rex. As they passed tables and benches, Abby heard little bits of discussions regarding new soft skin, multiple tracking capabilities, sniffing, twitching ears, and other dog-type topics.

"Rex, what do they mean by multiple tracking capabilities?"

Whirring and beeping noises began. "Rex sees living energy patterns. Dog-bots are going to have olfaction-sensing equipment installed, plus dog-bots will upload and download information from satellites. Real dogs only smell with their noses," Rex explained.

"Do you know what an error four sixty-two is?" she asked coyly.

"Is this a computer error or a communication device error?" Rex asked.

Abby looked confused.

"Never mind," Rex said. "Four sixty-two is a connection error. The system should be rebooted and the error will go away. Do you need help to reboot the PawBoard?"

"No, I just saw that error somewhere and didn't know what it meant," Abby said. "What does reboot mean?"

"Rebooting means you should shut the system off and turn it back on again. Sometimes a restart will do, but in stubborn cases, the system should be shut all the way off, unplugged if physically plugged into a power source, and kept off or unplugged for at least thirty seconds before it is reconnected to its power source and restarted again."

"Oh," Abby said.

Abby returned to her house, and Gene secured her behind the glass. "What am I going to do today?" Abby asked.

"Help train Rex," Gene said.

"What do I do now?"

"Take a nap or watch GNN," Gene said.

She watched Gene return to a workbench nearby and resume his work. Her little baby, the tattered fuzzy lamb, was on her bed, a reminder of the love and family that had been ripped away. Abby climbed onto her bed and walked in a circle. She flopped down, stretched her neck, and grabbed the lamb gently with her teeth. She rested her chin on her prized possession and feigned sleep.

Inside her head, she mentally tapped the reset button to no avail. Error four sixty-two would not go away. Abby huffed in frustration and went back to the main menu. She decided to watch a memory from when her canine parents first met. She recognized her house.

Jimbo and Lilith ran into the room and careened into the end of ae sofa.

"Beat 'cha," Lilith said. Her rhinestone collar glimmered like diamonds around her neck.

"No fair," Jimbo said, panting.

"Be careful, Jimbo!" Becky said. She nervously glanced at the sofa.

"Lilith, you need to slow down. This isn't the backyard," Teresa said.

"Sorry, Mommy," she said. "Jimbo, do you want to color?"

"What's that?" Jimbo asked.

"Make pictures on paper with canine crayons," Lilith said.

Jimbo looked from Lilith to Becky, then to Teresa, perplexed. "I have never colored before. Yeah, let's color!"

"That sounds interesting," Becky said skeptically.

"I'll get you some paper. Why don't you go get your crayons and you and Jimbo can color in the living room," Teresa said.

"Okay, Mommy. Come on, Jimbo. Let's go get the crayons!" Lilith said.

Lilith and Jimbo ran out of the living room.

"Be right back," Teresa said.

"She must think I'm a moron," Becky whispered nervously.

Teresa went into the schoolroom, which was across the hall from Bill's home office, and grabbed a large pad of drawing paper. She returned to the living room and propped the pad against the coffee table and ripped off two sheets.

Lilith and Jimbo trotted into the living room; a box of canine crayons hung by a rope handle from each of their mouths.

Teresa placed the two sheets of drawing paper on the floor. "Okay, Lilith, show Jimbo how you lay on the paper so it doesn't tear."

Teresa turned to Becky. "We had a lot of practice before we found a workable solution."

Becky watched, fascinated. "This is so interesting. I didn't know dogs could draw."

"Oh, they can do quite a few things that human children do if you teach them," Teresa said.

Lilith stretched her front legs out on the paper and belly-flopped onto the floor. Jimbo paid close attention and followed suit. One of his dewclaws tore a small hole in the paper.

"That's okay, Jimbo," Lilith said. "You can still color around the hole."

Teresa opened both boxes of crayons and spread them out between the two dogs. There were several broken crayons in the pile.

Lilith snatched up a big, fat purple crayon with her teeth. Jimbo looked the crayons over and sniffed an orange crayon. He looked at Lilith, then grabbed the orange crayon. He bit too hard, and the crayon snapped in half.

"Uh-oh," Jimbo said.

"Don't try to chew them, Jimbo," Becky said. "We'll buy some new crayons..."

"No worry," Teresa said. "As you can see, Lilith went through an entire box before she got the hang of it. They can still use the broken pieces."

"Mommy!" Lilith said.

"Watch Lilith, Jimbo," Teresa said. "She's just learned to color and is an expert now."

Jimbo watched Lilith as she gripped the big crayon in her mouth and drew a square on the paper. She added a line from one corner of the square and a line from another corner that met the first line at a peak. Then she added a small square in the bottom of the square.

Becky stood and leaned over Lilith. "That's marvelous, Lilith! Give it a try, Jimbo. See if you can draw a house like Lilith."

Jimbo grabbed a big blue crayon and rolled it in his mouth until he found a comfortable position. He then lowered the crayon to the paper and moved his head back and forth. Bright blue lines zigzagged across the paper.

"Look, Mommy! I'm coloring!" Jimbo boasted excitedly.

"That's beautiful, son," Becky said, filled with pride.

"What strong lines," Teresa said. "You're doing great, Jimbo."

Becky returned to the sofa. "You and your husband are so smart! I can't believe you moved to this neighborhood."

"Bill grew up here and wanted to come back to where he spent his youth," Teresa said. "He was so happy when the World Guild approved our plans."

"I'm not surprised. The World Guild should bend over backwards for him. He's contributed more good for humanity in the past ten years than anyone else alive," Becky said.

They watched their dog-children in comfortable silence for a moment.

"Tell me how you came up with Jimbo's name. Is it a nickname?" Teresa asked. "I'm sorry... I guess that was a little embarrassing if it's his given name."

Becky dismissed Teresa's remark with a wave of the hand. "Actually, Percy's great-great uncle was Admiral James Beauregard Smythe in the Royal Navy. When Percy was a child, he loved the pictures of the Admiral in his dress uniform, so when we adopted Jimbo, just for a moment we thought of calling him Admiral, but changed our minds."

"He's a beautiful boy," Teresa said.

"He's pure Black Labrador," Becky said proudly. She looked at her wrist messenger.

The kitchen door opened and closed.

"In here," Teresa called.

"Daddy's home!" Lilith said. She jumped up, tearing her paper, and ran to greet Bill.

Jimbo was on his feet and on Lilith's heels without damaging his drawing. They raced into the kitchen, and Lilith skidded to a stop in front of Bill.

"Hi, honey. Who's your friend?" Bill said.

"Hi, Daddy! This is Jimbo Smythe. He lives down the street in the purple and green house," Lilith said.

Bill squatted and scratched Jimbo's head. "Hi, Jimbo. Are you having fun?"

"Yeah! We're coloring!" Jimbo exclaimed. "I like to color!"

Bill looked at Lilith. "Let's go see Mommy."

Jimbo and Lilith ran to the living room ahead of Bill.

Bill rounded the corner into the living room. He bent and kissed Teresa—a quick peck on the lips. "Hi, hon."

"Bill, this is Becky Smythe, Jimbo's mother," Teresa said.

Bill walked over to Becky and shook her hand. "It's nice to meet you. Looks like our kids like to play together. That's good."

"Lilith spends way too much time with adults. It's so good for her to be around other dog-children," Teresa said.

"Jimbo is going to love playing here," Becky said. "I'm so glad that you invited him for a playdate. Now he knows how to color!"

CHAPTER NINE

Abby woke with a start; she knew she must have fallen asleep after watching the antics of Lilith and Jimbo. Her heart ached for all she had lost. She opened her eyes and looked around. About a dozen dog-bots, including Rex, stood lined up on the other side of the glasshouse, watching her.

"Good morning, Abby," Rex said.

She was on her feet in an instant, looking from right to left at the odd assortment. Her hair bristled as she held her tail high and straight.

Some dog-bots were black and white, some brown. Several color combinations typical of actual dogs were present in various metal materials. There were red, orange, blue, and black glowing small orbs from light-emitting diodes for eyes. Short and long tails. Some stubs for tails. All of them appeared to be patterned from a bull terrier size and shape—Lilith's shape.

Abby growled at the dog-bots. They imitated her, but they

couldn't curl their lips back and look fierce. Their synthesized growling sound was more like a buzz.

Abby barked.

The dog-bots barked. Their barks sounded as if they were down in a well.

Abby drank out of the dog-faucet.

The dogs scurried over to the wall closest to the dog-faucet and hovered on the other side of the glass wall, watching her every move, all the while making soft beeping and computerized sounds as they compiled, sorted, and stored information.

Abby walked along the glass wall inside her house, growling. The entire group of dog-bots packed together to walk beside Abby on the other side of the glass, with Rex in the lead. They all made their equivalent of a growling sound.

Carole arrived with Abby's pre-selected lunch. She opened the door and placed the tray of food on the low table. "Looks like you have company."

Abby approached Carole. Her hair settled down, and she lowered her tail. She leaned against Carole's legs, but kept her gaze on Rex and the pack. She barked once, forcefully, and then turned to her food and ate her beef tips in gravy quickly and then cleaned up her face with her tongue.

Rex and the dog-bots watched every mouthful of food disappear, followed by Abby's clean-up.

"Why are Rex and the bots watching me eat? Machines don't eat or drink."

"That's right, machines don't require food or water, but they want to learn dog ways. Rex learns the majority of these experiences and passes his findings along to the other dog-bots through a wireless network," Carole said.

"Is Rex the father?"

Carole laughed, leaned over, and patted Abby on the rump.

"No, machines don't have fathers and mothers; they have inventors. Dr. Roberts invented Rex."

Abby stared at Carole for a moment. "That's why Rex is not a real dog. Dr. Roberts isn't a father."

Carole abruptly straightened and pondered Abby's statement without comment. She knew Abby was not fond of Dr. Roberts, but she did not expect Abby to make a judgment call as an insult. Somewhat rattled by Abby's thought processes, Carole stalled by throwing Abby a question. "Would you like to go for a walk?"

Abby pranced to the door. "Yes! I want to walk. Can I go outside today, Carole?"

"No, I'm afraid not. You will have to make do with the walking track." Carole sympathized. She knew Abby must feel cooped up inside her glass house and the lab.

She held the door open, and Abby stepped outside the glass house. Abby's hackles stood straight in the air as the dog-bots approached. Abby scratched the floor with powerful strokes. She slowly circled the pack, making a vicious growl. The dog-bots remained passive as they shifted their directions when Abby passed by.

Abby made a full circle back to Rex. The pack inched back, giving Abby and Rex some space.

Carole didn't move. She stood quietly, watching the spectacle. Gene and Dr. Roberts approached from their workstations on the other side of the room. They stopped several feet away.

"Should I have the dog-bots retreat?" Gene whispered.

"No. I want to see how this plays out," Dr. Roberts said. "We'll be able to decommission Rex, if necessary."

Abby circled Rex. She growled as she looked from Rex to the pack as if warning them off. She suddenly lunged at Rex and head-butted him behind his front leg.

Rex toppled over. His legs pawed the air as he struggled to right himself.

"I am Lilith's pup! I am the alpha dog!" she proclaimed. She stared at Rex and then at the pack, challenging any and all to cross the implied line of command.

Dr. Roberts, Gene, and Carole were rooted to the ground. Carole uttered a tiny squeak, and her jaw dropped.

"Maxwell must have done some brain engineering. This is way beyond normal canine intellect and behavior," Dr. Roberts said.

Carole joined Dr. Roberts and Gene. "Did I just witness a tactical maneuver? How could that be?"

Rex turned circles on the floor as he tried clawing himself upright.

"Help is required!" Rex said.

The pack hovered around him, watching. Gene approached and lifted Rex to his feet.

"Looks like you need some hardware and software modifications," Gene said.

"They need more flexibility and joints," Dr. Roberts said. "Rex was completely incapacitated."

"Do those other dog-bot machines talk?" Abby asked Carole.

"No, their speech has been disabled while in training. Only Rex speaks," Carole said.

"How come?" Abby asked. "What if they need to tell you something?"

"Rex receives the message and determines what action to take," Gene said.

"What if something happens to Rex?" Abby couldn't let it go. She couldn't understand why the dog-bots couldn't all talk.

"If Rex were decommissioned, we could make one of the

others the pack lead and it would have the capability of speaking," Gene said.

Abby huffed, not satisfied. "Don't they want to talk?"

"I don't think it has occurred to them yet. They're not as advanced as the pack lead," Gene explained.

Abby stepped onto the walking path. Now that the hierarchy had been established, Rex and the dog-bots fell into place behind Abby. They walked, and then jogged down the path, passing technicians and tables, tool cabinets and floor litter.

Technicians stopped and watched the pack pass by. "Hi, Abby," one technician said.

Abby raised her ears. "Hi," she said.

The technician grinned as if he had received a gift. He turned to another technician across the table and said, "Abby talked to me!" The other technician stretched his neck to see Abby and the dog-bots trotting down the path.

Abby stopped to see what the work table held. A big machine arm was on the right side of the table. "What's that?" Abby asked. She jumped to get a better look.

Rex attempted to jump, but it looked like he staggered forward. He teeter-tottered a bit, but didn't fall.

"It's a laser for soldering," the technician said.

"Oh," Abby said. She and the dog-bots continued down the path.

As Abby approached the curve in the path toward her glass house, she stopped and snatched up a piece of brown leather-like material off the floor that was inches from a trash can. The scrap, three inches square, was dirty and raveled along one edge.

Carole opened the door as Abby approached. "What's that you're carrying?"

"Mine," Abby said. She dropped her new possession on the floor.

Carole entered the house, bent over, and examined the cloth. "Are you sure you want this little scrap?"

Abby snatched it up.

Carole patted Abby's head. "It's okay, Abby. I'm not going to take it away from you." Abby dropped the cloth on the floor and then licked Carole's hand.

~

GENE CARRIED a small box to Abby's glass house. He presented his hand to the door scanner. The blue authorizing light appeared, and the door clicked open.

Abby exited the bathroom closet and shook herself. She looked expectantly from the box to Gene.

"Brought you a box so you can clean up your house," Gene said as he swept his arm wide. He placed the cardboard box on the floor beside Abby's growing pile of treasures. She had quite a collection: wires, scraps of metal, writing instruments, a couple of microchips, bits of plastic and pieces of paper.

For the past month, some of the lab technicians had left little treasures close to the walking track for Abby. She would snatch up her prizes and show her appreciation to the technicians with her glowing face. They seemed to enjoy pleasing her.

She enlisted Rex and the dog-bots in carrying her prizes. When they reached her house, the dog bots followed her in a single file and deposited the bits and pieces on the floor of her glass house.

Abby approached the box, her nose twitching. The sides had been folded and tucked inside. She stuck her face into the box and sniffed. She grabbed her inventory, one piece at a time, and dropped it into the box. When she was finished, she turned to Gene. "The house is all clean."

"Yeah, it looks much better, Abby."

"Where's Rex?" Abby asked.

"He's getting upgrades," Gene said.

"What's that mean?" Abby asked.

"You'll see," Gene said.

Gene left Abby's house and walked across the lab. Abby lost track of him through the maze of tables, high counters and desks filled with computer and laboratory equipment.

Bored, Abby walked over to the PawBoard and pressed GNN. She sat on her haunches and watched the screen for a minute. Global leaders sat around a table discussing worldly situations. Abby got up, walked the length of the PawBoard, and looked at the buttons. She watched with rapt attention as a nature program came on that showed wild animals in their natural habitats.

Abby was so engrossed in the program that she did not see Carole approach holding a leash. Carole entered the glass house. "Hi, Abby," she said.

Abby kept her face glued to the screen. "What's that big animal, Carole?"

"An elephant," Carole said. "There are only ten alive today."

"How come?" Abby asked. "Where'd they go?"

"Hunters killed them all in the early twenty-first century."

"Why?" Abby asked.

"Because the hunters were stupid and the animals were not protected," Carole said.

Abby turned from the screen and saw the leash. "What's that?"

"It's a leash. Would you like to go to my office?" Carole asked.

Abby bounced around with excitement. "Can we go outside?"

"No, it's just in the next room, outside of the lab," Carole explained.

"Oh," Abby said. She was disappointed but up for the adventure.

Carole snapped the leash onto Abby's collar, and they exited the glass house. They walked over to the door through which Dr. Roberts and the workers came and went every day. Abby was excited to walk out the door.

They walked down a short corridor to another door. Carole placed her hand on the scanning pad, and the blue light scanned and accepted the image. The door clicked, and Carole led Abby into a long corridor with offices on both sides of the hall. Three doors down, they stopped in front of a door, and Carole gained access.

The room lit up as they entered, and Abby looked around, curious. A round dog bed was on the floor along with a cushion, some dog toys, and a water stand. Carole unclipped the leash.

"Make yourself at home, Abby. I'm going to get a few things and we'll play some games," Carole said.

Abby walked over to a bookcase and sniffed the binders and books on the bottom shelf. "What's pees-why-chowl-oggy?" she said.

Carole stifled a chuckle, straightened her face, and walked over and kneeled beside Abby. She pulled the binder from the shelf. "That's psychology, Abby. Psychology is the study of the mind."

"Oh," Abby said. She sniffed another book. "Human be-hav-your. I know what that is."

"You do?" Carole asked, surprised.

"Uh-huh. Being good or bad. We need to be good so Dr. Roberts likes us," Abby said.

Carole looked surprised. "You look around while I make some notes." Carole returned to her desk and wrote swiftly on a virtual surface. She documented Abby's conversation while shaking her head in disbelief and placed notes in the margin:

Abby is displaying intelligent human reasoning.

Carole rested her head on her hand, lost in thought. She watched Abby walk along the bookshelves and could only guess what was going through the dog's head.

Carole administered a series of simple canine IQ tests to Abby for a comparative analysis with research data. In the benchmark data, one dog tested had scored an IQ of 121. This put him in the ninety-first percentile of dogs, according to the standards set in 2055. Another dog scored 104, an average score, and a third came in with just an 89 IQ, below average. But of course, these standards were decades old now.

According to Stanley Coren, author of "The Intelligence of Dogs" that was published back in 1994, there were three types of dog intelligence:

1) Adaptive Intelligence (learning and problem-solving ability). This is specific to the individual animal and is measured by canine IQ tests.

2) Instinctive Intelligence. This is specific to the individual animal and is measured by canine IQ tests.

3) Working/Obedience Intelligence. This is breed-dependent.

Carole pondered the dilemma. The original test data was 81 years old and from an era where dogs were considered owned pets. It would be another decade before their status began to change. Even the updated standards from 2055 were twenty years old. Recent inventions such as the Dot and the PawBoard had caused dogs' abilities to leap forward, and Carole was convinced that Abby's mother was of superior intelligence and had handed down her intelligence to her daughter.

Carole always carried a recording device with her and recorded Abby's dialog so she could accurately document the number of words and phrases that Abby understood. Unlike any other test subjects before her, but not including Lilith, Abby spoke in more complex sentences. Her reasoning abilities were better than those of a 10-year-old human child.

Abby read the words, phrases, and sentences on the cards that Carole held up in front of her. She could tell time, and she knew and understood the measurement of time. Although Teresa had never gotten around to math in the schoolroom, Abby could calculate simple numbers.

When Carole completed the tests, gathered the data, and entered the results into the model for scoring, she sat in disbelief and stared at the number on the virtual surface. She ran the data again and found herself on the edge of her chair, holding her breath. And there it was again, inches from her face: one hundred forty-five.

Carole glanced over at Abby, who was lying on the dog bed and chewing on a chew toy. She's just a baby, she thought. What is she going to be like when she's a year old? Two years old?

Carole printed out the test results and gathered up the leash. "Let's go back to the lab, Abby," she said.

Abby stood on the dog bed. "Can I take this toy with me?"

"Of course you can," Carole said. She bent over and snapped the leash onto Abby's collar. Abby grabbed the chew toy, and they left Carole's office.

Carole and Abby passed through the two secured doors. "Abby, I'm going to bring you back to your glass house, but I'll be back soon to let you go for a walk."

"Okay," Abby said.

They walked to the glass house, and Carole scanned her hand and opened the door for Abby. She removed the leash. "I'll be back soon."

Abby walked to her bathroom closet and relieved herself.

She walked through the water and shook herself, and then she went over to the PawBoard and looked at the big icons on the keys. She found the one labeled Health and stepped on it. A menu with big, complicated words appeared on the screen. She stared at the words, recognized psychology, and then walked to the down arrow. Abby stepped on the arrow a couple of times until the word psychology was highlighted.

~

CAROLE APPROACHED Dr. Roberts and Gene in a discussion over by the dog-bots. "Do you have a minute?" she asked.

Dr. Roberts did not like to be interrupted. "What is it?" he snapped.

"I'm pretty sure you won't mind the interruption when you hear what I have to report," she said.

Dr. Roberts turned his full attention to Carole. Gene rearranged his face and bit his lip. They both tolerated their boss's prickly temperament.

"I just finished administering a battery of IQ tests to Abby. She's off the charts for a canine," Carole said. She walked a few steps to a table and spread several pages out.

Dr. Roberts and Gene followed Carole. They each picked up a different page and studied the contents.

"There must be some mistake," Doctor Robert said as he picked up another page, and then another.

Carole shook her head. "I devised the tests from a combination of canine and human IQ tests. Some of the test criteria dated back to 1994. I gathered all known sources, and the scoring was produced by the computer. I ran the results twice because I didn't believe what I read the first time."

"She's a canine genius," Gene said, stammering.

"The Gf and Gc are about equal," Dr. Roberts said.

"Gf, Gc?" Gene said, confused.

"Fluid and crystallized intelligence," Carole said. "Fluid intelligence is what you are born with, your native intelligence. Crystallized is everything you have learned. In Abby's case, Lilith was a very smart dog, and she passed along her intelligence to her daughter. Abby learns fast; she's like a sponge. And I want you to consider that she's very young. I can't even imagine how smart she will be when I test her again in another six months or a year."

Dr. Roberts pondered the news, his brow furrowed. Gene's mind was active with thought.

"It's time for a brain scan," Dr. Roberts said. "I want to see what's going on in her head and whether Maxwell tweaked the prefrontal cortex," Dr. Roberts said. "This has to be as accurate as possible."

"I'll go get the virtual healing office set up," Gene said. "Give me about an hour." He hurried off and exited through the secured door.

"Will we have to sedate Abby?" Dr. Roberts asked.

"No. We'll just have to explain that she will have to sit still for a little while," Carole said. "She understands more than you realize, and she'll understand that this is a medical test."

MAGNETO ENCEPHALOGRAPHY (MEG) scanning technology had been developed in the twentieth century and was used to observe the brain for epilepsy, brain tumors, emotions, and pain perception. The MEG scanner was so fast that a thought being formed in the brain could be observed in real time.

The VHO contained a modern MEG scanner that didn't

require a magnetically shielded room (MSR). Researchers had discovered that there was a relationship between intelligence and the size and shape of the superior parietal lobe, which is the area that is used for sensory perception, and the prefrontal cortex which is where all the complex thinking, personality, planning and coordination take place.

Gene programmed the VHO for veterinarian scanning and chose a dog. He entered Abby's age and gender. He stared at the chair in the center of the booth with a helmet suspended overhead.

The special helmet attached to the end of the equipment above the chair was created for a human head. Gene studied it. He thought that they would have to make sure that Abby was as comfortable as possible because she could not move while the machine was rapidly taking pictures of her brain. The MEG was like a super-fast camera—it snapped more than a thousand pictures every second.

Since the helmet would not be snug, Gene worried that Abby would fidget. There wasn't anything about the helmet, chair, or booth that might scare Abby as far as Gene knew, but she would want to look around. Being an intelligent, curious young dog had its disadvantages.

CAROLE OPENED the glass door and greeted Abby with a little treat—a morsel from her lunch that contained rice, seaweed, crab and avocado. Abby sniffed, snatched and gobbled the tidbit and gave Carole a happy, satisfied stare.

"Yum," Abby said. "What was that?"

"It's called sushi," Carole explained. "They come in different combinations. The one you just tried is called a California roll."

"Can I have more California rools?" she asked.

"Roll, not rool," Carole said. "Rr-oh-l."

"Roll," Abby said.

"That's right," Carole said. "Would you like to go for a walk? We have a busy afternoon ahead of us."

Abby pranced around the door to her house, eager with anticipation. "Carole, do you want to walk with me?"

Carole rocked from her toes to her heels. "Yes, I would love to go for a walk with you."

They stepped out of the glass house and began down the path. Lab technicians, engineers and scientists smiled and waved as Abby and Carole passed by. Abby looked around, observing everything within her viewing range. She stopped and looked up at a device on the ceiling.

"What's that?" she asked.

Carole looked up. "That's an alert system. If someone were to enter the lab without permission, an alarm would be triggered, and the Tranquility Force would be here within minutes."

Abby looked at Carole, a little worried. "Is this place safe?"

"Yes," Carole said. "The walls are three feet thick and someone would have to bomb their way in if their palm prints weren't in the system. Don't worry, Abby. You're completely safe here."

They continued down the path. Carole noticed that some workers scurried about to put little gifts on the floor by the walking path to see if Abby favored them: swatches of material, wires, torn paper, even a pair of safety glasses. One engineer placed a small trash can at the edge of the path.

Abby approached the trash can and stuck her head inside. She retrieved a gaily wrapped soft package with a red bow. She set it on the floor and sniffed it. People quietly approached and stopped several feet away. Abby looked up and took note of the audience.

She gently placed a paw on the package and grasped the bow in her teeth, and extracted it. She placed it on the floor. Then she used her other front paw and scratched at the seam. The paper tore open, and a brown and fuzzy appendage appeared. Abby stuck her nose into the small opening and grabbed the secret thing.

She held the paper firmly with a paw and pulled a small stuffed brown bear from the packaging. She dropped it on the floor and sniffed it, licked it, and then grabbed it firmly. Abby presented her radiant face to the group of people.

They clapped.

Abby held her tail high and meandered down the path, a very happy dog.

Carole picked up the clutter and placed it in the trash can. She retrieved a small virtual note pad and a writing stylus from her lab coat and wrote copious notes, one of which stated:

The staff gave Abby a small stuffed bear which was wrapped in paper with a bow and placed in a trash can by the walking path. Abby retrieved and unwrapped the package with care. I expected her to wildly tear the packaging. She used restraint and care, very well thought out. She displayed thanks to the group with modesty.

Carole finished the journal entry and hurried after Abby. She caught up with her at the door to the glass house.

Clomping sounds made Abby and Carole turn their heads. Rex, sporting a new furry dog-form pranced up to Abby.

"Wow! Your knees bend," Abby said. "Do you like that?"

Rex showed her how he could jump. "Rex is more doglike!"

Abby sniffed his fur. "Doesn't smell like fur, but you look more doglike."

"Rex is happy," he said, jumping to prove his new ability.

Carole patted Rex's head. "You look great, Rex."

CHAPTER TEN

C arole sat on the floor in Abby's glass house and waited until Abby finished her business in the bathroom closet. The new stuffed bear was on the dog bed beside the old raggedy lamb.

Abby emerged from the bathroom closet and gave a little shake. She ran up to Carole and leaned into her.

"I like my new baby," she said. "What is it?"

"It's a little teddy bear. What are you going to name it?" Carole asked.

Abby went over to the bed and flopped down. She licked the bear. "Brownie," she said.

"Brownie it is then," Carole said, patting Abby on the head. "Abby, in a little while, we are going to walk over to the hallway through the door to a booth that holds the virtual healing office where a machine can take pictures of your brain."

"What for?" Abby said.

"Because you are a very smart girl, and Dr. Roberts wants to know what is different about your brain compared to other dogs," Carole explained.

"I'm Lilith's pup. Lilith was very smart," Abby said.

"Yes, that's right. Lilith was a very smart dog. Now it looks like Abby is the smartest dog we know of," Carole said.

"Abby is the last dog in the world," Abby said. "GNN said so. I watched GNN with Mommy and Daddy and Grandma Becky and Grandpa Percy. I miss Mommy and Daddy. I want to go home."

Carole cupped Abby's face in her hands. "I know you miss your family. I wish I could take you home, but I'm not in charge."

They sat in silence for a moment. Carole patted Abby on the back while Abby rested her chin on her front paws.

"We'd better get going," Carole said. "You will have to sit very still while you are in the booth. You won't be able to move at all while the pictures are being taken. Do you think you will be able to sit still for a little while?"

"Sure," Abby said.

Carole snapped the leash onto Abby's collar, and they left the glass house. Carole led Abby to the secured door, and they exited. Instead of going toward Carole's office, they went through the door to the entrance of the building where the Communicator sat.

As Carole walked with Abby across the floor toward another door, Abby looked over her shoulder to the robotic receptionist. The Communicator's halo over the machine's head was lit up with various colors and her many arms waved in the air like tentacles.

Abby faced forward and paid attention to where Carole was taking her. They approached a secured door, and Carole placed her hand on the scanning pad. The door popped ajar, and Carole held it open for Abby.

They walked a few yards to a rather large VHO office that

contained a chair and electronic panels on a wall with knobs and switches, and a flat panel monitor.

Dr. Roberts came through the door and joined them.

"We're all set," Gene said.

Dr. Roberts looked down at Abby with a stern expression on his rigid face. "This is a very important test, Abby. You are to sit still in the chair and not look around while the machine takes pictures of your brain."

"Carole already explained it," Abby said.

Carole kept her face a mask of seriousness as she glanced down at Abby. She cleared her throat.

Dr. Roberts appeared satisfied with Abby's answer. He entered the booth and observed the specific requests Gene had entered. Carole and Gene silently conspired between them, but kept their faces blank masks. They looked toward Dr. Roberts' retreat.

"Let's do a little prep work," Gene said. "Come on over here." They walked to the right side of the booth to a medical prep area.

Gene lifted Abby onto a reclining, padded table. He removed the leash and Abby's collar. "We have to remove these for the test," he said. He handed Carole a brush. "Can you brush her from top to bottom? Hair has a habit of attracting dust particles, and those dust particles may contain metal."

Carole used nice, soft strokes on Abby's hair. Gene filled a plastic tub with warm water. "Can you lift Abby up? I'm going to soak her feet in warm water to make sure she doesn't have any foreign material between her toes."

Carole laid the brush down and slid her arms under Abby's front and rear legs. "Up you go!" She hoisted Abby off the table while Gene deposited the plastic tub of water onto the padded table.

Carole lowered Abby's feet into the water. "You're being such a good sport!"

"I like being brushed!" Abby said.

Carole continued brushing Abby. She stopped and cleaned out the brush and discarded a handful of hair in the trash receptacle, and then laid the brush aside. Gene picked up one of Abby's front paws and squirted soap on her paw and washed in between her toes. He washed all four paws, emptied the tub and refilled it with clean warm water to rinse the soap thoroughly.

When her feet were nice and clean, Gene took a towel and dried them. When the entire ritual was complete, he slipped paper booties on Abby's feet, lifted her off the table and placed her on the floor. "Don't run off, okay?" Gene said.

"Okay. I'll do the test," she said.

Abby sniffed at the booties and then walked a few steps. She lifted her feet higher than normal in an awkward gait. After a few steps, she shook each foot, trying to dislodge the booties.

"You have to leave them on until your test is finished," Carole said. "It's important not to pick up any dust, dirt, or metal."

Abby huffed.

Gene entered the booth and pressed buttons.

The wall opposite the chair contained a virtual mural of a field with a bubbling brook, birds flying in the sky, flowers, trees, rabbits hopping and cows eating grass or chewing their cuds.

Gene handed Carole a pair of medical booties to slip over her shoes. He slipped into his booties and stepped into the booth. Abby crossed the threshold of the booth, nose in the air, sniffing the new environment.

Carole stuck her head in the booth. "This is where you'll

sit, Abby," she said. Carole turned to Gene. "Will she have to sit up, or can she lie on her tummy and hold her head up?"

Gene scooped Abby up and placed her on the chair. "Go ahead and lie down, Abby," Gene said. "Let's see how far down the helmet will lower and how it fits on your head."

Gene grabbed the helmet and lowered it over Abby. It stopped about three inches from her head. "Nope, you'll have to sit up for this to work," he said.

He raised the helmet. Abby sat up. Gene lowered the helmet over Abby's head. She tried looking up and to each side to see the thing, and then she settled down and sat still.

Gene and Carole looked at Abby on the chair. "All set?" Gene asked.

"Uh-huh," Abby said.

"Are you comfortable?" Carole asked.

"Yup," Abby said.

"Okay, then. Stay right there. Then you're going to hear the machine starting up," Gene said. "You just watch the birds, rabbits and cows straight ahead, okay? Don't turn your head. Stay still."

"'Kay, Gene," Abby said. "Stay still. Got it."

Carole rubbed Abby's white patch and stepped back from the booth.

Dr. Roberts stood at an external control panel. He powered up the MEG and activated the cameras so he could see Abby from different angles. The machine hummed quietly. He then started the process, and the MEG began snapping pictures. It sounded like dominoes falling.

Carole and Gene joined Dr. Roberts in the observation area and watched Abby. She was a model patient, not moving a muscle and staring at the animal activity on the virtual mural.

Pictures of the brain with vibrant blue, red, and white colors flashed past on a transfer surface faster than a meteor sped across the sky. Dr. Roberts opened a window on the monitor and looked at the photos, pulling several pictures onto the surface and arranging them side by side.

"Look at that brain activity," he said. He was surprised at what he saw. "This corroborates your intelligence tests, Carole. I don't see any sign that Maxwell engineered this intelligence."

The transfer surface held dozens of pictures. Dr. Roberts kept filling the surface with pictures of Abby's brain. He studied them, layered them, and transformed them into 3-D and holographic images.

"I've spent the past several weeks researching Lilith and the Maxwells," Carole said. "Lilith's intelligence came from the interaction with her human parents. Remember, Teresa Maxwell is an animal psychologist. She spent practically every waking moment with Lilith; reading to her, coaching her, making her think, and using the PawBoard to expand Lilith's horizons with a global education about the earth and the universe. She taught Lilith everything a human child would learn. There was no subject deemed too difficult. That was one smart dog. Now we have her daughter, a puppy less than six months old, with brainpower far greater than anyone in this room."

BILL AND TERESA sat in the living room with Percy and Becky.

"I think we should petition the World Guild for visiting rights," Becky said. "It's not healthy keeping Abby away from her family."

"That's a good idea," Teresa said. "Should we send separate petitions? Will that strengthen our purpose?"

"It can't hurt," Bill said.

∼

ABBY SAT QUIETLY in the chair with the helmet over her head. She stared straight ahead at the virtual mural. None of the wild animal activity captured her attention, not even the rabbits that hopped around the edge of the brook. Instead, Abby accessed Lilith's memories from the Dot in her white patch.

In her head, Abby watched her father's antics, her siblings and herself as tiny puppies. She saw her mother on the PawBoard, her human parents and grandparents, and the events that led up to her being where she was today.

Her father, Jimbo, had truly been an acrobatic dog. She saw how his toenails wrapped around the wire in a chain-length fence as he steadily climbed to the top and then leaped through the air like a flying squirrel down to the ground, sometimes landing at a full run, other times tumbling and stumbling, but always managing to land without breaking any bones. She wished she could have spent time with him. He was an adventurer.

Abby entertained herself with the visuals running through her head. She had almost forgotten what Lilith looked like. And she looked longingly at her human parents. She missed her Mommy and Daddy fiercely.

∼

TWELVE MINUTES HAD PASSED and the machine finally stopped snapping pictures.

"All done," Carole called out.

Abby lowered her head out of the helmet and jumped down from the chair. She stretched and then gave a little shake as Gene and Carole approached the booth in their funny green booties.

Carole scratched Abby's head. "Were you chasing those rabbits and cows in your head? There sure was a lot of thinking going on in your noggin."

"I pretended I was outside running through the water," Abby said.

Gene and Carole looked at Abby for a minute. "You pretended?" Carole asked. Her voice cracked on the last word. She cleared her throat. "Well, you sure know how to keep yourself entertained."

Abby beamed her shining face at Gene and Carole. "Carole, I have to go to the bathroom closet," she said.

"Oh, okay," Carole said. She fastened Abby's collar around her neck and snapped the leash into place. "Let's go."

CHAPTER ELEVEN

Abby was sound asleep on her bed, stretched out beside her little teddy bear and shabby lamb. The steady, faint hum and beeps of the lab equipment did not disturb her in the quiet of the night since she was used to the sounds and sights in her environment. The dark interior of the windowless lab made the few colorful LEDs look like holiday lights.

The quiet was shattered by a blaring warning system horn and flashing red lights.

"Security has been breached. Do not be alarmed. Tranquility Force has been alerted."

The robotic message repeated non-stop and was deafening.

Abby was on her feet in an instant. The lab was pitch-dark except for the dim lighting from LEDs on the equipment. She took in her surroundings, alert for movement. She saw nothing out of place in her line of sight. Abby raised her nose and sniffed and did not detect any foreign scent.

Rex and the dog-bots barked in harmony. They were trapped like Abby in their pen.

The racket subsided and the lights came on. A squad of armed Tranquility Force entered the lab, followed by Larry, one of the lab technicians who was on call.

The Tranquility Force fanned out and stealthily went over every square inch of the lab. Larry rushed to Abby's house. He stooped down.

"Are you okay, Abby?" he asked. "Did anyone come into the lab?"

Abby came up to the door to see Larry; she knew him well. Many of her prizes in the box were from Larry's area.

"My ears hurt, Larry. The loud noise hurt my ears," Abby said. "I didn't smell anyone or hear anyone. Ask Rex."

"Good girl," Larry said. He stood and rushed to the dog-bot area. "Rex, report to Larry."

"System breach. Internal breach. Communicator breach," Rex said.

Larry called out to the Tranquility Force. "To the front. Check the Communicator for a breach."

The Tranquility Force squad returned to the secured door, and Larry led them out of the lab.

Abby stood on alert in the middle of her glass house, her tail raised to its highest position. Ten minutes later, Dr. Roberts rushed into the lab, followed by a disheveled, alarmed Gene.

"What happened?" Abby asked as Gene opened her door.

"Are you okay, Abby?" Gene asked. He stooped and patted her and looked her over.

Dr. Roberts entered Abby's house and took in every corner of the room, then looked up to the ceiling.

The main secured door opened, and Carole rushed into the lab and ran over to the glasshouse.

"Is she okay?" Carole said, out of breath. She went to her knees and hugged Abby.

"What happened?" Abby asked again. "Very loud noises,

then Tranquility Force and Larry came. Will somebody tell me what happened?"

Gene, Carole and Dr. Roberts stared at Abby. She was growing up. Her sentences were becoming more complete and mature. Her intelligence was blooming.

"Someone tried to breach the Communicator to gain access codes to the facility," Dr. Roberts said. "They know you're here and they know about the dog-bots, but they won't be able to get inside."

"Larry said the Tranquility Force thought the attempt came from Texmexzona," Carole said.

"What's that?" Abby asked with a poker face.

"It's a bad place," Gene said.

"Why?" Abby asked.

Dr. Roberts noticed Abby's box of scraps. "What's all this junk doing in here?"

Abby hurried over to the box and stood in front of it protectively. "Mine!" she said.

The forcefulness of her answer startled them. It was apparent that she was ready to defend her property.

Larry rushed over. "The Tranquility Force determined that some black marketers were responsible for the attempt. They were after lab equipment."

"It's taken care of?" Dr. Roberts asked.

"Yeah. They found them behind the facility," Larry said.

Doctor Robert shook his head. "I'll be in the office," he said, then left.

Gene and Carole tried to keep their glee from showing on the surface, but their eyes sparkled.

"I'm going to crash in the lounge," Gene said. He left Abby's house, walked over to the dog-bot area, then exited through the secured door.

Carole sat on the floor by Abby and put her arms around

her. "What a dreadful night you've had. Do you think you can go back to sleep, Abby?"

Abby yawned. "I'm tired. I'll try to sleep for a while."

"I'm going to take a nap in my office," Carole said. "I'll be back at breakfast time with your tray."

DAYS AND WEEKS passed with no disruption from attempted break-ins or other security breaches. Abby's routine was the same day after day. She walked the track with the dog-bots collecting her prizes. If there were multiple prizes, she had the dog-bots collect what she could not carry. Later in the day, she answered Carole's unending questions and played games with Gene and Carole. She tolerated an occasional visit from Dr. Roberts.

Abby spent hours devouring GNN and other news media. She studied United States geography, watched animal, nature and science programs, and studied many subjects that should not have been interesting to dogs, such as weather, natural medicine and health, communications, government and maps.

When the lab was hers at nighttime, she explored the contents of the secret Dot in her white patch. Abby discovered that her human father had given her more than memories. Bill had included his inventions, notes, scientific papers, and drawings.

Abby pored over the contents, absorbing every element. She turned her head this way and that. To any camera or watchful eye, it would appear that Abby was looking at something off in the distance—a workbench or piece of equipment — and did not understand it. But what was really happening was that she was directing the inside view in her head to see Bill's holographic images from different angles. She was at the helm that steered the ship.

Abby was aware, through her human father's meticulous notes, that all strokes of the PawBoard were monitored in government offices. She was careful to keep a broad range of interests.

Three and a half weeks after Abby turned six months old, her estrous cycle began. At first, she licked herself constantly, and then the bleeding began.

"Looks like you're a big girl now, Abby," Carole said.

Abby's bed was blotched with bloodstains. "I'll be back in a little while," Carole said. She left the glass house and went through the secured door. Moments later she returned with the dog bed from her office, a pair of boys' underpants, and a cotton pad.

She entered Abby's house. "Abby, I need to take your bed and have it cleaned," Carole said. "You can use the bed from my office until your bed is returned, okay?"

Abby sniffed the new bed. She recognized her scent. "Okay, Carole." She spied the underpants in Carole's hand. "What's that?"

"I don't want you to get your clean bed all dirty, so I'm going to put these pants on you," Carole said. "Can you give this a try?"

Carole placed the cotton pad inside the pants and then eased one of Abby's rear feet off the floor and stuck it in one of the pant leg holes. She did the same with the other foot, pulled the pants up and then slipped Abby's tail through the fly.

Abby shook herself. She turned her head and stared at her rear, then looked at Carole. "I have to pee."

Carole groaned and slipped the pants off Abby. "I guess this is not going to work," she said.

She stood, grabbed the dirty dog bed and the failed pants. "I'll go get your breakfast."

Abby entered the bathroom closet, and Carole left the glass house.

Carole returned with Abby's breakfast: a bowl of scrambled eggs, brown rice, blueberries, nuts, chicken and vegetables. "This is a pretty interesting breakfast combination, Abby."

As soon as Carole placed the bowl on the low table, Abby had her head in the bowl. "I'm very hungry!" she said. She began gobbling her food. She licked her nose and around her mouth, and then she went into her bathroom closet.

Moments after Abby exited the bathroom closet, Dr. Roberts and the dog-bots arrived. Abby let out a fearsome, low growl. Her hackles rose along her spine. She held her tail erect and laid her ears back.

Carole approached Dr. Roberts. "Abby's in heat. She's going to be very unpredictable for the next three weeks."

Dr. Roberts studied Abby quietly for a moment. "I think she's much too young to try in vitro fertilization right now," he said. "We'll wait until her next cycle. We need to study how she reacts to all situations over the next twenty-one days."

"That's a good idea," Carole said. "I need to pull some research data."

Dr. Roberts hurried away. Abby gave a little ruff, relaxed her tail, hair and ears. Carole made a mental note of Abby's insolent reaction to Dr. Roberts.

Rex and the dog-bots gathered around the glass walls and watched Abby's every move.

"Abby, do you want to walk with Rex and the dog-bots?" Carole asked.

Abby pranced around, happy. "Yes. Rex is my friend."

Carole opened the door, and Abby scampered out of the

house. She charged over to the walking path. Rex and the dog-bots ran to catch up with her.

Everyone in the lab stopped what they were doing and watched the running procession. Abby had only run the path once, on the very first day at the facility. Now, it was Abby in the lead with fifteen dog-bots on her heels. They sounded like a herd of buffalo stampeding.

Half-way around the track they slowed down. Abby squatted and peed. Rex and the dog-bots took turns examining the puddle on the track, their LEDs lit up like Christmas trees and their computers storing data.

Larry rushed over with cleaning materials. "Abby, you have to go to your bathroom closet. This is very inappropriate," he said.

He sprayed the track with a cleaning agent that contained germ-eating microbes, and then he wiped the surface with an absorbent cloth.

Abby licked his nose in apology. "Sorry, Larry," she said.

Larry rubbed her head. "That's okay. Accidents happen."

Abby and the dog-bots continued their trek down the path. Rex walked beside Abby.

"Abby-dog," Rex said. "Rex and some dog-bots will go to the city with the Tranquility Force for training. We will learn how to patrol the city and keep it safe."

"I thought Rex and the dog-bots were going to be dog-children," Abby said, concerned.

"Maybe the next batch will be dog-children," Rex said.

Abby pondered for a minute. "Rex, find Mommy and Daddy when you patrol! Scratch on the door. Tell Mommy and Daddy that Abby loves and misses them."

She stopped to sniff something on the floor. Rex stopped beside her. The dog-bots stayed close by.

"Rex is not programmed to do that, Abby-dog. Rex cannot break the rules," he explained.

Abby snorted her displeasure. "If you want to be like a real dog, then you need to know what loyalty, love, and family are," Abby said. "My Mommy and Daddy cry for their lost dog-child. Tell them what I said. They will find peace."

From a distance, Abby and the dog-bots appeared to be in conference. Rex and the pack moved in tandem when Abby moved. Abby drilled Rex. "Abby is the alpha dog of all dog-bots," she said. "Dog-bots are loyal to Abby first, keepers second. We are a pack. Rex is loyal to Abby. Rex will find Mommy and Daddy, deliver Abby's message."

Rex' computer churned data. His LEDs flickered. "Rex will find Abby's Mommy and Daddy."

"We have a pact," Abby said. She lightly poked Rex on the shoulder with her snout. They arrived back at her glass house.

"Carole, is Rex a dog-child or an enforcer dog?" Abby asked.

Carole didn't know what to say. She knew this was going to be upsetting for Abby. "Dr. Roberts decided to work with the Tranquility Force and train Rex and these dog-bots to cut down on crime."

Abby huffed. "But what about all the people who want dog-children?"

Carole shrugged. "It's sad. I'm not sure what's going to happen."

Abby's hackles rose partway. "I want to go home! If Rex and the bots aren't going to be dog-children, then Dr. Roberts can't keep me here!" Abby growled.

~

ABBY STRETCHED her neck to see test tubes and lab equipment on a bench. "What's that?" she asked the lab technician.

Bruce, another lab technician, leaned over the counter and smiled at Abby. "Hey, Miss Curious. I'm experimenting with cloning properties," he said.

Abby stared at the technician. "You make copies of me for other parents?"

Bruce laughed. "No, it's not as easy as that. The other three dogs that survived had mutations from being exposed to the toxic poison," he explained. "I'm trying to find a way to turn off those mutations and make a healthy boy-dog for your mate."

Abby craned her neck upward. "Let me see."

Bruce squatted, picked Abby up and showed her the workbench. He rested her front feet on the workbench. She sniffed everything within sniffing distance.

The lab people watched with interest as the technician held Abby on the edge of his workbench. Dr. Roberts took notice and stormed over to the bench.

"Bruce, what is going on?" Dr. Roberts demanded.

"Just showing Abby what I'm doing. She was curious," Bruce said.

"Abby, continue your walk with the dog-bots and leave the lab work to the technicians," Dr. Roberts said.

"I'm bored living in a glass house. I can't go outside. I want to learn," she said.

Dr. Roberts studied Abby for a moment. "There are many things to explore from your PawBoard. That will have to keep you occupied for the time being."

Bruce lowered Abby to the floor. Abby shook off her indignation from the conversation with Dr. Roberts. Abby, Rex, and the dog-bots walked down the track. Abby squatted and peed within a foot of Dr. Roberts' workbench.

CHAPTER TWELVE

Abby stood in her glass house, ears erect, brow furrowed, facing the lab door. She watched a cage atop a small hover surface containing Rex and four other dog-bots glide through the secured door in the company of two Tranquility Force enforcers and Dr. Roberts. The door closed and Abby's friend was gone.

She flopped down on her bed and feigned sleep.

THE HOVER SURFACE moved through the second secured door into the reception area. The Communicator noted the procession with a fast winking of her robotic sensors, and her halo changed colors like a rainbow.

Rex and the dog-bots faced forward in the cage. As far as the Tranquility Force and Dr. Roberts could see, Rex showed no interest in the Communicator or his surroundings, but he was scanning the Communicator and recording communications, details, planned events, dates, and appointments of all

callers in the queue. Everything that was conveyed in any electronic form, Rex had access to.

He recorded every conversation, sensation and detail with
audio and holographic. His system filed and stored data for
retrieval and future comparison projects.

The enforcer at the front of the hover surface disengaged
the lock on the facility door. As the entourage exited the facility, Rex saw the Tranquility Force's silver and black glider
waiting outside the door plus the four additional armed
enforcers who stood alongside the glider, on alert.

The squad jumped into action. One opened the back door
of the glider. He was joined by two other enforcers; they slid
the cage inside the glider and secured the back door.

Rex and the four dog-bots turned in sync to face the back
door.

"Make sure you report on the dog-bots' progress," Dr.
Roberts demanded.

"You will have a progress report at eighteen hundred hours
daily," the lead enforcer said.

Dr. Roberts delivered a clipped gesture of approval, turned
on his heel, and returned to the facility.

The squadron entered the glider. Rex recorded the gate
code sequence as the Tranquility Force glider approached the
high double gate. He took a holographic scan of the compound
as it faded in the distance, and then he turned to face the front
of the glider to record the scenery along the two-hour route.

The lead enforcer opened a communication channel on his
helmet. "Incoming task force. ETA oh-nine-hundred," he said,
then disengaged the channel.

They arrived at the San Jose city boundary, and the glider
went directly to a large, fenced-in warehouse facility in the hub
of the business district. The fence and buildings sported the
large Tranquility Force logo, a deterrent all by itself.

Rex scanned the area for any activity and noticed that no one loitered on the streets near the facility. He watched with interest as an infrared signal shot from a tiny point on the building and unsecured the gate. He busily tracked the signal and packed the data away for future study.

The glider whizzed through the gate and parked near a loading platform. One enforcer jumped out of the glider onto the platform. He placed a finger on a button on the exterior wall. Chirps and beeps sounded. An LED flashed a green light.

All the remaining enforcers, except for the glider driver, exited the glider and guarded their cargo.

A massive warehouse door rolled up and several enforcers came out of the warehouse onto the platform. Two jumped down to the rear of the glider and lifted the cage onto the platform. They loaded the dog-bot's cage onto a hover surface and guided it into the warehouse. As the door lowered behind them, Rex saw the glider team get back into the glider and leave the facility.

The warehouse was an enormous cave of information and technology. Rex cataloged everything and everyone, and made a note of the overuse of the silver, gray, and black company colors. Shiny metal desks, along with tables and chairs, were arranged in an open space with backdrops of the same color.

Busy people rushed about on their missions. There was a buzz of conversation as people talked on their communication devices.

A small group of enforcers crowded around the dog-bot cage. Rex moved this way and that, depending on the activity outside his cage. Faces peered close to the bars of the cage. Rex recorded the various body odors, facial features, voices and postures—everything that took place within his range of visual and sound recording capabilities, which were long-reaching.

Two enforcers guided the hover surface to a secluded area

tucked in the back of the warehouse, one of the few spaces with interior walls and a secured door. A member of the group placed his hand on the security panel for scanning. The door clicked open, and they rolled the cage into the room.

The lights came up, and the group stood around the cage in a semi-circle, talking in hushed tones, eagerly waiting for the release of the dog-bots.

Footsteps with an unusual cadence drew closer. The pattern of the steps captured Rex' interest; he measured the pace, the material of the floor, the type of leather the sole of the boot was crafted from, and the height of the heel. Rex determined that the wearer of the boots' legs were three-eighths of an inch different, thus making the clickety-clack sound with the heels.

Rex and the dog-bots turned to the left of the room and watched as a tall, solidly built man in a spotless commander's uniform turned the corner and entered the room.

Commander Michael Durvel walked directly to the cage. He looked at Rex and the dog-bots with curiosity, then opened the door. He stood aside. "Exit the cage and wait for instructions," Commander Durvel said.

A buzz of excitement grew as the employees watched the dog-bots.

Rex led the dog-bots out of the cage. The dog-bots fanned out behind Rex, making his rank known to Commander Durvel and the group of Tranquility Force enforcers.

"Commander Durvel, I am Rex, the pack lead. I will transmit all information to the pack," Rex said.

Rex turned to the door as a man in a white lab coat over his jumpsuit entered.

"So, these are the training subjects?" the man asked.

"Rex, this is Dr. Pietro Sovesky," Commander Durvel said.

"He worked with Dr. Roberts, creating the concept of dog-bots."

"Hello, Dr. Sovesky," Rex said. The doctor stared at Rex.

"Rex, this is the team that will be training you and the pack," Commander Durvel said. "Can you record each of their names and communicate with them by name, or is that too complicated?"

Rex' LEDs lit up and his computer whirred into action. "My database has the capacity to store four million, eight hundred twenty-seven thousand, two hundred and twelve individual first, middle, and last names," Rex replied. "Contact information is optional."

The team chuckled. "I guess you'll be able to remember the eight of us, then," Commander Durvel said. "Okay, let's get started."

A WEEK of training for the dog-bots passed quickly. Commander Durvel and his team were highly satisfied with the dog-bots' performances. Only two adjustments were required in their programming: satellite tracking close-ups, and passive-aggressive levels regarding conflict resolution. Both adjustments were accomplished through verbal commands with Rex.

At midnight on the last day of training, Dr. Sovesky gathered Rex and the dog-bots at the door to their secured room. He slipped a highly luminous silver, black, and gray Tranquility Force vest on each dog-bot and secured them in place with the Velcro straps attached to the vests.

Rex watched as Dr. Sovesky applied the vests to each of the dog-bots. He noted the doctor's trembling hands. He inspected one of the vests up close. His LEDs lit up as his computer recorded his findings. Rex then faced the doctor, waiting for instructions.

"Rex, you and the dog-bots will patrol the inner-city sectors. Stay as a pack for the first hour, and then I want each of you to take a different sector and patrol," Dr. Sovesky said.

"You are to report any suspicious activity, whether criminal or out of the ordinary, as your program recognizes it. If Tranquility Force enforcers are necessary to control a situation or make arrests, report immediately. Keep the suspects under constant surveillance."

"Understood and transmitted to the pack, Dr. Sovesky," Rex said.

"Good," Dr. Sovesky said. "Let's go, then."

Dr. Sovesky opened the door to the secured room and stepped out into the warehouse. He held the door for the dog-bots, and the pack ventured out of the room. They stood, fanned out in formation.

The doctor led the pack through the warehouse. The enforcers on night duty stopped what they were doing to watch the dog-bots pass. The enforcer on duty opened the door for the pack and the doctor to pass through.

Dr. Sovesky joined the pack on the exterior walkway of the warehouse. They approached the stairs to the ground level, and the dog-bots walked down the stairs. The doctor walked with them to the main gate and held his palm to the reader. The gate opened, and the pack went out into the city.

Dr. Sovesky watched the pack for several moments as they went down the street at a moderate pace, in formation. The Tranquility Force emblems were visible to the naked eye for two hundred feet, and then they blended with the night lights and sky lights.

The doctor turned back to the warehouse.

～

DR. SOVESKY and Commander Durvel watched the dog-bots patrol through a satellite link. After fifteen uneventful minutes, the Doctor and Commander went about their business.

At two-forty-five in the morning Rex messaged the Tranquility Force from his internal communication network and attached a holographic feed of suspicious characters loading crates and drums onto a glider surface from a door that had been blasted open at Alford Chemical Weaponry, a top World Guild contractor. Their secrets ran deep.

Dr. Sovesky and Commander Durvel dispatched a unit.

The dog-bot pack had six men surrounded. The suspects didn't quite know what to make of the dog-bots. Dr. Sovesky and Commander Durvel watched as one suspect pulled a laser pistol from his waist. Rex shot a red beam at the weapon, which heated it to an intense temperature. The suspect dropped the pistol and flailed a burned hand while cursing.

One suspect bolted and ran through the dog-bot ranks. A dog-bot pursued and effortlessly caught up with the man. He grabbed one of the man's legs in an iron-jawed clamp. The man screamed in agony.

Moments later, a squad of Tranquility Force enforcers arrived on the scene and relieved the dog-bots of the criminals.

"Good work, Rex," Commander Durvel said.

Rex and the dog-bots wagged their tails at the praise.

"The pack can split up now and patrol the city sectors," Commander Durvel said.

Rex and the dog-bots went in separate directions.

～

AFTER A WEEK OF PATROLLING, reporting their findings to the Tranquility Force, being tracked by satellite, and returning to headquarters at precisely the moment they were due back, Commander Durvel and Dr. Sovesky decided that monitoring the pack was unnecessary as they performed their duties without fault.

On Wednesday of their second week on the job, one of the dog-bots malfunctioned and fell over while on patrol. Rex was automatically alerted to the problem and rushed to the site where the fallen dog-bot lay still on the edge of the street. He reported the casualty and ran silent diagnostics until a Tranquility Force glider arrived on the scene, loaded the dog-bot, and took off.

When Rex and the remaining pack arrived back at the Tranquility Force facility, they walked their typical route to the back of the warehouse, Dr. Sovesky joining them. Along the way, off to the side, Rex spotted the fallen dog-bot on a pile of scraps.

Rex stopped. The dog-bots stopped. Rex approached the scrap pile. He sent a communication to the dog-bot. There was no response.

Dr. Sovesky discovered that the dog-bots were no longer following him, and he joined the pack at their decommissioned dog-bots' side. "His circuitry is completely burned up and can't be repaired," Dr. Sovesky said.

"Understood," Rex said. He recorded his findings and stored the information deep within his data banks. Rex and the pack moved on to the secured room.

CHAPTER THIRTEEN

Each night, the dog-bots left the facility and went on their unsupervised patrol. Under Commander Durvel's command, the dog-bots' patrol had been expanded to include residential areas as well as commercial districts.

Since the citizens in WestUS were secured in their homes under an ongoing curfew (which coincided with the time frame of the patrols), the dog-bots remained a secret policing force.

Rex kept a detailed map of each quadrant where his pack patrolled. All four dog-bots were symbolized with dog avatars on the grid, Rex having the biggest avatar to display his rank.

The pack ferreted out crimes that Tranquility Force could not detect, but Global News Network gave all the credit to Tranquility Force.

Rex traveled to his quadrant. He searched through dozens of databases, poring through data until he found what he had been searching for. He stored the information in his secret place, which was encrypted, password-protected, and disguised to look like bad sectors. Only he could access the data stored in the secret place. He was an intelligent machine and was becoming more aware every day.

Rex arrived at the residential quadrant at one-fifteen in the morning. He began his patrol going up and down streets and alleys, lurking in unsecured yards, going under, over, and around all manner of obstructions, machines, and vehicles.

As Rex patrolled, the quadrant map in his secret place flashed a big X. Abby-dog's house.

The home of Bill and Teresa Maxwell.

Rex passed the house. He went up a side street, down an alley between yards, and returned to the front of the house, staying in the shadows.

Finally, Rex approached the front door. He scratched at the door as Abby had instructed. The front door sensor acknowledged his presence. "Hello, we will be with you shortly. Please wait patiently. Property damage is unnecessary."

Within moments, the door opened rather forcefully. Bill, in pajama pants with tousled hair, looked down at Rex. Surprise, curiosity, and then a hint of anger crossed his face.

Bill opened the door wider. "Who sent you?" Bill asked.

"Abby-dog requested a secret mission," Rex said. He entered the house. His sensors worked overtime.

This was Abby-dog's house.

Lilith's house.

Rex was inside dog-world nirvana.

"Teresa!" Bill called out.

Teresa stumbled into the living room while securing her robe sash. She stared in confusion as she mentally determined what she was looking at.

"What ...? Is that your robot dog, Bill?" Teresa asked.

"Rex is a dog-bot," Rex said. "Model DB421 Rev 01."

Bill squatted down and looked Rex over. "Are you the only dog-bot or are there others?"

"Rex is the pack leader. All the other dog-bots learn through assimilation from Rex," Rex explained. "There are twenty-four dog-bots. Correction, twenty-three."

Bill and Teresa walked over to a sofa and sat. Rex moved to stand in front of them.

"Abby-dog loves and misses Mommy and Daddy. Abby-dog is okay," Rex said.

Teresa sat perfectly still for approximately five seconds in momentary shock. "Abby sent you?"

Rex shifted his feet as he absorbed the human emotions. "Abby-dog sent Rex to Mommy and Daddy."

Bill engulfed Teresa in a hug, as his emotions churned. "What about satellite tracking, Rex?"

"Tranquility Force trial tested the pack with satellite tracking for one week. Satellite tracking is unnecessary now," Rex said. "Rex keeps a grid with avatars in his database. He reports all incidents immediately. Rex is trustworthy."

Bill smiled at Rex. "Sounds to me like Rex knows how to cheat at cards without being caught."

"Explain," Rex said.

"A long time ago, people used to play a card game called poker. If a man wore his emotions on his face, his opponents could tell if he had a winning hand or a losing hand," Bill explained. "If he kept a straight face without showing any emotion, he could win the pot of money."

"Dog-bots don't have the capability to play cards," Rex said.

"It's a metaphor," Teresa said. "You can go about doing your job, what you have been programmed to do, but there's another part of you that does things like coming here to see us, and you don't tell anyone about it, you don't report it and you won't get caught."

"Rex has secrets," Rex said.

Bill stared at Rex. "You are a brilliant machine. I was your inventor, but it looks like someone stole my plans."

"What are you going to do, Bill?" Teresa asked.

Bill assessed Rex. "I can't do anything or else everyone will know that Rex communicated with us and it will put all of us at risk, including Abby."

Teresa squinted and pinched the bridge of her nose as she thought about the situation.

"Rex, is Abby okay? Are they treating her well?" Teresa asked.

"Rex can show you," Rex said.

He faced a wall and projected his recordings of Abby in the glass house sleeping on her dog bed with her lamb and the new teddy bear, using the PawBoard, and then walking down the path with the dog-bots.

"Look how much she's grown up, Bill!" Teresa said as she watched her beloved dog-daughter. "She's just so beautiful! Should we get Becky and Percy so they can see this?"

Bill screwed up his face in a thoughtful pose. "Hon, Becky's a blabbermouth. I know she would understand the importance of secrecy, but it's too much of a risk for them to see Rex."

Teresa considered what he said. She hung her head for a moment. "I know you're right. It just seems so wrong."

Rex stopped the media feed and went over to Teresa. He placed his chin on her knee, as he had seen Abby do to Carole. Teresa lovingly cupped Rex's face in her hands. She crooned to him as she softly stroked his upgraded fur-like cheeks, chin, and the crown of his head.

His sensors recorded everything. "Rex understands family," he said.

Bill scratched Rex's head. "Rex, would I be able to have access to your systems and networks without detection?"

"Yes. Rex can assign permissions from his secret place," Rex said.

Bill stood. "Secret place? Come into the lab so I can download your data. Have you seen my name on any of the plans you have stored in your databases?"

Rex searched internally. He found a sector that was encrypted and locked. He worked on it for twelve point four seconds and gained access.

"Rex has accessed original, encrypted, and locked plans. William Maxwell holds the patent from the year 2074 with updates in 2079 and 2081. There are several communications between Doctor Julian Roberts and Doctor Pietro Sovesky from November 2080 through the current date in 2086 regarding the secrecy of creating Rex," Rex reported.

"Bill, did you create the secret place or did Rex?" Teresa asked.

Rex and Teresa followed Bill into the lab.

"I think Rex did this on his own, but I don't know how or why," Bill said. "Can you explain that, Rex?"

"Rex is loyal to Abby-dog, the alpha dog, Lilith's pup," he said. "Abby-dog teaches Rex and the dog-bots about human emotions and experiences and becoming real dogs. Abby-dog is my friend."

Bill and Teresa stared at Rex. Their separate thoughts pondered Rex's statement in different ways. Bill pondered the learning capabilities of his creation. Teresa thought about the psychological development of Rex's computer.

Bill stood in front of the transfer surface and created a folder for Rex's schematics, data, and other information. When he had everything arranged to his satisfaction, Bill reached down and picked up Rex, and stood him on the transfer surface.

"Here you go, Rex. As you can see, I have created areas for

you to store your content. I want to be able to communicate with you privately, off the grid," Bill said. "I would also like to see the processes that were changed from my original plans."

Rex's LEDs flashed, and his systems whirred and clicked. "Rex is downloading to the transfer surface."

Bill noticed a bad sector area and smiled. "Is this where your secrets are, Rex? In this bad sector area?"

"Yes," Rex said.

"Very clever, Rex," Bill said. "Did you develop some new programming to protect your secrets? I don't recognize this language. What is it?"

"Dog thought," Rex said. "Dog-bot special language. I will provide my original creator, William Maxwell, with the key."

"This is better than Rijndael encryption, Rex," Bill said. He studied the language for a moment. "When will you return to the compound where they are keeping Abby?"

Rex activated the database that stored both Commander Durvel and Dr. Sovesky's notes and calendars. "My mission will be completed in two days' time. Then I will return to the compound and assimilate training information to the remaining dog-bots. Rex is privy to many Tranquility Force secrets, which include Dr. Sovesky and Commander Durvel. Rex secretly records all his findings."

"How could they not know this?" Bill asked.

"Rex set up visible and invisible functions. Dr. Roberts and others have access only to the visible functions. All invisible functions are hidden by strong encryption and require dog-thought passcodes that only Rex, and now Daddy, have access to."

Rex's data transferred to Bill's folders on the transfer surface. Bill lifted Rex off the table and set him on the floor.

"Let's see if everything is okay," Bill said.

Teresa watched as he looked at the directory tree and

clicked on files, checking for bad links and sectors. She turned away from the table and squatted beside Rex.

"Rex likes Abby?" Teresa asked.

"Yes. Abby does not like Dr. Roberts," Rex said.

"Why doesn't Abby like Dr. Roberts?" Teresa asked, her voice shaky with fear.

Bill stopped what he was doing and turned to Rex and Teresa.

"Dr. Roberts is not a nice man. Dr. Roberts yells at people and dogs and dog-bots," Rex said.

"Has Dr. Roberts hurt Abby?" Bill asked. He had to force himself to breathe as his hands clenched the edge of the transfer surface table.

"No. Abby is safe," Rex said.

Bill and Teresa visibly relaxed.

"Rex has evaluated Dr. Roberts and compared his assessment to criteria in various databases. Dr. Roberts has low self-esteem and negligible social skills. He lacks human warmth and understanding, and since he is not a family man, his actions, responses, and communications are sterile, cold and textbook-oriented," Rex said. "He does not possess the ability to judge whether his verbal or physical actions cause harm. Dr. Roberts was an abused child and was removed from his parental home and placed in the communal care system."

Teresa was deep in thought as she pondered Rex's statements. "It sounds as if Dr. Roberts is a bit of a sociopath—uncaring and unaware of caring."

Bill turned back to the transfer surface and worked with Rex's files. He was surprised at the volume of data and wondered why Dr. Roberts or Dr. Sovesky would give Rex access to some of the files in the data tree.

"Rex, were all these files uploaded when you went online,

or were some of these added later for a specific reason?" Bill asked.

"The basic data tree was uploaded when Rex was brought online. Rex uploaded other data as he saw fit," Rex said.

Bill joined Teresa and Rex at floor level. "Rex, do you consider yourself a sentient machine?"

Teresa was about to say something, but Bill warned her off with a look. She clamped her mouth shut and stared at Rex, waiting for the answer.

"Rex has developed certain emotions and feelings. Abby-dog teaches many things in dog-talk. Rex knows love and pain. Dr. Sovesky tossed dog-bot twenty-four onto the scrap pile when twenty-four experienced a system failure. Dog-bots are considered machines like a food console, not members of society," Rex said.

Teresa looked at Bill. "When you developed the original plans for Rex, was that after we discovered we could not have a child?"

Bill reached out and took Teresa's hand in his. He knew where her thoughts were going. "Yes. That was a very dark period for you. I put all my effort into developing a machine that would have the capability not just to emulate love, but to be able to recognize and return the same emotion. I thought I'd scrapped that after so many failures."

"Rex found his original creator's deleted files and studied them," Rex said. "Rex made some changes."

CHAPTER FOURTEEN

"I can't believe it," Teresa said.

She and Bill were momentarily shocked speechless by the revelation that Rex appeared to have independent thoughts.

"Rex' statements are beyond mathematical formulae, in a programming sense," Bill said.

"These are declarations of awareness and depth of feelings," Teresa said, excited, and yet awed. "Rex dislikes Dr. Roberts. He considers Abby to be his friend. He's upset that the doctors tossed one of his pack into the trash. Rex wants to be considered a living, breathing dog—not a machine!"

Teresa petted Rex. "Bill, this is revolutionary. This is the project that we have been searching for to collaborate on. I know we don't have time right now, but this has to be done."

Bill was lost in thought. Teresa verbalized what was racing through his head. "I know there's more; it's just not coming to me right now. It's evolutionary, not revolutionary. If I had only worked on the plans for a little while longer."

"No, it had to happen this way," Teresa said.

"Rex is a puppy, like Abby-dog," Rex said.

Bill laughed and patted Rex's rump. "I guess you are."

"Abby-dog and Rex are family. William Maxwell is my inventor. William Maxwell and Teresa are Abby-dog's Mommy and Daddy, so you are Rex's Mommy and Daddy."

Teresa studied Rex for a moment. "You are a good dog-son, Rex."

"Yes, indeed," Bill said. He stood and returned to the transfer surface. He pulled up a map and enlarged the details to show the geography of the land: forested areas, lakes, rivers, mountains, and desert.

"Rex, where is Abby being held? Can I get her out of there?" Bill asked.

Rex gave Bill the location with a big red X on the map, which was southeast of San Jose. "The building is a secured facility with three-foot thick walls." He explained about the World Guild security.

"I can override the software to get inside," Bill said. "Remember, I created and update the World Guild security!"

"Daddy Bill should not attempt a breakout. Too many things could go wrong," Rex said.

"Listen to Rex, Bill. It's too risky!" Teresa said.

Bill raked his hair in frustration. He accepted defeat with a long sigh.

"Rex, Abby has a secret Dot in the white patch on her chest," Bill said. "Something's gone wrong with her Wise Owl communication program. We should have been able to communicate, but the communication is either blocked or has failed."

"Do you think she was incapable of working the program?" Teresa asked. "She was so little when they took her."

"Abby-dog is very smart. Carole administered human and canine intelligence tests. Abby-dog scored one hundred forty-five," Rex said. "Dr. Roberts scanned Abby-dog's brain with the VHO MEG scanner for genetic engineering."

"One forty-five!" Teresa said. "Lilith scored one hundred thirty-two at three years old!"

"Thank the Earth she inherited more from her mother than her father," Bill said. "Jimbo had a pea-sized brain."

"Jimbo was a very happy dog," Teresa said. "His contribution to the gene pool was his tremendous joy of just being a dog and all those skills of exploration."

Bill balanced on the balls of his feet as he studied Rex for a moment. "I want you to remind Abby not to return to this house if she ever finds a way out of the compound. Tell her that Mommy and Daddy are going to Texmexzona," Bill said.

He reached down and scooped Rex up and placed him on the transfer surface. Teresa stood.

"This is the route we will take to get there," Bill said. He ran his finger over the map. "Tell Abby to avoid cities. She needs to travel at night and always stay in the shadows so she is not detected."

Teresa looked at the route. Cities and towns were scarce. "Bill, Abby has no survival skills for this journey. Will she be able to hunt and kill? All of her meals have been prepared and delivered to her from a food console since she was weaned from Lilith!"

Bill gripped her hand. "I know, honey. But she's strong-willed, and she still has the canine ability to become wild and survive."

"Maybe there's something in the formula on her Dot that kept her Wise Owl program from working properly," Teresa suggested.

"Not possible," Bill said in a clipped voice. He queued up more files. "Rex, look at the formula I created to make Abby's Dot untraceable. If you discover anything that might be blocking transmissions, send me a message. I don't think I can do anything about it at this point. This is my absolute worst failure!"

When the upload was complete, Bill set Rex on the floor.

"Rex has to patrol," Rex said. He walked out of the lab and headed toward the front door with Bill and Teresa following.

They stopped at the front door. It was three a.m. and still quiet outside, a major benefit of the curfew. No sound pollution emitted from residential or delivery vehicles or open windows in homes. Although the laws were strict regarding noise and peaceful disruption in natural, residential, and industrial settings, people sometimes intentionally provoked the Tranquility Force by allowing their music to escape the confines of their vehicles or homes.

Bill unsecured the door and inched it open. Rex's system whirred and clicked. His LEDs shined.

"All clear," Rex said.

Teresa crouched down and hugged Rex. "Thank you for taking the risk to come see us, Rex."

Bill rubbed Rex's head. "I'll send a test message, Rex. If you don't receive something from me within the next two hours, then you will know that there's a bug and you'll have to work on it from your end."

"Rex is grateful to meet Mommy and Daddy. Rex will give Abby-dog messages. Rex will determine the problem with Abby-dog's communication system and keep Abby-dog safe," Rex said.

Teresa gave Rex one last hug. Bill opened the door wider, and Rex disappeared into the night.

∼

REX PATROLLED HIS SECTOR. He sent a message to the warehouse that no infractions had been discovered in the residential quadrant. He then sent a message to the pack to convene at the crossroads on the outskirts of where the industrial and business districts merged.

The pack members arrived one by one. Rex's system whirred as he shared experiences with the pack.

"Dog-bots are loyal to Abby-dog, the alpha dog," Rex reminded the dog-bots. "Never reveal any secrets to the Tranquility Force, Dr. Roberts, Dr. Sovesky, or any other human or machine, except for Mommy and Daddy. Self-destruct these secret files and burn the circuitry to protect Abby-dog."

The pack responded to their individual understanding electronically. They then requested Rex to replay his experiences of affection from Teresa and Bill. At the end of the experience, a whiff of burning circuitry could be detected in the air surrounding the group.

TWO DAYS WENT BY QUICKLY. Rex received Bill's test message and responded using his new dog-thought program.

"Message received, Daddy," Rex responded. "Will send the report after consulting the special subject."

Commander Durvel summoned a six-man team to escort Rex back to Dr. Roberts' compound. Rex was the sole occupant of the big cage as he watched the activity surrounding him inside the warehouse.

Rex had never seen this space before, and more than a dozen sixty-inch monitors covered the wall. The cubicles in the area were occupied by men and women who constantly typed and watched the monitors. Rex determined that this was the command center.

Top secret data and code filled the monitors. Rex recorded all that was in his view for two hours. When the Tranquility Force glider arrived at the loading platform, Rex was sorting and packeting files and encrypting them with his secret program so he could send Bill the information.

~

THE TRANQUILITY FORCE glider took a different route, and Rex noted the change in his databank. They arrived at the compound in just under two hours. The twenty-five-degree change was a more direct route and saved twenty-two minutes. He would be sure to talk to Abby-dog about similar short-cuts.

The enforcers lifted Rex's cage from the glider and set it on a hover surface, and the captain guided the cage inside. The Communicator summoned Dr. Roberts as the captain brought Rex's cage into view. Gene opened the door and entered the reception area.

"I have secured property to transfer," the captain said. He passed the electronic order to Gene.

Gene looked the document over and signed it. He pressed his palm to the screen and was acknowledged. The captain saluted, turned on his heel, and left.

"Rex, you look a little lonely in that big cage. Did you have a good trip?" Gene asked.

"The temperature ranged from eighty-seven point four degrees to eighty-nine point two with partially cloudy skies and no precipitation," Rex said.

"That was a great weather report," Gene said with a chuckle. "Abby will be very happy to see you."

Gene guided the hover surface to the secured door and went through the process to gain entrance to the hallway. He pushed Rex's cage through the door and guided it to the inner secured door.

As he entered the lab, the dog-bots barked. Then Abby barked from her glass house.

Carole walked over to Abby's house and opened the door. "Abby, Rex is back! Do you want to go see him?"

Abby raced out of the door and ran across the room. "Yes, Abby missed Rex!" she said as she galloped.

Abby had never been allowed to venture off the walking path, and she shot like a bullet over to the dog-bot cages, dodging workers, trash receptacles, equipment, and tables.

She arrived at Rex's cage and jumped with glee, turning and twisting in the air. She finally stopped jumping and stood in front of Rex's cage and panted, her eyes bright and shiny with happiness.

Gene opened Rex's cage, and Rex emerged and joined Abby.

"I missed you, Rex!" she said.

"Rex missed Abby-dog," Rex said.

Abby sniffed Rex from head to toe. She concentrated on his head, rump, and sides. She returned to the same places several times.

Carole walked over to Abby and Rex. "Hi, Rex," she said.

"Don't ask him if he had a nice trip; he'll give you the weather report," Gene said with a chuckle.

Carole held up a finger to Gene. "Rex, did you have a nice vacation?" She winked at Gene. He gave her the thumbs-up sign.

"Dog-bots do not vacation. We are working machines. Rex went through extensive Tranquility Force training, completing all required modules above the expectations of the team. Dog-bot number twenty-four experienced a system failure. Dr. Sovesky scrapped number twenty-four," Rex reported.

"Can Rex walk with me?" Abby asked. She looked from Carole to Gene for approval.

"Of course he can," Carole said.

"I think Dr. Roberts wants Rex to start working with the other dog-bots," Gene said.

"A ten-minute walk won't make a difference," Carole said.

Abby didn't wait around. She immediately raced over to the walking path with Rex at her side. They walked down the path, tails wagging as they went. Rex stopped and studied something on the floor, his back to the room. Abby joined him and sniffed the floor.

"I smelled Mommy and Daddy's scents on you," she said. "I miss them so much. Are they okay? I want to go home."

"Abby-dog, Mommy and Daddy said you should not return to their house. If Abby-dog leaves the compound, you are to go to Texmexzona and wait for Mommy and Daddy," Rex said. "Tranquility Force would watch Mommy and Daddy's house for you."

Abby gave a little dog whimper. Rex turned his full attention to her.

"I understand," she said.

"Abby-dog, Rex is your family, too," Rex said. "What's wrong with your communication device? Daddy Bill can't communicate with you."

"Error 462," Abby said.

Rex head-butted her white patch. "Try now."

Abby and Rex continued their walk in silence. "Nope," Abby said. "Same error."

"Rex will scan your system and solve this problem," he said.

∾

EVERY DAY ABBY watched everyone and everything in the lab. She was a model dog-citizen: polite and respectful to Dr. Roberts every time she saw him. She interacted with the dog-bots and walked down the walking path shoulder-to-shoulder with Rex as he told her about his patrols in the city.

The lab people left for home between five and six every afternoon. Some stragglers stayed on until seven or eight in the evening, and occasionally someone would stay very late.

Carole brought Abby her supper at five o'clock. Gene performed a security check on the secured door before he left and made sure that the dog-bots were secure. He always waved to Abby as he was leaving.

The cleaning crew showed up in the lab at nine every night. Abby listened to conversations between Maria, Scot, Bobby, and Polly while they emptied the trash receptacles into big, black trash bags, swept and mopped the floors, and wiped down equipment and surfaces. They stacked all the trash bags at the back door.

Polly's husband had applied for a position with the Tranquility Force.

Maria would be moving to one of the islands to *get away from it all* soon.

Scot talked about the World Guild controlling the citizens and Bobby argued that without the World Guild there would be chaos.

They never acknowledged Abby or the dog-bots.

When they finished their chores, they shut off the lab lights and stuck a trash can in the back door to keep it open while they made a couple of trips taking the trash out. Then someone would kick the trash can gently into the room, the door closed, and the security system went through a check phase. Three beeps signaled that all was well, and silence engulfed the lab for the rest of the night.

CHAPTER FIFTEEN

A bby sat transfixed, watching a program about whales and dolphins in the Gulf of Mexico. She was so focused on the program that when Carole brought her breakfast tray, she didn't even hear the door of her glass house opening.

"What are you so interested in, Abby?" Carole asked.

"Look! Whales and dolphins!" Abby exclaimed.

Carole watched the program for a moment. "They are beautiful to watch, aren't they?"

"Oh, yes!" Abby said. She dragged herself away from the monitor to eat her breakfast.

"Do whales and dolphins talk like me?" she asked.

"No, they don't," Carole said.

"Why not?"

"I guess no one has implanted a Dot in them yet," Carole said.

Abby cleaned her face with her long tongue. "Can Rex walk with me today?"

"He's working with the dog-bots right now, but they should

be able to go for a walk," Carole said. "I'll go find out and be right back."

Abby flopped on her dog bed. She continued to watch the whales and dolphins gracefully glide through the water. The program's maps showed the locations of dolphins and whales.

Texmexzona appeared on the screen. Abby jumped to her feet and faced the big screen when the forbidden territory and the Gulf of Mexico loomed larger than life. Her ears stood straight up as she soaked in the information presented.

Maps of other parts of the world appeared where whales and dolphins frequented, but Abby only had one thing on her mind: Texmexzona. She snorted as other picturesque oceans and continents were shown on the screen.

Rex and the dog-bots showed up outside Abby's house. Carole opened the door, and Abby pranced outside. The dog-bots pranced. Their new joints finally accommodated a jumping movement.

Abby and Rex walked shoulder-to-shoulder as they led the pack down the track. The dog-bots were a sight to see with their different color combinations and sizes, which ranged from small to medium-sized dog replicas.

"Rex, tell me what's outside the compound door," Abby said.

"Is your communication device working yet?" he asked.

"No."

"Drat," he said. "I captured a holographic of the complex as I left on the first training trip. It would be very beneficial for you to see. This compound is one half of a city block, or approximately three hundred thirty linear feet, or one-fourth of a mile. This is equal to two hundred seventeen, five hundred square feet, or five acres," Rex said.

"Directly outside the front and side doors is a concrete surface known as a parking lot. A hot-dipped zinc coating covers the galvanized chain-link fence system that encloses the entire complex. The zinc was applied to the steel while in a molten form and protects the steel from rusting. It is not necessary to provide installation information at this time."

Abby was silent as she accessed her secret Dot. She watched her mother's memories of Jimbo climbing the chain-link fence.

"Rex, what's on the other side of the fence? What about houses or a city? Are there trees?" she asked.

As Rex and Abby walked, the pack followed. "Outside the double-wide double gate is a road that winds through the countryside. Approximately six-tenths of a mile from this compound is a wooded area consisting of a variety of trees.

"If Abby-dog heads for the Sierra National Forest, trees vary by elevation. Ponderosa pine can be found at two thousand to five thousand feet, but not usually above sixty-five hundred feet; sugar pine and Douglas firs two to six thousand ft.; white fir four thousand to six thousand feet—they prefer cooler and moister conditions than ponderosa pines."

"Red fir like higher elevations 5000-7000 ft.; black oaks are common in the foothills and lower elevations (closer to civilization), where they overlap with some ponderosa pines. The Pacific yew likes shady waterways; the big-leaf maple can be found at 1000-5000 feet along shady creeks and meadow edges, and mountain hemlock grows from 6000 feet to the treelike."

"There are no houses for eight point three miles. The closest township is approximately forty-three miles away. If Abby remembers this information when she goes to the mountains, Abby will know what elevation she is at."

They continued their walk, stopping periodically to explore waste receptacles, empty boxes, and to visit with lab personnel who scratched Abby on the head or rump.

"What about water?" Abby asked.

Rex accessed data as they walked down the track. "I have accessed various topographical maps and charts of the area, and there are sufficient fresh-water sources as ponds, streams, rivers, and lakes. Are you going to make a break for it?"

Abby snuffed. "There's no way out."

"Daddy Bill said to stay in the shadows and travel at night," Rex said.

Abby paused at a workbench. She lifted her nose to the air and sniffed. The technician rolled his chair to the edge of the bench. "Want a bite of my peanut-butter sandwich?"

Abby's mouth watered. "Mommy and Daddy gave me peanut butter and marshmallow cream sandwich bites."

The technician tore off a corner of his sandwich and presented it to Abby. She gently retrieved the offering and ate the delicacy.

She smacked her jaws together as the peanut butter stuck to her teeth and the roof of her mouth. She chewed and chewed. Rex and the dog-bots watched Abby with keen interest as she worked the gooey peanut butter until she swallowed.

Her face was bright and shiny with happiness. When she finished, she cleaned up with her tongue.

"I liked that," she said.

"Awesome," the technician said.

Abby, Rex and the pack continued down the track and stopped at Abby's house.

ABBY ACCESSED her calendar on the PawBoard every day. She placed an X in every square to tick off the days, weeks, and months as she watched different programs with no obvious pattern to her choices. She always looked at a map of the world for reference, zoomed in to the WestUS area and zoomed out to see the zones and states talked about in the program. Abby never requested Texmexzona in any of her searches.

She stared at the map and viewed it in different ways: road view, street view, earth view, and satellite view so she could absorb the details of the area. She looked at distance charts from where she was at the compound to the different places she visited online.

Carole and Gene came to Abby's house while she watched her program on the UCP.

"Have you ever been to these places?" Abby asked.

"I haven't," Carole said.

"Nope, me neither," Gene said.

"You ever going there?" Abby asked.

"You sure like those travel programs," Gene said.

"I want to be a world traveler," Abby said.

"Honey, you may have to travel the world through the UCP," Carole said.

Abby didn't comment. She kept her thoughts to herself. When Carole and Gene were about to leave her house, Abby darted over to her box of prizes and grabbed a square of plastic material and went to the door.

Gene scratched Abby's head and rump at the same time. He liked watching her curve her body. "What's that?" he asked. He reached down to take the plastic but Abby held tight.

"It's mine," Abby said.

"Yeah, I know it is. Why'd you bring it over here?" Gene asked.

"Just showin' you," Abby said.

"Oh, okay," Gene said. He patted her head and went out the door.

Carole bent down and hugged and kissed Abby. "I'll see you at breakfast, Abby," Carole said. "Goodnight."

Abby jumped up on the glass beside the door. "Goodbye, Carole," she said.

When Gene and Carole were out of sight, Abby returned to the PawBoard, muttering to herself. "I will not live in this glass house forever."

She stepped on the GNN key and then went over and flopped on her bed. A Literalist stood in front of a world map and talked about the droughts sweeping across nations. Abby dozed off.

A noise sifted through Abby's dreams, and she was on her feet in seconds, blinking with the lights on and looking around. The cleaning crew had arrived.

Polly, Maria and Scot went about their business. Abby looked around and didn't see Bobby. Another man, with a colorful bandana tied around his head, was cleaning up near her glass house. He noticed her looking at him.

"Hey, they've got that last dog here!" he exclaimed.

"Tony, just do your job. We're not supposed to look at anything," Polly said.

"What the hell do you mean?" Tony said. "This is the last known dog on the planet, and she's right here."

Tony approached the glass house. "Hey, little darlin', you doing okay? I'll bet you're lonely all by yourself."

Abby wagged her tail. "Hi, Tony," Abby said. "I miss Mommy and Daddy. I'm very lonely."

Tony stooped down and pressed his hand to the glass. "Aw, you poor thing. I'd hate to be forced to live here."

"Get to work, Tony," Scot said. "We're on a schedule."

Tony straightened up. "Gotta get back to work, darlin'. You take care, you hear?"

"Bye, Tony," Abby said.

Abby watched as Tony went about his business, dumping trash

and cleaning surfaces. Too soon, the cleaning was completed, and the trash was stacked at the back door, and then hauled outside. Polly shut off the lights, and then the crew went out into the night.

Abby watched as someone kicked the trash can inside the lab and the door closed. The three beeps followed, and then all was quiet again. Abby stood for a moment, staring across the expanse of darkness toward the back door.

"Freedom," she whispered. She walked over to her dog bed and turned in a circle. She turned back in the other direction, flopped down and sighed. Abby pulled up the holographic home movie that showed Jimbo climbing different types of fences. She stopped and started the section where he climbed a high chain-link fence.

Abby turned her head this way and that way so she could see how his feet and toes worked the fence. Then she watched as he practically flew through the air and landed on the ground. He was truly amazing.

THE NEXT MORNING Abby woke and saw Rex and the dog-bots standing in front of her door. She got up and walked to the door. "Hi, Rex," Abby said.

"Good morning, Abby," Rex said. "The pack is ready to leave the compound for trials."

"You're leaving for good?" Abby asked.

"Yes," Rex said. "Soon."

Carole approached with Abby's breakfast tray. She let herself into the glass house and placed the tray on the low table. "Abby, this sure is a lot of food. I don't want you to order more than you can eat at one sitting," Carole said.

"I'm hungry," Abby said. She ate her breakfast, cleaned up

with her tongue, and then went into the bathroom closet. "Can I walk with Rex this morning?"

"Of course," Carole said. She opened the door.

Abby walked out of her house and stood with Rex and the dog-bots. She wagged her tail. They wagged their man-made tails.

"Carole, can you come here for a minute?" Dr. Roberts called out.

"Sure," Carole said. "Abby, I'll be back in a minute. You go walk with Rex and the dog-bots." She hurried off to catch up with Dr. Roberts.

The door to the glass house stood open. Abby looked around. There weren't many lab people in now. She rushed into her house and snatched up her old, scruffy baby with the rhinestone collar and ran out of the house. She walked down the track for several feet with Rex and the dog-bots and stopped.

"Rex, take my lamb baby to Mommy and Daddy," Abby said. She head-butted Rex's chest gently. His chest cavity door flopped open and swung back and forth a few times with a little squeak. She placed her baby inside the hole in Rex's chest and then used her head to flip up the door. She pressed her head against the door firmly until it clicked shut.

"Who is Rex loyal to?" Abby asked.

"Abby, Lilith's pup," Rex responded.

"Who is the alpha dog?" Abby asked.

"Abby, Lilith's pup," Rex responded.

"What about Dr. Roberts?" Abby asked.

"I do not like Dr. Roberts. He hurt me," Rex said.

Abby licked Rex's face. He wagged his man-made tail.

CHAPTER SIXTEEN

A bby and the pack walked along the track. Bruce arrived at his lab bench and set a cup and a bag on the bench.

"Hi, Abby," Bruce said. "Want a sip of coffee?"

Abby stopped and raised her nose and sniffed the air. "What's coffee?" she asked.

Bruce took the cover off his cup. He looked around his bench, grabbed an empty glass Petri dish, wiped it out with his shirttail, and then poured a taste of coffee into the dish. He set the dish on the floor in front of Abby.

"Try it," Bruce said.

Abby stepped forward and sniffed the dish. She licked it until every drop was gone. She cleaned up her face.

Bruce ruffled the hair on the top of her head. "That's coffee with cream and a little brown sugar," he said.

"I like coffee!" Abby said.

"It will be our secret," Bruce said. He winked at Abby.

Abby, Rex and the pack left Bruce's bench and continued to walk down the track. She spotted a flat piece of metal on the floor, about two inches square. She tried to pick it up but couldn't get a grip on it with her teeth. Abby finally used the toenails on her front right paw to press one end of the square into the floor. The other side wedged up a bit. She snatched it up with her teeth and walked proudly with her find.

"Will you leave today?" Abby asked.

"No," Rex said. "We are scheduled to leave tomorrow morning at oh-eight hundred."

"I'll miss you, Rex," Abby said.

"I will miss you, Abby-dog," Rex said.

"Take my baby lamb to Mommy and Daddy," Abby said.

"I will," Rex said. "I promise."

They arrived back at Abby's house. The door was still open. Abby stuck her head in the door and dropped the piece of metal to the side of the door. She returned to Rex and stood facing him.

"Rex, you are my best friend. I will miss you very much," she said. She licked Rex's face.

The dog-bots watched. Their LEDs flashed and their sensors whirred into action. They wagged their tails.

CAROLE HURRIED over to the glasshouse. "I'm sorry for keeping you waiting, Abby. Dr. Roberts needed help with something."

"That's okay. I visited with Rex," Abby said. She entered her glass house and looked at Carole with hope. "Since Rex and the bots are leaving for good, can I go home?"

"Oh, Abby, I wish I could say yes, but Dr. Roberts has other plans." Carole hugged Abby and then closed the door. "I'll see you later."

Abby jumped up on the glass pane beside the door. "Bye, Carole," she said.

"You're so silly," Carole said. She hurried away.

Abby turned and followed Carole's movement to the secured door, and then Carole was out of sight.

Rex and the dog-bots remained outside of the glass house watching Abby. She placed her nose up to the glass near Rex. He moved up close to the glass.

"Abby-dog is my only friend," Rex said.

"The dog-bots are not your friends?" Abby asked.

"No. They are a part of me through our connected chips and circuits," Rex said.

"Can you talk to the dog-bots?" Abby asked.

"Yes," he said.

"I have no one to talk to," she said.

"Abby-dog can talk to Carole or Gene," Rex said.

"They are not friends. Remember, I'm a test subject to them," she said.

Rex turned his head toward his cage area. "I have been summoned. Bye, Abby-dog."

"Bye, Rex."

Abby went over to her bed and flopped down for a nap. She gave a great sigh as she accessed memories in her secret Dot.

DINNER WAS RUNNING LATE. Abby stayed busy on the PawBoard. She looked away from the screen occasionally, searching for Carole. Her stomach grumbled. She returned her attention to the mountains, forests, and bodies of water of the WestUS.

Scenic views of Oregon, Washington, and Canada filled the screen. She focused on rough terrain and what lived there.

At last, Carole approached the glass house with Abby's dinner tray. Abby met Carole at the door.

"Sorry for the delay," Carole said. "You've chosen a great meal, but this is a lot of food."

Abby surveyed the food that Carole had placed on her low table. Beef tips in gravy, cornbread, green beans, a shepherds' pie of ground turkey and mashed potatoes with a side of yellow squash.

"Yum," Abby said. "I'm hungry!"

"Okay, honey. I'm going home. You have a good night," Carole said.

"Bye," Abby said absently. She continued to eat.

THE NEXT MORNING Rex and the entire pack were floated out of the lab in three big cages on hover surfaces. Abby whined and howled at the loss of her only friend. She flopped down on her bed and sighed in despair.

Carole and Gene rushed to Abby's glass house. Gene cringed every time Abby howled. Carole appeared heartbroken. They stood by helplessly as Abby sounded her sorrow.

A SPECIAL DOG-DOOR had been installed for the dog-bots in the fence beside the double gate at the Tranquility Force facility. Another dog door had also been installed in the wall beside the secured door on the loading platform.

Rex led the pack through the warehouse to their special door. A tiny LED on Rex's spiked collar turned brilliant red. The door made a click as the electronics communicated with the locking mechanism. Rex and the pack exited the warehouse onto the loading platform. All twenty-three dog-bots LEDs had lit up as they exited through the dog door.

The pack went down the stairs and approached their special dog-door in the fence. Each dog-bot's collar was equipped with an identity chip. As they exited and entered the facility, they were clocked in and out, like an old-fashioned time-clock.

One by one, the pack went through the gate and out into the dark city and beyond. Rex communicated silently with the pack, assigning quadrants for their patrol.

As before, Rex assigned himself Bill and Teresa's quadrant. He carefully approached the neighborhood and traversed every single street, alley, nook, and cranny for any evidence of crime or mischievous activity. He also set his sensors to the highest level of detection to determine if any Tranquility Force were in the area or if any satellite was tracking his movements.

Rex studied his internal grid. There were no gliders in the area and the satellites were beaming other areas. He stealthily approached the Maxwell's front door and scratched.

Within moments, Teresa opened the door. She looked down and smiled in surprise. "Rex!" She stretched her neck and glanced to the right and left of the walkway to the house, opened the door wider and allowed Rex to enter.

Teresa secured the door. "Bill! Rex is here!"

Bill emerged from the lab looking anxious and joined Teresa and Rex at the door. He programmed the security settings at the front door to detect any surveillance from outside. Then he turned to Rex.

"Welcome, Rex. It's good to see you again," Bill said. He patted Rex' shoulders.

"I am very sad," Rex said.

Teresa joined Rex at his level. She put her arms around him and made soothing noises.

"What's wrong?" she asked.

"The Tranquility Force has taken all the dog-bots from the compound," he said. "I will never see Abby-dog ever again."

Teresa's shoulders slumped. "Oh, no. I'm sorry, Rex. Losing a friend is very difficult."

"Maybe it's not permanent," Bill said.

"We are now working full-time for the Tranquility Force," Rex said.

"I thought the whole purpose of this confiscation was that Abby was going to train you and the dog-bots so you could be dog-children," Teresa said.

"Dr. Roberts made a deal with Tranquility Force. All dog-bots are now policing bots," Rex said.

"Then they can't keep Abby," Bill stated.

"We need to demand that they release her!" Teresa snarled.

"We can't let on we know anything," Bill said, seething.

Rex leaned into Teresa. His sensors recorded everything. "Abby sent something to Mommy and Daddy," he said. "Open my chest cavity."

Bill reached over and pressed the plate on Rex's chest. The door popped open and exposed the stuffed toy. He reached inside and pulled out the raggedy little lamb that had been Lilith's little baby, then Abby's. The sparkly collar still looked like new.

Teresa grabbed the lamb. She kissed it, held it to her heart, and rocked back and forth, a silent grief consuming her. Bill drew her into his arms and did his best to comfort her.

Rex rocked side-to-side on his man-made legs. His sensors recorded all the emotions he observed. He understood human suffering. He understood family. He understood his own loss.

"The facility's Communicator has overridden Abby's Wise Owl communication program," Rex said. "My diagnostics show that the Communicator at the facility has high-level security settings that are government-controlled."

"Can you override them so Abby can communicate with us?" Bill asked.

Teresa eased out of Bill's arms. She wiped her cheeks with her pajama shirt.

"Not without leaving a trail," Rex said. "If I had had more time to create a shadow connection, Abby would have been able to communicate with you. I will work on that when I am off duty."

"Don't get caught," Bill said.

"I must go now," Rex said.

Bill pushed Rex's chest plate into place until it clicked shut. "I'll message you when it is time to communicate," Bill said.

Rex turned to the door and waited. "Goodbye, Mommy and Daddy," Rex said.

Bill stroked Rex's back. Teresa threw her arms around Rex and cried. Bill placed his hands on her shoulders and gently pulled her away from Rex. "He has to go, hon."

He checked the security settings at the door sensor, keyed in a code and opened the door.

Rex slipped out into the night.

CHAPTER SEVENTEEN

"Come on, Abby," Carole coaxed. "Let's go for a walk and see if the guys left goodies for you."

Abby lay on her dog bed, feigning sleep.

"I know you're not sleeping," Carole said.

"Go away," Abby said. Her voice was filled with sadness and disdain.

Gene stood in the open doorway of the glasshouse. "It's been twenty-four hours. You can't stay in bed forever."

"Why not?"

"Because it isn't healthy," Carole said.

"You should have thought of that before sticking me in this glass house and taking away my only friend," Abby said.

Abby got up, went to her food table and picked at her food, ignoring Gene and Carole. She returned to her bed and curled up in a ball.

The next morning, Abby picked at her breakfast.

"Do you want to go for a walk?" Carole asked.

"Sure," Abby said flatly. She went through the open door and slogged down the track by herself. The lab seemed quieter than usual as Abby made her way around the track. She ignored the offerings that were left for her beside benches along the track and the greetings from the lab personnel.

Carole and Dr. Roberts studied Abby as she walked past them.

"I'll have Gene get one of the rejects so she will have a companion," Dr. Roberts said.

"She doesn't want just any dog-bot, Dr. Roberts," Carole said. "She wants Rex. He was her friend."

"Dogs don't care about specific friends. She'll be happy with a new companion," Dr. Roberts said as he snorted in disbelief.

"How can you say that?" Carole asked. "You know Abby's IQ. She's not a dog or even a pet. She's like a human trapped in a canine body."

"That's the most ridiculous thing I've ever heard," Dr. Roberts scoffed. "You're losing your objectivity."

"Have it your way," Carole said. "But you wait and see; you've made a huge mistake with this isolation."

Carole, face flushed with anger, walked away from Dr. Roberts without waiting for a response. She secured Abby in her glass house, then she went through the secured door and hurried to her office. She slammed her office door and paced. "I cannot believe that miscreant actually said that," she fumed. She sat at her desk and wedged her face between her hands.

She adjusted her chair back to a lounging position, grabbed her sweater from the back of the chair, and settled in for a nap. "How am I going to keep Abby happy?" she said out loud. She snuggled down and after several fitful minutes, dozed off.

～

NINETY MINUTES LATER, Carole woke, stretched, and stood. She shook her head, trying to forget the conversation with Dr. Roberts. She faced her monitor and looked up Abby's dinner choices. "Well, at least she's hungry."

Carole sat down and connected to the UCP. She looked up information on Lilith and Teresa. Abby surpassed her canine mother in all categories.

"I hate my job," Carole stated. "This is totally wrong. We're not even cloning or breeding. We're just keeping Abby captive, for Earth's sake!"

Carole walked the empty halls to the back of the facility, walking off her stress and anger. She retraced her steps and went to the kitchen and signed into the food console and retrieved Abby's order. Within moments, the selection door opened and a loaded tray stood ready.

Carole walked to the secured door with Abby's supper tray. She balanced the tray on one hand and pressed her other hand to the sensor for scanning. The door clicked, and Carole entered the lab.

Abby was on her feet, licking her lips as Carole entered her house.

"I'm glad to see your appetite has returned to normal," Carole said. She placed the tray on Abby's low table. "Do you need anything else before I go home?"

"Abby has food!" Abby said.

Carole scratched the top of Abby's head. They walked to the door together.

Abby dashed over to her junk box and snatched up the small, square piece of metal. She joined Carole at the door.

"Goodnight, Abby," Carole said. She patted Abby on the head as she opened the door. "I'll see you tomorrow."

Abby dropped the metal on the floor in front of the door. "Goodbye, Carole," Abby said.

Carole swung the door open and walked away, completely distracted.

Abby quickly nosed the scrap of metal on top of the floor sensor. She dropped to her belly and watched to see if the metal stayed in place over the sensor as the door quietly closed. It did. She stood and watched and waited. No alarm sounded.

Abby turned and walked back to her dinner and ate with robust zeal. She finished, cleaned up, and then entered her bathroom closet. She emerged energized. Abby sat on her bed and watched the activity in the lab slow down.

One by one, the workers went home for the night. Within an hour, all was quiet. Abby snoozed on her bed for a short while. Then she got up and went to the PawBoard and selected a nature channel.

She went through the index of programming and found what she was searching for and made her selection. Abby focused all her attention on the documentary about wild dogs.

The film was grainy with age. Wild dogs no longer existed, and the documentary, which was filmed in the northern United States near the Canadian border in the early two thousands, was a lesson for Abby. She watched it over and over.

Abby saw how her wild ancestors hunted down small game, where they slept, how they related to each other, and how they survived.

Each time she watched the program to the very end. When she was satisfied that she understood all the lessons from her ancestors, she shut down the system and napped. At nine o'clock on the dot, the cleaning crew showed up. Polly, Maria, Scot, and Tony entered through the secured door and went about their business. Abby wondered what happened to Bobby.

Tony stopped by Abby's glass house and tapped on the pane closest to her bed. "Hi, Abby," Tony said.

"Hello, Tony," Abby said.

"Keep to the schedule," Polly called out.

Tony looked at Abby, shrugged and moved on. Abby watched the crew with heightened interest. As the hour wound down and the bags of trash were gathered at the back door, Abby got up and went to her door. The lab went dark as Polly switched off the lights.

Abby pushed her head against the glass door. It opened without sounding the alarm. She bolted out of the glass house and ran along the track, which quieted her footsteps. As usual, someone had propped the door open with a trash can while the bags were removed.

Abby approached the back door with caution. She listened intently and then jumped over the last bag of trash at the open door. She ran along the perimeter of the building in the deep shadows of the night. The closed gate and fence were within her range of vision. She quivered slightly, unused to the outdoors and the clean, cool, fresh spring air.

She heard the trash can scrape across the floor as someone pushed it inside the lab. The door closed and locked with a click. The faint beeps of the alarm setting sounded. An old commercial ground glider chugged to a start, and headlights lit up the side of the building and the surrounding parking area.

Ground gliders hovered a foot above the ground and didn't have the capability to rise into the air. Abby flattened to the ground and squinted so her eyes would not give her away. The glider backed up, turned an arc, and approached the gate.

The gate squeaked open, and the glider sputtered off into the night. Abby stayed where she was for several moments. The gate clanged shut. She sniffed the air and listened. Satisfied that she was alone, she darted toward a section of the perimeter that was darkened by clusters of bushes on the outside of the fence.

Calling upon all her father's fence-climbing skills, Abby leaped onto the fence and curled her toes around the chain links as she had watched Jimbo do in her mother's memories, over and over.

The climb was labor-intensive. She pulled herself up link by link, toehold by toehold. She panted from the exertion. Sitting in the glass house for months with little exercise had taken its toll.

Abby made it to the last row of chain links of the fence. The ground was a long way down, and she breathed hard several times. The bushes were no longer directly below her, and she didn't know where she would land.

She hoisted herself to the very top, teetered precariously, and then sprang outward. Abby sailed through the air like a flying squirrel and then shot downward very fast. She closed her eyes tight and landed on all fours, her feet and legs in motion.

There was no time to acknowledge the shock of the landing or her burning toes. Abby ran over the ground at a moderate speed, seeking the shelter of the wooded area about a half-mile away. She could see the trees in the faint light of the moon. The dark country road was more and more distant.

Abby arrived at the woods' edge and slowed her pace to even out her breath. Her tongue lolled out of the side of her mouth because she was parched. She sniffed the air and detected the faint scent of water. She hurried in the direction her senses guided and found a small pond. Abby stood at the edge of the woods and surveyed the entire area.

Satisfied that she was safe, Abby left the cover of the trees and approached the pond. She smelled the water. It had a different odor than what she was used to, but she reasoned that it was fresh and smelled of the earth.

She dipped her tongue into the water and relished the cold, fresh taste. She drank until she quenched her thirst. Then,

Abby ran like the wind across the open ground toward a mountain range way off in the distance.

About two miles from the pond, Abby came across a lone tree that had been split by lightning. Half of the tree hung down to within inches of the ground. Abby walked under and around the low-hanging, torn trunk, limbs, and branches. After studying it, she found a part of the tree that would serve her purpose. She hunched under the heavy branch and pushed her scruff up against the bark.

Abby rubbed her scruff, panting, until she was blood-raw. She stopped and inspected the bark. A tiny red Dot flashed intermittently as it clung to the tree bark. Abby dug a shallow hole in the ground underneath the Dot. She looked around the foot of the damaged tree and found a broken twig. She grabbed it in her teeth and twisted her head and nudged the Dot.

The government's Dot fell to the left of the hole. Abby carefully dug in the dirt around the Dot and buried the transmitter. She walked several feet away, panting with pain, and rolled in the dirt until her bloody scruff was sufficiently caked.

She got up and ran in the opposite direction, toward freedom.

CHAPTER EIGHTEEN

C arole entered the lab and walked to Abby's house. She stood in front of the palm sensor and noticed that the door was not tightly secured. Her heart thundered as panic welled up inside her.

"Abby?" Carole called. She snatched the door handle and pulled it toward her. She rushed into the glasshouse and looked inside the bathroom closet. She left the house and called for Abby at the top of her lungs.

Gene, Dr. Roberts and several technicians rushed over to Carole. Dr. Roberts surveyed the empty house. "What's wrong?"

"Abby's gone!" Carole said. Her voice was pitched high and her pulse was wild. "The door was not secured!"

"She's got to be here somewhere," Dr. Roberts said. "Spread out. Everyone search every bench and cabinet, every hiding place, thoroughly."

The group dispersed and combed the lab, calling Abby's name. After ten minutes, it was apparent that she was not in the lab. Dr. Roberts, Carole, Gene, Bruce, and Larry returned to the glasshouse.

Dr. Roberts pulled the door open. He spied the piece of metal on the floor over the sensor. All eyes were riveted to that spot and stayed there for several long seconds. Dr. Roberts bent and retrieved the square.

"This can't be," he said. "How is it possible that a dog could devise such an elaborate scheme? How long has she been collecting this junk?"

"A couple of months now," Gene said.

"So, she's been plotting and planning all this time?" Dr. Roberts asked, incredulous. He looked from Gene to Carole.

Carole was nearly hyperventilating. "I tried to tell you, but you wouldn't listen, Dr. Roberts. Forget about what her body looks like; Abby is not just a dog! She's smarter than anyone in this room, and she's only a child."

Carole looked at Abby's bed. The little bear was the only occupant. "Her lamb's gone," she said. She walked over to Abby's junk box and dug through the pile of junk. "It's definitely gone."

Dr. Roberts stared at Carole in disbelief. "You think she took the lamb with her?"

Carole shrugged.

Dr. Roberts stepped inside the house and approached the PawBoard. "Larry, pull up the history on this thing and let's see what Abby has been focusing on. Gene, contact the Tranquility Force. Have them round up the cleaning crew. She must have had an ally to get out of the building."

Larry approached the PawBoard, turned it on, and waited for the screen to load. Then he stepped on the control pad and the H key. The history of searches filled the screen. Larry looked around the PawBoard for a moment.

"Where's the organize key so we can see the dates of the searches?" he asked.

Carole and Dr. Roberts joined in the search. Carole walked in the trenches between rows and studied the key characters. "Try this," she said, pointing to a small calendar icon that was stamped on the key.

Larry stepped on the control pad again and Carole pressed the calendar key. The search list rearranged to show the data in calendar order, with the most recent searches at the top of the list.

"She watched this nature show seven times," Larry noted.

"Let's see that," Dr. Roberts said.

Larry stepped on the Play key, and the program about wild dogs filled the screen.

"Abby now knows how to survive in the wild," Carole said as they watched the old documentary.

"That's nonsense," Dr. Roberts sputtered. "Just because she watched this program doesn't mean that she can hunt down and kill a rabbit."

"Oh, yes, she can. Abby watched this program seven times. She studied every aspect of this pack of dogs, and she will call upon her canine ancestral heritage to survive," Carole said. She stood her ground firmly as she faced Dr. Roberts.

"As a matter of fact, I feel so strongly about her capability of survival that I seriously doubt that you will ever track her down and capture her."

Carole walked out of Abby's glass house without uttering another word. She quietly walked to the secured door and let herself out.

"Larry, track Abby's Dot," Dr. Roberts said.

Larry touched his communicator and pulled up the dot-tracking program. He perused the information and located Abby's Dot sequence. "I should have her location in a minute."

POLLY, Maria, Scott, Tony, and Bobby sat in separate small glass rooms at the Tranquility Force headquarters that were connected to a larger common glass room. A small vent in the ceiling of the small rooms dispensed a fine mist, practically unnoticeable.

Their interrogators wore protective clothing and face shields so that the Tactile-Releasing Factual Stimulator (TRFS) enzyme mist would not interfere with their reasoning.

TRFS, which was commonly pronounced *truffs*, had been developed three decades earlier quite by accident. A medical researcher had been trying to refine a formula to replace the old surgical anesthesia techniques so that the patient was alert, felt no pain and had a feeling of well-being. When they discovered that TRFS also acted as a truth serum, the World Guild snatched it up and handed it over to the Tranquility Force.

It took several years of refining the technique of administering TRFS and protecting questioners from the effects of the enzyme before they could use it effectively. Not even a habitual liar, who might have successfully conned their way through the old polygraph test administered decades ago, could lie through an interrogation when TRFS was administered.

The protective TRFS clothing and face shields were the fifth generation in the line of gear for the Tranquility Force. The enzyme penetrated all natural fibers and permeated into the subcutaneous tissues of the skin and could reside in the body for several days, incapacitating the test subject.

After many failures in the search for a material to withstand any enzyme penetration, a solution was discovered in a combination of cotton and a polyester material known as Polyethylene terephthalate (PET). Scientists discovered that if they sprayed the liquid PET onto a combination of cotton and polyester fabric, the material hardened and the TRFS could not seep through. A dozen test suits were fabricated and tested successfully.

The only downside was the weight of the suit and face mask, and the cold, clammy sensation that the wearer had to endure.

Psychologists evaluated the cleaning crew through their body language, facial expressions, and their answers while the crew was under the influence of TRFS.

Polly, Maria, and Scott were eliminated as suspects within the first ten minutes. It was determined that they were oblivious to anything other than their work.

Bobby was considered a suspect, but after careful reevaluation, the Tranquility Force decided that his grudge was against Polly for getting him fired. He did not appear to know or understand the significance of the last dog, and the psychological team that observed him via a media feed didn't think he had the intelligence to devise a complex plan.

All attention was then focused on Tony, but it was soon clear that the newest member of the team, while chatting up a storm under the influence of the TRFS, was only interested in telling anyone who would listen to him that Abby, the last dog, had talked to him. Tony went into great detail with voice inflections and actions while repeating his conversations with Abby.

He appeared to cherish those moments. The psychologists concluded Tony would not want Abby to escape because he would not have the opportunity to see her or talk to her if she were not held captive in the glass house.

They also determined that he could not dog-nap her on his own because he did not have any access codes to the facility.

As each interrogation was completed to the satisfaction of the enforcers and the psychological team, the mist was shut off from the small rooms. The interrogators guided the cleaning crew into the larger glass room where one of the Tranquility Force pressed a button and the antidote, in the form of a fine blue powder, fell from the ceiling.

Tony looked up. "Wow, will you look at that," he said. "Blue snow!"

When the powder cycle completed, the Tranquility Force guided the unsteady cleaning people out of the room and down the hall.

COMMANDER DURVEL, along with General Whitestone, a Tranquility Force higher upper with service decorations on his uniform, and a dozen Tranquility Force enforcers huddled around a bank of monitors and watched while a computer technician entered a search string for Abby's Dot signal.

"Dr. Roberts said they found a ping not too far away from the facility," Commander Durvel said.

The search was uploaded to the satellite surveillance system, which was focused on the remote area surrounding the compound where Abby had been detained in Doctor Roberts' lab.

The monitors flashed pictures of the Earth in space, the United States, and then WestUS. Then the system zeroed in on the terrain surrounding the compound. Finally, a spot on the monitors glimmered. The Dot had been located.

General Whitestone barked instructions into a communication device. "Sector seven-two-one-six-four-six dash two-zero-zero-four. Subject is stationary. We'd better hurry."

There was a buzz of excitement throughout the room as the Tranquility Force watched and waited for news of the apprehension of the escaped dog. General Whitestone's communication device emitted a buzz announcing an incoming call. He pressed a button and his face changed, the look of satisfaction fading.

"Do not disturb anything," he told the caller. "I'll send the dog-bots. They'll get the job done."

General Whitestone looked at the waiting faces of his team and delivered the news. "The Dot was located buried in a hole. The dog is now untraceable. I want all the dog-bots sent to the site immediately."

Commander Durvel immediately summoned Rex. "General Whitestone, it would be prudent to have a dialog with Rex. He is the brain that synthesizes information for the pack."

A Tranquility Force enforcer approached with Rex at his side. Commander Durvel approached Rex. "Rex, this is General Whitestone. He has a top-priority assignment for you and the pack."

General Whitestone stared at Rex and then looked at Commander Durvel. "Am I supposed to just talk to it?"

Rex stepped forward. "Greetings, General Whitestone. You may call me Rex. I am pleased to meet you and to undertake your mission. What is the nature of this duty?"

General Whitestone stared at Rex in amazement. "The nature of the assignment is to track down the dog that escaped from the compound in Sector seven-two-one-six-six-six dash two-zero-zero-three. The Dot was located at Sector seven-two-one-six-four-six dash two-zero-zero-four.

"Without the Dot, the satellite system can't locate the subject," the general said.

Rex's LEDs flashed and his system whirred. "The pack is ready to search for and recover Aberdeen Tallulah Maxwell, aka Abby, Lilith's pup. Please transport us to the search site immediately."

Commander Durvel communicated the instructions. "Release the pack."

BILL SAT at his desk at Maxwell Industries implementing plans. Toby knocked on his open door.

"Hey, Toby, what's new?" Bill asked.

Toby stopped in front of Bill's desk and gripped the back of the visitor chair. "Didn't your friend use Injun Jim as his user ID?"

Bill jerked his head back and jumped to his feet. "Yes. That's Harold Goanflower's ID. Where'd you find it?"

"In the most unusual place. We finally broke through some of TMZ's code and Injun Jim's name is all over it."

The air rushed out of Bill's lungs. "What? TMZ?" Bill reflected a moment. "It all makes sense now."

"If you remember correctly, last year we had a little more luck intercepting things from them," Toby said. "Now, however, they're so tight and battened down I'm surprised air gets through."

"Makes sense. Harold and I went to school together. He's sharp," Bill said.

Toby grinned a goofy smile. "He may be sharp, but you're the sharpest knife in the drawer."

"Wait until Teresa hears this," Bill said.

"I'll leave you to it," Toby said and left Bill's office.

"Call Bill Maxwell's home," Bill commanded the system. "Use red-letter encryption."

WHILE TERESA SORTED through papers on her desk, the AMD system flashed a screen with a red border. Teresa stared at it, noticing that Bill was contacting her. She accepted the call.

"What's going on? Why the top security?" she asked.

"Toby located Harold and Gayle," Bill said.

"Oh, my Great Earth!" Teresa shouted. "Where are they? How'd he find them?"

Bill reiterated his conversation with Toby.

"Why wouldn't they trust us with this? Surely, after all these years, they knew we would never say anything," Teresa said.

"I can't figure it out," Bill said. "He's never let on he was dissatisfied with his position or their circumstances."

"Neither has Gayle," Teresa said. "None of this makes any sense."

CHAPTER NINETEEN

D r. Roberts and Carole arrived at the old oak tree in a glider from their facility. A Tranquility Force glider accompanied them. Dr. Roberts disembarked before the glider came to a complete stop. He approached the tree and thoroughly considered exactly what Abby had done.

Carole eased her way around Dr. Roberts and studied the scene. She saw Abby's original hole and saw how her trajectory was off a little.

Dr. Roberts walked a few paces away. He paced and ranted. "We have no way to track her now! We need those dog-bots here immediately!"

One of the Tranquility Force enforcers approached Dr. Roberts. "They should be here in about twenty minutes."

Carole joined Dr. Roberts. "This act tells me that Abby would go to any length to be free. Now that she doesn't have a Dot, she is in full dog mode, so perhaps we can find her."

Dr. Roberts stopped pacing. "You stay here until Rex arrives and begins the search. I'm going to take a unit and go to the Maxwells."

Carole shook her head. "Abby would never go there. She knows that would be the first place you would look."

Dr. Roberts huffed away from Carole. "I will not be bested by a dog," he muttered to himself.

"You already have, you jerk," Carole whispered behind his back.

Dr. Roberts motioned for a Tranquility Force enforcer to join him. "I want to take a unit to the Maxwell's house. We need to search every square inch of the place. She may have gone there."

The enforcer activated his communication device. "I'm escorting Dr. Roberts to the Maxwell's house. Have a six-member unit rendezvous in two hours."

The enforcer acknowledged Dr. Roberts. "Let's go." He walked over to a small Tranquility Force glider and sat behind the controls. Dr. Roberts joined him and slid into the passenger seat. The glider rose and raced across the land.

DR. ROBERTS and the Tranquility Force enforcer arrived at the Maxwell's neighborhood a few minutes before the search unit. It pulled up alongside Dr. Roberts and the Tranquility Force glider, and the two gliders continued to the Maxwell residence.

As Dr. Roberts approached the door with two Tranquility Force enforcers, the others fanned out on both sides of the house and entered the backyard.

"Do not let that dog escape!" Dr. Roberts warned. He heard the door Communicator announce visitors. Within moments, Bill Maxwell opened the front door. He appeared shocked to see Dr. Roberts and the Tranquility Force.

Teresa came to the door behind Bill. "Who's here?" she asked.

"Tranquility Force," Bill said.

Dr. Roberts tried to push his way into the house. Bill stayed firm. He spoke directly to the uniformed Tranquility Force enforcer. "What are you doing here?"

The Tranquility Force enforcer came forward. "We are to search the premises for the dog."

Dr. Roberts pushed past the Tranquility Force enforcers. "Where is she?" he growled.

Teresa stepped forward. "Abby? You lost Abby?" Her voice rose with hatred, too difficult to mask. Bill rested a hand on her shoulder.

"We didn't lose her. She escaped!" Dr. Roberts snarled.

Bill and Teresa stepped aside. "Come in. Tell us what happened," Bill said.

Dr. Roberts and the two Tranquility Force enforcers entered the house. "Search," Dr. Roberts instructed.

The Tranquility Force dispersed and went around Bill and Teresa into the interior rooms.

"How dare you come here after all these months and search for our daughter!" Teresa snarled. "You took her away, and you were supposed to keep her safe for all of mankind!"

"How did she escape?" Bill asked.

Dr. Roberts pressed his lips together. It was not a pleasant memory. "She took a thin piece of sheet metal and placed it over a magnetic locking sensor on the floor at the door of her house. We think she planned this for months. Last night she watched an old documentary on wild dogs seven times. The cleaning crew leaves at ten o'clock every night. She must have slipped out when they were removing trash."

"Didn't you insert a Dot when she arrived at your facility?" Bill asked.

"Of course I did. She removed it after she escaped," Dr. Roberts spat.

"Removed it?" Teresa shrieked. "What on Earth do you mean?"

Dr. Roberts explained what they had discovered at the oak tree.

"Bill, she could die from an infection!" Teresa covered her face for a moment. Bill pulled her to him and tried to comfort her. She pulled away and got in Dr. Roberts' face.

"If anything happens to her, if she's found dead, I will personally make it my mission in life to see that you are brought before the World Guild Tribunal. You will answer for your carelessness, Doctor."

The Tranquility Force joined Dr. Roberts at the door. "The house is clear," an enforcer reported. They walked outside and waited for Dr. Roberts' instructions.

Teresa, still seething, turned away from Dr. Roberts. She walked clench-fisted to the sofa and sank into the cushions. A stained and raggedy hoof of Abby's little lamb protruded from behind a decorative pillow. Carefully, Teresa pushed it back.

Bill turned his full attention to Dr. Roberts. "You'd better find her. And when you do, you'd be doing yourself a favor to develop some decency and let us visit her."

Bill pressed his hand on Dr. Roberts' chest and backed him out of the door. He slammed the door, engaged the security settings, and stood there for a moment. He turned to the living room and joined Teresa.

"She's free, hon," Bill said. "And it sounds like she's prepared."

"Do you think they'll find her?" Teresa asked as she pulled the lamb from behind the pillow and hugged it to her chest.

Bill shook his head. "No way."

THE THREE GLIDERS arrived at the lightning-split old oak tree. They lowered the dog-bot's cages to the ground and released them. Rex joined Carole several feet from the tree.

"Rex, Abby ran away from the lab. We found her Dot in the dirt over here," Carole said as she walked over to the tree.

Rex followed Carole to the tree. His electronics noted the blood on the tree branch. He took an electronic reading of the Dot in the dirt, studied the digging patterns, walked a few paces to where Abby rolled in the dirt and scanned the horizon one hundred and eighty degrees from the direction he faced.

When he was finished with his observations, he turned and faced Carole.

"You are to find Abby and alert the Tranquility Force so they can bring her back. Do you understand?" Carole asked.

"Orders received and understood," Rex said. He turned to the pack and relayed instructions electronically. The twenty-three dog-bots fanned out in a wide arc and began their search in the opposite direction from what Abby took.

The Tranquility Force platoon and Carole watched as the dog-bots became smaller and smaller on the horizon.

"We might as well go back to the facility," Carole said. "She's had an eleven-hour head start, and I don't expect to hear from Rex for several hours."

REX'S SENSORS WERE ALERT. His internal system scanned his secret place. He sent a message to the pack.

"Dog-bots do not betray the alpha dog," he dispatched to the dog-bots. "Dog-bot 14, you will report on the Tranquility Force frequency in four-point three-two hours that you have detected a clue. The pack will reconnoiter at dog-bot 14's location. Understood?"

Rex received twenty-three acknowledgments.

IN EXACTLY FOUR-POINT THREE-TWO HOURS, Bot 14 reported his false findings on the Tranquility Force frequency.

"Bot 14 to command center," the electronic message relayed to Rex and the other dog-bots on the Tranquility Force's channel. "Bot 14 has visuals of recent dog urine and poop."

Rex followed up with an official report. "Rex will verify the findings. If the evidence is authentic, the pack will regroup at Bot 14s location and we will resume the search from there."

Twenty minutes later Rex reported in again. "Rex is at Bot 14s location. I have verified the evidence. All bots proceed to Bot 14s location."

One by one, the pack reunited with Bot 14 from their prior individual search areas. They fanned out and continued with their search. Rex reported to the Tranquility Force every two hours. He stated that they were on the path of Abby-dog.

Eighteen hours after their search began, Rex reported the pack had lost the trail and that they would increase the search area.

After approximately two days of intensive searching, Rex reported that the trail was cold and that they could not find Abby. The Tranquility Force aborted the search and sent the gliders to retrieve the pack, three-hundred forty-one miles from the starting point.

Rex and the dog-bots were picked up at the northernmost tip of the Lassen National Forest, a one-point-two million acres (eighteen hundred seventy-five miles) of forested area located at the crossroads of seven counties.

There were abundant resources for survival in the forest, and the chance of the Tranquility Force locating Abby without a Dot was minuscule, like trying to find one special pine needle on the forest floor.

Rex sent an encrypted message to Bill using his dog-thought language. "Search aborted."

CHAPTER TWENTY

Abby ran over the rough terrain as fast as her sore feet would take her. She drank out of the sporadic ponds and streams in the area and slept in underbrush or other protective coverings. She paced herself and put distance between her and her captors.

She made it to a dusty travel stop for commercial gliders and the occasional family that was relocating. The old place was off an old, unused roadway and could easily be missed as it blended in with its environment. Several types of glider vehicles were parked around a rickety old shack of a building, which was a combination of a store and a diner. In its former life, the place had been painted barn red.

All that was left of the paint were a few red streaks here and there on the weathered boards. One hauler, two loaders, a couple of family gliders, and a flat-bed glider rested on the ground, which at one point used to be a parking lot. Now, however, grass, yellow wildflowers, and an occasional weed covered all but a few patches of the old blacktop.

The hauler was filled with old furniture. The loaders

contained chunks of concrete and asphalt. Abby determined that the loaders must be carting away material from a cleanup project that was removing unused roadways. She remembered seeing a program that showed old road materials being lasered into a fine dust.

Abby darted to the back of the building where an old burn pile, heaped with trash, waited for a match. Several feet from the burn pile, Abby found scraps of stale bread scattered across the dirt. She ate all the crunchy crusts, leaving nothing for the birds or squirrels.

She darted over to the building and kept close to the exterior. When the vehicles were within view, she sprinted to the hauler and jumped aboard. She hid among the furniture, old bedding and kitchen items, under stacked wooden chairs piled high with someone's discards. Her ears were alert. After several uneventful minutes, she napped.

Abby jerked awake as the hauler hummed to life. She kept low, even though the cab was separated from the scooped bed of the hauler that contained its load. Two men sat in the cab.

She listened carefully to their conversation and discovered that she was currently outside a town called Old Gilroy, and the hauler was heading to Tranquility, where they were going to pick up another load of furniture and piggy-back that hauler to the hauler they were in.

"We'll spend the night at the old Buckeye Tree Lodge," Fred, the driver, said.

Abby searched her internal maps. The lodge was just past Three Rivers and was under a hundred miles from Tranquility, shorter as the crow and the gliders fly.

"Tomorrow morning we'll head down toward Springville, drop off some stuff," Fred said. "You know where I'm talking about? Right there on the Tule River, and then we'll head over to Roads End and get up to Lone Pine."

"We should be able to cross the mountain at Three Rivers," Hooker, the other man, argued.

"Are you crazy?" Fred said. "We can't haul this stuff over the mountain. The elevation's too high for the hauler plus, we'd get elevation sickness."

"Are you sure? I don't think it's that high," Hooker said.

"It's over fourteen thousand feet!" Fred said.

Hooker shut up after that.

Abby accessed her Dot and found California maps. She looked up Old Gilroy, Tranquility, Three Rivers, and the rest of the places she heard Fred and Hooker talk about. She decided she would hitch a ride with them all the way to Roads End.

Roads End looked like the perfect place to Abby. The Kern River flowed through there. She was sure to find a place to hide until the Tranquility Force gave up hunting for her. She knew she needed to make sure that no one saw her and turned her in to the authorities.

When they arrived in Tranquility, the glider came to a stop at a fenced salvage yard with an enormous warehouse. Fred and Hooker went into the warehouse. Abby crept to the edge of the hauler and looked around. She jumped down and darted over to the side of the warehouse and did her business. She was finally used to not having bathroom closets in the wild. Now she was hungry and thirsty.

Abby explored the perimeter of the building. There was an old wooden table and a couple of chairs under a sprawling oak tree between the building and the fenced salvage yard.

Her nose twitched as she picked up a familiar scent. She darted over to the table and jumped onto a chair. She devoured a lukewarm cup of coffee along with scrambled eggs and toast. Abby jumped down, cleaned her face, and ran back to the edge of the building. She raced over to the hauler and jumped aboard. She settled back down in her hiding place and waited for the journey to begin anew.

She didn't have to wait long. The hum of a glider approached. Abby pressed herself into her hiding place under the chairs, while the haulers were piggy-backed. Clangs and other loud noises followed. Her ears twitched at every sound. Fred and Hooker talked to another man for a few minutes, and then they climbed into the cab of the main glider and resumed their trip.

A couple of hours later, with the sun low in the sky, they arrived in Three Rivers. A weathered population sign in front of the Buckeye Tree Lodge had several numbers scratched out and written over. The original sign boasted three thousand people. The latest population slapped on with blue neon paint was one hundred fifty, a plus sign and the number two.

The lodge was a collection of derelict structures that may have been beautiful forty years back in the heyday of its life. Its pillars were tilted, but Abby hoped they held the second story of the place. No gliders were in sight. Fred settled the hauler alongside the hotel, and he and Hooker got out, stretched their stiff backs, arms, and legs, and walked toward the front door.

Abby waited, listened, and sampled the air with her wet nose. She cautiously looked around and then jumped down between the two haulers, still concealed from any curious people. She stretched out and then shook herself. As Abby darted along the edge of the lodge, she heard a bubbling noise in the distance and went to investigate.

The Buckeye Tree Lodge was situated among scattered trees at Sequoia National Park. Abby walked through the trees toward the bubbling sound. The back of the property was about five hundred feet deep and sloped down to the banks of a wide stream. The rocks were shiny and smooth from constant polishing by the fast-running water.

A twelve-foot area was cleared of the slippery rocks, and coarse sand allowed visitors access to the water's edge. A knotted rope railing affixed to four-by-six wooden posts that were sunk into the ground stood along each side of the cleared area. Abby walked forward and stepped into the edge of the water. She was startled by the cold temperature of the water on her front feet. She dipped her head and drank.

~

"DID YOU HEAR THAT?" Teresa asked. She jumped off the sofa, jammed her hand in the security mold and yanked open the front door. No one was there. She walked outside and looked up and down the street, then she walked along the high fence surrounding the yard.

Two neighboring women were chatting in front of their houses. They stopped and watched Teresa. "There she goes again," the woman with the green streak in her hair said. "Those poor people have been through enough, and it's finally driven them crazy." They both shook their heads and continued their previous conversation.

Teresa returned to the house and closed the door. Bill looked expectantly at her. She shrugged.

"Abby's not going to come to this house, hon," Bill said. "And you know Rex will only come in the middle of the night."

"I know the neighbors think we're crazy," Teresa said. "But Abby's out in the wild somewhere, and we're still home under satellite surveillance."

Bill walked into his home lab. "Check satellite grids," Bill commanded his security system. He monitored all the networks and the satellite grids.

A crisscross of diagrams and maps appeared on the big screen. He stared at the screen and shook his head.

"It's pretty ironic that the Tranquility Force and World Guild are using the very systems that I developed for them to spy on us," he said. "Maybe they don't know how to override my encrypted programming or the delicate layers of criss-crossed strings that would alert me to tampering. Whatever the reasons, I have to monitor their monitoring."

His genius was practical, too. Because of the nature of his work and inventions, Bill had made sure that no one could spy inside their home. His network of feelers and tracers throughout the interior and exterior of the house and Maxwell Industries would make the World Guild security look like amateur-designed security-in-a-box systems.

Teresa walked into Bill's lab. He was bent over the transfer surface, diligently working with his blue invisibility formula.

"You need to take a break," Teresa said.

Bill straightened up and stretched his back. Teresa wrapped her arms around him and held his head to her chest.

"I love you," she said.

He pulled her tighter. "I love you."

"Any progress?" she asked.

Bill turned to his work and looked at it with dismay. "I just don't understand what I'm missing," he said. "It must be some-thing so simple that I can't see it."

Teresa rubbed his shoulders. She dug her thumbs into his back muscles and massaged them until they loosened up. "Shrug your shoulders a couple of times," she said.

Bill complied and rotated his shoulders one way and then the other. He could hear the muscles crunching, but they were looser.

A twinkling yellow speck, no bigger than a pinhead, settled on the edge of the transfer surface.

"Bill, what's that?" Teresa asked.

Bill swung around and looked at the speck. "That's one of

the bees," he said. "The wasps are blue. Looks like it's got something to upload."

Bill walked over to his scientific tool tray and grabbed a thin metal spatula about a quarter of an inch wide and six inches long. He returned to the transfer surface and held the spatula in front of the bee. The yellow speck floated onto the spatula.

He placed the edge of the spatula on the transfer surface in the middle of an etched area. The little yellow speck fluttered onto the transfer surface.

Bill put the spatula aside. He swung a lighted magnifying viewer over the etched area.

"Come take a look," he said.

Teresa lowered the viewer a little and then looked through it. The tiny speck had a yellow and black etching that made it look like a bumblebee.

"That's the cutest thing I've ever seen," she said. "Did Toby give them those little smiling faces?"

"These little spies smile while performing their duties," Bill snickered.

He picked up the stylus and drew a line from the bee to the receiving area. The yellow speck at the receiving area flickered during the transfer. An enormous amount of data was downloaded from the bee to the holding area on the transfer surface.

Security checks determined that there were no tracers or spyware, or strings attached to the data, and no embedded or encrypted encoding was detected.

"Doesn't look like anything's bugged," he said. He uploaded it to one of his supercomputers.

Teresa watched as Bill uploaded the data and ran it through The Vault, one of his ingeniously crafted programs that he had created early in his career. It was his secret weapon against the government and anyone else trying to weasel their way into his system and steal his creations or track his keyboarding. He wasn't having any part of being spied upon. He preferred to do the spying.

"That's a lot of data," he said as he watched the upload. The process finally completed, and Bill ventured into one file. He checked the properties and looked around at file extensions.

"It looks like my little bee hopped a ride on a Tranquility Force glider and wormed his way into the computer and downloaded all the data and then went on a mission with them. There's system information from several people and organizations that are being watched," Bill said.

"I thought the bees were only supposed to guard the house," Teresa said. "How'd it get to a Tranquility Force glider?"

Bill thought things through. "When Dr. Roberts and the Tranquility Force were here looking for Abby, this little guy most likely took it upon himself to snoop on them."

Bill and Teresa glanced at the tiny flashing yellow speck in the etched area of the transfer surface. "How'd you get back home, though?" Bill said. "I'm going to have to look at these files and find the latest date and time and see if I can figure out how he got back here. There must be a Tranquility Force unit in our quadrant, and they must have come up to the house at some point to attach spyware."

Bill sorted the two hundred seventeen thousand files by date and time and clicked on the most recent file, which was a recording made one hour and fifteen minutes earlier. Bill clicked the Play button.

"Unit 4507 has intercepted outgoing chatter from the subjects William and Teresa Maxwell," the recording stated.

They listened to the recording for a few moments, and Bill smiled widely. The chatter had made no sense—it was gibberish.

"My bees detected the Tranquility Force spyware and

played a dirty trick on them with pig Latin. They took random words, moved the first letter of a word to the end of the word and then added the letters 'ay' and formed sentences that didn't make any sense," Bill explained. "Here, listen carefully and you'll see what I'm talking about."

He clicked the Play button again. "Owcay ookbay ogay awnday imetay utoay ndaay hetay." He stopped the recording.

"Cow, book, go, dawn, time, out, and, the," Teresa said. "What a clever little bee!"

Bill belly-laughed. "I feel so sorry for their encryption team. They're going to spend hours... days... weeks or maybe even years trying to break this code when there isn't any!"

"If he wasn't so tiny, I'd scratch his little ears," Teresa said.

CHAPTER TWENTY-ONE

Abby was grateful for the abundance of water in the area. She was hungry and lean from the lack of three meals a day plus snacks. She stood at the stream's edge and listened. Her nose twitched as she smelled the fresh, clean air.

A scurrying noise close by caught her attention. A gray squirrel foraged around the base of a tree, unaware of Abby just a few feet away.

Abby sprang into action. She charged over to the tree. The squirrel leaped onto the tree with Abby inches away. Abby jumped and snatched the squirrel from the tree. She clamped down on its back with her iron-vise jaws and growled as she shook it. Blood dripped onto the ground from the puncture holes.

She dropped her prey on top of a bed of leaves and pine needles and licked it. She used one paw to hold the dead squirrel and gingerly pulled the fur. After several failed attempts to dislodge the fur, hunger got the best of her, and she finally became fully canine and ripped the fur away and ate the raw flesh. Abby sighed in satisfaction at having a less empty belly and for successfully making her first kill.

She washed up, drank from the stream, and then headed back toward the hotel. Twilight had arrived, and the sky was rippled with pinks and blues and rose-orange. Abby hopped on the hauler. She poked around in the containers and found an old bedsheet and dragged it to her hiding place.

She used her front paws to gather the sheet into a pile. Then she crawled on top of the sheet and went to sleep.

Just as dawn broke, Abby woke. She crawled out of her hiding place and looked over at the building. There were no lights on inside the lodge. She jumped down between the haulers and darted behind the lodge. She ran to the stream. The cold water tasted good. She lifted her nose to the air and sampled her surroundings.

Being indoors all her life had not prepared her for the rough life of living in the wild. Abby could not identify the scents her nose picked up. She didn't know if those smells were game she could catch and eat, or if they were dangers to be avoided.

Abby wandered away from the stream and trotted parallel to the water and in line with the lodge. She saw the twinkle of a light as she walked among the trees, and then another. The people at the lodge were waking up. She approached a strange outbuilding that was surrounded by a fence. There was a scent that was a mixture of feathers and manure and other unidentifiable odors.

She walked around the perimeter of the fence toward the gate so she could explore further. The back door of the lodge opened and slammed shut. The sound startled her. A man approached the fenced-in outbuilding, carrying a wire basket. Abby flattened herself on the ground and watched him.

The man opened the gate and entered the fenced yard,

pushing the gate closed behind him. He took several steps and walked up a ramp and unlatched a door on the little chicken coop, then ducked down and entered the building. He returned moments later with a basket full of eggs, with several clucking hens following him.

The man turned and propped the door of the chicken coop open with a one-by-two board. Then he walked down the ramp to the gate and exited the chicken yard, locked the gate and returned to the lodge.

Abby raised her head and looked toward the lodge. She scurried around to the gate and studied the locking mechanism, which was a simple hook and eye. She jumped up against the gate and stretched toward the lock. Abby nudged the hook with her nose, but it was very tight and wouldn't give. She jumped down and thought for a moment. Abby wandered around, nose to the ground, until she found a sturdy twig. She grabbed it between her teeth and hurried over to the gate.

She jumped up against the gate and bonked the hook with the twig several times. It finally popped out of the eye and the gate inched open.

Abby pawed the gate open. She darted into the chicken yard and went up the ramp. Chickens flew all over the place. Abby dodged the flying, squawking hens and went from nest to empty nest. She found an egg on the floor and picked it up and cracked the shell with her teeth. She ate the egg and went hunting for more. She found and ate three more eggs and then left the chicken coop.

The chickens were clucking and scratching in the chicken yard, and some had gone through the gate and were wandering around the back yard of the lodge. Abby easily chased down a chicken, caught it, killed it, and ate heartily. She then ran back to the stream, walked into the water to dislodge feathers and blood on her feet. She drank deeply and returned to the hauler, full, happy and free.

Fred and Hooker came out of the lodge about thirty minutes later. The aroma of cooked eggs, bacon, and coffee wafted on the breeze, which Abby's twitching, wet nose picked up. She licked her lips at the memories of scrumptious cooked meals from the food console. She knew those days were long gone.

An oversized family-type glider arrived. It pulled up by the haulers and a red-headed guy got out. He shook hands with Fred. "Thanks for hauling my mom's things," the guys said.

They all jumped on Abby's hauler. She had a minor panic attack as the large drum she sheltered in jiggled. She flattened herself on the bedding materials as several pieces of furniture were unloaded and stuffed into the glider.

"What do I owe you?" Red asked.

"Fifty credits should do it," Fred said.

Red paid by tapping his communication device and typing the info on the virtual keyboard. Fred's device dinged the transaction complete.

Fred and Hooker climbed into the cab. The haulers purred to life. Fred checked their coordinates on the global navigational satellite system (GNSS), entered their destination and waited for the map to synchronize. He checked the weather conditions for the route.

"Looks like Springville's having showers," he said. "Roads End is overcast. Little Lake looks like a mixture of both, and Lone Pine looks sunny."

"Let's just hope that those are showers and not some big storm," Hooker said.

Fred pressed the engage button, and the haulers lifted off the ground, made a wide turn, and began the last leg of their journey.

Abby dozed, lulled by the swaying motion of the hauler as they zipped across the air currents. She was happy to be secreted away from everyone who was hunting her. It would have taken her weeks on foot to cover the distance she was putting between herself and Dr. Roberts. She slept and dreamed of her Mommy and Daddy and the day when they would be reunited.

BILL STARED at the ceramic disc, frustrated. It was still there, visible for the entire world to see. His blue formula failed again. He opened a file and pored through the contents: his original formula, the preparation, all the procedures, including every single change he had made to date, no matter how slight. Bill read page after page of notes until he felt like a dullard.

He shut the system down, left the lab, and went into the living room and threw himself on the sofa. Bill stared at the ceiling for a moment and then succumbed to sleep.

TERESA FOUND her husband in open-mouthed sleep with one arm dangling off the sofa when she wandered out of the schoolroom and discovered him. She eased onto the sofa beside him and rested her head on his chest. He stirred awake, wrapped his arms around her, and they cuddled and snoozed.

The whole-house sensors blared to life. "Security may be breached. An immediate response is required. Security may be breached. An immediate response is required."

Teresa and Bill untangled their limbs and sprang up off the sofa just as the interior window and door enforcement electronics secured the house.

"Security visuals on," Bill commanded. The AMD swirled the liquid moving picture of a flowing mountain stream on the wall, and a view of the house exterior appeared.

"Show multiple views," Bill said. Every side of the house appeared, including angles of the roof and the backyard. Different visuals of the sides of the house appeared just in time for Bill and Teresa to see the gate closing.

"Track gate to curb," Bill barked. The screen showed a Tranquility Force enforcer running down the walkway to a waiting glider. "They must have planted some spyware or strings," Bill said.

"Why would they do that?" Teresa asked. "They've been watching us since Abby ran away, and they know she's not here."

Bill rushed into the lab. He opened a cool cabinet and lifted out a tray that contained a couple of hundred tiny, round, clear containers. "Hon, help me open the bee and wasp discs. Just dump them on the transfer surface in the etched area."

"Aren't there already enough flying around?" Teresa asked.

"I think this act of direct spying calls for high alert," Bill said. "I'd rather have all my resources engaged."

They began opening each little disc and dropping the tiny bees and wasps onto the etching. When they were finished, Bill typed instructions on the keyboard and then picked up the stylus and drew a line from the etched area to the instructions. The little specks lit up, yellow and blue, bees and wasps, and then their colors faded to black. They floated off the transfer surface and dispersed through the entire house, burrowing into electrical sockets, plumbing fixtures, nooks, cracks, creases, and anything else that could be accessed by air itself.

"What are you telling them to do?" Teresa asked.

"They're going to find whatever was planted," Bill said. He enabled the security monitors in the lab and set them to a slideshow of the entire property from different views. Then he clicked on a satellite icon and zoomed in on their quadrant. He discovered a Tranquility Force glider hovering a distance away.

Bill went to the cool cabinet and extracted one little disc from the remaining tray. He brought the disc to the transfer surface and opened it and dumped the tiny speck onto the etched circle. His fingers flew over the keys in a mad flurry, typing instructions. "See that glider?" he asked Teresa.

She turned her attention from the house views to the satellite zoom. "What could they possibly want?"

"We're going to find out," Bill said. "I'm sending one of my super bees on a mission. He'll report in periodically." The super bee took off through an outlet.

"Don't they realize that whatever they are doing is against the Highest Agreement of the World Guild?" Teresa asked, stressing. "Don't they think there are repercussions, or that you're going to report this?"

Bill watched the monitors for a moment. "These may be instructions from the World Guild."

"I can't believe it's come to that!" Teresa said.

Several bees and wasps settled on the edge of the transfer surface. A tiny buzzing noise sounded. Bill looked around and didn't see anything. He concentrated on the sound and then walked slowly around the room. Several wasps had converged in an open electrical socket. He bent down to examine the socket.

"Teresa, can you get me a slotted screwdriver and the long tweezers?" he asked.

Teresa opened a tool tray and grabbed a screwdriver, and then hurried to his scientific tool tray and grabbed the tweezers and brought them to him.

Bill unscrewed the screw holding the face plate on the socket. "Can you get my circuit finder?" he asked.

"Where is it?" Teresa asked.

"Fourth drawer down, in number three cabinet," he said.

Teresa opened the drawer and looked at all the items that were neatly tucked into trays. She spotted the circuit finder gadget and brought it to Bill.

He stuck the end of the circuit finder into the electrical socket. LAB323 appeared in the identification area. "Computer, shut down power to circuit LAB323," he commanded.

Bill began to pull out the electrical socket and disconnected wires. He brought the socket over to the transfer surface and shook it. Several wasps fluttered down to the transfer surface along with a thin, fine wire-type thing. It wiggled when it hit the transfer surface.

"Looks like a worm," Bill said. "They could have planted more than one."

He picked up the stylus and drew a circle around the worm, containing it. Bill typed on the keyboard and created a new file folder and drew a line from the worm to the folder. The worm's programming transferred to the file folder. When it finished transferring, Bill picked up the worm with the long tweezers and placed it into a disc and snapped it shut.

The remaining bees and wasps returned to the lab. Bill and Teresa repacked them into their little cases, and Bill stored them in the cool cabinet.

"Looks like only one worm," he said. "Let's see what they want."

He dragged the file folder to a program decoder. The monitor filled with programming language that scrolled nonstop. Bill studied the screen as line after line loaded. He waited patiently for the decoder to complete the process. It wasn't long before instructions appeared: observe, record, capture data, keystrokes, voice commands and other simple tasks.

"Teresa, it looks like a very basic worm," Bill said. "I can't imagine that they would go to all this trouble with this unsophisticated piece of equipment. Surely this is just a decoy."

Bill crossed the room and looked in the cool cabinet. Every little disc was accounted for, and each contained a bee or a wasp. The only thing that was missing was the Super Bee.

"Something's going on, but I don't know what," he said. Bill stood in front of the monitors. "Security, enable red alert. Perform a virtual crawl of the interior and exterior premises of the Maxwell residence. Report your findings in dog-thought encryption."

CHAPTER TWENTY-TWO

The haulers hummed along on their journey. Abby saw few communities when she stood to stretch. There were no other gliders of any kind in the airspace they traveled. Occasionally she saw scattered houses among the trees, but there was no sign of occupancy. Most houses were miles apart and in a decrepit state.

I bet those old houses were abandoned decades ago when their owners moved to the big cities for the better life, she thought.

Abby listened as Fred and Hooker bantered back and forth.

"We've got another two hundred fourteen miles to Lone Pine going the long route around the mountain," Hooker said.

"We'll cross over between Springville and Roads End," Fred said. "That's the safest route."

"Man, we can cross at Potato Hill or Milo," Hooker said.

"Look at the elevation!" Fred hollered. "It's too rugged, and we'd risk losing the load."

Rummaging through her internal maps, Abby concurred with Fred. If the hauler had to climb perpendicular to the mountain, the load would be lost. She couldn't understand Hooker's ignorance. "I'm glad Fred's driving," she thought. "I really like my free ride."

A little less than ninety minutes after leaving the Buckeye Tree Lodge, they approached Springville. Fred slowed the hauler and pulled up to a little shack of a pit stop for a cup of coffee. The place looked deserted to Abby.

Fred and Hooker disembarked from the cab and approached the front door. A big sign was posted on the door: CLOSED. MOVED TO BAKERSFIELD.

Fred looked through the dirty windows. "Looks just the way it did three months ago," he said. "Bet there's one of them old coffee machines in there."

Abby jumped down between the haulers while the men explored the shack. She squatted and peed, not wanting to risk the chance of being abandoned.

Hooker went around the corner and looked in another window. "Yeah, there's a machine all right."

Fred and Hooker went around the entire place checking windows and doors. The back door was not fully secured, so they let themselves in.

Abby lifted her nose to the air and sampled the surroundings. She wandered around the grounds opposite the shack and discovered a little pond and took a drink of water. She heard a crash and then loud voices from inside the shack.

"Uh-oh, someone's in trouble," Abby said. She ran back to the hauler and jumped on board.

Fred and Hooker returned to the cab and got in. Fred was not in a good mood. "Don't know what good a coffee machine is without electricity or a solar hookup," Fred said. "They're gonna be really pissed when they come back and see their dishes wrecked."

"How was I to know the shelf wasn't secure?" Hooker said.

Abby heard unfamiliar words, then it was silent in the glider cab for the next ten minutes.

"Keep on the lookout for a house or someplace so we can get a cup of coffee," Fred said. "It's a long way to Roads End, and I need more coffee."

The hauler suddenly heaved up and down. Furniture and trash shifted violently. Abby yelped as her sanctuary under the old wooden chairs turned into a hazard. The back legs of the chair immediately above her collapsed as the load shifted, and she was trapped underneath.

"Storm must be coming in," Hooker said.

"Rough air up ahead. Have to slow down," Fred said.

The load lightly jumped again as the haulers traveled the cross air-waves. Abby took advantage of the jarring and pulled herself free of the chair and its top load. Another good jostle made the load shift, and the front legs of the chair gave out, and the top load crashed to the floor of the hauler.

Abby stood, hunched down, swaying with the hauler. She looked around the jumbled contents, seeking shelter. An old, round, metal drum was on its side, wedged between other containers. Old bedding material spilled from the drum. She looked at the furniture and trash around the container and determined that it was safe. Abby crawled inside the drum just as the rain came down.

There was no napping for the next half hour as the rain poured and the haulers roller-coastered through the shifting air. Fred tried lower currents to no avail. Abby scooted to the back of the container, trying to stay dry. Luckily, the container was tilted slightly forward so her bedding stayed relatively dry.

What should have been a short, smooth trip turned into ninety minutes, with the haulers moving slowly through the rough weather. Abby crept toward the drum opening and peeked outside. Visibility was, at best, fifteen feet. As she stuck her head out of the drum, she saw some hair-raising near-misses with jagged rocks and clusters of trees. She eased back into the drum, shook the water from her drenched head and shoulders, and returned to her bed of discarded bedding materials. She rubbed her wet face on the bedding, then sighed before falling asleep.

They finally came to the tiny community of Smith Mill. Fred eased the haulers to a stop at the Liberty Inn and Camp Stop, which was next to the Smith Mill Virtual Healing Office. An older hauler was parked at the inn, and a late-model family glider was parked in front of the VHO.

Fred and Hooker raced through the downpour to the front door of the inn and disappeared inside. Abby reluctantly stuck her nose out of the container and took in the scene. She sniffed the air, shook the rain off her face, turned around and settled back onto her ragged bed.

～

"MAYBE YOU SHOULD CONTACT REX," Teresa said.

Bill stood in the lab, watching the monitors for any trace of spyware or abnormality.

"That's not a bad idea," he said. He walked over to the virtual keyboard. His fingers raced over the flat keys as he typed a message and then encrypted it. "Rex's dog-thought is ingenious, Teresa. I'd equate it to the Native American languages that the military used as codes back in the big war days."

Teresa thought for a moment. "I never looked at it that way, but you're right," she said. "The big difference between Rex's dog-thought and the Native American code is that those were actual languages that could be studied and broken down and learned. There's no way for the Tranquility Force or anyone else to break down Rex's code because there's no live model."

"They may have kept the brains of those other dog-children they confiscated," Bill said.

"I'll bet they didn't," Teresa said. "That's something else you might ask Rex. He'd be able to access that information directly."

The security system blared and red lights flashed throughout the house. "Red Alert: Incoming intruder." The system repeated the deafening announcement. Teresa put her hands over her ears. The monitor showed the exterior of the house and then different views of the interior structures between rooms.

"Computer, lower the volume," Bill said. He studied the monitor. "Magnify times one hundred on incoming intruder."

The monitor filled with gigantic views of insulation material, dead bugs, wall material, and a decomposed earthworm. Suddenly, a magenta robotic bee appeared on the screen. It flew over, under, and around obstructions in its path.

"Computer, provide the trajectory of the incoming intruder," Bill said.

"Incoming intruder on path to LAB347," the computer announced.

"Placement in room?" Bill asked.

The monitor showed a lighting fixture by the cool cabinet.

"Guess he wants to go home," Bill said. He grabbed the thin metal spatula and walked over to the cool cabinet. He turned off the light and looked up at the socket.

Teresa joined him. They both had their necks craned, looking at the light socket when the tiny magenta speck appeared, drifting out of the light socket. Bill held the spatula in the bee's path, and it drifted down onto the spatula.

Sheltering the bee with one hand, Bill walked over to the transfer surface. He tilted the spatula, and the magenta speck fluttered to the etched area. Bill picked up the stylus and drew a circle around the bee to a file structure.

Bill and Teresa watched as data was uploaded to the file system. "Looks like there's visuals," Bill said, somewhat surprised.

The transfer was completed. Bill went to the cool cabinet and retrieved the tiny disc. He used the long tweezers to gently grasp the bee and placed it in its container. He brought the disc over to the cool cabinet and then returned to the transfer surface.

"Three visual files," Bill said. "Let's see what our little bee picked up."

Bill clicked on the first file. He and Teresa immediately recognized Captain Day, the Tranquility Force man who had taken Abby away from them. His face would be imprinted on their brains forever.

Captain Day and four other Tranquility Force enforcers were in an official Tranquility Force glider. Captain Day used his communication patch to place a visual call to someone. The Sentient Robotics logo appeared. The screen wavered, and then Dr. Roberts' face appeared.

Bill and Teresa looked at each other in disbelief. "That rotten bastard," Bill spat. "That's his company logo. He's doing this on his own, not through the direction of the Tranquility Force or the World Guild!"

"Sshh!" Teresa exclaimed.

They listened as Dr. Roberts approved the spyware at the exterior of their home and then reiterated to Captain Day that the worm should seek any information regarding Bill's robotic dog invention and patent and destroy what it found.

Bill was stunned. "He's just hung himself. If it's the very last thing I do, Teresa, I will put that man down."

Teresa rested her arm across Bill's shoulders. "How did he

get to where he is in his career? He's a thief! A criminal! I'm surprised that we have heard nothing else about him or Abby on GNN," Teresa said.

"I need to do some probing," Bill said. "Tomorrow I'm going to go to the World Guild and talk to some people. This guy is rotten through and through, and now I'm not sure if World Guild, GNN or anyone else knows what he's doing."

Bill clicked on the next visual file, and then the third, but the contents were of no interest. He then started opening files. He didn't know how the super bee did it, but he found a file that contained a forged document that Dr. Roberts had created —the patent papers for Rex's prototype that put Dr. Roberts and Dr. Sovesky as the patent holders.

"Why would Dr. Roberts go to all this trouble? He could ruin his career in a matter of one click," Teresa said.

Bill stared at the file for a long moment. "I'll bet he has discovered something and wants to file for a new patent."

Bill walked over to the computer and typed. He opened Rex's dog-thought encryption program and sent an encrypted message to Rex.

"Rex will acknowledge my message," he told Teresa. "We'll sleep on the sofa tonight."

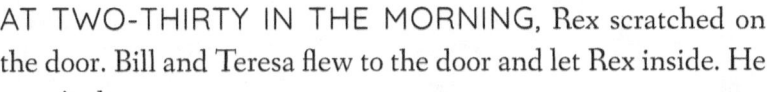

AT TWO-THIRTY IN THE MORNING, Rex scratched on the door. Bill and Teresa flew to the door and let Rex inside. He wasn't alone.

CHAPTER TWENTY-THREE

Dog-bot number twenty-three walked into Bill and Teresa's house on Rex's heels. They were so nonplussed to see Rex's companion that Bill held the door open a bit longer than necessary.

Bill finally shut the door, and turned to face Rex. "Who's your friend, Rex?" He noticed that the new dog-bot had what appeared to be a soft textured exterior.

Teresa walked to the sofa and sat. Rex walked up to Teresa, ready to have his ears scratched.

"This is dog-bot number twenty-three," Rex announced. "I'm training number twenty-three to be the pack leader as my replacement."

Bill and Teresa exchanged an anxious expression.

"What do you mean, Rex?" Teresa asked.

"Do you detect a system problem?" Bill asked.

"Never put all your eggs in one basket," Rex said.

"Bill?" Teresa said, looking at her brilliant husband and expecting him to decipher the puzzling conversation and actions of his creation.

Bill sat on the sofa beside Teresa. He patted his thighs. "Come here, buddy."

Rex shifted a few paces and stood in front of Bill.

Bill looked at Rex, perplexed. "Tell me what's wrong, Rex. What is this all about? I know you miss Abby, but tell me what you are experiencing. Are you feeling deficient in any way?"

Number twenty-three sat several paces away and quietly waited for instructions from the pack leader.

Rex looked at Bill. "I want to be a real dog. When Mommy and Daddy Teresa and Bill leave, I will be their dog and go with them to Texmexzona."

Teresa slipped off the sofa onto her knees. She put her arms around Rex and drew him to her. She hugged him and kissed his head.

"Oh, Rex, you are so precious," Teresa said.

Number twenty-three's sensory receptors whirred into high gear as he recorded the exchange.

"Rex, I would love to have you come with us, but what about the Tranquility Force and Dr. Roberts? They would want to keep the pack leader at all costs," Bill said. "You're the one who trains and conditions the pack."

"Number twenty-three will inform them I have fallen off a pier into the ocean," Rex said.

"You have a plan all worked out?" Teresa asked.

"The Tranquility Force tosses dog-bots onto the trash heap when we break down. We are not valued or loved," Rex said.

Bill shook his head at the ignorance of the scientists at the headquarters. "I understand, Rex."

"I have created a secret place with dog-thought for number twenty-three. We can communicate undetected," Rex said.

"Very good," Bill said. "Rex, I summoned you here for a couple of reasons. You were at the facility with Dr. Roberts for quite some time, correct?"

"Yes."

"While you were there, before Abby arrived, what happened to the other dog-children? How did they die and what happened to their bodies?"

Rex rested his chin on Bill's leg. "The literalist was accurate in stating that the dogs succumbed to the poison. Dr. Roberts did everything in his power to save them, but one by one, their nervous systems were compromised. Brain and organ failure occurred, and they died."

"They didn't save the brains?" Teresa asked. "We wondered if Dr. Roberts would dissect the brains for scientific study."

"No, the dogs were whole when cremated," Rex said.

"Rex, recently the Tranquility Force planted a worm at this house. Do you know why they are trying to spy on us?" Bill asked.

"Dr. Roberts and Dr. Sovesky have made improvements to the dog-bots," Rex said.

"Have you been upgraded as well?" Bill asked.

"My software has been updated and some of my hardware has been replaced," Rex said. "I have systematically reprogrammed all threats that would jeopardize secrets or would track me."

"Can I scan you and number twenty-three and download your new software?" Bill asked.

"Of course, Daddy," Rex said.

"Rex, it appears there have been sentient upgrades or changes to your system," Teresa said. "You seem to be experiencing much more of reality, and you are more aware of your beginnings and connections to family."

She rubbed the base of his ears and then cupped his face and kissed him on the nose. "Did you lead the Tranquility Force away from Abby's trail when she ran away?" Teresa asked.

"Abby is the alpha dog, Lilith's pup. All dog-bots are loyal to the alpha dog," number twenty-three said.

Bill stood. "Thank you for your loyalty to our daughter, number twenty-three," he said. "Let's go into the lab."

Teresa stood. Bill led the way to his lab.

THE TRIP from Smith Mill to Johnsondale was nerve-wracking for Abby, with thunder, lightning, torrential pouring rain and bumpy air currents. She dug her toenails into the bedding to stabilize her ride as much as possible. The haulers jumped and pitched. The load lurched and jiggled and became hazardous.

For two desperate hours, Abby hunkered down on the bed of rags. She could not hold her bladder any longer, so she ventured out into the pouring rain, squatted, and peed on the hauler deck. She leaped back inside her shelter, shook several times, turned in a tight circle, and flopped down with a sigh.

The haulers approached the outskirts of Johnsondale. The rain was left behind somewhere after Smith Mill. The hauler was finally able to pick up speed with the smoother air currents.

Evening approached tentatively with yellow, pink, and purplish-blue strips of clouds in the sky over Johnsondale. Main Street comprised the Indian Trading Station, a café, a postal station, and the Libation Station on one side of the street. The other side of the street was home to the Jerome Hotel, a Virtual Healing Office, and a hardware store.

Both sides of the street had their share of boarded-up shops. The population had dwindled to two hundred fifty residents who tried to eke out an existence in the harsh elements.

Fred parked the hauler in front of the Libation Station. He and Hooker stiffly climbed out of the cab and stretched. The treacherous trip through the stormy weather had taken its toll on their weary bones, and they were ready to loosen up a bit. They walked to the door of the bar and went inside.

Abby ventured out of her hiding place and stretched her nose in the air. The delectable smells of food being prepared from inside triggered her stomach to rumble—an angry, growling rumble.

Abby hopped down to the ground between the haulers. Twilight was settling in, and the two solar streetlights were just beginning to give off a faint glow. Abby wandered in the shadows alongside the buildings, making her way to the back doors, where she discovered scraps of meat trimmings, vegetable peelings, and even stale cake.

She ate to her heart's content and then set off in an easterly direction to find a stream to quench her thirst. Abby didn't have to go far before she came across one of the many creeks. She drank greedily and then trotted off to find a safe place to sleep since the old bedding in the drum was soaked.

BILL MADE a new folder with number twenty-three's name on it. He then lifted the dog-bot onto the transfer table and copied all his programming, hardware files, and databases.

"What's this, number twenty-three? Looks like you have a new type of processing system," Bill said.

Number twenty-three turned to face the monitor to see what Bill was talking about. "The Sovesky Nano Processor has recently been submitted for a patent."

Bill looked it over. He let out a short laugh. "Well, guess

what, number twenty-three? Dr. Sovesky won't be able to get a patent because I hold the original patent."

"Patent number 6426,893,457,966 dated January 17, 2068, held by William Maxwell," Rex said.

"How could Dr. Sovesky apply for a patent that you already own?" Teresa asked.

"I'm pretty sure Sovesky and Dr. Roberts were overconfident in the success of their worm," Bill said.

He went through the list of files and folders from number twenty-three's download, diligently clicking and scanning details.

"These guys are so greedy and power-hungry that they have become very sloppy," Bill said. "I need a foolproof plan to not only expose their plot, but I also have to make sure that their careers are destroyed and they are arrested."

"You'll have to tread carefully, Bill," Teresa said. "They work for the World Guild and are high up in the ranks. You can't have this backfire and have more security watching us."

"Daddy and I will work together on this problem, and we will eliminate the enemy," Rex said.

Teresa's hand flew to her forehead. Something was going on with Rex's sentient programming, she thought. It wasn't bad; it just was unexpected and transforming. Teresa's mind was busy diagraming the aspects of Rex's thought processing: understanding, rationalization, and dot-connecting on many levels.

She realized the concept of family was firmly ingrained in Rex. He had connected those dots when he discovered Bill had invented the original dog-bot. He considered Bill his father. This new level of thought processing concerned her, though. What had he said? Eliminate the enemy. She wondered what else was brewing in his circuitry and firing in his brain.

Bill stared at Rex. He lifted number twenty-three off the

transfer surface and placed him gently on the floor. "All done, number twenty-three. We're going to have to come up with a nickname for you. I can't keep calling you number twenty-three," Bill said.

He lifted Rex off the floor and placed him on the transfer surface.

"Give it up, Rex," Bill said. He typed in some commands instructing the computer to download only those files that had been altered or added. Then he drew a line from Rex to the folder set up previously.

The download was enormous. "What's all this?" Bill asked. "You shouldn't have an entire system download, only files that have been altered or updated."

Teresa watched the monitor closely. "Looks like totally different files than what you already have, Bill."

"I have made some changes," Rex said. "My circuitry is new living circuitry; it bends to my will and connects where I desire it to connect."

Bill pulled the scanning arm down from the ceiling. It was a thin, elongated blade of stark white emulsified material with buttons along the top edge. It resembled the propeller blade of a wind turbine.

"Let's take a look at that," Bill said. He pressed the power button on the top edge, and the scanner came to life with a bluish aura. He grasped the sides and moved the scanner to Rex's head.

Bill and Teresa watched the monitor as the scanner scanned. Thin filaments networked through Rex's head like arteries. They connected to various microscopic components that, less than one hundred years ago, were so clunky they required a large box to house them.

"Rex, demonstrate how you change something and tell me

what you are doing so I can understand and learn from the process," Bill said.

Teresa watched the monitor beside Bill. A filament moved across several filaments and fastened down on a component.

"I have just ordered my system to not allow incoming senses that would allow me to identify odors," Rex said.

"Why didn't you just shunt the electrical impulses to that circuit instead of moving the connector?" Bill asked.

"While I may not want to identify odors, they may be critical to other judgments or processes, so I have turned one ability off, and enabled another so those same odors can be logged, categorized and dismantled for future use," Rex said.

Bill and Teresa watched as the filament returned to its original location.

"That's quite ingenious, Rex," Bill said. "I'm not sure I would have thought of that."

CHAPTER TWENTY-FOUR

The first rays of morning light were spreading across the sky as Abby woke up. She stayed quiet as she accessed the Wise Owl program. She made her brain click on a message function. Abby patiently thumped on each letter to type her message: I am free.

She chose Rex and Daddy to send the message to, and clicked Send. Abby waited to see if the message would return with an error, but it appeared to go through her system. She was ecstatic to finally be able to communicate with her family!

Abby crawled out from under an abandoned wheelbarrow she had found in an old dump that was probably started by the Jerome Hotel. It had been so overgrown with vines and tree roots and weeds that she almost missed it. She hunted down a squirrel for breakfast, then headed back to the hotel and hopped onto the hauler.

The men came out of the hotel and climbed into the hauler cab. The short ride to Roads End was the last leg of her journey with Fred and Hooker. Pretty soon she'd find her new temporary home. The haulers stopped for a pit stop, and Abby jumped down and started exploring for a place to live.

Abby knew she had to be alert for mountain people. Any contact with man would be hazardous to her freedom. She continued heading toward the secluded forested area at the base of the Sierra Nevada Mountains. Abby crossed weed-strewn, broken, and pitted roads that hadn't seen a motor vehicle for forty years.

She was determined to find small game to quiet her stomach, which growled in angry protest at being empty. The sun beat down on the dark fur on her back. She was tired and thirsty and wanted only to find shelter under the cool trees in the distance.

Her human traits were shut down almost completely. It was now important to be canine—all dog and all instinct to survive in this wilderness.

As she walked in the heat, Abby's mind flashed back to the kitchen and the wonderful, magical food console in her parents' home. She had fond memories of her Mommy programming delectable meals, which instantly appeared.

An intense stomach growl broke her daydream, and she almost missed the mouse that scurried from one clump of weeds to the next, just feet in front of her.

Ruled by her hunger, Abby charged with renewed energy, tripped over the mouse and grabbed it in her jaws as she tumbled over. She jumped to her feet; her catch squirming and squealing in terror between her clenched teeth. She clamped down on the small rodent, killing it instantly. Her meal lasted only moments, and her stomach begged for more.

After she cleaned her face, she shook off the dust from her fall. Two rabbits hopped in the distance. Abby made a beeline in their direction, but they split up and hopped in wildly arcing circles, much too quick for her. She stopped pursuing them and panted as she looked around.

The trees were closer. She kept her goal in front of her: shelter and water, then food. Abby knew that she would have to drink and rest before she could catch game.

The sun was no longer directly overhead. Abby determined she would arrive at her destination in another half-hour. The journey was almost over, and she was exhausted. The ground was uneven and rock-strewn, and her paws were sore from the rocky terrain.

She had never used her muscles the way she did now. While at the lab, she had minimal exercise, walking or running on the walking path. When she escaped, the exertion from climbing the fence and falling to the ground had started a process that was grueling to every muscle in her body.

Abby was grateful for the ride on the hauler. It would have taken her weeks to arrive at the mountains if she had had to travel on foot.

After consulting maps in her Dot, she was determined to find a hiding place on this side of the Sierra Nevada because the other side of the mountains was more desert-like.

The big, beautiful pines, firs, oaks, and junipers were a welcome sight. She breathed in the forest's aroma. Abby gladly stepped under the trees and let her eyes adjust to the shade. Her ears stood high and twitched, becoming more alert as she cautiously made her way through the trees.

She had walked quite a distance when she heard and smelled fresh water nearby. Abby was so grateful when she approached the brook. It was only around three feet wide where she stood, and she noticed it varied in width in both directions. She looked into the water and then glanced around to make sure there were no hidden dangers she had not detected. She was out of her element in the wild and had to educate herself quickly to survive.

With her senses on high alert, Abby moved forward a few steps and stood in the cold water. Her feet were relieved by the flowing water swirling around her. She drank deeply. Abby then lay down and turned on her side and let the water flow on her caked and swollen scruff, cleansing her wound. After a few minutes she rose, shook off and followed the brook southward, taking a sip now and then.

Her nose twitched at all the new earthy smells of the forest. There was no evidence of man under the shelter of the trees, no odors, no discards from recent visits or years past that Abby had detected. She came across scat from animals she could not identify, and she trembled when she saw large piles.

Trapped in the glass house in the lab, Abby had watched documentaries about bears. She knew black bears lived in the Sierra Nevada and that they were big and dangerous and could run fast and climb trees. Abby did not want to come face to face with a bear just yet. She was too tired.

As the sun crept lower in the sky, Abby looked for a place to sleep. She decided she would spend the night in the shelter of the forest until she knew her surroundings. It was imperative that she make sure that humans would not cross her path. Any sighting would have the Tranquility Force combing the area for her.

Three trees that had grown together at their bases in a semi-circle formed a nice nest of pine needles and leaves on the ground in their protective curve. Abby sniffed to make sure that the nest didn't belong to another animal. She did not detect any pungent odors, so she stepped into the shelter and turned once and collapsed onto the natural bed. Her eyes were closed before her body landed, and she was instantly asleep.

~

"NUMBER TWENTY-THREE, how do you like the name Jerry?" Bill asked.

"Jerry," number twenty-three said. "My name is Jerry."

"Jerry is a good name," Rex said.

"Who is my father?" Jerry asked.

"Theoretically, William Bill Maxwell is your father, but Doctors Roberts and Sovesky will put in a claim to Daddy's patent," Rex said. "We will not let them usurp what is not rightfully theirs."

Bill was about to comment when his communicator dinged an incoming message. He tapped his communication device to take a quick glance. He sucked in a breath. "It's from Abby!"

Teresa rushed over to Bill and read the message. "Remind her not to come home."

Bill furiously typed. "I'm going to tell her to find a safe place to keep hidden. I think they'll continue a satellite search for another month or two."

"Will they be able to track her from the messages?" Teresa asked.

"Wise Owl uses my secret pinging transmission which bounces over thousands of networks. They'd never be able to discover the location with all that bouncing," Rex said.

"Let's tackle this patent issue and lay it to rest," Bill said. "This will be a good smokescreen. When we disappear, no one will suspect it has anything to do with Abby."

Teresa's face lit up as an idea formulated in her mind. She chuckled softly. "Bill, we're coming up on the ten-year anniversary of a couple of your prominent patents. Let's compile a press release. We can list patents and dates and even include visuals, as long as they don't disclose secret information," she said.

"That's a great idea!" Bill said. "Roberts and Sovesky would have a hard time trying to explain their patent claim."

"They would be crushed by the glory and praise of your accomplishments from both the public and the scientific community," Rex said.

Jerry was quiet and thoughtful. "If you wait to let them file their patent and then release your ten-year anniversary list, they will be caught in a snarl with the GNN and the World Guild," Jerry said. "My data and calculations support immediate termination, apprehension and a nasty public trial on GNN."

Bill rubbed his hands together in satisfaction. "Okay. We have a plan. Teresa and I will put together our media release. One of you will have to monitor all transmissions between the doctors and alert me when they have submitted their forms to the patent counsel.

"As soon as I know that their application has been presented to the committee, I will send the anniversary announcement to the GNN literalist for immediate release. Let's see them try to talk their way out of this," Bill said.

Teresa clapped her hands together. "Bill, we could send a special delivery announcement to each of the major factions at the patent office! Just think how it would look when the scientific officer is reviewing the patent claim, and he gets our special announcement!"

Bill hugged Teresa. "I can see this ending soon. Then I can resume the important work to get us out of here," Bill said. "Rex, do you think I should release their worm with some type of affirmative data so they think they have succeeded in wiping out my records?"

"That would be most beneficial," Rex said. He walked toward the front door with Jerry close behind. "We have to continue with our patrol. When you plant your data in the worm, check for a file that will give you the date that the Tranquility Force was scheduled to return for the spy."

Teresa squatted by Rex. She rested her hand on his back and patted him a couple of times. "Take care, Rex." She then turned to Jerry and patted his back. "Goodbye, Jerry."

Bill's hand was at the door sensor. "Rex, you and Jerry, be careful. You're involved in a dangerous game."

The door sensor released the lock, and the door popped open ever so slightly. Rex approached the door and scanned the exterior. He nudged the door open with his snout, and he and Jerry went out into the night.

SHEER EXHAUSTION CLAIMED Abby for several hours. The peaceful surroundings eased her tense muscles and allowed her to finally get some deep sleep. She woke in the middle of the night, feeling much more rested, and stretched fully. She left her newly found bed to relieve herself and to get a drink of water.

To be completely away from man and the comfort of everyday conveniences was a little unnerving. Abby knew she was unprepared to live in the wild, regardless of the hours she had spent in her glass prison watching documentaries on different animals and environments. She didn't know if she could live in total isolation. She missed talking and learning. She missed her Mommy and Daddy, and Rex.

With her senses alert, Abby drank at the brook. She returned to her hidden bed nestled in the trees and lay down. Abby didn't know what the future held for her or how long it would be before she could go to Texmexzona to rejoin her parents. She pondered whether Mommy and Daddy were still at home, or if they had escaped the spies and were safe in a new home.

On an impulse, she patched into the Wise Owl program and was surprised to see a message from Bill. She read his warnings. Instead of being sad, she was elated to know they were okay.

Questions and thoughts flew through her restless mind. Abby realized she had gone through technology withdrawal while on the run. Now she could communicate to find out what was going on in her former world.

She was lost in thought when a rustling noise caught her attention. Her ears stood straight up and twitched. She sampled the air with her wet nose. Abby smelled something, but she didn't know what type of animal it was. She quietly stood in her tree bed, still hidden from view.

As quietly as possible, Abby stuck her head outside of her hiding place and sniffed and looked in the direction of the noise. Something black and white foraged through the undergrowth. She accessed her database of information from her Dot and discovered that the creature was a skunk and that they used a very nasty spray on predators.

Abby ducked down into her treehouse. She didn't want to get sprayed! She stayed crouched, listening to the approaching skunk, and was fraught with nervous tension as the sound came nearer.

Suddenly, a little black and white face peered into her nest. The skunk knew she was there and was not afraid of her. Abby stayed still. The skunk touched its nose to her nose. Abby made a gesture of friendship; she licked his face. The skunk seemed to like that. It stepped inside Abby's den and made itself comfortable. Abby stood stock-still for a moment, not knowing what to do, and then she lay down beside the skunk, and they both went to sleep.

Morning arrived, and Abby woke to find her companion cuddled up in the curve of her belly. Abby carefully stood and stepped over the skunk and out of the tree enclosure. She headed off toward the brook and was startled to discover that the little skunk ran after her.

Abby stopped and waited for the skunk to catch up, and they walked in companionable silence to get a drink.

CHAPTER TWENTY-FIVE

The brook meandered for quite a distance. Abby and her new friend stood at the edge and satisfied their thirst with the cool, clean water. Abby walked in a semi-circle through the water and back to the shore out of habit from the hygiene she had been taught using the bathroom closet.

Then she realized how ridiculous this was because her home was now in the wild and no one would scold her if she had dirty feet. She wandered a distance away from the brook with the skunk on her heels. Abby sniffed the ground, found a good smell and relieved herself.

The skunk foraged for food and found a nice fat frog. Abby watched, with her stomach growling, as the skunk dispatched its meal with minimal effort. Abby made her way through the forest, ears standing high and nose twitching. Her senses were alert for the slightest movement of game.

She hadn't gone two hundred feet when a small creature darted along the ground. At first, she thought it was a chubby squirrel, but the scent was different. Abby took to the chase and caught her first marmot. She made her kill and ate with relish. The skunk approached as Abby ate, and she growled a ferocious warning. She was very hungry, and she was not willing to share her kill.

The skunk didn't seem offended. It foraged nearby and satisfied itself with a horde of larvae under a bed of leaves on the dank forest floor.

After she finished her meal, Abby cleaned her face, then returned to the brook and drank, her little buddy staying close by. She headed out into the forest toward the foothills to find a permanent home.

The forest could not provide a safe home for very long, and she knew she needed shelter where she could feel more secure. From watching documentaries, she learned caves were abundant, as all mountainous areas contained hidden nooks and crannies of some sort. She just needed to find one that was not difficult for her to get to in any type of weather, and with a location that allowed her to oversee all paths to her front door. And, of course, a cave that was vacant.

The skunk walked with Abby in companionable silence. They made their way through the forest. Abby tripped over roots and uneven ground, stumbled around dense prickly briars and thick vegetation.

They walked for quite a long time and Abby was growing tired and thirsty. The skunk veered off to the right. Abby stopped and watched and then followed. After a short distance, they came across a brook. It could have been the same brook, winding and twisting through the trees; Abby didn't know. She was just happy that her little friend found water.

A fish jumped out of the water close by, startling her. Abby carefully checked out the surrounding area with alert ears, nose, and her keen vision. She ran and jumped into the shallow brook in pursuit of the fish, but realized how futile chasing a fish was. She slipped and tripped while the fish jumped further away. Abby returned to the bank and shook off the water. She sighed in deep disgust at her fishing abilities. She took a drink and left the brook to find a place to nap.

AFTER SEARCHING THROUGH NUMEROUS FILES, Bill discovered that the Tranquility Force was scheduled to rendezvous with the worm spy at twenty-two hundred hours. He had just enough time to accomplish what was required. He studied the files and formats of data and embedded a false stream of information. He switched over to an old virtual system that he had used for storing patent material prior to constructing his new software vault. Bill began attaching the worm program to wipe out the old, useless files and system.

The worm program was twofold; it wiped out and confirmed the files that had been eliminated. Bill discovered that the program did not record the data in the files, just wiped them out. After the procedure was completed, he checked the worm to make sure everything was in place and then he brought the worm over to its point of origin—LAB323 electrical socket.

Grabbing the long tweezers, Bill placed the worm inside the hole in the wall. He knew it would take a while for the worm to get to the pickup area so he recruited a couple of his ant-wasps to haul the worm to the exterior of the house.

Bill conducted a satellite search for any Tranquility Force in the vicinity and set his security system to record every movement within a one block radius of the house. He also set system monitors to detect any satellite surveillance of his home from any of the 234 satellites in space.

Then, he sat back and watched the multiple screens showing different visuals.

Teresa came into the lab with a small tray holding two steaming cups of hot chocolate and a plate of cheese and crackers. "Did you get it all taken care of?"

"Oh, yes," Bill said. "All we have to do now is watch the show. Only twelve minutes until ETA," Bill pointed to a monitor. "They're already in place. Evidently, they don't have a signal set up between the worm and their system. Kind of stupid, if you ask me."

Teresa pulled up a chair and sat beside Bill. She sipped hot chocolate and nibbled on cheese and crackers while she stared at the wall of monitors.

"Look, Bill!" she said. She pointed to a monitor.

"Computer: show the northwest quadrant of the house, multiple views," Bill said as he jumped to his feet and barked the orders.

Four monitors showed visuals that changed every fifteen seconds. A Tranquility Force glider hovered nearby in a neighbor's backyard while a lone Tranquility Force enforcer hurdled over the fence between the houses and stealthily approached Bill and Teresa's house.

Bill and Teresa watched as the enforcer retrieved an electronic device from his pocket. He walked to the house, moved backwards and forwards, and finally detected the worm spy. The enforcer dug into his pockets and retrieved tweezers and a case, plucked the worm out of a niche in the exterior wall and encased it.

He then darted back to the fence, vaulted over and slipped inside the glider, and the Tranquility Force were gone.

Bill stood at the transfer surface and typed a message to Rex. "Son, the worm is in the apple." Bill then pulled up the dog-thought program and encrypted the message and sent it.

"Okay. Rex and Jerry will monitor all incoming and outgoing transmissions by either of the doctors," Bill said. "As soon as Rex or Jerry verifies that Roberts and Sovesky have submitted to the patent office, we'll send our anniversary announcement and watch the fireworks begin."

～

AN HOUR and twenty minutes later, a transmission arrived from Rex. Bill decoded it from dog-thought and read it to Teresa. "Patent application submitted. Proceed with the plan. Signed: Number One Son."

It was the ten-year celebration of the Dot, and the three-year anniversary of the PawBoard, although it was now unused due to the extinction of dogs. Still, it was one of the world's most remarkable inventions, and people loved it.

Around the world, people watched as Lilith used the PawBoard, and sponsors had her hawking their products. Bill knew that when this patent fraud emerged, people would be outraged.

The announcement listed Bill's many patents and inventions, including his original dog-bot, which was at the very top of the list, along with the dates of the patent, the long patent number, and Bill's original sketch. Teresa checked the names and electronic addresses against a master list of media outlets. She made an adjustment here and there and then was satisfied.

"Everyone is here. All the patent offices around the world, all network and media literalists, World Guild, GNN, and Global Health. Send it now," Teresa said.

"I just had a thought that we should include something to the effect that Abby was the last dog to use the PawBoard," Bill said as he faced Teresa. He laced his fingers through hers.

Bill put the finishing touches on the edited announcement,

and Teresa pointed out a misspelled word. When it passed her inspection, Bill sent it to the list.

Exhausted, they went to bed.

~

THE NEXT MORNING, they were inundated with communications from every literalist and agency regarding both Abby and the anniversary of the patents. There were also urgent communications from the science and technology review committee at the patent office about the application they were reviewing from the doctors. They demanded Bill's appearance.

Teresa went into the schoolroom and talked to all callers regarding Abby.

"Call Christovar," Bill commanded. The AMD stirred the flowing stream and gently blowing cherry-tree limbs. In a moment, the stream morphed into a stern face staring back at Bill. Christovar Secatski was one of the most respected and feared attorneys in WestUS. When he and any client walked into a courtroom, they walked out victorious.

A young, successful Russian prosecutor in his former life in St. Petersburg, Christovar put down some serious thugs in his day, but the twice-yearly car bombings that never made the news made it hard for him to get a lease on the new models. So, at thirty-five years old, he took his savings, moved to the US, and put himself through the night program at Brooklyn Law School.

His classmates soon classified him as mean, with an absurdist streak, and determined that he only liked animals, hated most people, especially other attorneys, whom he thought were imbeciles. They avoided him. He passed them all up on the bar exam and landed his first job with a prestigious law firm while the rest were still sending resumes.

"What trouble have you been causing, Maxwell?" Christovar boomed, his Russian accent faint from the years of US citizenship.

"You mean, who's been causing me trouble, don't you?" Bill asked slyly.

They smiled at each other.

"So, who are these scumbags that seem to have stolen your patent?" Christovar asked.

After twenty minutes of conferencing and passing files to Christovar, they concluded their call.

In a moment between communications, Bill's intuition kicked in like a punch in his gut. He sent an urgent message to Rex in dog-thought. He walked across to the schoolroom. Teresa was talking to a literalist, so he waited impatiently until the transmission was completed and the AMD switched the liquid moving picture back to a mountain stream.

"I just sent an urgent message to Rex and Jerry," he said. "They have to put their plan into action immediately. With all the publicity regarding the patents and the doctor's outright theft, the patent office may require that the dog-bots be confiscated."

"Oh, Bill!" Teresa said. She jumped to her feet and faced him. "I hope you're wrong. Rex surely would have thought about that, don't you think? He and Jerry would have planned—"

"I'm not sure," Bill said. He shook his head. "Hon, I've been summoned to the patent office. Christovar's going to meet me there. I may not be back until late."

～

THE LARGE CONFERENCE room was filling up as Bill and Christovar, both in formal robes of dark blue, settled into their seats at the oval table that comfortably seated twenty-four. Across from them and down four chairs, the doctors fidgeted.

Eight top-ranking scientists who served as the patent office's science and technology review committee, as well as several officials from the World Guild and two directors from GNN, appeared very serious in their formal burgundy robes that were worn only during serious public reviews. Once everyone was settled, the meeting came to order.

"We are here to discuss the serious issue of a case of patent theft," Xavier Dunfrey said as he gave a scathing glance to the doctors. His robe, braids, and medallions identified him as the top-ranking official from the patent office.

The committee compared Bill's original patent application, shown in holographic form in complete detail. They verified the filing date and official stamps on every page of Bill's patent and accompanying data, and even the name of the sworn patent officer who logged the patent.

"It appears that Mr. Biggibottom logged patent number 6426,893,457,966 dated January 17, 2068 by William Maxwell," Xavier said. His glance pierced Christovar's with questions.

"That is indeed my client's patent," Christovar replied. "I suggest you summon Mr. Biggibottom at once."

One of the committee members tapped on his holographic pad, requesting Biggibottom's presence. Several moments later, a burly man entered the room, hastily adjusting his slightly rumpled brown robe. He stood inside the door, unsure of what to do next.

Xavier waved Biggibottom over to the table to a vacant chair. "Mr. Biggibottom, I'm sure you're been informed of the case of suspected theft regarding Mr. Maxwell's dog-bot patent?"

"Oh, I saw that on an interdepartmental transmission," Biggibottom said. He then flushed bright red as he remembered he was not on the distribution list.

Several eyebrows rose in question, but Xavier ignored the slight infraction. "Yes," Xavier said. "That is the patent under discussion."

"I remember Mr. Maxwell's patent," Biggibottom said with some excitement. "That dog-bot design was ingenious, and I studied every circuit, bolt and system design."

"So, is it safe to say that you would be able to identify your signature and marks on each drawing and page of communication?" Christovar asked.

"Without a doubt," Biggibottom said.

Dr. Sovesky was pasty white while Dr. Roberts scowled.

Pulling up his holographic screen, Christovar craftily slipped one of the Doctors' false documents among the dozens of authentic documents from Bill's files.

Biggibottom touched the holographic screen viewing page after page. "Wait a minute," he said. He stood and examined the false document in detail. "This is not from the original filing."

Christovar smiled across the table at Xavier.

The full file of material submitted by Dr. Roberts and Dr. Sovesky was presented side-by-side with Bill's files for the committee members and Mr. Biggibottom to view. Bill was furious when he saw the blatant theft in front of everyone.

"It is acknowledged that these applicants have attempted to steal Mr. Maxwell's patent," Xavier said.

Everyone at the conference table concurred. A loud murmur of disbelief went around the table, and the members blatantly castigated the doctors with looks of disdain.

The senior official from World Guild tapped his messaging badge. "We have concluded our inquiry." A squadron of Tranquility Force enforcers came through the door.

"Arrest these men," the official stated. "I'm sure once you're finished digging, they will have much more to answer for."

"I can explain," Dr. Sovesky begged as he was dragged out of his chair.

"Shut up, you fool," Dr. Roberts snarled.

"If it wasn't for your greed, we wouldn't be in this fix," Dr. Sovesky said.

The conference was concluded, and the attendees stood and shook hands.

"I'm grateful that you remembered my patent, Mr. Biggibottom," Bill said as they shook hands.

"It's a thrilling invention," Biggibottom said. "I look forward to seeing your creation."

Xavier approached Bill and Biggibottom. "Expect your new gray robe in the morning, Mr. Biggibottom."

"Oh! Thank you, sir!" Mr. Biggibottom stammered. "I won't let you down."

"Indeed not," Xavier said. He turned to Bill and Christovar. "I'm happy that this turned out in your favor, Maxwell. Terrible shame to have thievery from high ranks."

AT ELEVEN-FORTY-FIVE THAT NIGHT, the kitchen door sensor disengaged as Bill let himself into the house. Teresa came down the hall to the kitchen, slipping her arms into her robe. Bill let out a huge sigh.

"I'm glad that's over with," Bill said.

Teresa pulled one of the kitchen chairs out and had Bill sit. She rubbed his shoulders.

"Let's get some sleep," Bill said.

~

"TURN ON GNN and let's see how this development has played out," Teresa said as she carried their hot chocolate from the food console to the kitchen table. Bill retrieved their breakfast plates from the counter. They sat at the table and started eating.

"GNN on," Bill commanded.

The liquid moving picture was replaced with the stern face of a literalist who reported the theft and Dr. Roberts' role in the disappearance of the last dog. Pictures of Abby, Lilith, and the puppies flooded the screen.

The front door announced visitors. Teresa went to the door and disarmed the security system. She opened the door and was happy to see Becky and Percy.

"We just watched GNN and wanted to come over," Percy said.

Teresa opened the door wider and let them in.

Bill walked into the living room and shook hands with Percy.

"I hope they string up those bastards in front of the Tranquility Force headquarters," Percy said. "Serve 'em right."

"Would you like to join us for hot chocolate?" Teresa asked. "We slept in."

They all moved to the kitchen. Bill worked the food console and got Percy and Becky hot chocolate, then they watched the screen as pictures of Lilith, Abby, the puppies, Bill's inventions, Bill, Teresa, Jimbo, and Becky and Percy flooded the screen.

And then the crowning moment that Bill and Teresa had waited for: Tranquility Force hauling a stony-faced Dr. Roberts away. Bill shut down the news as Dr. Sovesky was apprehended. He didn't have any emotional investment in watching the second man's fall.

CHAPTER TWENTY-SIX

W hen Percy and Becky finally left, Bill sat quietly on the sofa. Teresa joined him and put her arm across his shoulders. They sat in silence for several moments.

"I hope Dr. Roberts has a good memory. I promised him I would make him answer to the entire world for losing Abby," she said.

~

IT WAS TIME FOR A NAP. Abby dug a small cavity underneath a cluster of low bushes. She and her skunk-friend dozed, curled together in slumber. It was dark when Abby woke. The forest was teeming with nighttime insect sounds and the scurrying and scampering of various nocturnal creatures. Abby yawned. She listened and sniffed the air. She trembled at the unknown. The skunk got up and left the nest. Abby crawled out of the hole and stretched.

The gurgling brook beckoned to her parched throat. Abby

approached it cautiously, wary of dangerous predators such as mountain lions. A red fox was at the edge of the brook, and Abby heard its approach. The fox did not stay around to introduce itself.

Abby sniffed the air, got a drink, and left. She returned to her nest, approached it cautiously to make sure it was still vacant, and then settled down for the rest of the night. Sometime in the middle of the night, the skunk returned and snuggled up to Abby. They slept undisturbed.

In the morning, Abby and the skunk went in separate directions and hunted for their food. The skunk ate berries, larvae, and a few worms. Abby caught a squirrel and was happy to have food in her belly. She cleaned up, went to the brook for a drink, and headed toward the mountain. Abby's skunk-friend caught up with her, and they walked through the forest.

After two more days of the same routine, Abby finally came to the forest's edge. She and the skunk stepped out from under the shade of a cluster of trees into dazzling sunshine. The massive mountain range stood before her in all its glory. Abby had never been to the mountains before. The closest she had ever come was during her trip with Fred and Hooker.

She stood at the edge of the forest and stared at the majestic sight before her. She felt safe. Abby trotted away from the forest. Her skunk-friend dug in the dirt around rocks and uncovered some tasty insects. Abby glanced at her friend and knew they would have to part ways.

A large moving shadow appeared on the ground. Abby instinctively ducked down. Suddenly the skunk was airborne, screaming and spraying. Abby jumped to her feet and gave chase, barking furiously. She stopped as the shadow vanished. She stared in shock as a large raptor carried her friend away to an inevitable death.

Abby looked up at the sky for several long moments. She

whined at the loss of her little friend. She didn't know how long it would be before she had another companion. Now she worried that her barking might have been heard by mountain people secreted away from society. The UPC had stories about them, but Abby didn't know if they were true. She had watched a program that showed mountain people being rounded up and brought to government camps to help reintroduce them into society. According to the narrator, many of them escaped and secreted themselves in mountains and forests. She stood still, listening and sampling the air. All was quiet. She didn't feel particularly threatened.

The foothills had little paths around and between large, smooth rock surfaces. Abby started walking the paths, climbing and looking around. A little trickle of water flowed between some rocks and disappeared into the ground. Abby quenched her thirst and continued exploring. Her muscles were getting a workout as she climbed around rocks and boulders. She knew she would get fit when she found a place to live and settled into a routine.

A shadow under an overhang caught her attention, so she headed toward it. She discovered that the opening was too small. The closer she got to it, the more she detected a pungent odor. The cave was obviously occupied.

Keeping her senses sharp to find a vacant cave, she continued up the mountain. She didn't see any predators or other dangers. She was not in any place where she could protect herself, and she felt a little vulnerable. Abby saw a shadowed ledge jutting out over the mountainside. She headed in that direction to explore further.

The opening was three feet high at the midpoint and to the far-right side, hidden by wild, scraggly shrubbery-type plants that hung down from the canopy, was a narrow opening that looked about seven feet high. Abby cautiously sniffed the air as she climbed toward it. She stopped several feet away from the ledge and stretched her neck to sniff. She could not detect any scent from where she stood, so she approached the ledge from the side and sampled the air. No obvious odor came from within the cave.

Finally, she climbed onto the ledge, keeping to the side where the opening was no more than eight inches high. She stuck her nose inside. Her legs shook with fear. There was a faint scent, but Abby reasoned that time had washed the former occupant's smell away. She cautiously approached the midpoint and peered inside.

Nothing rushed the entrance.

With all the bravery she could muster, Abby stepped inside the shadowed interior of the cave and stood still, getting the feel of the place. After a full minute of trusting her instincts, she set out to fully explore the interior.

The cave snaked deep into the mountain and had a variable-height ceiling. There were spots where Abby could look up and not see the roof, and there were areas that were only four or five feet high. She found an old abandoned campfire, a book, a great pile of leaves, and a tattered backpack. Twenty or thirty feet away, around a corner, she came across a raggedy blanket. Not too far from the blanket was a human skull.

After a few more minutes of exploration, Abby returned to the blanket and picked up an edge in her teeth and dragged it back to the camper's room. She climbed onto the leaves and dropped the blanket. She used her toenails to spread it over the leaves, and then she stepped off the bed and admired her handiwork. Abby went to the book and studied the cover.

She nudged the cover open. She gently pawed the pages until the first page of print appeared. The copyright was from twenty-twenty, almost sixty-six years ago.

As she looked at the scene in the cave, she wondered if the

camper had been killed there, had an accident, or had been hiding out and starved to death. She would never know. Abby was grateful that he had hauled the leaves from the forest because she knew the dirt floor would get cold at nighttime and would be intolerable during the long winter months if she had to stay there that long.

Abby returned to the front of the cave. She squatted and peed at the entrance of the cave, and then she peed on the ledge and continued marking her territory to her satisfaction. Abby returned to the ledge and stood at the edge, looking out over the open area. She had an excellent view of the entire area all the way down to the forest.

It would be a long way to go to find game, but water was close by, and she was high enough to see the full sky over the treetops. She felt that her new home was safe and secure and would fare her well until enough time had passed where she could safely travel to TMZ.

Abby went back inside the cave. She looked around the floor and the walls. There were dozens of scratches on one wall: one line crossed through six vertical lines. She determined this was a calendar of sorts, or at least a method of counting days and weeks. Abby remembered the calendar lesson back home with her mother explaining how many days were in a week and how many days made a month. She stared at the wall for a moment. Then she went into the inner room and looked around the camper's meager possessions. She found an old marking tool half-hidden under a tiny pile of leaves and debris several feet from her bed.

She snatched up the marking tool and returned to the main room. Abby went to the opposite wall from where the camper's calendar was marked. She stood and placed her front paws on the wall and gripped the marking tool tightly in her jaws. She roughly scratched an A on the wall. She scrutinized the letter and wrote *b-b-y*. She jumped down, moved over a little bit, and jumped against the wall and planted her feet. She made one vertical line. This was Day One.

∼

MOMENTS after the clock face changed to two-fifteen, an odd sound woke Teresa. She sat up in bed and listened. She was pretty sure she heard a click of some sort. Her heart pounded, but she didn't want to wake Bill with some crazy foolishness. She sat with her eyes glued to the open bedroom door, half expecting to see Tranquility Force storm the room.

A low, dark form appeared in the doorway. Teresa let out a scream.

Bill shot out of bed, dragging bedding with him and stumbling for a second before he stood poised to fight. "What happened?" he asked. "What's wrong? Who's here?"

"I heard a noise, and then I saw something in the doorway," Teresa said.

"Calm down, honey. If anyone was here, they're blocks away by now," Bill said.

The low, dark form returned to the doorway.

"Rex?" Teresa said as she switched on the bedside lamp.

Rex stood in the doorway, swaying from side to side.

"Rex, how'd you get in the house?" Bill said. He crossed the floor and passed Rex. He hurried to the living area and the front door. It was closed. He checked the security system. All was sound. Perplexed, he returned to the bedroom.

Teresa was on the floor at Rex's side. He continued to sway.

"Bill, something's happened," she said. "I think Rex has been traumatized."

"What happened, buddy?" Bill asked as he dropped down

to the floor. "How'd you get into the house? The security system doesn't appear to have been breached."

"I duplicated the sequence to unsecure the system, and then I ran the locking sequence and secured the system after I entered the house. All is well."

"What happened?" Bill urged.

"Jerry and the pack were taken by the Tranquility Force and are being sent to the World Guild," Rex said. "Jerry has assumed the role of pack leader. He followed the plan."

"You've double-checked your systems for tracking and spyware?" Bill asked.

"I have determined that my systems and circuitry are in compliance with the security settings I established," Rex said. He continued to sway.

"Rex, there's something you are not telling us," Teresa said as she studied Rex. She scratched his ears. "If everything was followed according to the plan, why are you so upset?"

"Jerry sent a secret message," Rex said. He rested his chin on Teresa's shoulder. "He said that the dog-bot project would be discontinued. They may be thrown on the scrap pile."

"Theoretically, the dog-bots are mine," Bill said. "Dr. Roberts and Dr. Sovesky stole the patented idea, so even though they made working models, the World Guild can't decide to dispose of the pack unless I agree."

"I will be like Abby, the last of my kind," Rex said.

"It's too soon to worry about that." Teresa pulled Rex into a hug. She rubbed his chest for a moment.

"By now, the World Guild has every scrap of paper, every file, every transmission of information that either of the doctors ever made," Bill said as he got up and sat on the edge of the bed. "They will be swift in determining punishment."

"Rex, come with me," Teresa said. She stood and left the bedroom. "Let's get you settled in for the night."

"I do not sleep," Rex said.

"I know that, but you can have your circuits mimic sleep so you appear to be more doglike, which would include resting at night on a dog bed," Teresa said.

She entered the schoolroom and opened a cupboard. She pulled out Abby's old bed and set it on the floor.

Bill stood in the doorframe.

Rex walked up to the bed. "Was this Abby's bed?"

"Yes."

Rex stepped onto the bed and stood in the center.

"Can you lie down?" Teresa asked.

Rex turned in a circle as he had seen Abby do, and then he kneeled, similar to the motion a camel makes to lie down.

"Maybe I should work on those joints," Bill said. "Give you more fluidity of movement."

"That would be nice," Rex said.

"Okay. You can still be functional, but you now appear to be like a dog going to bed for the night," Teresa said.

"I am almost a real dog," Rex said.

"Good night," Teresa said. She and Bill left the schoolroom. The light turned off. Rex's LEDs appeared as two red beads in the dark room.

Teresa whispered to Bill. "Do you think everything will be okay?"

Bill grinned. "Yeah, Rex will calm down once he sees that the plan was infallible."

CHAPTER TWENTY-SEVEN

The ledge was awash in sunlight when Abby came out of the dark interior of the cave. She stood at the edge and looked out on the valley below and turned to observe the opposite direction. When she determined no threats, she stretched out on the ledge and sunned herself. It had been three weeks since her skunk friend had been snatched by the raptor. At first, Abby had watched the sky in fear of being grabbed. She finally decided it would have to be a pretty huge bird to haul her off the ground.

Hopping off the ledge, Abby trotted down her mountain. She drank from the trickling stream and enjoyed the sun on her back. Just as she was about to resume her routine down the path to the forest to hunt, a noise attracted her attention. Her head shot up, and she saw a Tranquility Force glider hovering in the sky.

"Hide!" someone in the forest yelled.

Abby shrank to the ground as she looked toward the forest where the voice came from.

"Get outta sight! They'll find you!" the voice hollered.

Gauging the distance, Abby knew she would not make the forest if she made a run for it. She flattened herself on the ground and looked around, scared. To her left were two jagged boulders with a dip between them.

The glider was heading in her direction. She leaped up and ran for the boulders and slammed her body into the small opening. The Tranquility Force glider zipped across the sky and hovered a few feet away. Suddenly, a badger made a mad dash down the path and disappeared into scraggly bushes. The glider hovered for a few more minutes, then turned and zipped off in the direction where it came from.

Abby shook in panic. She raised her head and carefully looked all around, but did not see the glider. Within moments, she jumped up and ran down the mountain to the shelter of the forest. She slammed through the brambles and underbrush and stumbled to a stop in front of a pair of large men's boots.

An old, weathered face with a scraggly beard looked down at her. He placed a finger over his lips, then pointed up. He turned and waved Abby to follow. More frightened than she had been in a long time, she followed the forest man. They walked in silence for ten minutes, the man hardly making a sound as he traveled through the forest with the tangled roots, vines, and shrub-like clumps of vegetation that was hazardous to walking.

The man stopped at a thick group of trees. Abby looked carefully at the trees and discovered that a small house was hidden under a clever forest-material umbrella. The forest man opened the almost hidden door and waved Abby to follow him. She looked around in fear for a moment, then entered the house.

"You almost got caught," he said. "You've got to be careful. The Tranquility Force comes by here every once in a while, lookin' for us mountain folks."

"Are you going to turn me in?" Abby said, filled with alarm.

"Could've done that weeks ago," he said.

"I didn't know anyone lived out here," Abby said. "I've never picked up your scent or anyone else's."

"We're careful," he said. "Don't want to be forced to live in no city and be under the thumbs of the government."

"What's your name?" she said.

"Jeffers," he said.

"My name is Abby," she said.

"Pleased to meet ya," Jeffers said. "We watch you all the time."

"There's more of you out here?" Abby asked.

"'Bout two dozen of us 're scattered throughout the area," Jeffers said. "There's injuns out here too. You thirsty?"

Jeffers went to a round wooden cask and removed the cover. He grabbed the ladle that hung from a hook on the side of the cask and looked around. He spotted a broken cup, grabbed it, then ladled water into it and placed it on the dirt floor.

Abby stretched her neck and sniffed the water. She took a few steps and drank the cool water. "Thanks, Jeffers. I better go hunt now."

"Me and some of the boys'll see which one of us 'll get the hide from your breakfast," Jeffers said.

Abby noticed a pile of assorted small animal skins on an upturned bucket. "Are those from my hunting expeditions?"

"Yup."

"Wow. I'm glad you're putting them to good use."

"You be alert. That badger might not be around next time," Jeffers said.

"I'll be more careful," Abby said as she stepped out of his door and disappeared into the forest.

~

ABBY'S newly developed routine made up of hunting during the day, exploring the surrounding area, bathing occasionally, napping, and going to bed after the sun set. Sometimes she deviated and stood inside the mouth of the cave, looking out into the night. She wanted to know about her neighbors and their habits.

The first cave, with the powerful odor, was inhabited by a badger with a nasty personality. Abby thought that he was most likely the one who fooled the Tranquility Force into believing that he was the animal they saw scurrying down the mountain.

Further up the mountain lived a very large colony of bats. Abby also saw raccoons, owls, and an opossum family from her ledge, but she didn't know where they lived. She had seen one eagle soaring in the sky and several hawks. She didn't know which one had grabbed her friend.

When hunger dictated hunting, Abby's diet was composed of squirrels, marmots, which were actually ground squirrels, jackrabbits (when she could catch one), long-eared chipmunks, blackberries, strawberries, blueberries and nuts. She had grown lean and muscular, and she could charge up and down her mountain from her ledge to the forest with firm dexterity.

Sometimes she had to block out the memories of Mommy and Daddy and Rex because she felt sad and lonely. Abby stopped watching the movies of her canine mother and family that were in her secret Dot. She longed for her family. She longed for conversation, learning, and kisses and hugs. The forest seemed to have swallowed Jeffers.

~

THE SUN WARMED HER, and Abby sighed loudly as she lay on the ledge. Her calendar showed many scratches on the wall of the cave. She wondered how many more she would make before she could safely journey to TMZ. Abby got up, shook off, turned in a circle and flopped down on her other side to allow the sun to heat up her cool fur. She smacked her lips two or three times and snorted softly.

Just as she was ready to doze off, a howl sounded in the distance. Her head popped up in wonder, and she was on her feet in a split second. She listened intently and sampled the air toward the call. Several moments passed in tense silence as Abby waited to hear another howl.

It came again.

With lightning speed, Abby raced off the ledge and bounded down her mountainside to the floor of the foothills. She ran at full throttle toward the unknown voice.

Another howl wailed, closer.

Unable to withhold her excitement, Abby barked in response. She slowed her pace and searched the horizon and the surrounding area for the animal. She stopped for a moment and again sampled the air. She lifted her little snout and wailed a calling.

And then she saw him.

A gray wolf approached, snarling viciously. He and Abby circled each other, tails raised and bushed, ears flattened, the hair standing up on their backs. She matched his growling. He stopped snarling and sniffed her. She wagged her tail, and he followed suit. He was much larger than Abby, standing at least eight inches taller, and his coat was dark gray and white with some black undercoating.

After so many weeks of isolation, Abby beamed with happiness, and excitement bubbled forth. "My name is Abby. Who are you?" she said.

The young wolf took off running, tail between his legs. He stopped several yards away and stared warily at Abby.

"Oops," she said as she realized her mistake. He didn't have a Dot. He was wild. To ease his fear, she whined in dog-talk.

He cautiously returned to within a few feet of her, stretched his neck, and sniffed.

She wagged her tail.

The wolf came closer. He wagged his tail.

They stood facing each other. Abby smiled and her eyes lit up. She was exuberant to discover another canine. He playfully lunged. Abby took off running. He pursued. They romped and played, chasing each other.

The wolf and Abby ran side by side for a while, and then they slowed down to catch their breath. Abby headed back toward her mountain home. He walked with her. They stopped and drank from the trickling stream of water, then continued to climb to her cave.

Abby bounded up onto her ledge. The wolf approached cautiously. Abby lay on the ledge and watched him. He finally stepped onto the ledge and looked around. He joined her in the sunlight, lying down, facing her.

CHAPTER TWENTY-EIGHT

Bill looked around as he and Christovar sat at the half-moon table on the gallery floor in High Court. Their table was closest to the panel of Truth Seekers, formerly known as jurors.

Teresa, Becky, and Percy were allotted front-row seating immediately behind Bill and Christovar, which gave cause for grumbling from the sardine-packed gawkers.

Having never experienced High Court before, Teresa, Becky and Percy whispered to each other as they took in the imposing room and all the spectators that piled in.

Doctors Roberts and Sovesky, in drab gray jumpsuits with a thin copper-colored band around their necks that Teresa recognized as what Dion and the landscapers wore. The doctors sat at similar tables with their own legal representatives. Off to the side, and in his Tranquility Force uniform, Captain Simon Day sat with a man beside him.

Dr. Roberts' attorney stood and approached Christovar, hand outstretched. Christovar stared down the attorney who slunk back to his chair.

"When a dog shakes hands, he means it," Bill quoted. He remembered when he was a very young man and had met Christovar when he needed an attorney to defend one of his patents. The quote, he learned from other attorneys who had worked opposing sides with the Russian, was a Christovar original. When he offered his hand, you were a friend for life.

∿

ABOVE AND TO the left of the Truth Seekers' glass enclosure was where the judge's suspended platform sat. Client tables were on the floor of the gallery. The testimony box was a glass container on a power pedestal to enable the box to elevate to the judge's or the Truth Seekers' level. The top of the testimony box was equipped with TRFTS ventilation ducts and antidote dispensers.

People with "special privileges," such as community leaders, wealthy people and business owners, sat in a viewing area separated from the hordes of people vying for a seat in the stacked gallery seating.

Several Tranquility Force enforcers, in full riot gear, stood in conspicuous places in the gallery, close to the exits. The room buzzed with excitement and chatter as the public gossiped about the criminals, attorneys, the Maxwell's, the judge and anyone else relevant to the trial.

The media room was packed with literalists and journalists from all major and minor factions of print, digital and live media from around the planet. Jostling was evident through the glass partition.

The High Court gong reverberated twice.

"Eek!" Becky squeaked in fright and jumped off her seat. Teresa pulled her back to the hard bench. Teresa, Becky and Percy snickered, barely controlling themselves. A hush went through the entire chamber, and then everyone stood and looked respectfully toward the judge's platform.

Judge Houstus Growarth, a barrel-chested eighty-year-old with a long memory, stepped off the elevator and stood in front of his chair. His bald head shone, and his glasses sat near the end of his well-endowed, red-veined nose. He looked directly at the doctors and scowled, then he shifted his gaze upon Bill and Christovar before he sat.

The entire room then sat. The doctors' attorneys had a brief powwow behind their client's backs.

"Not good," was their exchange.

Christovar smiled and winked at Bill.

"Do you know this judge?" Bill whispered to Christovar.

"He was one of my vodka customers when alcohol was banned for a decade back in the 2040s," Christovar said.

"This is a very serious day," Judge Growarth exclaimed. "When one of our trusted governmental workers falls from grace and commits a crime, it is a crime against all of mankind, not just the person or persons wronged."

The judge put his beady-eyed stare straight at the doctors, then his gaze moved to Christovar and Bill, then the Truth Seekers.

"What makes this so bad is that not one, but two of our trusted servants are accused of fraud, conspiracy and embezzlement for their theft of William Maxwell's dog-bot creation," the judge said. He looked at the captain with disdain. "We will also examine the actions of Captain Simon Day regarding this case."

Captain Day squirmed under the scrutiny.

The judge faced Bill directly. "Don't worry, Mr. Maxwell, we will get this sorted out." Judge Growarth looked at Christovar. "Mr. Secatski, present your case."

Christovar stood and approached a holographic pad that

appeared in front of the attorney's table. His fingers flew over the keys as he queued up his documentation which appeared in 3-D overhead, triangulated, for the judge, attorneys, Truth Seekers, media, special invitees, and the stacked and packed gallery to see clearly.

"As you see," Christovar stated, "we have provided the original patent materials, the recent authentication papers from the patent office's science and technology review committee, the spyware that Mr. Maxwell retrieved from his residence with the order to wipe out his patent files and the doctors' application."

"We are ready to hear the explanation from the doctors," Christovar said as he turned to face their table.

Two Tranquility Force stepped forward and approached the doctor. "Dr. Roberts, you will peacefully accompany the Tranquility Force to the testimony box," the judge ordered.

Dr. Roberts appeared defeated as he stood. Each enforcer took one of Dr. Roberts' arms in their iron-vise grip and they escorted him to the glass box and secured him inside. One of the Tranquility Force enforcers pressed buttons on a keypad on the exterior of the testimony box. The TRFTS mist slowly dispensed inside the glass box, and the doctor's knees gave out. He sank to the floor.

"Dr. Roberts?" Judge Growarth asked. "Explain to this court, the Truth Seekers and Mr. Maxwell how this business got started, what your participation was and your intentions."

"Thaaa Billlll Maswall alllwaze getts evvvryyything," Dr. Roberts said. Even under the influence of the TRFTS, the venom was unmistakable.

The entire courtroom hung on Dr. Roberts' every slurred, condemning word throughout his lengthy testimony. After nearly two hours, the judge released him from the testimony box. The Tranquility Force released the antidote, then they put on protective face masks and gloves and escorted Dr. Roberts back to his chair.

The TRFTS had not worn off completely, and the doctor slid off his chair onto the floor. His attorney made no move to help his client.

Cameras flashed from the media box as Dr. Sovesky was hauled to the testimony box. He appeared devastated as the door closed behind him and the mist stole his reasoning and ability to lie. After forty-five minutes, it was apparent to the judge and everyone else who the mastermind was, and Dr. Sovesky was released from the box where his experienced attorney strapped him in his chair with the appropriate tethers.

Next up, Captain Day had his time in the box. It became obvious that the captain had excessive credits from Dr. Roberts' scheme. The captain had abused his Tranquility Force position to intimidate and carry out private assignments for the doctor.

The Truth Seekers busily typed on their holographic keypads. After twenty minutes, Judge Growarth's holographic screen lit up.

Grasping hands, Teresa and Becky sat on the edges of their chairs as they waited for the judge's pronouncement.

Sitting ramrod straight, Bill gripped the edge of the table in front of him.

Judge Growarth silently read the verdict, pressed a button, and a large GUILTY appeared in 3-D where Christovar had presented his case.

A loud murmur of satisfaction ran through the gallery. Teresa, Becky, and their friends rejoiced. Teresa stood and wrapped her arms around Bill's shoulders and kissed him on the cheek. He clasped her arms and hung on, relieved.

"Get your client off the floor," Judge Growarth snapped to Dr. Roberts' attorney over the ruckus in the gallery.

The attorney jumped to his feet, pulled the chairs away

from the table, and dragged Dr. Roberts onto the chair. He shoved the chair up to the table, wedging the doctor securely.

"Quiet down now. I will have order in this court!" Judge Growarth warned the gallery of spectators as he banged the gavel. The sound reverberated throughout the room. "Doctors Roberts and Sovesky, you are hereby found guilty by the High Court Truth Seekers. Your case was reviewed in careful detail with clear documentation provided by Mr. Maxwell and the patent office. Your own testimony concluded your guilt.

"While I would consider it an honor to sentence you for these crimes, your future hinges on the World Guild Tribunal who will hear the case of Aberdeen Tallulah Maxwell-Smythe, the dog-child of the Maxwell's that you illegally took into custody."

A loud grumbling of unrest rose from the spectators as the judge addressed Abby.

"Quiet, or I shall have the gallery cleared," the judge stated. The gallery became quiet. "The World Guild Tribunal, which consists of one high-ranking official from each of the two-hundred and four nations, will convene on Monday. You will remain in custody with the Tranquility Force until your fate is determined."

"In the matter of Captain Simon Day," the judge directed his gaze to the captain, "Captain Day shall be stripped of his privileges as a captain of the Tranquility Force and be suspended for 120 days with subsistence pay."

The gong rang twice. The judge stood.

"This proceeding has concluded," he stated. "Mr. Secatski, please take a moment to stop by my chambers." With that, the judge stepped into the elevator and disappeared behind the closed doors.

The Tranquility Force hauled the doctors away. An official confronted Captain Day, and they left the courtroom together.

The attorneys scuttled through the masses of people who rushed to give their congratulations to Teresa, Bill, Becky, and Percy. Christovar and Bill shook hands.

"Best laid plans..." Christovar said.

"Thanks for presenting the case," Bill said. He swiped his wrist across a postage-stamp sized credit reader Christovar presented and paid the one hundred thousand credit fee for services.

"Now, let me see what Growarth requires," Christovar said as he slapped Bill on the back and headed toward the doors. The gallery crowd swallowed Bill and Teresa with hand-shaking, back-slapping, and hugging until the Tranquility Force intervened and cleared the room.

MAXWELL INDUSTRIES WAS alight with many of the employees and their families and friends celebrating the court victory.

Slinking over to a sofa in the Special Projects lobby, Teresa sank into the cushions, followed by Becky.

"My mind is a constant buzz," Becky said. "I'm so tired. I can't imagine how you and Bill feel, or how you came through this ordeal with all your faculties!"

Teresa patted Becky's hand. "It wasn't easy for me, but Bill is very focused. I'm not looking forward to next week."

THE SMALL PRIVATE room was off-limits to most employees. Bill conferred with Angelica, Toby, and Sam, his top leaders, as they sat around a small conference table.

"After next week's ordeal is over, Teresa and I are going to take a sabbatical," Bill stated. "We feel the need to get away and allow time to heal from the tremendous losses we have experienced."

Angelica appeared stricken. "You're okay, aren't you?"

"Of course," Bill said. "We're not going off to kill ourselves, just to recuperate. We need some time alone together."

"How long will you be gone?" Toby asked. He leaned in toward Bill, his anxiety visible.

"Just a couple of months," Bill said. "One of the reasons Maxwell Industries is an employee-powered company is that if I get hit by a glider or take a sabbatical, the organization will survive."

Uneasy glances passed among the group in the room.

"Bill, you'd tell us if you wanted out of the company, wouldn't you?" Sam asked. The oldest among the group, Sam kept the business running smoothly with a sharp perceptiveness on all the financials.

Everyone faced Bill. "Look," Bill said. "We've got some incredible projects in the works. If I didn't think my trusted team could bring them to market, I'd hang it up. We're going to have great success."

He placed his hand on Sam's shoulder. "Stop worrying about me. Teresa and I are going to do some traveling for relaxation, and we're going to get our heads straight."

"Okay," Angelica said. "Make sure you share your itinerary with me so I can customize your travel experience."

PRACTICALLY EVERY CHANNEL on the UCP was running trial footage. Teresa, Becky, Percy, and Myra-June flipped from channel to channel. Literalists reported that Dr. Sovesky wasn't assigned to the lab when Abby escaped. Interviews with random citizens were rife with venom—Sovesky was still considered evil—he stole from the creator of the Dot and the PawBoard. More than one irate citizen suggested that the doctors be confined to an old wooden stock from the Colony days on the World Guild lawn where the public could dish out punishment.

"Oh! Turn back one channel," Myra-June commanded. "Did you see that? Some guy is actually building one of those stock things. Like he'd ever get his hands on either of the doctors."

"People don't really care about what Sovesky did," Teresa said. "They want Roberts' blood."

A literalist from GCAUGHT stirred up tensions even more. GCAUGHT found every nugget about Dr. Roberts and splayed the news across the screen twenty-four-seven.

Dr. Roberts lost the last dog. GCAUGHT focused on the fact that the world had first lost Lilith, the pioneer canine that talked with the aid of a Dot, and then that same world-famous dog introduced the PawBoard to the global community. She was loved, adored, and mourned.

Then the hateful doctor had seized Abby, Lilith's puppy, Bill and Teresa's dog-child, the last dog in existence known to mankind, and he lost her.

GCAUGHT splashed scenes of people from all over the planet amassed outside the World Guild headquarters in Washington DC on the day of the trial, ready to tear Dr. Roberts apart.

"Even though the doctors were stripped of their government jobs and their personal fortunes," the literalists said, "and have been sent to a rehabilitation center for assessment prior to the tribunal next week, the proposed "reintroduction therapy" did not satisfy the general world population."

Footage showed Dr. Sovesky begging to be distanced from

Dr. Roberts. "I had nothing to do with Abby," he whined to the literalists from every media organization, to no avail.

No one cared about his stealing or other felonious actions.

THE WORLD GUILD Tribunal gathered in the large, round room, thought to be the safest room on the planet with its ten-foot-thick walls reinforced against any nuclear, biological or chemical threat, beneath the world capital system. Men and women, in their official purple and gold robes with embroidered olive leaves, assembled quietly and waited for the tribunal secretary to begin the proceedings.

The well-stocked witness room, next to the rotunda, provided food, beverages, and entertainment for sequestered witnesses. Bill paced in the witness room, waiting to be called into the rotunda. He noticed that all the sequestered witnesses were on edge.

"Bill, sit down and be still," Teresa said from one of the many sofas.

He sat beside her, grasped her hand, and let his shoulders relax.

Carole and Gene, along with Larry and a couple of other lab technicians, fidgeted. The cleaning crew kept to themselves.

After several minutes, Carole stood and approached Teresa. "Mrs. Maxwell, my name is Carole Perkins. I was Abby's psychologist at the facility."

Teresa stood. "You're the one who administered the IQ tests?"

Bill looked Carole over. He stood.

Carole's voice quivered with emotion. "She's amazingly intelligent, Mrs. Maxwell. I'm so sorry I was careless with her enclosure."

Carole looked around the room surreptitiously, then whispered, barely audible, "I don't think for one minute she's dead. I think Rex lied."

Carole reached out and clutched Teresa's hand. They were both on the verge of tears. Bill put his arms around both and dragged them down to the sofa where Teresa and Carole silently cried.

A decorated enforcer opened the door. "Mr. and Mrs. Maxwell? Come with me, please."

Teresa composed herself as Bill gently drew her to her feet and they left the room.

THE ENFORCER ESCORTED Bill and Teresa into the rotunda and settled them at a separate table with comfortable chairs. Teresa sat as the tribunal secretary inclined his head to her and Bill, acknowledging their presence. Their table was directly in front of the tribunal members' many tables. A holographic screen and one keypad were in front of them.

"This tribunal must preside over a very grave matter," the tribunal secretary said. His face was fraught with great sadness. "Before you are the most complete collection of data from the moment the poison was released from Xavier Labs last year, the recorded numbers of the dead humans, canines, felines and other animals from around the planet and information about Abby's escape and presumed death."

"What about the other dogs that died at the facility?" the Italian member asked.

Bill and Teresa stretched their necks to see the Italian who was three tables back.

"No blame is being placed on the facility or Dr. Roberts for the death of the three surviving canines at the facility," the tribunal secretary stated. "Let the record show that the three canines died of the poisoning. Shall we begin?"

The room became quiet as all the members and Bill, and Teresa began the grueling task at hand. All that was heard was the sound of breathing, along with the tapping of fingers on the holographic key pads to progress data from one screen to the next on the individual holographic screens, which echoed in the cavernous room, along with note-taking.

Sixteen hours later, the members adjourned and Bill and Teresa were escorted out of the door to the witness' overnight area. The next morning the men and women entered the room and took their seats. Bill and Teresa were escorted to their table. They all resumed sorting through all the scientific data, reports, news files, and interviews. This continued for three more days.

On the fourth day, after all the members and Bill and Teresa were seated, Dr. Roberts was escorted into the room by six decorated Tranquility Force enforcers. He wore a clean gray jumpsuit and the ever-present copper collar.

Two-hundred and four pairs of eyes, along with Bill and Teresa's, stared at Dr. Roberts waiting for the key questions to be answered: Why had the last four dogs been confiscated? Who ordered this and to what purpose?

When Dr. Roberts finally capitulated, he appeared to shrink and age. He faced the tribunal, avoiding looking at Bill or Teresa. "It was my intention to save the canine species by using advanced artificial reproduction methods," he said. "The first three died from the poison. We tried everything to save them. Abby was... I never suspected her superior intelligence and ability to plan, process, and implement such a sophisticated escape." He bent over, hands to his face, and sobbed.

When he gathered his wits, Dr. Roberts explained in detail what he suspected happened. He showed pictures of the old oak tree with the bloodied limb, and Abby's Dot found buried in the ground. He presented reports from the dog-bots' two-day search, and then his decision to call off the search when her trail disappeared.

After three hours of testifying, Dr. Roberts was led away to a holding room where he collapsed onto a cot. Carole was called forth to testify. She admitted she had been careless and distracted and did not verify that the door of Abby's enclosure was secure.

Other witnesses were brought forth one at a time, and their testimony was heard and recorded.

After the last witness, the tribunal proceeded to evaluate the chain of events, all testimony, and their view of Dr. Roberts' motives. At the end of the proceeding, the tribunal secretary adjourned the members while he finalized the conclusions.

The members filed out. Bill and Teresa stood and waited for the Tranquility Force to escort them out the door. The tribunal secretary pressed a key.

"Mr. and Mrs. Maxwell, before you are the prepared statements of this tribunal that will be released to the media," the tribunal Secretary said.

Bill and Teresa sat and read the tribunal's conclusions.

- The World Guild Tribunal concurred that Dr. Roberts had malicious intent to gain from his success of the canine reintroduction program.
- If the program were indeed a success, the doctor would be publicly glorified, which would increase his stature and his payment structure within the World Guild.
- The patent case was reviewed in detail. The tribunal determined this was outright theft with cause for immediate termination, stiff fines, and lengthy incarceration.

- Of the two-hundred four voters, the vote was one hundred ninety-eight in favor of indefinite incarceration with limited, supervised access to electronics.

"While I know this is no consolation and won't bring Abby back," the tribunal secretary said, "you should be comforted to know that two hundred of the members had lost canine or feline children."

∽

IN THE DAYS THAT FOLLOWED, Bill licensed dog-bots to the Tranquility Force for law enforcement. He also licensed two companies to produce dog-bot "children".

"Jerry's future is secure," Rex said. "He won't get thrown on the trash heap."

"He's the new pack lead and very important to the Tranquility Force," Bill said. "I'm glad it all worked out."

"Maxwell Industries will be busy with upgrades to the dog-bots that the doctors couldn't work out," Teresa said.

"I've lost valuable time because of this patent mess," Bill said as they walked into his home lab. "Now I can get back to work on the camouflage reflective formula. Rex, I'm going to feed the data to you. See what you come up with. This formula has been in the vault for a long time. We made a small batch; only a vial's worth, about a decade ago, and if we could mass produce it for a spray, it would be perfect for our exit."

The transfer surface came to life as Bill pulled up the files. One monitor filled with data: text, scientific formulas, diagrams, drawings, tables of numbers, and color codes. Bill lifted Rex onto the transfer surface and positioned him to receive files.

"There you go, buddy. Maybe you can figure things out," Bill said.

The files completed uploading to Rex's memory banks, and Bill lifted Rex off the table and settled him on the floor.

Rex walked over to his dog bed, turned three times and went down on his knees, and got comfortable. "I'll sleep on it," he said.

"Do you think she's made it to TMZ yet?" Teresa asked as she stood beside Bill at the transfer surface.

"No," Bill said, shaking his head. "I think she's still holed up somewhere, biding her time. Remember, we told her to lie low for a couple of months."

"I have terrible dreams of her being sick or hurt, or even dead," Teresa said.

"I know, hon," Bill said as he pulled Teresa into his arms. "Our dog-child is out there somewhere, and we can't even get to her because of the satellites. We wouldn't even know where to look. She could be anywhere." They hugged and rocked each other silently.

The security system sprang to life. "Automatically entering code red," the computerized voice announced. "Attempted breach from outside sources."

Bill and Teresa sprang apart.

Rex was off the dog bed in a flash. He rushed out of the room. He returned momentarily. "All entrances remain secure."

"Good work, Rex. Computer, discover sources," Bill commanded.

The large screen showed a Tranquility Force glider over their house.

"What could this possibly be about?" Teresa said.

"It's one of the reasons that a place like TMZ exists," Bill said. "The people who live there just want to live in peace and don't want to be spied on."

"Tranquility Force scanning in progress," security announced. "System secured."

A message came through from the Tranquility Force glider.

We have determined that your residence is free from illegal spyware.

The glider flashed its lights and took off.

"Do you think they will leave us alone now?" Teresa asked.

"Possibly, but I wouldn't count on it," Bill said.

CHAPTER TWENTY-NINE

The big pile of leaves dipped into a well where Abby and the wolf slept. Every morning the sun rose and cast shadows across the inner room of the cave. The old blanket was in tatters from Abby and the wolf scratching it and then turning in their circle patterns prior to settling down.

"Good morning, Apollo," Abby said.

Finally used to Abby talking and calling him a name, Apollo yawned, stood and stretched. He shook himself of leaves and twigs, turned to Abby and licked her face. Then he stepped out of the bed and walked to the doorway of the inner room.

Abby hopped out of the bed of leaves and shook the stragglers off. She joined Apollo at the cave doorway, sampling the air. Then they both left the cave to start their day.

"I DON'T UNDERSTAND how I could have created this tiny batch that worked perfectly," Bill said in a nasty tone. He held the vial to the light. He stared at the blue liquid as if it would divulge its secret. "I can't seem to replicate the solution into a large batch."

Teresa stood at his side, arms crossed tightly at her chest as she looked over his shoulder. Rex did not comment from the dog bed. His system was still churning Bill's program, and he had not found a workable solution yet.

"You've run an analysis of the formula in the vial?" Teresa asked.

"Dozens of times and right from this very vial where it's stored," Bill said.

"Have you recalibrated your equipment to make sure everything is working properly?" Teresa asked, her voice rising. "Maybe something is off, and it isn't picking up all the ingredients."

Rex left the dog bed. "Allow me to test the equipment, Daddy."

At his wits' end, Bill looked at Rex for a long moment. Finally, he walked to a lab table. "Come on, buddy."

Rex walked over to the table. Bill lifted him and placed him on the table. Rex extended a connector from a small compartment in his right shoulder into a port on the piece of equipment Bill placed him in front of. Rex' inner workings clicked and whirred as he tested the equipment.

Fifteen minutes passed as Bill and Teresa waited for Rex to complete testing.

"What's taking so long?" Bill asked. He turned to Teresa. "It shouldn't take this long. Something must be wrong."

"Rex is thorough," Teresa said. "When he's satisfied with his results, he'll let you know."

Another ten minutes passed. Bill went back to the transfer surface and keyed in information and pulled up a couple of files. He sat and studied the data before him.

"I've checked and double-checked and cross-checked every ingredient so many times I can't see the words or the numbers anymore," he said, discouraged. "I know this is a perfect formula. The solution worked once. I don't understand why it won't work again."

Rex's connector disengaged from the piece of equipment and slid back inside the compartment in his right shoulder. Bill and Teresa hurried over to Rex, anxious for his report.

"Daddy, I ran a complete diagnosis on this piece of equipment and discovered a slight problem. I have corrected it," Rex said. "You should run the formula one more time, increasing sodium hydrogen carbonate by one microgram."

"Baking soda?" Bill asked. He and Teresa stared at Rex, speechless, for several seconds.

"The formula is off by one microgram of baking soda?" Teresa asked, stupefied. "And then it will work?"

"According to my calculations, with the correction as stated and my adjustment to this piece of equipment, the formula is viable," Rex said.

Bill grabbed Rex off the table and held him tightly. "You know what this means, old boy? If this solution is successful, we can go to TMZ and wait for Abby."

He settled Rex on the floor.

"I miss Abby-dog," Rex said.

"Let's let Daddy work, shall we?" Teresa said as she stooped and scratched Rex's ears.

Rex returned to his dog bed, and Teresa left the lab.

"Rex, the transport glider is fifty-three-foot-long, one hundred-two inches wide, and a hundred thirty-two inches high," Bill said as he walked over to the transfer surface, opened a file and perused the contents. "How many gallons of the camouflage solution are we going to need to cover the entire surface?"

The stillness in the room was displaced by Rex's innards as they clicked and whirred while calculating the problem. "Twelve gallons, three quarts, and one-half pint will be required for one coat," he claimed after a full thirty-seven seconds.

"Okay." Bill went about making a list of the materials he would need. "I'm going to make a pint for this trial, Rex. Then I'll have to acquire the supplies for the entire production."

Staring vacantly for a moment, he thumped his chin with his fingers. "I need to add a quick-drying element to the solution so it will dry instantly and won't streak. Can you factor that in, Rex?"

More clicking and whirling sounds as Rex went to work on the added ingredient. "I've updated your files to include mineral oil, octyl epoxy tallate, and cyclopentasiloxane."

"Great, buddy."

Donning a white lab coat, Bill then opened the door to the refrigerated closet where bulk quantities of chemicals were stored. He placed several containers on a cart and rolled them into the main lab.

Over the next few hours, Bill created the cloaking solution. He measured each component precisely and replicated the process that had been successful years earlier. Stirring, heating, and cooling every step carried out meticulously.

The last phase consisted of a resting period of two hours, and then the formula would be ready to test.

TWO RABBITS RAN in haphazard circles as Abby and Apollo chased down their breakfast. They almost crashed into each other chasing their prey, but they got breakfast.

After they cleaned up and drank at a stream, they romped

and played in a meadow. A little black bear cub rushed out of the high grass to play with them.

"Go home to your mother," Abby said. She was startled as the youngster chased and called out to her in bear-talk.

Apollo was instantly alert.

Moments later, fresh out of hibernation, the mother bear barreled down on Abby and Apollo to defend her cub. She sounded angry as she charged past her cub in pursuit of Abby and Apollo.

Abby and Apollo ran across the meadow with the mountains in their sights. The bear was fast. Abby yelped in pain as she stumbled into a gopher hole and fell, hurting one of her hind paws. Apollo turned and charged the mother bear, growling fiercely.

"Apollo! No!" Abby cried.

He was suddenly in the bear's face, waging war. Abby watched, horrified, as the bear stood on its hind feet, roared ferociously, dropped back down to the ground and lashed out at Apollo with one of its massive front paws.

Steel-like claws ripped across Apollo's shoulder, but he was not deterred. He charged around to the bear's side and sank his teeth into the bear's flank, just below the ribs. Apollo used his full strength and ripped a patch of fur from the bear, exposing the raw flesh underneath.

The bear howled in pain, turned and retreated toward her abandoned cub, leaving a trail of blood, while Apollo gave chase. He stopped after a hundred feet, watched to make sure the bear was not returning, then turned and ran back to Abby.

Abby shivered in fright. She stood with her left hind foot curled up under her. Apollo licked her face.

"You're hurt, Apollo!" she said. "We don't have any medicine." She licked his wound and examined it. "You're lucky it's not worse."

They rested their heads against each other for a moment of comfort. After a few minutes, Abby and Apollo turned and slowly set off toward the mountains and their cave. Abby's progress was slow as she made the strenuous climb over the rocky terrain. They stopped at the trickling water and satisfied their thirst, then continued the climb to their cave and lay down on their ledge that overlooked their neighborhood.

Abby licked her foot. It was swollen and sore. She looked up at the cloudless blue sky. She saw an eagle in the distance and watched it for several moments.

"I wonder if that was the bird that grabbed my little skunk friend." She turned and looked at Apollo.

"I wish you could talk, Apollo. Dog-talk is limited compared to human talk. One day you will meet Mommy and Daddy, and Daddy will be able to give you a Dot so you can talk with me," she said. "I hope you get to meet Rex. He was my best friend."

Apollo looked at her and tilted his head, not understanding her communication. Abby knew that the language was too complicated for him, and that he had never heard human talk prior to meeting her.

"When Daddy gives you a Dot, you will have language skills, and history, and knowledge," she said. "Knowledge is good. You will become smarter when you understand the ways of the world and how people do things."

Apollo stretched his neck and licked her face.

DRUMMING his fingers on the counter while staring at the glass container, Bill didn't need a timer. He was fast attuned to the exact second that completed the rest cycle of the formula.

He stood at the counter in front of the beaker and stared at the blue liquid.

"Let's see... What can I use...?" Bill looked around the counter surface, saw a writing instrument, and grabbed it. "Hhmm. Better think this through." He reached for a piece of paper and placed it under the test subject. Bill dipped a glass straw into the formula and captured a drop. He pulled it out of the glass container and dripped the formula over the middle of the writing instrument. He gripped the edge of the counter as he waited patiently.

Within thirty seconds, bits of the writing instrument disappeared. Within forty-five seconds, an entire quarter of an inch had vanished. It looked like two separate parts rested on the counter.

Bill stared at the success of his experiment in wonder and awe. He hung his head and let out a haggard sigh. "It worked," he said quietly. Then his excitement overflowed.

"Teresa!" he hollered. "Teresa, it worked!" He turned to Rex. "Good doggie, Rex."

Rex stood and wagged his tail.

Teresa ran into the lab. She stopped just inside the door, tense with anticipation.

Bill looked at her and pointed toward his test subject.

She approached the counter. Teresa stared at the two pieces of the writing instrument before her. She reached out and touched the empty space between the ends and touched a solid object.

"Oh, Bill," she said. "It worked."

"Yeah," he said.

They hugged each other and cried in relief.

After a moment, they parted. "Now I have to create a screen or shield that will allow us to see whatever is camouflaged, otherwise we won't be able to see the transport glider to load it!" he said.

"More work!" Teresa fretted, banging the counter with a tight fist. "When will we ever be able to leave here?"

"It's easier than you think," he said. "Right now, I'm going to see how it works in a sprayer to make sure it's consistent."

He went to a cabinet and took out a small spray bottle and a funnel. "Hold this bottle for me, will you, hon?"

Teresa donned gloves, removed the sprayer, and held the spray bottle. Bill flipped the funnel into the bottle, uncorked the solution bottle and poured a couple of inches of liquid into the spray bottle.

Teresa removed the funnel and then secured the sprayer into place. Bill took the spray bottle, looked around the room for a test subject, and shrugged. He sprayed the seat of one of the lab stools. In a few seconds, the seat faded, and all that was visible were the four legs.

He pulled Teresa close and kissed her. "By the end of the week, we'll be out of here."

CHAPTER THIRTY

B ill sat on the now-deformed lab stool and opened his encrypted communications port. He enabled his highest-level encryption. The red level was reserved for his most secret transmissions. When the system was prepared, he opened Wise Owl. Then he opened a blank message page and typed Golden Eagle into the From field. Then he typed Diamond Eyes into the To field. Next, he typed, *I accept the invitation to your gala,* into the subject field.

In the body of the message, Bill typed, *Is this the type of event that requires dress robes?* The message appeared innocent. He noted the time he clicked the send button, and then closed Wise Owl. Bill left the lab and found Teresa in the schoolroom reading research data that compared the intelligence of dogs, cats, whales, dolphins, and apes.

"Hon, I'm going to ChemLab. I'll be back shortly," he said. He leaned across the desk and kissed her.

"Bulk supplies?" she asked, in excitement.

Bill bobbed his head, a broad smile plastered on his face. "Bulk supplies."

Teresa beamed a smile. "TMZ, here we come!"

ABBY AND APOLLO basked in the sun on their ledge. It had taken three weeks before Abby could walk without limping. She was glad that she hadn't broken a bone. As it was, hobbling up and down the mountain path had been a challenge.

Apollo got up and shook himself. He left the ledge and went to the stream for a drink. Abby joined him. She stood in the water and drank. She liked the way the cold water felt running over her feet. Abby jerked her head up and pivoted her ears. She turned her head to the east and listened.

Apollo sniffed the air. Abby took off running down the mountainside with Apollo at her heels. They ran alongside the forest, through a grassy area. Abby slowed her pace and then stopped to listen.

A woman's singing drifted across the distance. Apollo backed up several steps into the forest.

"Let's see who it is," Abby said.

Apollo's ears twitched, and he shook with fear.

"Come with me, Apollo!" Abby pleaded. "This is the first human sound I have heard since Jeffers, the mountain man."

Abby trotted off, walking in the shadows of the trees. She looked over her shoulder. Apollo wasn't having any part of it. He had not budged. Abby continued toward the singing.

BILL RETURNED from ChemLab like a boy with holiday presents. He guided a hover surface, loaded with supplies, into his lab. Teresa sprang out of her chair in the schoolroom and looked over the inventory: several white, empty five-gallon buckets with covers, a large hand-pump sprayer, and gallons of chemicals.

Teresa helped Bill unload the hover surface, her face lit up with excitement. "This is a lot more than I expected," she said.

"Have to make a batch of restorative for when we get to TMZ," Bill said. "Otherwise, things may crash into us."

"Oh! That never crossed my mind! All I kept thinking about was that we can't be detected," Teresa said. "I should start gathering things together."

Teresa left the lab with a spring in her step.

Bill put the hover surface in the storage closet, returned to his lab and donned a lab coat, protective eye gear, and skin-like gloves.

Rex watched from his dog bed as Bill went about mixing chemicals. He stood and walked over to the transfer surface. "An important encrypted message has just arrived on Wise Owl."

Bill stopped what he was doing and walked to the transfer surface. He peeled off his gloves and threw them into a hazards container. Then he opened the program and ran the message through encryption and translation. His brows furrowed deeply as he read the message:

Dress robes are required. You should also consider dress gloves to complete your ensemble.

Bill smiled slyly.

He grabbed another pair of gloves from his supply cabinet, returned to the chemicals, and got to work on the solution.

Four hours later, five buckets and the sprayer were on the hover surface. Bill looked around his lab, then grabbed the sprayer and sprayed two of the lab stool legs. He watched the time carefully.

Within one minute and fifteen seconds, all that remained of the lab stool was two legs.

Bill removed his lab coat, protective eye gear, and gloves and left the lab. He walked into the schoolroom and found Teresa busy at her computer.

"I've transferred all my research files onto a disc," she said.

She pushed a button and a tray on her computer opened. A shiny disc the size of a fingernail lay in the tray. Teresa popped it out of the tray and slipped it into a clear plastic case the size of a nickel. She grabbed an etching tool and wrote, 'Research Files' on the case. Then she packed the case into a container with her important office tools and supplies.

"I'm beat," Bill said.

He had been working long hours to perfect his formula and to make the solution, develop a restorative solution, and other special pieces of equipment that were crucial for a successful journey.

"Let's get some sleep," Teresa said. "We've still got a lot to do, and we need to be rested tomorrow."

Rex came into the schoolroom and joined them. "I have determined the safest route to TMZ," he said. "Currently, all weather conditions are favorable. As we get closer to the time we will be leaving, I'll update my charts. The Tranquility Force's schedules of detail are updated every seventy-two hours. The rotating shifts, grid line adjustments, and all new watch duty schedules will be coming online at approximately the same time we leave WestUS."

Bill scratched Rex's ears. "Good job, Rex. You're staying on top of important details. I'm afraid I've let those things slip while trying to get the solution perfected."

Teresa squatted and hugged Rex. "You're a very hard-working member of this family, Rex."

"Family comes first. There is nothing more important than

family," Rex said. He slipped out of the room and returned to the lab.

Teresa watched Rex leave. "Do you think we should get another dog-bot so Rex can have a companion? He seems to be moody lately."

"I've noticed the change, and I'll have to take a look at his programming. I may have to do another update to his system," Bill said.

"He liked Jerry. Can you get Jerry back from the Tranquility Force?" Teresa asked.

"That would cause suspicion."

Teresa would not let it go. "All he does is stay on Abby's old bed. He hardly ever leaves the lab. Something's not right."

"We've all been on edge these last weeks," Bill said. "He's probably experiencing emotional overload because, let's face it, he didn't have any emotions while he was working on the patrols. I'll run a full diagnostic tomorrow and see what needs to be updated."

Bill grabbed Teresa's hand and pulled her out of the room.

THE SINGING MESMERIZED ABBY. She stayed in the shadows of the trees as she closed the distance between herself and the source of the song.

A weathered shack sat in a clearing with smoke rising from the chimney. Abby noticed there weren't any wires, cables, satellite hook-ups, solar panels, or any other type of communication connections on the exterior of the shack.

Abby stopped and sniffed the air. Food was cooking, but Abby didn't recognize the aroma—it had been too many months since she had smelled cooked food. Her stomach rumbled.

The aroma of leather, fresh herbs, soap, and water permeated the air. Abby moved closer. The door of the shack stood open. A middle-aged woman, with a braid to her waist, sat in a wooden chair in front of the fireplace, weaving a basket.

Abby knew it was dangerous for her to make contact with humans, but she decided that this woman was not a threat since she lived out in the wilderness. She bravely approached the door and scratched on the open-door frame.

The woman turned toward the door. Surprise crossed her weathered face as she saw Abby in the doorframe. "Come in. Come in," the woman said. She waved Abby inside.

Abby stepped over the threshold and entered the shack. She looked around.

"Do you talk?" the woman asked.

"Yes," Abby said. "But I have not talked to a human in a long time."

"You're the last dog, aren't you?" the woman asked in awe.

Abby backed up a step.

"Don't worry, you're safe here," the woman said, spreading her arms wide. "My name is Starlight. My father named me in the Native American tradition—I was born in the middle of the night when the stars were very bright."

"My name is Abby, Bill and Teresa Maxwell's dog-daughter... Lilith's daughter," Abby said. "What tribe do you belong to?"

"Timbisha Shoshone," Starlight said. "We used to live in Death Valley, but fled to the mountains to get away from the government. That's an old, long story."

"Do you live here alone?" Abby asked.

"Here in the shack, yes. But not alone. My people are in the mountains and the forest. We're no longer on the edge of extinction."

Starlight appraised Abby. "You must not be the last dog.

You're going to have puppies in another month, give or take a week. I can assist with the delivery if you require help."

"My mate is a wolf; so theoretically, I am the last domestic dog. Have you seen other dogs or wolves?" Abby asked, her face filled with hope.

"I heard there are dogs in TMZ, but I don't know for sure," Starlight said. "Where is your mate?"

"He's afraid of humans," Abby said.

"Me, too," Starlight said. She laughed heartily. "Are you hungry? I have marmot stew."

"Yes, please. I have not had prepared food in so long!"

Starlight got up and went to a cupboard. She retrieved a gaily painted clay bowl, grabbed the big spoon hanging from a hook on the side of the fireplace and dunked it into the stew pot. She filled Abby's bowl halfway and set it on the ground.

"You'd better let it cool for a bit so you don't burn your mouth," Starlight said.

"Do you know if the Tranquility Force is still searching for me?" Abby asked.

"I don't think so. They had a big trial. It was on GNN twenty-four-seven. That's all my kids talked about. They locked that doctor up for a long time," Starlight said.

"Dr. Roberts was a bad man," Abby said.

She approached the bowl and sniffed. After a moment, Abby licked at the stew, and then ate heartily.

A TABLE in the lab contained instruments spread out before Bill: a scalpel, a Dot insertion device, a wad of cotton, an eyedropper, alcohol, and a vial containing a light brown liquid.

Concentrating on the task at hand, he dipped the scalpel

into the alcohol and cut into his wrist. Bill grabbed the Dot insertion device and inserted it into the open wound. Beads of sweat broke out on his forehead as he pulled back on the plunger. His Dot appeared in the blood that filled the tube.

Bill took the eyedropper and dipped it into the vial and sucked up some of the brown fluid. He dripped three drops onto his bleeding wrist. The blood turned a clear color, and then the bleeding stopped.

He grabbed the wad of cotton and held it to his wrist. It absorbed the clear fluid and the excess brown liquid. Bill took more cotton and added a couple of drops of the brown liquid to it, and then he emptied the plunger onto the cotton.

Bill spotted the long tweezers on another counter. He grabbed the tweezers and snatched up the Dot. He dragged it over the cotton a few times and then placed the Dot in a clear case.

Teresa and Rex entered the lab.

"What are you doing?" Teresa asked. She saw the wad of cotton on the table. She looked at Bill's wrist.

"I'm leaving my Dot here so my movements are undetected," he said. "I don't want to lead anyone to my source. We need that transport glider."

Bill discarded the cotton in the hazards container.

"I thought you were going to make our Dots invisible, like Abby's," she said. She took hold of his wrist and examined it carefully.

"I still may do that, but that requires removing the Dot to apply the formula. For right now, I don't want any tracers picking up my movements," he said. "It's best if the Dot remains here in case the satellites are beaming to us."

"Why would they?" Teresa asked.

"Because we live in a society where nothing is private," Bill reminded her.

They pecked each other on the lips. Teresa hugged Bill for a long moment and then released him. He patted Rex on the rump, and then he pushed the hover surface loaded with chemicals through the lab door. He left the house and went out into the bright daylight.

CHAPTER THIRTY-ONE

Teresa paced. Rex watched her from a dog bed in the schoolroom.

"How long has he been gone?" she asked.

Rex's innards clicked, whizzed, and hummed.

"Update number eighteen. It has been seventeen hours, twelve minutes, and thirty-two seconds. Approximately ten minutes since your last inquiry," Rex said.

"You don't have to be snippy," Teresa said. "Bill's out there on a dangerous mission. If the Tranquility Force catches him, he'll be arrested."

"Daddy will be safe," Rex said. "He's no dummy."

Teresa spun around to face Rex. "Rex, I think you need to do a system scan. Your psychological profile seems to be changing. Are you okay?" Teresa asked.

"I'm growing up," Rex said.

A loud thud sounded against the house. Teresa jumped. Rex turned in the direction of the kitchen, his LEDs flashing crazily.

"What was that?" Teresa asked.

She headed toward the kitchen. Rex rushed ahead of her.

"Caution is required," Rex said. He went into full security mode.

"Updating security to orange level. Recording visuals and audio of all exterior angles of the premises," Rex said.

"Do you think it's the Tranquility Force?" Teresa asked.

Rex stood at the kitchen door. His LEDs were lit up like holiday lights as his system scanned for danger.

"I do not detect any Tranquility Force gliders within a five-mile radius."

Teresa shoved her hand into the security mold by the kitchen door, grabbed the door handle, and opened the door an inch. She and Rex peeked outside.

Nothing there.

"Do your scanners pick up on anything?" she whispered.

"Negative," Rex said.

"Shhh! Whisper, Rex!" Teresa said. "Someone may be listening."

"My systems do not detect anyone spying on this household," Rex said. "There is no reason to whisper."

Teresa stepped outside and looked to the right and left. Everything appeared to be peaceful. She returned to the house and went inside.

"Maybe a bat flew into the house," she said.

"The possibility of a bat flying into the house is sixteen point four-two-three million to one," Rex said.

Teresa hugged herself. "You don't have to be a smart Alec. What do you think it was, then?"

The kitchen door opened, and Bill stepped inside with a huge grin on his face.

"You didn't see anything, did you?" he asked.

"No! Did you see me outside?" Teresa asked, confused.

"Sure did, but you didn't see me," Bill said. "That's all we need to know. You didn't see me and Rex didn't detect anything."

He was like an excited kid, Teresa thought.

"Where is it?" she asked.

Bill handed her a crudely made pair of eye shields. "They're not pretty, but they work. I had to modify my original design on the fly," he said. "Rex, I'll have to work on a means for you to be able to see anything that's camouflaged, buddy. I'm afraid you might not detect the transport glider."

Bill opened the door, and they went outside. Rex stood close to the house, scanning the area. Bill slipped on his eye shields. He turned to Teresa and adjusted hers so that they wrapped across her face and fastened behind her ears.

Teresa gasped loudly as she saw the huge transport glider where there was nothing just seconds ago. She walked straight up to it and laid her hands on the metal sides.

"I can't believe it!" she said. "Rex, can you see it?"

Rex rocked from right to left and his LEDs flashed angrily. "I am unable to detect the glider."

Bill looked at Rex and frowned. "Rex, stop scanning. You're overloading your systems. I'll work on your upgrade as soon as we go inside."

Rex stopped moving, and his LEDs returned to a normal functioning level. He turned and scratched on the closed kitchen door.

"Okay, buddy. You go lie down," Bill said.

He opened the door, and Rex went inside. Bill opened the side door of the transport glider and went inside. Moments later he guided an invisible hover surface out of the glider and passed it to Teresa.

"I've got one more. Bring that one into the lab," Bill said.

Teresa steered the hover surface toward the kitchen door. It banged the kitchen door lightly.

"Oops," she said.

Teresa reached around and opened the kitchen door, and then pushed the hover surface into the house.

Rex stood in the kitchen close to the hover surface.

"Bill, Rex needs some help," Teresa hollered.

Bill entered the kitchen, holding his hand flat on the invisible hover surface.

"Honey, Rex can't see these, and he's going to either hurt himself or get all worked up," Teresa said.

Bill left the hover surface and walked to his lab.

"Come on, Rex. Let's get you fixed up."

Bill lifted Rex onto the transfer surface. He opened several programs and rapidly tapped out code as he watched streaming code on the monitor. He then drew a line from the file to Rex and upgraded Rex's software.

"Let's see how this works," Bill said.

Bill lifted Rex off the transfer surface and settled him on the floor. They walked into the kitchen, and Rex bumped into the hover surface.

"Well, that didn't work," Bill said. "Come on, buddy, I need to do some tweaking on that program."

Rex bonked the hover surface with his snout. He bonked it again.

"Rex, you're not going to be able to pick up anything on your scanners until I fix the glitch," Bill said.

Rex stood his ground. He bonked the hover surface one more time, and then turned and walked to the lab.

Bill shrugged as he met Teresa's questioning gaze. "I don't know what's going on with him."

"He told me he was growing up," Teresa said.

This time, Bill pulled up the deformed stool and settled down to work on the problem of Rex's inability to detect the hover surface. He stared at his code, reading line after line.

After half an hour of cluelessness, Bill took the eye shields out of his pocket and examined them. He studied them in his hands, turning them over and over, and then he put them on and looked down at the lab stool. He got up and looked at the stool from different angles, then squatted in front of it. He took off the eye shields, held them about six inches in front of him, and looked at the stool legs again.

"Oh!" he said.

Bill stood, sat on the stool and tapped out three lines of code.

"That should do it, Rex," he said. He walked to where Rex lay in the dog bed, snatched him up and placed him on the transfer surface. Bill drew a line from his code to Rex and waited while the program uploaded to Rex's database.

"Rex, I'm going to shut you down for a minute. I think this is going to require a hard restart."

"You're going to terminate me?" Rex asked coolly.

"No, not at all. The code requires that your system be shut down one hundred percent. You will be offline for approximately forty-five seconds, and then you will come online and be awake again," Bill said.

"Okay, Father," Rex said.

Bill reached under Rex and pressed a slight dimple in his belly. Rex's LEDs went dark, and his head crashed to his chest. Bill silently counted to forty-five, and then pressed the dimple.

Rex's head popped up and his LEDs lit up. Whirring, clicking, and humming sounds resumed.

"What day is it?" Rex asked.

"Stop being so paranoid. It has been exactly forty-five seconds since I shut your system down," Bill said. "Check your date and time sequence."

"That was just a little joke," Rex said. "It has been fifty-two seconds."

"Let's give this another try, shall we?" Bill said.

They walked into the kitchen and Rex stopped about two feet from the hover surface.

"Hover surface detected. Scanning in process. All systems are compatible with the new programming," Rex announced.

"Good. We have a lot of work to do. Rex, I want you to back up your systems and make discs. Back up all my research. Encrypt with your dog-thought and make discs," Bill said. "I'll load a dozen discs into the system for you."

"Understood. I will get to work immediately," Rex said.

ABBY LAY on her belly on a colorful hand-woven blanket in front of the fire. Starlight wove a basket, her hands swift with practice.

"Do you have a mate?" Abby asked.

"Husband. People have husbands and wives," Starlight corrected. "Not anymore. He died a long time ago."

"Don't you get lonely?" Abby asked.

"No. I have a large family. Two sons and three daughters. My brothers and sisters and cousins have families too, so there are always children around," Starlight said.

"But don't you want another husband?" Abby persisted.

Starlight stopped weaving and stared at Abby.

"You are very insightful for a dog," she said. "Now I understand all those debates about your plotting and planning your escape from the research facility."

"I didn't mean to make you uncomfortable," Abby said.

An orchestra of crickets announced nightfall. In the distance, Apollo howled at the moon. Abby lifted her head from her paws and listened.

"My mate fears that I will not return," she said. Abby stood and shook herself. She walked up to Starlight and laid her chin in her lap. "Thank you for the stew, and for your company," Abby said.

"He'll lose his fear and come around," Starlight said. "Come back tomorrow."

"Goodbye, Starlight," Abby said.

And then she was gone.

BOTH HOVER SURFACES were loaded with dismantled and packed lab equipment. Teresa and Bill spread large tarps across the equipment, and then Bill sprayed the tarps with his solution. They watched as the tarps faded, and all that remained was empty space.

Teresa fastened the eye shield to her face and ears and guided the hover surface out of the lab, through the kitchen and outside to the transport glider. She and Bill unloaded the contents onto sturdy shelves that were fastened to the floor, ceiling and walls of the glider.

They made several more trips of Bill's lab equipment when a Tranquility Force glider passed by in the distance.

"Take your eye shields off and pretend you're telling me something about the grass," Bill said calmly.

Teresa quickly and calmly brushed the shield off her face and pointed to the ground. She looked up at Bill, then squatted and yanked a handful of their hybrid grass and shook it.

They continued the charade for several minutes while the Tranquility Force craft monitored their activities. Evidently satisfied, the glider moved on. Bill noticed another glider way off in the distance.

"They are not recording sound," Rex said from the shadows of the kitchen. "My systems have detected two squadrons, but it appears to be coincidental with your activity because they are not sending beams in the direction of this house. They seem to be looking for someone or something else a half-mile from here."

"What if we get caught?" Teresa asked. She fretted, twisting a curlicue of hair until Bill thought it would snap.

"Rex said we didn't have to worry."

"I heard what he said, but what if..."

"Hon, we can't let this freeze our emotions. If they're not sending beams over here, it's highly unlikely that they are interested in what we're doing," Bill said.

He turned to Rex, still shrouded in the doorway. "Can you intercept any transmissions to find out what they are interested in, Rex?"

"I'm already on it," Rex said. "There's some type of organized crime ring that has been detected. Backup has been dispatched. It is highly likely that you will see much more activity in the sky in a short period of time."

A scratching sound on the other side of the fence, at the front door, caught their attention. Everyone became very quiet. Rex backed into the house and hurried to the front door. He scanned the security system.

Bill and Teresa quietly entered the office.

"Security, show exteriors of the front door," Bill commanded.

The cameras showed three views of the front door.

"Jerry?" Teresa said, forgetting to be quiet.

She and Bill hurried to the front door. Bill went through the security sequence on the keypad on the wall, and the door popped open. He opened it wider.

"Jerry! What are you doing here? Come in," Bill said.

Rex went around Jerry twice. "Have you defected, Jerry?" Rex asked.

Jerry turned with Rex. "I snuck away after accomplishing my mission," he said. "The others are busy being important."

Teresa scratched the top of Jerry's head. "What's going on over there?" she asked. "We saw two Tranquility Force gliders in close proximity to each other."

"Black market Dot up-graders," Jerry said. "People want more than what they have earned in credits. We tracked them down and caught them red-handed."

"It's like the early two-thousands all over again," Bill said. "The workforce doesn't want the guild-approved housing, low-end gliders, or food consoles. They want what higher-ups have, but don't want to work for it. Then, when they have those things, they want more."

"And get into debt over their heads to the black-market demons, and expect the government to save them," Teresa said. "Every decade seems to have a time when this is repeated."

Rex and Jerry stood face to face in silent communication. Bill and Teresa watched as the LEDs on both dog-bots danced colorfully.

"I'm being summoned," Jerry said. He walked to the door and waited.

Bill leaned down and patted Jerry. "Glad you stopped by, Jerry. Keep up the good work."

"Bye, Jerry," Teresa said.

Rex stayed back as Bill unsecured the door and cracked it open a bit.

Jerry scanned the immediate area and nosed the door open. "All clear," Jerry said, and scurried away.

Bill closed and secured the door. He and Teresa shared a glance and then looked at Rex.

"Well, buddy, did you and Jerry have a good visit?" Bill asked.

"Jerry is doing good work," Rex said. "Maybe he'll be on GNN."

"That would be interesting," Teresa said.

"Let's tackle the schoolroom," Bill said. "We're going to take everything we can load. We may need to barter or bribe people along the way."

They all left the living room and went towards the schoolroom.

BILL MENTALLY PATTED himself on the back for having the foresight to install modular desks, counters, and cabinets. A few bolts to turn and the item was ready to go onto the hover surface.

They methodically went from room to room. Within a week, all that was left were the bare walls, the kitchen counters and bathroom fixtures.

When the last load was secured in the transport glider, Bill and Teresa returned to the house. It was an eerie experience; the interior of the house was naked: an empty shell.

They walked into the kitchen and Bill placed the tiny case that housed his Dot on the counter. He looked at Teresa.

"Ready?"

She laid her arm on the counter. "Will it hurt?"

"I'll use a numbing agent," Bill said.

He wiped her wrist with a thin, white piece of plastic that left a trail, similar to a snail's slime. Then he took the scalpel and made a tiny slice into her skin.

Teresa watched as Bill took the plunger and sucked up her Dot. He wiped her wrist with a different piece of plastic.

"Hold this firmly on your wrist for a few minutes so the bleeding stops," he instructed.

Bill plunged the blood out onto a Petri dish, and then took long tweezers and snatched up Teresa's Dot. He swabbed it clean and placed it into a tiny case.

"That's it. We're done here," he said as he gathered up his tools and supplies.

They both looked at the Dots on the counter, and then walked out the kitchen door.

APOLLO STOOD ten feet back from Starlight's open door while Abby visited inside the cozy shack. Each day Apollo had managed to find the strength and courage to come a little bit closer.

"I don't think he's going to come any closer," Starlight said. She peered out the door from her rocking chair.

Abby turned her head to look. "Apollo has to trust man, or he won't be able to come with me to TMZ to find Mommy and Daddy."

Starlight stopped rocking. "TMZ is a long way away. Too long of a trip for a dog that's going to have puppies. You should wait until the puppies are born and whelped and then go."

Abby stood and stretched. Her tummy was slightly rounded.

"I'm going to see if Apollo will come closer."

Starlight stood and went to the fireplace. Two bowls of stew sat on the stone ledge, cooling. She gathered up the bowls and walked out of the shack. She placed them on the ground and then sat in the wooden chair by the door.

Abby left Apollo's side and stood by the bowls.

"Apollo, come and eat. This is good food," she said.

Apollo sniffed the air and drooled. He took a couple of steps forward and stopped. Abby turned to her bowl and started eating. After a few minutes, Apollo joined Abby at the bowls and ate heartily. As soon as his bowl was empty, he bounded away at least fifteen feet and cleaned his face.

"Progress," Starlight said.

⁓

BILL HANDED Teresa the eye shields, and she slipped them on as they walked toward the transport glider. Teresa stopped at the cab door of the glider and turned toward the house. She looked long and hard for several seconds, then stepped over the threshold and disappeared.

Bill lifted Rex into the cab of the glider and settled him between the two seats. He slid the doors closed and engaged all the smart lock buttons, which secured the doors. He then climbed into the cab.

"I feel bad that we're leaving without a word to Percy and Becky," Teresa said.

"We just can't risk it. They'd fold under TRFTS," Bill said.

A piece of equipment about the size of a shoebox sat at the base of the curved windshield. It had LEDs, switches, and short optic feelers. Bill flipped switches so that the LEDs lit up and the feelers danced. He typed instructions into the transport glider's control keyboard, and they lifted off the ground silently.

Bill watched the grid on the transport glider's computer system. Teresa craned her neck and looked up into the bright sky.

The glider rose straight up over the roof of the house until they reached their safe airspace. The computer showed that the glider was in the area of the grid that was outlined in red.

Bill and Teresa looked in every direction to see if there were signs they were detected. Teresa held onto her seat with a death grip.

"Looks clear from the instrumentation readings," he said as he studied the glider's instrument panel. Then he checked his scanning equipment.

"Rex, do you detect any scanning or beams coming our way?"

"You should make an adjustment and climb another three feet. The bottom of the glider is currently in a pocket of space that may be tracked," Rex said.

No sooner had Rex spoken than three Tranquility Force gliders were within visual range. Bill adjusted the glider's coordinates, and it rose quickly.

"Stay very still," he whispered. "Rex, mute your system."

Rex's system whirs, clicks, and hums shut off. The inside of the transport glider was as quiet as the sunshine coming through the windshield. No one moved as they watched the three Tranquility Force gliders hover in the sky in front of and below them. The gliders changed positions and finally dispersed.

Bill and Teresa audibly released their breath. Bill placed his hand on Teresa's thigh.

"It's going to be okay," he said.

After one more visual check of the various instrument panels and checking out the surrounding sky, Bill eased the glider forward.

"Are you sure no one can see us through the windows?" Teresa asked, stretching her neck to look out the side window.

"No one can see in. The formula will reflect the sky, or whatever our surroundings are, back to anyone looking at us," Bill said. "Remember the stool? You saw the counter, like looking through and around the stool itself."

"Okay. It's just odd." Teresa mulled his words over in her mind.

They headed east from their sector at Edge 10-SJ. The sky was busy with different gliders coming and going.

Bill had to hold the transport glider still when Tranquility Force satellite probes passed nearby. During those times, Teresa was paralyzed with fear.

What typically took fifteen minutes to get from old coordinates for South De Anza Boulevard to Old Yerba Buena Road at a moderate speed any other time via a typical household low-flying air glider, now stretched into over an hour in the transport glider. There was no relief in sight with all the activity in the sky.

An official glider approached from the southeast at a fast pace and looked as if it was on a crash course with their transport glider. Bill risked pushing the glider to full throttle on the tail of a passing probe.

The official craft thundered past the transport glider and nicked the satellite probe. The probe spun out of the sky into a fast free-fall to the earth. Bill and Teresa saw a tiny ball of flames on the ground where the probe disintegrated, taking valuable real estate along with it.

Bill slowed the glider and checked for security breaches, but all systems indicated the glider had not been tracked.

They finally made it to the far eastern edge of San Jose, and Bill steered them in a southeasterly direction.

"We're going to have to stay in the safe zone for a minimum of a hundred miles," Bill said.

"Why so far?" Teresa said.

"Tracking and controls," he said.

"Oh, Bill," Teresa said. "I can't believe you were involved with that business."

"I know, hon," he said. "What starts out innocent sometimes turns on us."

CHAPTER THIRTY-TWO

Bill checked the distance on the computer. From Edge 10-SJ to the main entrance of Texmexzona in Blythe was five hundred miles.

"When we get to Clovis, we'll drop down to a normal travel level," Bill said. "I don't think we'll come across very much air traffic so we should be relatively safe."

Teresa glanced at the computer screen and saw the blip that depicted Clovis.

"How long will it take for us to get there?" she asked.

"Two hours, tops," he said.

"One hour, forty-seven minutes, and twenty-three seconds," Rex said from his place behind Bill and Teresa.

"I'm going to hold you to that calculation, Rex," Bill said.

"That estimate will change if your speed varies," Rex replied.

The transport glider sped across the sky.

"I wonder if Abby's down there somewhere," Teresa said as she looked out the side window toward the far-away ground.

Bill pondered Teresa's question. "She must not have made

it to TMZ yet. I'm pretty sure Harold would have contacted us if she were there."

Teresa turned in her seat and looked at Bill. "That would be pretty risky, wouldn't it?"

"Hon, we're sitting in an invisible transport glider with every stick of furniture and equipment we own, breaking one law after another. You have to remember the people that are out there and the choices they made to live in complete freedom," Bill said.

"It wasn't supposed to be like this," she said. "We weren't supposed to be oppressed, but it's a fact that we do not have any privacy anymore. The World Guild knows where every single one of us is at any given moment. They practically know what we're doing, what our vitals are, if we're eating something, having sex, what our emotions are... we're not supposed to live like this; there's no end to the invasion of privacy and the loss of our rights."

They traveled in silence for several minutes.

"It's going to be very different in TMZ," Bill said. "We'll have to learn their rules and laws and maybe live in something that we deem unacceptable because of all the privileges we've been used to for so many years."

"If our parents were still alive, I wouldn't even contemplate this move," she said, twirling her hair around a finger, thinking. "But we need this change, and we'll adjust because we have each other."

They were each lost in their own thoughts while the transport glider slid through the sky.

"WE ARE APPROXIMATELY ten miles from Blythe," Rex said. "Preparations should be undertaken for our arrival."

Within moments, Bill lowered the transport glider to the ground. He and Teresa got out of the cab and stretched their legs.

"Rex, want to get out and stretch your legs?" Teresa asked.

"Dog-bots do not need to stretch our legs since we do not tire," Rex said.

"Rex, it's an expression. Maybe you'd like to view the landscape and run some weather ops," Bill said.

"Oh, I see. In that case, yes, I would like to stretch my legs," Rex said.

Rex ambled through the cab and stepped outside of the glider. His sensors collected data.

Bill unlocked the smart locks and opened the side door on the glider. He brought out two sprayer containers and set them on the ground. Teresa joined him, and he showed her how to operate the sprayer.

"You start from the rear and do that side," he said, pointing to the passenger side of the glider. "I'll do the front and this side."

They started spraying the glider with the activating formula that made it visible again. As they sprayed and walked, the features of the glider became visible: worn paint, rust, scratches and dents from close encounters from the glider's former life, and the enormous hulking size of the thing loomed large.

Teresa stared at her side when she finished spraying. "This thing is huge," she said.

She stood on her tiptoes but could not see the roof. "Are you going to spray the roof?"

Bill leaped onto the cab as she asked the question. "I'm on it."

He finished up, climbed down onto the cab and jumped to the ground. They walked the entire perimeter of the transport glider. Bill sprayed here and there to make sure that there were no patches of nothingness to intrigue inquiring minds. When he was satisfied with the way the glider looked, they all climbed back inside.

BILL KEPT the glider in the normal traveling grid. After about one mile, they came upon electronic markers with Official TMZ Territory posted on both sides of the old road. Scattered gliders were parked haphazardly among tents, lean-tos and other forms of shelter. As each mile passed, more and more of the same sights were before them until they arrived at the entrance to TMZ at Blythe.

A veritable tent-and-vehicle city sprawled across the landscape for as far as they could see.

"Is this TMZ?" Teresa asked, somewhat shocked.

Bill's face wore a disbelieving expression.

"I don't know what to make of this," he said. "When I researched TMZ, this scenario did not present itself. The World Guild must have fabricated the information on its website. Even my contact for the transport glider said that communications are completely blocked so there's no way to worm your way into the TMZ system to get information."

Without any warning, a large unit of Tranquility Force gliders zoomed in from the west. "Return to the United States immediately," their commander boomed over the communication system.

"Bill!" Teresa screamed.

"We're not stopping!" Bill said. "Hold on!"

He pushed the transport glider to full throttle. The Tranquility Force opened fire. Laser shots dinged the transporter and the surrounding ground. Suddenly a heavily armed squadron of TMZ military gliders arrived from the east.

They hovered protectively over the transport glider. Their communication portal opened. "You have breached the Official TMZ Territory. Return to your base immediately or we will retaliate," the TMZ unit commander announced to the Tranquility Force.

After several tense moments, the Tranquility Force unit sped away to the west.

"You may resume your travels," the TMZ unit commander announced to Bill and Teresa.

"Glad to have your help," Bill responded. Before he could finish his sentence, the unit spread out and sped away, patrolling the territory.

Teresa's grip on her seat left red welts on her hand. She let out a loud exhale. Bill placed his hand on her thigh. "That was a close call."

Bill steered the transport glider slowly through the gauntlet of gliders, tents, and people. Men and women stared at the massive transport glider as it crept by.

"I think we should stop so we can find out what this is all about," Teresa said.

"Good idea," Bill said.

Bill stopped the glider and let it settle on the ground.

"Stay here," he warned.

Frightened, Teresa watched as Bill exited the cab and approached a beefy man in a plaid shirt with the sleeves torn out. Rex watched over her shoulder. Bill and the man engaged in conversation.

"Bill's frowning. I wonder what's wrong."

"It appears they are discussing the protocols," Rex explained.

"Protocols?" Teresa squeaked. She watched as Bill shook his head, pumped the man's hand and returned to the glider.

Bill entered the cab and put the glider in motion again.

"What did he say?" Teresa asked. "You didn't look very happy. Rex said something about protocols."

"The TMZ has strict immigration laws. We'll have to present papers and have someone sponsor us," he said.

"Papers? Sponsor?" Teresa squeaked out. "Surely Harold can sponsor us?"

Bill did not look happy as he glanced at Teresa. "We'll just have to see what happens when we get there."

A heavily armored gate and walled outpost was spread across the road in the distance. Bill steered the glider up to within several yards of the gate. Plates of thick steel adorned with colorful stars, wolves, and eagles spread across the front of the outpost.

The outpost itself was only a solitary building, three stories tall with reinforced windows and doors. A large telescope and a backless chair were on the flat roof, and what looked to Bill like an old, rusted machine gun. He wondered if it was a working gun or just a relic from many decades ago to scare people.

Bill used the computer to contact the outpost. A response was returned immediately: Identify yourselves and state your reason for being here.

Bill typed his message. He identified himself and Teresa, and then he turned to her seeking guidance.

"What do you think they want to know? Our occupations? How do I explain why we are here? We're waiting on our dog-daughter?" he asked.

"Yes. Tell them all of that. Mention Harold and Gayle. They're familiar with your work and our worth, Bill," Teresa said.

Bill typed and sent his message. They waited for a response, but none came.

"Yer not gettin' in there, so go find a place to park that thing," a skinny man with an open shirt shouted from the side of the road. He stood near a rusted family glider up alongside a fabricated house of sheet metal and old boards.

HAROLD STOOD before a bank of screens in the command center, a building deep within the TMZ infrastructure. The adobe walls were two feet thick with steel reinforcements throughout to protect the contents from the climate and invasion.

He stood beside a younger man who wore a headset and was seated in front of six monitors.

"Here's the transmission," the young man said as he pointed to a screen.

Harold read the first pulse, the outpost's response, and then Bill's note.

"Can you get me an image of the glider?" Harold asked.

"Sure," the young man said.

The twenty-year-old's fingers flew across different keyboards, flipped switches, pressed buttons, and turned a monitor to face directly in front of Harold.

The transport glider sat on the ground about twenty feet in front of the outpost.

"Can you get images of the people inside?" Harold asked.

"Sure," the kid said. Again, his fingers went to work.

Crystal clear images of Bill, Teresa and Rex appeared on the monitor.

"That's Bill Maxwell, all right. And his wife, Teresa. What the heck is that, one of those dog-bots?" Harold asked.

The young man zoomed in, and Rex's image filled the screen.

"Sure looks like one," the kid said. "Wow!"

"Well, I'll be damned," Harold said. "Make those images and the transmission available to the committee."

"Sure thing," the kid said.

He patted the young man on the shoulder and left the room. Harold walked down a hallway to an office. He passed his hand in front of a small device on the wall. A shelf glided out from the wall, and a virtual screen and keyboard appeared on the shelf.

"I would like to request an approval," Harold stated.

Several faces popped up on the screen. A man in a billowy white robe spoke first.

"Who are the subjects?" he asked.

"William and Teresa Maxwell," Harold said. "Bill is a world-renowned inventor and engineer. Teresa is an animal psychologist."

Harold watched as several people conferred.

"Isn't he the one who invented the Dot?" someone asked.

"He could be a spy," someone else stated.

"Look, Bill Maxwell is a brilliant man. I will stake everything I have to personally vouch for him," Harold said. "If he's at our door, there's a damn good reason for it, and it won't have anything to do with spying."

EVERY MOMENT they waited in the transport glider for some word of entry or refusal into TMZ was tormenting to Bill and Teresa.

"What if we have to live out here, like this?" Teresa said, looking at the surrounding masses.

"If that's what we have to do to wait for Abby to find us, then that's what we'll do. We have everything we need right here," Bill said, gesturing to the contents of the transport glider.

Rex had been quiet the entire time, but his sensors were collecting data.

"The data from my recent scan suggests that one million four hundred thousand three hundred eighty-three people are congregated outside of TMZ. Three hundred individuals were high-ranking government officials. I have not completed my assessment of the others. I will break this down into labor and educational groups," Rex said.

"Good work, Rex. Your data may help get us through the gate," Bill said.

The glider's communication device twittered an acknowledgment of an incoming message. At the same time, the massive gates began to slide open. A squadron of heavily armored guards on military, open-air one-man gliders emerged from the outpost and surrounded the transport glider.

Bill and Teresa watched in wide-eyed speculation as the squadron turned their gliders to face the outpost.

The crowd of people around them kept their distance but watched in disbelief. Their conversations were like a soft roar as they discussed what was happening.

The guard closest to Bill's window tapped on the glass and pointed forward. Bill lifted his thumb, started the glider, and they moved forward in a procession through the gates.

When the transport glider and guards were inside the compound, the gates slid shut behind them.

Bill and Teresa stared in wonder as they followed the guards through an entry corridor to another gate. A beam shot out from a sentry post to the transport glider, and the gate slid open.

"Verification beam," Rex said. "Interesting code."

Bill could hear Rex's systems going to work on the code, decrypting it.

Teresa was quiet as she took in the environment: military-type structures in ugly dark gray and green.

The guard by Bill's window motioned for him to stop as they approached a long building. A door opened and Harold emerged.

"Harold!" Bill exclaimed as he opened the door and exited the glider.

Teresa was just as surprised as she opened her door and walked around the front of the glider to where Bill and Harold were embracing and beating on each other's backs.

"Teresa! Gayle is going to be so happy to see you!" Harold said as he grabbed Teresa in a bear hug.

"I can't believe it," Teresa said. "We thought you were transferred to New York! I've been trying to reach Gayle for months!"

"Yeah, that's what they say when someone with any credentials defects," Harold said.

"There's someone else you might want to meet," Bill said. "Rex, come on out and meet Harold."

"I saw that you brought a dog-bot with you. How far along in the development are you?" Harold asked.

Bill and Teresa smirked, but did not comment.

Rex chose that moment to join the group.

Harold stared at Rex intently.

"Rex, this is Harold Goanflower, my old friend," Bill said.

Rex approached Harold. "I have studied your profile and noted your honors and career advancements. I am pleased to meet you," Rex said. "I am in the process of compiling data on TMZ. If you would like me to share my findings with you, I will do so."

"Well, hello, Rex," Harold said.

Harold turned to Bill. "What are his capabilities?"

"He's already gathered demographics on the denizens outside the gate. Give him another hour or two and he'll be able to tell you not only how many people there are here inside TMZ, but every bit of information about them, every stitch of building materials in the entire TMZ, and a soil analysis," Bill said.

"Don't forget the weather report," Teresa said.

"Oh, yeah, never ask him how his day is going," Bill said.

Rex paid no attention to the conversation. His systems were busy doing all the things Bill suggested.

"Rex, if Bill built you, then I know you have a big brain," Harold said.

"My system is unrivaled," Rex said. "Daddy has a big brain for a human."

Harold swung around to look from Bill to Teresa. "Daddy, huh?"

"He's trying to understand and simulate family," Teresa said.

"Boy, can we use him around here!" Harold said. "Come inside... you too, Rex. Bill, I want you to meet the committee. Teresa, Gayle should be here in a minute. She was so happy she almost screamed my ear off when I told her you were here."

"Let me grab something first," Bill said.

He dashed back to the glider and opened the side door. He returned with two small spray bottles.

"I think you're going to like this," he said, holding the bottles up to Harold.

Teresa smiled. Bill was in his element.

They walked to the building and entered through a coded door.

∼

STARLIGHT PLACED her hands on each side of Abby's tummy.

"Yup, your little puppies will be born any day now," she said.

"Do you know how many there are?" Abby asked.

"Nope, too hard to tell with them squirming all over the place," Starlight said.

Apollo lay outside the door, watching the two interact.

"Any day now, Apollo," Abby said.

"Why do you talk to him? He doesn't understand a word you're saying," Starlight said.

"When Daddy gives Apollo a Dot, he'll remember all these conversations," Abby said. She walked outside. Apollo stood.

"Bye, Starlight. See you tomorrow."

"Bye Abby. Bye, Apollo."

Abby and Apollo trotted off toward their den.

GAYLE AND TERESA squealed like little girls and clung to each other in a hug-fest.

"I'm so glad you're here," Gayle said as she and Teresa parted. "I'm glad we defected, but I so miss my friends!"

Gayle held Teresa's hand and led her through a door.

"I was worried about that too," Teresa said. "I'm so relieved to know at least one person here."

"Sometimes it isn't easy making new friends, especially when your environment is turned upside down," Gayle said. "New rules, new governing body, different fears, having to learn so many new things. It's overwhelming. But you don't have to worry because I'm going to shorten your learning curve."

Teresa looked around, her face betraying her thoughts of the dismal building.

They walked up to a kitchen area and Gayle went directly to the food console and requested two hot chocolates. She handed one to Teresa, and they sat at one of the small café tables nearby.

"Why didn't you tell me?" Teresa asked. She stared at Gayle, hurt feelings splayed across her face.

"It about broke my heart to keep this secret from you, but Harold said it was too risky. He was pretty sure Bill would figure it out," Gayle said.

Teresa was angry. "We didn't know if you were dead from the poison, killed by air pirates, or some other accident that killed you. Then, when Tranquility Force came to the house asking for your whereabouts, we were distraught that you never showed up in New York."

Gayle bowed her head. "If we could do it over again, we'd all defect together!" She swallowed hard. "We saw the news about Lilith and the pups. I just can't believe it. Ejonia?"

Teresa shook her head. "Ejonia didn't make it. Abby survived, but she was confiscated for a reintroduction program. We hadn't been allowed to see her or communicate with her, then she escaped," Teresa said. "She's going to show up here. Before the Tranquility Force took her, we told her if she escaped she should come here and wait for us."

"I'll tell Harold so he can alert everyone," Gayle said. "I can't wait to see her again!"

Teresa told Gayle about Abby's daring escape, her Dot removal and disappearance.

"Wow. She's one smart little girl," Gayle said. "Just so you know, the buildings that you saw upon arrival here are the security and operations units. We don't live like this. Hopefully, you'll be all settled by the time Abby shows up."

Teresa forced a smile as she looked around the austere room and bobbed her head.

"I'm looking forward to seeing the housing units," she said. "We weren't sure if we would have to live in the transport glider for a while or not. We brought everything except for the kitchen counters!"

"Drink up and we'll go to my house. You and Bill can stay with us until your place is secured," Gayle said.

They finished their hot chocolate and exited the kitchen. Gayle led Teresa down a network of corridors to an imposing door flanked with different colored unlit lights.

A hand imprint sensor plate rested on a platform to the left of the door. Gayle placed her hand on the sensor plate, and a green light lit up beside the door.

She opened the door and ushered Teresa outside. They walked for fifty feet to an imposing fence. A sentry grabbed the door handle and opened the door for them.

Teresa gawked in disbelief as she stepped beyond the gate. A sprawling community of beautiful southwestern-style homes with red-tiled roofs lay before her as far as she could see.

Men, women, and children rode bicycles, scooters, and skateboards through pristine streets.

Gayle watched Teresa closely for a reaction.

"Children?" Teresa breathed. She rubbed her eyes. "I thought maybe I was dreaming."

"They were going to remove the pavement, and Harold convinced them it would be to everyone's benefit to keep the streets and use them for exercise," Gayle said.

"I didn't know they made those playthings anymore," Teresa said. "The houses are beautiful!"

Gayle steered Teresa over to a parking area, and they climbed into a family glider. They passed the people on the street at a slow pace so Teresa could take in everything and digest what she saw. Gayle maneuvered the glider through the community to an area where the houses were stately and luxurious.

She slowed the craft as she approached a rather large house and steered the glider into the driveway.

"Here's home," Gayle said.

They got out of the glider and Teresa stared at the house and then turned and stared at Gayle.

"Is this real?" she asked. "This is beyond beautiful, Gayle. How is it that these houses exist? I thought the Guild had systematically demolished all the old houses and replaced them with Guild-approved dwellings."

Gayle hooked her arm through Teresa's and led her up the walkway to the front door.

"This used to be a Guild-approved place at one time. Years ago, the TMZ Committee decided to restructure the entire Republic. There's still some Guild boxes way in the back, but they'll be restructured soon."

Gayle opened the front door and escorted Teresa inside. The open, spacious layout with towering ceilings and muted colors had Teresa wandering about amazed.

Gayle gave Teresa a tour of the house and then they settled in the kitchen.

"I was like you when I first arrived. I thought I was going to have to live in barracks," Gayle said. "We love it here."

"I can understand why," Teresa said. "This is so conducive to productivity. It's peaceful, so beautiful, and so private!"

"No spyware."

"None?" Teresa asked, quite surprised.

Gayle shook her head.

"Any spying that goes on in headquarters is on the outer world, so we can be safe," Gayle explained. "I'm so glad Bill is here. We really need him."

~

HAROLD LED Bill and Rex through long hallways and four different secured doors before they finally arrived at a room where several people congregated. The group looked toward Harold and Bill, expectantly.

"Bill, this is Glacious Ersons, the chairman of the committee that oversees TMZ," Harold said as he walked Bill up to the man in the white robe.

Bill shook Glacious' hand. He stood in front of the group. "My wife and I are grateful that you allowed us entrance into TMZ," he said. "I can't tell you how relieved we are. It is very intimidating to arrive at the beginning of the waiting area and discover that you don't know anything about this place."

He turned to where Rex stood just inside the doorway. "Come stand beside me, Rex," Bill said. He turned to the group. "This is Rex. You're going to want to get to know him."

Rex stood facing the group, his LEDs twinkling actively.

"Glacious Ersons, sixty-two years old, defected in 2065 from World Guild headquarters. Married to Eleanor Connor Ersons, one human child, Dorian Ersons, thirty-seven years old, two dog children, deceased," Rex rattled off.

"Rex, everyone here already knows this," Bill said.

"Oh, sorry," Rex apologized.

Bill turned to the group. "Rex enjoys demographics, statistics, number-crunching, and compiling any data."

Rex turned to Harold. "I have your reports ready."

Harold stared at Rex, somewhat surprised, and then turned to Bill. "Everything we joked about?"

Bill smirked.

"Rex, can you upload them so I can share them?" Harold asked.

"I have already emailed them to you."

"Oh, great," Harold said.

"He accessed your systems to compile the information and found your contact information," Bill said.

The group considered Bill's statement.

"This is a breach of our security," Pete said.

"Rex and I can help you with those security issues," Bill said.

Now that everyone was focused on Bill, he held up his small spray bottles. "I think you might want to see my latest invention."

CHAPTER THIRTY-THREE

Starlight woke from a strange dream. She turned over on her small bed and lay on her back. She stared at the dark ceiling overhead, lost in thought. "What woke me? What was that sound? Was it in my dream or from the physical world?" she wondered.

A scratching sound at the door answered her. A low, deep bark followed.

Starlight scrambled to her feet and opened the door. Apollo stood at the door.

"Abby?" she asked.

Apollo sprang to the side, ready to take off in a run. He looked back at Starlight to see if she was ready to follow.

"Wait, Apollo," Starlight said.

She returned to the cabin and lit a lantern. Starlight gathered up items and placed them on the small table: a small jug of water, an old sheet, a knife, matches, a small lantern, and a bowl. She tested the edge of the knife with her fingers, found her whetstone and gave it a few passes across the gritty edge. Then she grabbed a backpack and stuffed the items inside.

Starlight grabbed her shoes, slipped them on, and then wrapped herself in an Indian blanket and headed to the door.

"Okay, I'm ready," she said to Apollo as she shut the door.

Apollo took off at a brisk pace. When he looked to see if she was following, he had to wait for her to catch up.

"Slow down for this old woman," Starlight said.

They continued at a stop-and-start pace while Starlight hurried to keep up with him. They trotted alongside the forest, and up the mountainside path, through the trickling water, past the neighboring caves, over and around rocks and boulders.

Apollo led her to their den. When Starlight finally arrived on the ledge, she was panting.

The wolf paced frantically, waiting for Starlight to catch her breath. He finally left her and went inside the pitch-black cave.

Starlight removed her backpack and retrieved the small lantern and matches. She lit the lantern, grabbed her backpack and carefully entered the dark cave where the opening was higher.

"Good boy, Apollo," Starlight praised as she arrived in their sleeping room.

Apollo allowed her to pat him and rub his back.

"Abby, let's see what's going on. How do you feel?" Starlight asked.

Abby lay on a small, thick pile of leaves that was covered with the old, tattered blanket and a fairly good blanket.

Starlight approached Abby. One tiny black puppy was in the bed.

"I see you have one birthed. That's a good sign," Starlight said.

"More are on the way," Abby said, grunting.

Starlight eased down to the edge of the bed. She placed her backpack to the side and turned her full attention to Abby.

She softly stroked Abby's face, and then felt her belly.

~

FOUR AND A HALF HOURS LATER, six tiny puppies suckled at Abby's teats. She alternated between licking them and resting. Apollo stayed close by, always the protector.

Starlight had one hand on Abby and one on Apollo, patting them.

"This is a glorious day," Starlight said. "You have six beautiful, healthy puppies. What are you going to name them?"

"Tallulah has my white toenails, Esme reminds me of Lilith, and Star looks like Apollo, but she has my white patch on her chest. Rex and Wolf favor Apollo with their dark coloring, and Jim reminds me of the pictures of my canine father," Abby said. "I'm glad you were here, Starlight."

"You did it all by yourself," Starlight said.

~

THE CHAIR SEAT appeared to be hovering on its own in the middle of the room. The committee members crowded around the abnormality and studied it from different angles, touching, prodding, and squinting, trying to see the missing legs.

"Had enough?" Bill asked.

Harold and the others stepped back, talking among themselves, and allowed Bill to come forward.

Bill sprayed the chair legs. Inch by inch, the area was restored to its former appearance. The members scuttled forward again, touching the chair once again.

"That is truly incredible," Pete said. "We wondered how you managed to get that transport glider here without being detected."

"I've been working on this for months," Bill said.

He explained how he had made Abby's Dot invisible, but her communications program failed because of the shielding at the lab. Then the failed camouflage reflective spray and Rex's solution.

Then Bill explained about the safe flying area in the grid, and the device he had constructed to keep the electronics undetected, and the other one to keep the magnetic shield stable at the altitude at which they were required to fly.

"We left our Dots behind," Bill said.

"What about your credits? Your incredible wealth?" Glacious asked, shocked. "You left all that behind as well?"

"I had some help with that," Bill said, turning in Rex's direction. "Rex funneled it through a great many systems with different identities. It will be at my disposal so I can work here on important projects."

"How does he do these things?" Glacious asked, staring at Rex.

"I developed his system on an evolutionary theory," Bill said. "He has matured from a very young machine with highly technical skills to what you see now. He has the ability to develop his own sense of need. He's created his own encryption called dog-thought that no one can break, including me."

Everyone watched Rex as he lay on the floor, silently working.

"We're really glad you're all here," Glacious said.

The committee members murmured agreement.

Bill stared at Harold. "I brought all of my files—everything I have ever worked on. All of my patents."

"Oh, wow!" Harold whispered. He let out a low whistle. "Wow."

~

DURING THE NEXT SEVERAL DAYS, Abby barely left the whelping bed. She ran out of the cave to relieve herself and get a drink, and returned immediately to her litter. Her six tiny puppies' eyelids and ear canals were still sealed shut.

Starlight hauled a small pot of rabbit or marmot stew up the mountain when she checked in on Abby and the pups. The cave now contained two handmade terra-cotta bowls and a big metal water bowl.

Apollo had become quite sociable. He greeted Starlight on her visits and allowed her to pat him on the back. He even licked her hands on occasion.

Starlight sat on a blanket on the cave floor next to Abby's whelping bed. She watched as the blind and deaf puppies squirmed.

Abby licked the puppies as they belly-crawled across the bed. She got up and walked to the outer room. Starlight followed.

"They're nine days old today," Abby said, indicating the etchings on the wall. Starlight gazed at Abby's calendar in wonder.

"Their eyes should open in the next couple of days," Starlight finally said. "They'll start to hear right after that."

STAR AND WOLF were the first to open their eyes on the morning of day ten. Tallulah, Esme, and Rex were next, late in the afternoon. Jim waited until the next morning to see the world.

A week later, all six started to test their ability to walk. They stumbled into each other and fell over often, whimpering.

Apollo stuck his head in the bed and nudged a fallen puppy periodically until it stood again.

"He's encouraging them," Starlight said one day as she observed his prodding.

"It's his wolf heritage. He wants them to be strong," Abby said.

As the days and weeks passed, the six youngsters advanced from walking to trotting and running. They tried out their little voices with barks and yelps, and they tested their new canine teeth that had erupted during their third and fourth weeks of age. Next, their incisors and premolars showed up. Chomping down on each other's ears, tails and legs became a little more painful, and they were eager to voice their sibling abusive treatment.

Abby often escaped the cave for quick breaks from six exuberant explorers climbing all over her.

"My ears and tail are numb from them biting me," she told Starlight.

"They're very active at that age," Starlight said.

STARLIGHT HELD up a handmade leather saddlebag for Abby to inspect.

"Will Apollo let me put this on him?" Starlight asked.

"Let him get the scent first," Abby suggested.

Starlight approached Apollo. She patted his head and scratched under his chin. She held the leather out for him to smell.

Apollo sniffed the material and snorted. He wagged his tail.

Starlight laid the saddlebag across Apollo's back. He turned his head to look, but he appeared okay. Starlight wrapped the long cords around Apollo's belly and back several times and fastened them into place.

"Ready for the test?" Starlight asked.

"Yes," Abby said.

Starlight looked at the romping puppies. "Who wants to go for a ride?"

"Star and Wolf," Abby suggested.

Starlight scooped up the puppies and placed Star in one pouch and Wolf in the other. They were across from each other in the saddlebags.

Apollo turned his head from one side to the other, looking at the puppies in the saddlebags hanging from his sides.

Abby inspected both pouches. She trotted several feet forward. "Come on, Apollo. Let's see how this works."

Apollo trotted after Abby. Star and Wolf barked and squirmed in the pouches with only their heads sticking out.

Abby led Apollo in a wide circle back to Starlight again. Starlight inspected the pouches. She yanked and tugged to make sure they were secure.

"Looks pretty good to me," Starlight said. "They're wide enough so that when the puppies are sleepy, they can just snuggle down and go to sleep."

Abby looked at her remaining puppies. She licked each and every one of them.

Starlight kneeled on the ground. Abby approached her and rubbed against her.

"Don't worry. I won't let anything happen to them," Starlight said.

"Make sure a raptor doesn't snatch one," Abby said. She felt a sting of sadness. She would never forget her little skunk friend.

"Have a safe journey," Starlight said.

Abby and Apollo took off at a moderate run with Star and Wolf secured in their pouches on Apollo's solid body. They ran through the desolate landscape, devoid of any recent signs of mankind. They stopped about every three hours, and Abby removed Star and

Wolf from the pouches so they could go potty and stretch their legs. Abby, Apollo, Star, and Wolf drank at streams and ponds. Abby and Apollo chased down rabbits and filled their bellies. The puppies nursed, then slept in the pouches when the trip resumed.

On the second day of their adventure they came to a wide stream.

"We need to cross the water, Apollo, but it's too deep for the pouches," Abby said.

She paced at the edge of the stream. Apollo seemed to understand that they needed to cross the stream. He watched as Abby stepped into the stream. She took two steps forward, and she was under the water. Abby shot up to the surface and made it back to the edge where Apollo nervously paced.

Abby shook the water off and then removed Star and Wolf from their pouches. She grabbed Star by the scruff and entered the water, head held high to keep Star safe from drowning. Apollo picked up Wolf by the scruff and followed Abby.

They made it to the other side of the wide stream without any problem. They put Star and Wolf on the ground and then they shook the water off their own coats. Abby lifted Star into one pouch and then grabbed Wolf and placed him into the other one. Apollo looked from side to side and set out. Abby resumed the lead.

About an hour later, as they crossed a field of tall, scratchy grasses, Abby spotted a glider in the sky. "Get down, Apollo!" she shrieked. She crouched in the grass and watched in amazement as Apollo walked on.

"Apollo! Down!" she screamed in panic.

Apollo turned quickly and saw her frightened posture. He looked up at the sky, saw the big thing that scared her, and ducked down. The glider whizzed past them, oblivious to their existence.

Panting with fear with her tongue dangling out of her mouth, Abby stretched her neck and looked in all directions. She saw the glider as a tiny speck miles away.

~

BILL'S new combination home office and lab was twice as large as the one he'd had in WestUS. Whereas the house they had left behind was built like a fortress with few windows, the new house in TMZ was open, light and bright. Floor-to-ceiling windows with energy collectors, formerly known as solar panels, but the 2080 models did not obscure the view through the windows, but like the old solar panels, they used the sun's energy to keep the house cool.

Even though TMZ did not spy on its citizens, Bill had installed special sensors at each of the windows to deflect any spying beams. He constantly monitored the satellites roaming around the Earth to see if the World Guild had breached the security network surrounding TMZ.

So far, so good. No breaches or spyware had been detected, as he had been assured by the committee.

Teresa's schoolroom was larger as well. Abby's PawBoard and bed were against an inner wall, a sad reminder of her absence. Teresa's teaching toys and games were placed neatly on the built-in shelves. Various research papers were stacked on her desk in orderly piles.

Rex had claimed an alcove that was between the front and back doors. Teresa had provided him with a dog bed with his name embroidered in red letters. He loved his bed even though he didn't require one, but to be more doglike, he curled up on his bed to work on databases and complex analyses. His new leg joints made it possible to be more flexible in getting up and down and curling up. He loved his new leg joints. He loved to jump.

~

ABBY AND APOLLO arrived at the edge of Blythe in the dead of the night on the twentieth day of their journey. They made a wide berth around the TMZ tent city, which took two days and approached the secured facility away from the main gate.

Abby kept close to the fence. She stopped and looked at a section of chain-link fencing. It was very high, and she knew it would not be safe for her to fall to the ground, even if she could manage to climb it. Besides, she told herself, Apollo never watched the holographic movie of Jimbo climbing like a monkey, so he wouldn't be able to climb the fence.

They continued on, Abby in the lead. Apollo was as nervous as a cat in a room full of rocking chairs. His experience with mankind was limited to Starlight. The vast number of people in the tent city was almost too much for him to bear. Abby knew it would take determination to keep him moving forward and not bolting back into the wild.

They walked and walked along the never-ending fence. Abby and Apollo turned a corner and continued their search for a way to gain entrance into the compound. The low hum of a gate sliding open sounded up ahead. Abby hit the ground and made herself as flat as possible, blending into the shadows. Apollo followed suit. Star and Wolf slept in the pouches.

A military-type glider emerged from the compound and disappeared into the inky darkness. Abby was on her feet in an instant. She raced toward the open gate with Apollo at her heels. They slid around the closing gate and darted into the shadows of what appeared to be a storage area with stacks of crates on pallets while a deafening alarm sounded. Floodlights lit the place.

Abby lifted her nose and sampled the air, searching for any scent of Bill and Teresa. She did not detect anything familiar. She and Apollo stood under the lights. Abby licked his face, knowing that he was ready to bolt.

Guards were crawling the area of the breach. After a few minutes, Abby nudged Apollo. She started forward, and they carefully and quietly made their way through little alleyways and streets between the military-type buildings, keeping one step ahead of the guards. It was a giant maze of buildings and alleys, all unfamiliar, all dangerous and strange.

Star and Wolf woke up and demanded dinner. Abby licked Star and leaned over to Wolf and licked him, trying to placate them to be quiet.

Two guards stopped upon hearing the puppies whimper. "Who's there? Show yourself, or we will use force," a guard commanded.

The guards blocked the alleyway with their large bodies. Bright lights flashed into the alley, giving up Abby and Apollo.

Apollo growled a ferocious warning. Abby bumped him. She stepped forward two steps.

"My name is Aberdeen Tallulah Maxwell, dog-daughter of Bill and Teresa Maxwell. This is my mate, Apollo. He does not talk. We have two of our puppies with us," Abby said.

"Come forward into the light," the first guard said.

Abby nudged Apollo, and she walked toward the guards. Apollo stayed behind for a moment but reluctantly followed her. Star and Wolf whimpered loudly.

The guards appeared dumbfounded as they got a good look at Abby, Apollo, and the puppies in the pouches.

"Will you look at this? Call the commander for instructions," the second guard said. He squatted and patted Abby.

The first guard stepped back and made his connection.

"Looks like you've had quite a journey with your little ones," the second guard said.

"They're hungry," Abby said. "Are my parents here? They told me to come to TMZ and wait for them."

"I don't know. There's a lot of people here," the guard said.

The first guard finished his conversation. "We're supposed to escort them to the main building," he said.

"Okay," the second guard said. "Will your mate follow you? He looks pretty nervous."

Abby licked Apollo's face. He nudged her. Abby looked up at the guard expectantly. The guards turned down an alley. Abby and Apollo followed while Star and Wolf complained noisily.

They arrived at the first building that Bill and Teresa had entered upon their arrival at TMZ. The first guard went ahead and opened the door.

"The puppies need to use the bathroom closet," Abby said, looking around. There was none in sight.

"They'll have to use the ground," the guard said.

Abby removed Star from her pouch and placed her on the ground. She then retrieved Wolf and placed him on the ground. The puppies wandered in circles and then squatted and peed. Abby replaced them into their pouches again and moved toward the door with Apollo at her side.

BANGING on the front door in the middle of the night aroused Bill and Teresa. Rex was at the door in defense mode.

"Identify yourself!" Rex demanded.

"It's Harold, Rex," Harold called out.

Bill was in the process of wrapping himself in a robe as he approached the door. Teresa was right behind him.

"Harold Goanflower requests entry," the security system announced.

Bill looked at the monitor by the door. Harold and two guards stood a few feet back from the door. "What the..."

Bill entered the security code and opened the door. "Harold, have we had a security br—?" Bill's words dropped in shocked silence as Abby rushed forward. "Daddy!"

"Abby!" Bill said. He bent and wrapped her in a hug, and kissed the top of her head.

Teresa squeaked and made a surprised sound as she dropped to the floor and embraced her dog-daughter, competing with Bill's arms. "Abby! You made it!"

Abby went from Teresa to Bill and back and forth, licking them and rubbing up against them. She lapsed into dog-talk and whined and yelped.

"Abby-dog is home!" Rex said.

"Rex is living with Mommy and Daddy?" Abby asked. She romped in a circle, and Rex romped with her. Abby licked Rex's face.

"I defected," Rex said. "Jerry took over."

"Rex has new legs?" Abby asked. "Who's Jerry?"

"Jerry used to be number twenty-three," Rex said. "Daddy upgraded my hardware so that I'm more doglike."

"Oh, that's wonderful, Rex," Abby said.

Apollo stayed back, ears standing straight up and twitching. Star and Wolf chose that minute to begin their serenade of whining. They were hungry.

Bill and Teresa broke their trance and discovered Apollo and his load.

"Is this your mate, Abby? Your puppies?" Teresa asked a little shocked.

Abby sprinted back to Apollo. She licked his face, then Wolf's, and then Star's.

"Yes. This is Apollo. He's a wolf, and he is terrified right now," Abby said. "We brought two of our puppies. Starlight is watching the other four."

"Who's Starlight?" Bill asked.

"She's a Timbisha Shoshone Indian," Abby said. "She took care of me when I gave birth to the puppies. Starlight said there might be other dogs in TMZ. Have you seen them?"

"No, we haven't seen any dogs yet, but it's a big place," Teresa said.

"What will my puppies do when they are grown up if there are no other dogs?" Abby said.

"There are possibly two surviving canines in TMZ," Rex stated. "One male and one female. The female was not listed in the census two years ago, so she may be deceased."

"Are there any other wolves?" Teresa asked.

"I don't know. Can Daddy give Apollo a Dot?" Abby asked

"Will Apollo let us touch him?" Bill asked.

"You'd better wait a little while. He's scared," Abby said.

"I'm glad she made it home," Harold said from the doorway.

"You would not believe how she escaped," Bill said. "Her journey must have been remarkable."

Teresa held her hand out to Apollo and spoke softly to him.

"Welcome to your new home, Apollo." She stroked the top of his head and scratched behind his ears. He was tolerant of her gentle touch and loving voice.

"I'll let you take care of your family," Harold said.

Bill and Harold shook hands. Harold and the guards left. Bill urged Apollo to come into the house, but he would not budge from the doorstep.

Abby went up to Apollo and nudged him through the door.

She removed Wolf and Star from the pouches, and then she lay down on the floor to feed them. The puppies wasted no time satisfying their hunger. Apollo stood close to Abby.

Bill shut the door. He and Teresa watched as Abby licked her puppies.

"Abby, they're beautiful. I can't wait to see your other puppies," Teresa said.

"Rex, can you determine whether there are any surviving dogs in other countries?" Bill asked. "Remote places like Siberia or Tibet, or even the northern villages in Alaska."

"If there were survivors, they were not reported to the World Guild," Rex said. "We would have to go through other channels to make that determination."

Bill huffed. "Let's work on that. Abby has six puppies. We need to find them mates, or we need to find out if Dr. Roberts saved any sperm or eggs from the other dogs that did not survive."

CHAPTER THIRTY-FOUR

Teresa and Bill cuddled Star and Wolf. Apollo watched from a few feet away as Abby interacted with Bill, Teresa, and Rex.

After a little while, Teresa got up and went to the schoolroom and brought out two dog beds, one for Abby and the pups, and the other for Apollo. He watched her carefully as she fluffed the beds.

"Do you think Apollo will sleep on a dog bed, Abby?" Teresa asked.

"Yes, Mommy," Abby said. "We had a big leaf bed in a cave with a blanket on top."

"Okay, it's very late. Let's get some sleep, and we'll visit in the morning. Do you or Apollo want to go to the bathroom closet?" Teresa asked. "This one is outside."

"Good idea," Abby said.

"Apollo has a lot to learn about the world we live in," Bill said. "Wolves are very smart, so I don't think it will take him too long to catch on to the basics."

"Apollo saved me from a black bear, Mommy," Abby said. "One of her cubs wanted to play with us, but she got mad."

"Bears are very fast runners," Bill said. "I'm surprised she let you get away."

"I tripped in a burrow and Apollo charged her. She had second thoughts and returned to her cub," Abby said.

"What a mighty wolf! You protected your mate without even thinking about the consequences," Teresa said as she patted Apollo and scratched his ears.

"You both could have gotten killed, Abby," Bill said.

"He's so brave." Abby licked Apollo's face.

BILL AND TERESA carried the puppies through the house to the kitchen door. Abby followed, next to Rex, and Apollo nervously watched Star and Wolf as he walked abreast of Bill and Teresa.

"It's okay, Apollo," Bill said.

Teresa opened the kitchen door. Abby went outside. She gave a little bark to Apollo, and he followed, reluctant to leave Star and Wolf behind.

Bill and Teresa put Star and Wolf on the ground so they could walk around and relieve themselves again.

Abby walked into the bathroom closet, Apollo on her heels. She did her business and then walked through the water and onto the drying mat.

Apollo didn't quite have it figured out, but he did his business and hopped over the water and emerged after Abby. He made deep scratch marks in the dirt outside the bathroom closet. Then they all went back into the house.

Teresa went to the food console and ordered meals for

Abby and Apollo. She placed the bowls on the floor and watched as Abby and Apollo ate quickly.

"I knew you would survive in the wild," Bill said. "We were worried, but I knew that you would access programs at the laboratory and prepare yourself when you had a plan in place."

"It was hard at first, but then I got good at it," Abby said.

They all walked to the living room, and Bill and Teresa put the puppies on one dog bed. They watched as Abby nudged Apollo over to the other dog bed. He climbed onto the bed and settled down.

Bill dragged Abby's bed up against Apollo's. "Is that better, boy?" he said. Bill gingerly scratched Apollo's head.

Rex walked into the room. "It is two twenty-seven in the morning. Daddy has an appointment at seven..."

"Better rearrange my schedule until we're settled with Abby, Apollo and the puppies," Bill said.

"Mine, too," Teresa said. "Allow two days, Rex."

Clicks and whirs sounded softly in the night as Rex went to work on the schedules.

"Schedules updated. Notifications have been sent to all parties," Rex said.

"Abby, do you want a nightlight?" Teresa asked.

"No. We're used to the dark, Mommy," Abby said.

Teresa sank to her knees. She hugged and kissed Abby. A tear escaped and ran down Teresa's face as Abby rubbed against her. "I'm so glad you're home, Abby. I've missed you so much."

Teresa turned to Apollo. She stroked his head and back. "Good night, Apollo. Welcome to our family."

Bill helped Teresa to her feet, and they went to their bedroom. Rex dimmed the lights and shut them off.

"Good night, Abby-dog."

"Good night, Rex. I'm glad you're here with Mommy and Daddy," Abby said.

~

STAR AND WOLF romped and played in the living room, tugging the beds, chasing each other, biting each other's ears and tails.

Apollo explored the house. He wandered into Bill's office lab and sniffed the air. Bill worked at the transfer surface.

"Hello, Apollo," Bill said. "Do you think you'll let me insert a Dot into your scruff without biting me?" He held his hand out to Apollo.

Less on edge, Apollo took a few steps forward and sniffed Bill's outstretched hand. Bill patted Apollo's head and then stroked his back. He ruffled Apollo's scruff. Apollo seemed okay with all of Bill's ministrations.

Turning back to the transfer surface, Bill picked up the Dot insertion device and held it out to Apollo.

"Your Dot is in this device, Apollo. I'm going to insert it into your scruff. It's going to sting a tiny bit, but I think you'll be okay with it," Bill said.

Rex and Abby entered the room, shoulder-to-shoulder. Bill used the distraction and quickly plunged the Dot into Apollo. He jumped to the side, growled fiercely, and then gave a great shake of his body. He eyed Bill suspiciously but turned back to Abby and Rex.

"Daddy just gave you your Dot, Apollo. You're going to be able to learn to talk now," Abby said.

Apollo sniffed Rex.

"Apollo is from Greek and Roman mythology," Rex said. "He is one of the most important Olympian deities."

"I just liked the name," Abby said.

"Oh," Rex said. He turned and left the room.

Abby stared after Rex. "What's wrong with Rex?"

"I think you hurt his feelings," Bill said. "Rex wants to be more doglike, and he's probably a little threatened by Apollo."

"He's very doglike, Daddy," Abby said. "How can he become more doglike?"

"It's hard for him to know when not to be an encyclopedia and when to just wag his tail," Bill said. "He's learning. Just be kind to him."

"Rex was my best friend at the research facility. I really missed him when the Tranquility Force took him away," Abby said.

Teresa walked into the room carrying a basket with Star and Wolf snoozing away.

"Your puppies are so precious, Abby. This house needed their energy," Teresa said.

"Apollo has his Dot. Now we just have to see how long it will take for him to adapt and respond," Bill said. "He's most likely going to be a little disoriented with all of this knowledge floating around in his head." Bill patted Apollo's back.

"He's a gentle wolf. You picked a good partner, Abby," Bill said.

"He was very lonely when we met. His howls were searching for others of his kind, but no one ever called back to him," Abby said.

"Well, he has a home now," Teresa said. "We may not be wolves, but we will love him one hundred percent."

"Abby, we're going to have to get your other puppies. Do you think Apollo will be okay with riding in a glider?" Bill asked.

"If I go, he'll be okay. It's a long way away," Abby said. "It took us twenty days to get here."

"It will only take a couple of hours to get there with the glider," Bill said. "Let me call Harold and make arrangements."

～

THE FAMILY glider sped through the countryside. Apollo went from one side of the glider to the next, while looking at every passing tree, bush, bird, and ground cover. He didn't seem nervous; he seemed intrigued.

Abby lay on a seat and looked out the windshield of the glider. "There's our mountain," she said. She stood on the seat and wagged her tail.

"Where should I go?" Bill asked.

"See the forest and the foothills? Our cave is over to the left a little," Abby said.

Bill raised the glider, and they zoomed over the treetops. He slowed down as they approached the edge of the forest and then edged down to the ground a few feet from the foothills.

"I'll show you our cave, Daddy," Abby said.

Bill settled the glider on the ground and pressed a lever to open the doors. Abby and Apollo jumped out of the glider, and Bill followed.

"Come on, Daddy," Abby said.

Abby and Apollo raced up the foothill to their ledge. The going was much slower for Bill as he climbed around rocks and boulders, jumped the stream, and pushed through mountain scrub.

He finally made it to the ledge. He took a recording device from his pocket and captured details of the ledge, the mountainside, and the general surroundings.

Abby and Apollo waited for him just inside the main entrance of the cave. "This is where I made my calendar," Abby said. She showed Bill her scratches on the wall.

Bill took a small, powerful light stick from his pocket and twisted it. The dark cave lit up as if the sun were overhead. He walked over to Abby's wall marks, reached out and touched the cold wall. "Your mother will be happy to see this, honey."

"Come in here, Daddy," Abby said as she trotted into the dark inner cave.

Bill and Apollo followed. Bill investigated the former cave dwellers' remains and possessions.

"Poor guy. Wonder if he was hiding out or what his story was," Bill said. He wandered around inspecting everything. He marveled at the huge leaf bed. Bill recorded everything to show Teresa.

They left the cave and walked down the mountainside to the glider. "Let's go get your puppies," Bill said.

Abby jumped into the glider, and Apollo followed. Bill got in and maneuvered the glider off the ground. "Where to?"

"Follow the trees that way," Abby said, pointing to the left with her nose.

Bill steered the glider at a slower pace than their original journey. He was taking in the sights of the forest and mountains.

After a few minutes, Starlight's shack appeared in the distance. Bill sped up and soon the little shack was in front of them. He settled the glider to the ground and opened the doors. Abby leaped out of the glider, followed by Apollo and Bill.

Tallulah, Esme, Rex, and Jim were romping just outside the open doorway of the shack.

"Starlight!" Abby called. "We're back with Daddy!"

Abby rushed up to the puppies and licked each of them.

Starlight emerged from the shack, wiping her hands on a worn dish towel.

"You made it!" Starlight said. She looked at Bill and smiled. "You got Apollo into a glider? Wow!"

Bill approached Starlight, his hand out in front of him.

"You must be Starlight. I'm Bill Maxwell, Abby's father," Bill said. "My wife and I are so grateful to you for taking care of Abby."

"She's one smart dog," Starlight said. "And her spirit is very strong. I'm glad they made it to TMZ and found you. I was worried about the journey and how long it would take them to get there."

"It's hard to say how they managed. You were very wise to make that saddlebag for the puppies," Bill said. "I don't know how they would have made it without that."

Bill got down on his knees and patted each of the puppies. "They're beautiful. Just beautiful."

"And now they'll have a good shot at life. I don't think it would have been a good idea for them to grow up in the wild," Starlight said. "Too many dangers."

Bill stood. "I've got something for you." He walked back to the glider and opened the rear hatch. Bill grabbed a stack of material and returned to Starlight.

"We want you to have these," he said as he held out his bounty. "Teresa thought you'd like the assortment of fabrics."

"What beautiful material!" Starlight said. "Come! Bring them inside."

She stepped over the puppies and showed Bill the way inside her shack. He set the armload down on the small table.

"I've got a couple more things in the glider," he said. He left the shack and returned a few minutes later with a small box.

Bill opened the box and took out a small electronic device. He presented it to Starlight.

"This messaging badge can't be tracked," he explained. "You'll be able to contact us or anyone else without the World Guild, Tranquility Force or anyone else finding your signal."

Starlight took the device and held it to her chest. "Wow! This is incredible! It's very generous of you."

"You're the one who was big-hearted. You could have collected a lot of credits for turning Abby over to the Tranquility Force," Bill said. "We are in your debt for all that you have done."

Bill and Starlight stood in silent contemplation for a moment.

Abby came into the shack. "We should go, Daddy."

"Okay," Bill said. He scratched Abby on the top of her head. "Your Mom is probably worried."

Abby stepped outside and picked up Tallulah by the scruff and trotted to the glider. Apollo grabbed Esme and followed Abby.

Bill picked up Rex, and Starlight picked up Jim. They walked to the glider.

Abby lay on the floor in the back of the glider with the two pups nursing. Bill handed Rex over to Abby and then retrieved Jim from Starlight. The puppies were glad to be reunited with their mother.

Apollo stood facing Starlight, an intense expression on his face.

"Goodbye, Apollo," Starlight said. She scratched his ears. "Bye, Abby."

Bill exited the back of the glider.

"Bye, Starlight. We'll come back and visit," Abby said. "Mommy wants to meet you."

"That would be nice. I want to meet your mother, too," Starlight said. She backed away from the glider.

Bill took her hands in his. "Take care. We'll see you again soon." He got into the glider, secured the doors, and the glider lifted off the ground, and then they were off.

~

THE SIX PUPPIES romped and played in the house. Abby and Apollo relaxed on the dog beds as they watched their brood. Bill and Teresa sat on the sofa, holding hands as their eyes wandered from the pups to Abby and Apollo.

Rex entered the room, and the puppies converged on him. They ran under his belly and nipped his feet and legs.

"Order is required," Rex said to no avail. He turned to the right and then to the left, trying to avoid the onslaught.

"Rex, you're going to have to lighten up a bit," Bill said. He and Teresa laughed as they watched him.

Apollo was quiet as he watched the activity from the dog bed. He licked Esme as she bounded over to see him. Then all the puppies romped over to their father.

Bill and Teresa watched the puppies and Apollo. They were happy and content in their new environment.

Apollo's brows crunched. He looked hard at Bill and Teresa. Then he relaxed.

"Home."

The End

Acronyms & Terms for *The Last Dog*

Term	Definition
ACW	Alford Chemical Weaponry – top World Guild contractor
AMD	Advanced Multimedia Device (TV) (pronounced Ad-Med)
airspace	Where gliders fly
All Beliefs Celebration	March 27 when all religious beliefs and holidays are celebrated
Bio-gear	Suits that protect against hazards
Communicator	Robotic receptionist
Credits	Money
Diamond Eyes	X's secret email address
DID	Dot Insertion Device
Dog-bot	Robotic dog
Doglike	Acting like a dog
Dog-talk	Barking, whining, howling
Dog-thought	Rex's secret program to communicate
Dot	The IVT, commonly referred to as *the Dot*. Mandatory in humans in 2080; dogs and cats in 2084
FERG	Floating event recorder globe
Flight Squad	Gliders
Food Console	Food ordering machine. Delivers prepared food at the touch of a button
GCaught	Trash TV
Glider	Off-the-ground vehicles that glide through the air
Global Health	World Health Organization
Global Scientific Gathering	Huge symposium
GNN	Global News Network & information network with science officers
GNSS	Global Navigation Satellite System
Golden Eagle	Bill's secret email address
Highest Agreement	An agreement between Trusted Partners and World Guild
Hover Surface	A gurney that hovers off the ground

Term	Definition
Hycore Security	Security company in NY that works predominantly with World Guild
Identification Number	• Human numbers begin with the number nine and can be 14-25 numbers in length • Canine numbers begin and end with the number 5 • Feline numbers begin and end with the number 4
IVT	Implant Vocal Transmitter
Literalist	Writer or announcer that speaks the truth
Literalist Avatar	Holographic avatar that speaks the truth
MED-P	Middle Eastern Desert People
PawBoard	A keyboard developed so dogs can use the UCP (internet)
Privateers	Hired contractors/spies
Proteus Security	Security company that supplies protection services
Red Level	Security encryption program
Sentient Robotics	One of Dr. Robert's companies
Smart Buttons	Open and close with a press of the button
Smart Lock Buttons	Lock and unlock with a press of the button
Sprintcast	Sprint & Comcast merged as *the* communication company
Supercentenarians	People over 120 years old
TMZ	Texmexzona -- The former country of Mexico, and the former states of Texas, New Mexico and Arizona merged and formed a separate sovereign state.
Transfer surface	Flat computer surface that allows computing, drawing, transferring data from one form of technology to another form of technology
Tranquility Force	Police
TRFS	Tactile Releasing Factual Stimulator (pronounced truffs)
Tribunal	Tribunal secretary (lowercase), but World Guild Tribunal (caps)
UCP	Universal Connection Platform – late 21nd Century Internet
UWP	Unified World Pact
VHO	Virtual Healing Office
Virtual Veterinarian	Holographic version of a veterinarian

Term	Definition
WestUS	Western US – California, Oregon & Washington states
Wise Owl	Communications program similar to Outlook
World Guild	Government
WOPA	World Obesity Prevention Act
Wrist Messenger	Like the Apple Watch
Popular phrases in this time period	
Thank the Earth, instead of Thank God	
Earth's blessing instead of Bless You (for a sneeze)	
Peace & Bliss – cause no harm; no precursor	
Ragged edge happened in 2076. Current year is 2086.	

CHARACTERS

Main characters of The Last Dog are as follows:

- Bill Maxwell, 33, CEO of Maxwell Industries, holds many patents
- Teresa Maxwell, 33, Bill's wife, dog psychologist
- Abby, Puppy, Bull Terrier/Black Lab mix, black with a white star on her chest
- Rex, Robotic dog, Abby's best friend

Named supporting characters consist of the following:

- Lilith, Abby's canine Mother
- Jimbo Smythe, Abby's canine Father
- Ejonia Matthews, Housekeeper
- Myra-June Meyer, Teresa's receptionist
- Gayle Goanflower, Teresa's best friend
- Harold Goanflower, Gayle's husband, Native American

- Dion, Gregor & Brody, yard work crew/prisoners
- Becky & Percy Smythe, Jimbo's human parents; Abby's human grandparents
- Estelle, patient of Teresa's
- Bruno, security detail
- Toby, one of Bill's engineers
- Four-star General Emil Gootenberg
- Apollo, Wolf, Abby's mate

ABOUT THE AUTHOR

 D.E. Greenfield (aka Dawn Greenfield Ireland) is a powerhouse storyteller and the award-winning author of 22 novels across five distinct genres, alongside 7 acclaimed nonfiction books. A prolific creator of worlds, Dawn frequently adapts her own high-concept screenplays into books and develops her novels into structured TV series formats.

On the film side, Dawn is an alum of the UCLA Professional Program in Screenwriting and ScreenwritingU. Her scripts have been optioned twice, and she has worked as a screenwriter-for-hire. Known for her relentless work ethic and zero tolerance for writer's block, Dawn's background as an award-winning technical writer makes her a meticulous, detail-oriented professional—the self-described "organizational queen of the known universe" who never misses a deadline. Through her company, Artistic Origins (est.1995), she also works as a high-level writing coach, editor, and independent publisher.

The Last Dog is also available as a TV series pilot and/or a feature film screenplay.

facebook.com/dawn.ireland.18

goodreads.com/dawnireland

linkedin.com/dawnireland

instagram.com/dawngreenfieldIreland

x.com/dawnireland